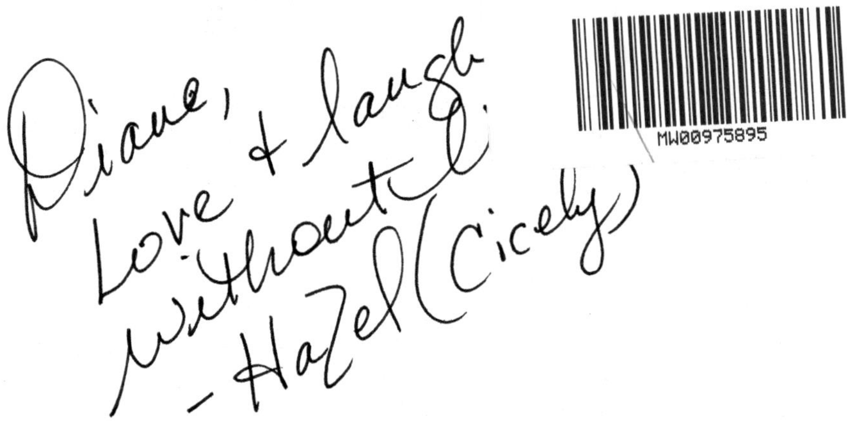

The Church Chronicles of Iris and Locke: The Complete Jackie Black Trilogy

By

Hazel Lindey and Rosee Garfield

The Church Chronicles of Iris and Locke

The Complete Jackie Black Trilogy

ISBN-13: 978-1511524520

ISBN-10: 1511524529

DEDICATION

Lord, we thank you for giving us imaginations that allow us to bring laughter to others.

NOVELLA I: WELCOME TO SWEET FIELDS

CHAPTER 1: IRIS

Iris sat primly on the end of the fifth pew in the middle section of St. Andrew Baptist Church—the oldest African American church in the state of Georgia. She smoothed her taupe sheath dress on her lap once more and adjusted her clutch at her side. This was her first service at St. Andrew since her grandmother, Margaret "Maggie" Murphy, died a month earlier. Iris had decided to stay on in Sweet Fields and live in the large Victorian house she inherited from her grandmother. Now, it was time for her to join the community, and attending a church service was the first step. A pupil of human behavior, Iris couldn't help but observe and analyze the congregation of her granny's church.

A motley collection of twelve women in white shirtdresses and white hats with scarlet trim sat to the far left of the pulpit. Each wore a magnolia on her lapel to further signify her affiliation with the deaconess board. A few were fanning themselves, and two elderly ladies were already nodding off, even though the service had just begun. Others were enjoying the choir's lively rendition of Andrae Crouch's "Soon and Very Soon."

As Iris scanned the faces of the congregation, one face demanded her attention. A pair of active bulbous eyes sat beneath a dramatically low blond widow's peak. The woman with the eyes was the color of vanilla custard, and she glared at Iris as if she were interrogating her. She held the carriage of a deaconess, an influential deaconess. Iris' suspicion of the big-eyed woman's position was confirmed by the magnolia. The custard colored woman also wore a shirtwaist dress like the other deaconess members; however, Iris noted that her dress was noticeably shorter when she walked into the church. The dress stopped at a dangerous height, several inches above the knees, revealing the longest pair of bird legs Iris had ever seen. The legs were covered by thick flesh tone stockings, the kind that dancers for football teams often wore underneath their small shorts. Her eyes continued to question Iris. Not one to back down, Iris returned the woman's glare and eventually slid the corners of her mouth upward into a dry smile that did not fully reach her eyes. She smoothed her dress again and turned her attention to the choir.

It had been a long time since she had heard the song they were singing. The organist, a robust woman with a large dark burgundy colored bouffant looked straight ahead as she played. She paid no attention to the director or the choir. *Odd*, Iris thought. *Did the choir sing the song so often that the director and organist need not communicate about its nuances?* Iris tried to follow the organist's gaze; it looked as if the organist and the large-eyed deaconess were glaring at each other. But the organist was no match for the deaconess, as the organist eventually looked away first. She banged on the keys with more gusto when the showdown came to its disappointing end.

Iris weaved a story in her head about the two ladies. They both looked to be about the same age—early to mid forties. In a fist fight, Iris' money would be on the organist. She was a large woman, solid—not soft and pillowy. In a battle of wits, Iris would put her money on the large-eyed woman. She seemed clever; her eyes never stopped moving and taking in information. It was a man, Iris figured. It was always a man. *Was one the wife and the other "the other woman?" Or were they both single and after the same man? Did this man attend the St. Andrew? Yes. Most likely. Anyone who was anyone attended St. Andrew.*

Iris scanned the deacon's board. About twenty men of all ages sat in their Sunday's best suits and ties, clapping and singing. *Perhaps the object of the women's affections sat on the deacon board. But which one?*

Iris had begun an analysis of each man but was interrupted on the third gentleman when she was distracted by the pastor who was approaching the podium. The pastor, Prentiss LeBeaux, was tall and broad-shouldered with a thick mustache. He was an attractive gentleman with an athletic build, honey-colored skin, and thick wavy hair sprinkled with touches of gray throughout. The honey wasn't just in his skin; it was also in his voice. Iris was sure he had used the combination of his baritone voice and long-lashed gray eyes to charm countless women. She let her eyes trail the pastor's frame from the shoulders of his navy suit down to his fingers. His fingers. They were not adorned. No wedding ring, but still a visible quarter inch indentation of commitment. *That explains the slight droop of his neck, and the way his large hands dangle from the wrists--lonely hands,* Iris thought. His shirt collar was neatly tucked, except for a slight puckle of white at the neck, on the back right side. Iris knew what this meant. There was no one at home to tuck and dust him--to be sure his collar was completely tucked and the small bits of lint were dusted from his back and shoulders.

She was almost sure of it. He was the man.

Iris glanced at the thin frog-faced woman just in time to see her eyes alight with admiration and respect onto the pastor's distinguished figure. There was something Iris saw in the bulging eyes, a wildness restrained by fetters too loose. There was wildness and something else. Iris looked at the woman's mouth and saw her tongue peak out to subtly lick her lips--top and bottom. The woman then pressed her lips together into a slight pucker. Lust. That's the other thing Iris saw in the deaconess' eyes. Iris shot a glance to the right of the pulpit at the organist who had stretched her lips into a wide, toothy grin. Right. Of course, it was the pastor. The two women were vying for the attention of the pastor of St. Andrew. Who wouldn't be? He was very handsome, and from what Iris heard from her grandmother, the pastor was quite charming too. Grandma Maggs had called the pastor, "a very nice man, nice to his own detriment."

Throughout the service, Iris continued her survey of various people in the sanctuary. She noticed a small lady tucked into the pew across the aisle from her. She repeatedly sanitized her hands after every handshake, hug, or touch. Iris was content to watch the little lady with the gray sister locs, but someone whispered for her to stand.

"We'd like to welcome Mother Murphy's granddaughter back to St. Andrew. As you know, Mother Murphy went to her heavenly reward last month, and don't we miss her, church?" The congregation shouted hearty amens. The pastor continued, "Well, her granddaughter, Iris, moved back to Sweet Fields and decided to make

St. Andrew her church home." The congregation clapped and shouted, "amen." Iris wanted to crawl under the pew or better yet, walk right out of there. It was, in fact, very hard for her to keep her feet planted at her seat. *I will not walk out. I will not walk out*, she thought. She felt there was no need for this kind of public display, and hoped she was smiling as she smoothed her dress over her lap.

"Sister Iris, come up here so we can greet you and welcome you into the St. Andrew fold," the pastor urged. Iris did not move. She nodded and smiled. "Come on, dear. Don't be shy. Everyone remembers you from the time you were knee-high to a grasshopper." Iris stood and stepped out into the aisle. She did not walk out of the church, but she refused to look at any of the faces watching her. When she finally reached the front of the church, the pastor stepped down from the pulpit and pulled her into a bear hug. His cologne filled her nostrils. His large arms were squeezing her ribcage. She wanted to pummel his muscular back with her fists, but fought back the urge. When he finally released her, she gasped for air, but the freedom didn't last long.

Soon she was bombarded with unsolicited affections from men, women, and children—none of whom she knew. Hugs, handshakes, and, to her dismay, a kiss on the cheek! *Who did that? How dare they!* Finally, the parade of strangers was over. Iris did not run back to her seat at the end of the fifth row like she wanted to. Instead, she regained control and took long confident strides back to her seat. The little lady with the sanitizer stuck out a green-gloved hand as Iris passed her. She did not look at Iris, only straight ahead. Iris got a good enough look at the little lady to note her smooth walnut colored skin, her small triangular wooden earrings, and the hint of soft pink gloss on her lips. The woman slipped a tiny vial of sanitizer into Iris' trembling hands. "Use this," she said in a voice almost too loud for worship service. Only then did the woman turn to take Iris in, fully. Iris noted her quick nod of approval, the kind that only people with long money, as her granny would say, could give. The loc'ed lady then turned her tiny head toward the pulpit as if the exchange never happened.

CHAPTER 2: LOCKE

Belle Lynne Locke arrived at St. Andrew Church of Sweet Fields exactly twenty-seven minutes early. She needed time to settle in. It had been seven years since she attended worship services there and two years since her Clive had died. Her entire being was centered around Clive, and she liked it that way. They were a pair who had done well together, in everything. The kind of couple that people didn't think really existed. Clive and Belle Lynne Locke, though they'd been married forty-three years, had always looked like newlyweds. When they went out to eat, it was rare they'd finish their entire meal, because they talked the entire time. Often, the salads would wilt and the soups would grow cold underneath the energy of their vibrant conversations. Up until the last time Clive drove, he still made Belle Lynne wait inside the car while he made his way around to open the door for her. Belle Lynne reached for the door of the church and paused. She observed her hands, protected by a favorite pair of soft kelly green gloves. As she extended the right one to turn the knob, she realized that in all her years with her Clive, she never had to touch the door knob of St. Andrew, the lever of her own car, or the first MACK truck Clive bought to drive across country. Clive made that so. Yes, he had his way, Locke thought, but he was good to her.

While during their early years of marriage, Locke was content to live happily in a small cottage with her small gardens and small pots of basil, parsley, and rosemary, Clive thought big. He was a gargantuan man, with dreams to match. Only seven years after they'd married Clive bought them a large Victorian home, three streets away from St. Andrew, and only one block away from her very best friend, Maggie Murphy. He was determined she be near the most important things in her life.

Often Clive's big dreams arrested Locke's want to live simply. He wanted not just to own one big truck to drive as a carrier, but an entire fleet of trucks "to put on the road." He wanted not one rental home, but a community of luxury row houses in downtown Sweet

Fields. He made not a few safe investments, but several risky leaps that yielded more money than even Locke knew they had. Clive made their money long, even though his own life was relatively short. He said he did it for her, but Locke told him he didn't have to do all that. *No need to make such a fuss. And for what? We have no children. It was just me and you, Clive. That is the way we wanted it, at first. Me beside you in that stinking eighteen wheeler, bumbling around the country, with one of your hands on the wheel and the other on my lap. Us spending time together. All our time together.*

"I have to spend a little time away from you now, so that I can spend a lot of time with you later." Her Clive had said. And that he did. "You'll get sick of having me around." And that, she did not.

The doorknob of the church reminded Locke of what she'd lost. But that same doorknob at St. Andrew would give Locke an opportunity to plug into life again and regain some semblance of usefulness.

Locke had never really thought of herself as useful, until Clive died. She took care of him, even before the colon cancer. She made sure he ate well, even though he would sneak away and eat pounds of choice cut beef and slabs of pork ribs. She cut his hair. She ordered his custom made shoes--the ones that did not rub his right pinky toe and make him walk funny. What use was she to anyone, now that her Clive was gone?

Locke mourned Clive's death deeply and for a very long time. Yes there were suitors, but their advances annoyed her. The men who came to call looked their age. Often they would have to take an extra quick step to climb the stairs leading to her front porch, a wide span of bamboo floors, cushioned rocking chairs and aromatic plants in exotic looking pots. The men who attempted to woo Locke shuffled and grunted. They farted without discretion, following each wind breaking with awful laughter of the *heh, heh, heh* sort. *Clive never "heh, heh, heh-ed,"* Locke thought. His laughter was a big round cloud. He threw it into the air where it exploded and filled the room.

But these men, they tried to hang on to hair that should have long been shorn away. They ate bad meat and probably took Viagra. Clive had never taken Viagra. After a year, the men stopped calling and Locke was content to sip mint julep tea, make strong cherry wine, and watch Lawrence Welk reruns on the large flat screen TV she'd had Pastor LeBeaux mount on the sun porch at the back of her home.

So Locke grieved hard, and even Pastor LeBeaux thought she may grieve herself to death, but Belle Lynne Locke never did anything to death. It was not her way. Still, Pastor Prentiss LeBeaux didn't know that. He tried to mother her. She was one of the reasons he came to Sweet Fields in the first place, and his investment in her livelihood was almost a necessity. Payback. On their many trips to New Orleans, Clive and Locke visited Pastor LeBeaux's church, and after he lost his wife, they were the first people he called, even before his own father. The Lockes saw Pastor LeBeaux cry. They saw him become infantile in his grief, his sufferings from separation anxiety. They supported him after he handed his church over to the associate pastor. They called him when St. Andrew of Sweet Fields needed a new pastor, new blood to help rejuvenate the church after a scandalous split.

Locke took a quick deep breath, but it didn't slow down the beating of her heart. She tugged at the thick bun of gray locks at the nape of her neck. *Yes, every strand is tucked and tethered,* she thought. She planted her gloved palm on the knob, gripped it and turned. She heard the suction of the door opening and sighed in relief as she looked at the empty sanctuary of St. Andrew.

She walked down the center aisle toward her seat. The church's smell had not changed, and the carpet was still plush under her feet. Locke abhorred floors that were not made to dampen the sound of footsteps. She reverenced God's house, almost to the point of obsession. In God's house, even your footsteps should be sacred, quiet. *This carpet, the carpet I chose, added sanctity to every footstep,* Locke thought.

Locke was pleased. One, two, three, four, five. To the right. End seat. The brass plate flanking the side gleamed. "Clive & Belle Lynne Locke," it read. That was the only inscription the Lockes wanted on the pew. Locke thought it unnecessary to make such a fuss over words. The name was enough.

Locke pulled out a vial of sanitizing spray from her purse (it was her own customized concoction, made special to accommodate her unique immune system), sanitized her seat, and stood for a moment to allow the air to settle. Members began to file in; they were surprised to see Belle Lynne Locke, and her standing at the end of the pew, looking at almost invisible droplets of liquid descend, gave them pause. But Locke remained unaffected by her audience. She would not move until she was satisfied that her seat had been properly consecrated by the sanitizer. After Locke was pleased with the sanitation, she gathered the wide legs of her brown linen pants, slid between the pews, and sat down, confident that no one would attempt to shuffle by her, grazing her knees and stepping on her toes, once she'd sat down; they knew better.

She did not pray. She'd made it to church, just as God moved her to do. But, Locke was still a little mad at God for taking her Clive. God understood the beauty of their love. He made it that way, so Locke didn't understand why He'd take that from her. She was disappointed in God, and sometimes, when she felt God's spirit upon her, she would tilt her head upward and say out loud, "I am still pouting," to make Him go away. She and God had worked out a unique and special relationship. They had deep roots, ones that left room for a little bit of pouting. God would not go away and neither did she.

Across the aisle in the fifth row sat a new woman--a selfassured woman who almost belied her own confidence, as she looked as if she would fold up into herself. She was pretty enough, especially her hair which looked like it had not been touched by a hot comb in quite some time. The lady's hair was black and thick with dense coils throughout. She wore it like an afro, but with shape and moisture. The heavy bangs fell across neatly arched eyebrows that framed a set of deep brown eyes that never stopped scanning the church and it's inhabitants. The woman had a healthy head of hair, and though the curls were dense, the slightest turn of the woman's head allowed the hair to greet its audience with a small wave. The woman was fit but not in a hard way. She still held onto some of her softness. Locke thought that all women, no matter how hard their lives, should hold on to some of their softness. This woman had, and while her dewy brown skin almost blended into the taupe shift she wore, Locke considered her a classic, like her when she was young. But then again, the new woman looked like Maggie, her one true friend--the oldest and the dearest. Surely, Locke thought, it couldn't be.

Locke's thoughts about the new woman were interrupted by Pastor LeBeaux's voice. In that gentle way, that sometimes annoyed Locke, he babbled on about something. *For God's sake what was he talking about, now*, she thought, *I've told him about extending service unnecessarily with information he should put in the church newsletter.* Then reluctantly, the new woman rose from her seat. She kept smoothing her clothes and hair and looking back at her spot on the pew, as if her seat would up and run away. Locke could see the moment when the new woman shook off her anxiety and walked up to the front of the church with a cool confidence that covered her anxieties well. *That's a good girl*, Locke thought. "Never let them see you sweat. Or they will make you sweat." Locke said out loud. So, it was, Maggie Murphy's mysterious granddaughter. Locke looked toward the ceiling and said, "I may be alright, now."

The sermon and another choir song ended before Iris was able to collect herself. She did not like crowds. She did not like strangers. She did not like people intruding on her personal space. Lloyd's reclusiveness had rubbed off on her. She couldn't help but smile a bit thinking about Lloyd Sutton. She smoothed her dress and stood with the rest of the congregation when she realized the service was about to end. She watched as everyone, or almost everyone, bowed their heads for the benediction. The small grayhaired, loc'ed lady was looking directly at her…and so was the bigeyed, long-legged, deaconess.

Iris gathered her clutch and bible and turned to exit her pew when a tall male usher put a hand to her elbow.

"Good afternoon, Sister Murphy. I'm Melvin Collier, head usher here at St. Andrew. Won't you join the pastor and new members in the ladies' parlor for light refreshments?" Melvin Collier held out a very official looking gloved hand toward a door in the wings.

"Oh. Thank you, but I will not be staying." Iris kept moving toward the church exit to make her point.

"The pastor insists, sister. Just stay a few minutes," he said with a charming smile. He moved slightly in front of Iris. She followed the usher to a room furnished like a Victorian parlor— complete with tapestry wingback chairs, small mahogany tables, and lace curtains. "This is the Women's Ministry room," Melvin announced. "Make yourself comfortable. Refreshments will be served momentarily," the usher said before leaving her in front of a massive ornate bookshelf. And there she stood.

Ladies wearing slim rectangular pins, which read, *New Members Committee*, on their suit lapels, entered through a pair of French doors. They carried an assortment of petit fours, tea sandwiches, and drinks. Other new members and visitors meandered in moving past her unnoticed. The room began to fill up, but Iris recognized no one. No one except the small lady with the hand sanitizer.

She watched her take a seat in a high-backed wing chair nestled in a far corner. She rifled through her handbag for a moment before lifting her eyes to look directly at Iris. She smiled and nodded. Iris nodded back. As soon as Iris prepared to take a step out of her cozy place on the wall, she was blocked by a large pink hat. The wearer of the hat turned to face Iris and said, "Oh! Theeeere are you are! I've been looking all over for you!" The woman's voice was a high shrill C-minor. She reached out with both arms and pulled Iris into a hug. "Your grandmother was one of my best friends. I'm Luceal Baxter, but everyone calls me Ceal. "It is nice to meet you Ms. Baxter."
"No. It's a pleasure to meet YOU. I've read—oh—I mean
I've heard so much about you. I feel like I'm meeting a celebrity." She was holding Iris' hand tightly when she turned and yelled across the room. "Laura! Come here and meet Maggie's grand!" Iris tried to pull her hand back, but Luceal tightened her grip.

"Oh! Ceal, she's a pretty lil thang. Lil' chocolate self!" the lady called Laura said. She was wearing a white shirtdress and deaconess' hat.

"Iris, I want you to meet my sister, Laura. We're fraternal twins in case you're wondering." But Iris was not wondering. She was only thinking, *Oh no, there are two of them*! She did not want there to be two of them. Or one of them. Nor did she want to meet any of these people. In fact, she had never said St. Andrew would be her church home. She merely said she would stay on in Sweet Fields since her granny had left her the house and everything she owned. Iris was on the verge of panic. She did not like crowds, strangers, or questions; she knew questions would be coming soon.

The one called Laura spoke first. Her makeup was too perfect. This is what made Iris nervous. "Now, Iris. Your grandmother, God bless the dead, hosted all of our Tuesday Tea meetings and our Saturday Sewing Circle meetings. You know Maggie was the only one who had a house large enough to host such gatherings. We were hoping you would be willing to host next month's meetings," Laura asked leaning in but speaking rather loudly. Laura's voice went up on the word *meeting*, and the collar of her little white shirt dress vibrated with excitement and anticipation. Laura's perfectly manicured left eyebrow remained raised as she waited for Iris' answer.

"I will not." Iris said shortly. Tea? Sewing? What year were they in? She would not have nosy biddies in her granny's home to snoop and ask for things. Laura's eyebrow dropped, and Iris thought she heard the woman growl. Iris reaffirmed her position about the manifold meetings the woman proposed. "Absolutely not." She arched a brow at the one called Luceal, the one who said she had "read" about her. SHE most definitely was not coming into her Granny's home. While her sister, Laura, was much too made up to be comfortable with, Iris thought that the one called Luceal could use a visit from Clinton and Kelly of "What Not to Wear."

"You've been here a month. We'll give you another month to get yourself together, and we'll talk about it over brunch. We know you've got to move your family down here with you."

"There is no family. There will be no Tuesday Teas, nor will there be Saturday Sewing," Iris said having finally snatched her hand from Luceal's grasp. Using that same hand, she smoothed the hair at the nape of her neck and looked for some salvation in the room.

"But why?" Laura wanted to know. "Maggie would have wanted it that way, don't you think? You—her granddaughter carrying on her community traditions. "

"Oh quit harassing her, already Laura and Luceal. And stand back! Are you trying to steal her breath? Jesus!" Laura and Luceal stepped aside to reveal the small lady with the hand sanitizer. "Let the girl breathe some FRESH air and get her bearings," she said while taking a small vial from her neck and spraying the air around the twins.

The two sisters slunk away leaving Iris standing with the small, gray-haired lady. Iris, already tall and wearing stilettos, stood head and shoulders over her. For closure, Locke yelled at the twins' backs, "...and how would you mewing cats know what Maggie wanted. Just, please…" Iris observed how the loc'ed woman threw those words at the women as if she were throwing out old pot liquor. She had never felt more grateful since she moved to Sweet Fields.

"I'm Belle. Belle Lynne Locke. You may call me Belle. I would shake your hand, but I don't have my gloves on." She said shifting her eyes from her hands to Iris' hands. "No offense, dear. I'm rather particular about germs and such."

"I am rather particular too," Iris said, not explaining exactly what she was so particular about.

"I noticed. Now, those two sisters are trouble. Stay away from them; they are full of germs of evil. Don't tell them anything.
Not even the time." Belle said, rolling her eyes in their direction. Locke began to walk in the direction of the two wing backed chairs, and Iris followed, almost dutifully. "The stories I could tell you about the Baxter sisters will curdle your blood, but we'll save that for another day," she said turning to look at Iris full on. So, you're Maggie Murphy's granddaughter. Maggs and I were thick as thieves in our girlhood days. She was a clever woman, your grandmother. And it looks like you're particular just like her."

"What do you mean by that?" Iris asked arching a thick eyebrow.

"Oh calm down. I mean the way you kept smoothing your dress. Maggs did that all the time. She couldn't bear to have lines or wrinkles in things—table linens, bed linens, clothes, kitchen towels, you name it. I also noticed you can be quite terse. You said 'There is no family and there will be no teas or sewing'. Very short and to the point. And no contractions! I like that most. That's how city people talk. Quick, sharp, and rude. I mean, by southern standards, that was rude, but you can't be rude enough to the Baxter sisters. You keep that city-sharp tongue of yours ready. You're going to need it."

Before Locke could continue, Prentiss LeBeaux was at her side. "Sister Locke." His voice smiled when he said Locke's name. He was warm toward her, and while he never once touched Belle Lynne Locke, his hovering way let Iris know they had history. Rev. LeBeaux turned to greet Iris. "Hello again, Sister Iris. I can't tell you how good it is to have you in our midst. Now, if you'll excuse Ms. Belle and me, we're going to step away for a moment. You don't mind do you?"

"Oh no," Iris breathed. Belle Lynne Locke's forwardness had made Iris uncomfortable, but she couldn't help think about how relieved she was to see the stately little woman and her sanitizer during service and how thankful she was to be the recipient of her rescue mission afterward. She watched Pastor LeBeaux as he walked away with Locke. He bent his head down toward the small woman, listening tentatively. Iris noticed how his right hand hovered ever so gently under Locke's left elbow, which was crooked just enough to allow her Louis Vuitton pouchette to dangle from her arm. While the chatter of the gathering never stopped, all eyes were on the pair as they continued on in quiet conversation, as if no one else was in the room. *Long money*, Iris heard her granny's voice speak gently in her ear.

Later, Iris stood on the church steps, slid on her Kate Spade sunglasses, and decided to walk home through the park. Pendleton Park was lovely this time of year. Though she wished they had been grouped by color, she couldn't help but smile at the tulips that lined her path through the park.

The Pendleton was directly across the street from St. Andrew and her home—it still felt funny to call granny's home hers—was just two blocks away. She strolled along carefully and admired her grandmother's house when it came into view. The large Victorian house sat on the corner of Magnolia and Cuyler. The olive green paint looked fresh and the whitewashed trim and fence, crisp. It was a beautiful house, and her granny was meticulous about its curb appeal. She eyed the porch swing and decided she would have her Sunday dinner al fresco.

Iris enjoyed the porch swing well into the evening. A few children rode by on their bikes. The adults walked by and waved to her. She nodded in response afraid that a warm smile and hearty wave would be misinterpreted as a welcome for them to join her on the large porch. When the sun shined its final light, she turned to go inside and recognized the slightest flutter of curtains in the front window of the house across the street. Her grandmother told her about him. Bennett Banks, the man who watched all things and said nothing. Iris decided that she would deal with him later, on an evening when she was not so sleepy and over worn from the day.

Just as she climbed into her grandmother's California kingsized bed, the phone rang. She stared at the cordless phone blinking green lights at her for a long moment before answering.

"Hello," she clipped out.

"That's interesting. You don't ASK 'hello?' like most people when they answer the phone. This is Belle. I hope I'm not disturbing you."

"I am just getting into bed. How may I help you?" Iris asked flatly.

"I have a question for you. Did you notice the two ladies trying to kill each other during service today?" Belle sounded like she was smiling.

"Kill each other?" Iris asked while propping herself up against a mountain of pillows.

"Oh, yes. If looks could kill, the deaconess and the organist would be at the Willie Richmond's Funeral Home." Belle giggled.

"Oh yes! I did notice them. Did you notice how they both reacted when the reverend stood up?"

Belle cackled loudly. "I knew I was right about you. You don't miss a thing! What do you think it's all about?"

"Well, I don't know any of them, but it seems like the ladies both want the reverend's attentions. Is he married?"

"Rev. LeBeaux? No. He lost his wife of 20 years about 5 years ago. They had been married since they were 18 years old. Clive and I had been married 43 wonderful years." There was a long pause. Finally, Belle continued. "I hear Jacqueline Black, the deaconess, is fairly new in town. She came about a year ago. That woman is on a mission. You mark my words."

"How do you know all of this? I thought you were new to the church."

"I am new…somewhat. This is my hometown. I grew up here. Got married here. Clive and I visited often, but I decided to come back for good when Clive died. "

"So how long have you been back in Sweet Fields?

"Not long. Today was my first Sunday back in church. You want to know how I could possibly know the goings on of St. Andrew if I don't talk to people, don't you? Well, I read lips. I don't have to talk TO people to know what's going on. I just look at them while they talk. I can stand at a safe distance—away from germs and viruses and STILL be in the proverbial loop." Belle laughed an eerie giggle. "Now don't you go telling people my secret," she chided.

"Your secret is safe with me. You're the only person I've had a conversation with since I've been here. I, uh, prefer to keep to myself." Even as Iris spoke these words, she wondered how was it that this woman had drawn her in with such a short exchange over the phone.

"I see. 'You, uh, prefer to keep to yourself.' Well, I think something's made you that way; we don't have to talk about it tonight. But we will talk about it 'cause I like to know who I'm friends with."

"Friends? Who me? You don't even know me."

"Child, I know all I need to know for now. You keep to yourself. You tell it just like it is, and your eyes move 'cross people faster than mine do. That means you see a lot that other people don't see." There was silence. Belle had read Iris like a book and in doing so shut down the conversation for a few moments. Finally, Belle broke the uncomfortable silence. "Well, Iris. You know I like that name. It's an old lady's name, but you'll grow into it. I'm going to bed. I will see you tomorrow." And with a click of a button, Belle was gone.

Tomorrow? What was tomorrow? Iris had plans for tomorrow. Apparently, Belle did too.

CHAPTER 3: SHOES

Iris woke up to the urgent ringing of a doorbell. She frowned and covered her head. "Oh my God! Who the devil is it?" she growled rolling out of bed. She murmured and blasphemed the ringer of the bells as she slipped on a robe and stomped, barefoot, down the stairs. The wood floors were cool against her feet. She snatched the massive oak door open and yelled through the screen door "what?!" She saw no one. She looked to the sides of the porch and found Belle sitting in the porch swing. Belle looked as if she'd been sitting on the swing for hours, as if it were her home. She had on gloves.

"My, my. Aren't we testy in the morning?" she teased smiling. "Where are your shoes?"

"What? Shoes? I was in bed asleep!"

"That's the problem with young folk. They don't take care of themselves. You should never walk around barefoot! It's bad for the reproductive organs."

"That doesn't make any sense, Mrs. Locke. What do you want?" Iris asked still frowning.

"I want you to go put some shoes on is what I want. What I **need** is for you to get dressed and come with me downtown."

"Downtown? What's downtown?" Iris recalled the frustration of the downtown shops—Mom and Pop shops.

"My favorite shoe store. *Dolce Chasseurs.*"

"I see. But why must I come with you?"

"I need to get to know you. What better way to get to know someone than while shoe shopping? If you require more conversation about it, can you at least put on some socks?" Iris sighed loudly and went back inside and up the stairs. Belle remained in the swing.

Moments later, Iris returned to the porch to find Belle bending over the azalea bushes in the yard. "Mrs. Locke. What are you doing?"

"Beautiful azaleas, Iris. Just beautiful. Your grandmother always did have a green thumb." She stood up and realigned her long linen blouse. "Did you know they were poisonous? Just as pretty as

they can be, but that kind of pretty right there," Locke pointed at the azaleas again, "will kill you dead…come on. Genevieve is waiting for us." Locke skipped down the steps. This surprised Iris, but not a lot. Locke snapped her head around to Iris on the last step and said crisply, "And do not call me Mrs.
Locke. It's either Belle Lynne or Locke for YOU. For you, only."

Iris slipped into the passenger seat of Belle's special edition navy Cadillac CTS coupe. She admired the tan leather craftsmanship and said so.

"I absolutely detest Cadillacs, but Clive, bless his heart, insisted that I have one. Navy is my favorite color, so he made a special order. I can't bring myself to do anything with it except drive it. My Clive…he was such a sweetheart."

Belle's voice got a little shaky when she spoke of Clive. Iris knew how that felt—to speak of a loved one and get choked up with tears. Iris, unsure of what to say, said nothing. Eventually, the car glided soundlessly out of the residential area and onto Sweet Field's main street. The historic downtown was home to many quaint boutiques, cafes, and shops. The clientele consisted mainly of tourists and upper crust residents. Most people shopped at the mall on the west end of town. Sweet Fields Galleria was a good collection of the popular retail and department stores. Iris had visited the galleria mall once or twice and had been sorely disappointed. She resorted to online shopping. It had never occurred to her to visit the Shops of Sweet Fields on Main Street.

Locke parked the coupe in front of a coffee shop, and the two ladies prepared to exit the car. As Locke walked around the front of the car to join Iris on the sidewalk, she said "what in blue blazes is she wearing?"

"Who?" Iris asked looking around. Locke tipped her sunglasses, little round ones like John Lennon used to wear, and looked across the street at the *Majestic Divine Dancers of Heavenly Bodies.* Iris looked in the direction of Locke's gesture and saw the tall thin lady from church emerging from a red Ford Thunderbird convertible. Her long, graceful form was draped in a yellow chiffon duster over yellow leotards. Her head and neck were wrapped in a yellow floral scarf. She wore a black pair of round shades that nearly covered the entire top half of her face.

"That's the lady from church yesterday. Who is she?"

"Trouble. That's who she is." Belle said grabbing Iris' elbow. She visualized the words "Bubonic Banana" along the side of Jackie Black's body.

They made an odd pair, Iris thought—Locke in her early sixties and she in her late twenties. Locke with her short, petite frame, and Iris with her height and curves.

"Jean Claude and his sister Genevieve are lovely people. The customer service is legendary." Belle said pausing in front of the store *Dolce Chasseurs.*

A gentleman with a silver beard and curly mop of white hair opened the door as Iris reached for the handle.

"Ah! Belle! Bonjour! Comment êtes-vous?" the man said air kissing Locke. "Et qui est votre ami?" He said turning to Iris.

"Jean Paul, I am so glad to see you again! This is my new friend, Iris Murphy. Iris, this is Jean Paul Babineuax." Locke said standing between the two. The Frenchman kissed the back of Iris' hand and flashed her a brilliant white smile.

"It is a pleasure to meet you, Iris. Any friend of Belle's is a friend of ours." Jean Paul said not taking his eyes away from Iris'.

"Yes, yes, Jean Paul. Stop flirting. She's young enough to be your daughter," Locke said rapping him lightly on his chest with her knuckles. "Where is your gorgeous sister, Genevieve?"

"She is in the parlor preparing for you. Please, ladies do go through," he said gesturing towards a pair of green velvet curtains. "Oh, we shall, Jean, but I want to show Iris your beautiful shoe boutique," Locke said as she grabbed Iris' elbow again with a pink gloved hand.

They perused the shoes on display. Iris was teeming with excitement. She noted the brands of the finely crafted leather shoes and decided right away this was her favorite place in Sweet Fields. The disadvantage of online shopping for Iris was that she couldn't touch or smell the leather. For her, that was one of the most exciting parts of shoe shopping, and she missed it. Locke was telling Iris about her favorite shoemaker in the United Kingdom when they heard a woman's voice address them.

"Well, hello, ladies," said the voice. Locke and Iris turned to face the tall woman in banana yellow. Her eyes bulged anxiously as Locke and Iris took in the sight of her.

Locke spoke first. "Hello, Jacqueline. Don't you look, er…like the picture of spring this morning."

"Why, thank you, Belle. I shall value that compliment, as I hear they are rare coming from you." Jacqueline turned to Iris. "I don't believe we have met. I'm Jackie Black," she said extending a slender hand.

"I'm Iris Murphy. It's a pleasure to meet you."

"You know," Jackie said trailing her fingers over a lowheeled pump on display. "I never knew this was a shoe store."

"I'm sure you didn't, dear. Most people visit the mall for their footwear. Only those with more discriminating tastes shop here."

Iris watched Jackie fondle the shoes on the shelf in front of her. Locke noted the way Jackie turned each shoe over to check for prices.

"Oh no, dear. Jean Paul doesn't disrespect his shoes by placing stickers on them. Surely you've heard the saying, 'If you have to ask...' I'm sure Macy's has what you need." Jackie whirled around to face Locke, but Locke had already turned away and was smiling at a woman near a curtained entryway. "Come, Iris. Genevieve is ready for us." As the two ladies walked toward the curtains, Locke turned to look at Jackie over her shoulder.

"I'm so sorry we can't continue this little chat, but Iris and I have appointments."

"Appointments with a shoe clerk? Belle, if I make you uncomfortable, I understand. You don't have to make things up." Jackie said with a smirk on her lips. Jackie started to follow the women beyond the velvet rope and curtain of the shoe store. She spun around dramatically, and the banana yellow chiffon whipped around as she turned to go through the curtains along with Iris and Locke. Jean Paul met her twirl with a smirk and wink.

"Non, non, non, Madame," Locke said in a surprisingly spot-on French accent. "You, Jacqueline, may continue your window shopping out here, whilst we have our tea and select our shoes in privacy and comfort." She and Iris disappeared through the velvet curtains. Jackie watched the bullion fringe swing until Jean Paul approached her.

"Madame, perhaps you would like to try the shoe?" he said looking at the leather ballet flat Jackie was bending and twisting in her hands. Jackie threw the shoe at Jean Paul's chest and stormed out of the shop with her banana yellow chiffon scarf trailing after her.

Genevieve waited for them on the other side of the green velvet curtains in a cozy parlor warmly decorated in tapestries and lace. She brought iced tea, sherry, and mimosas in crystal pitchers with crystal glasses on a silver serving tray. She gestured for them to sit in the upholstered armchairs and gathered their handbags— Locke's brown MZ Wallace satchel and Iris' black Kate Spade cross body—and hung them carefully on a nearby coat rack. While the ladies sipped their sweet tea, Genevieve brought out boxes of shoes and placed them on a nearby table. She brought Locke a pair of exquisite handmade shandals first. Then, she brought Iris a pair of nude Louboutin pointed toe slingbacks. When Iris smiled and sighed, Genevieve smiled and nodded.

"Oh! These are beautiful!" Iris giggled. "Did you tell her what I like?"

"No. That's Genevieve's power of deduction. She's mute, you know. But she can read a woman's feet like a book. The more she gets to know you, the more she will amaze you by discerning your likes, dislikes, and what will look and feel good on you," Locke said nodding her approval to Genevieve.

The forty-year-old French woman with waist length hair gathered the boxes and set them aside. She refilled Iris' glasses with sweet tea, poured Locke a fresh glass of sherry, and disappeared behind the curtain again.

"You can only shop with Genevieve by appointment. I've been knowing her and Jean Paul for years." Locke sniffed awkwardly. "My Clive was Genevieve and Jean Paul's investors, you could say."

Genevieve returned with two smaller boxes. Sandals. She opened the box for Locke and slipped the leather thong on her foot. Then Iris, but Iris had already opened her box and was sliding her foot into the shoe. Genevieve smiled and nodded. When the appointment was over, Genevieve had sold Locke a pair of RED shandals and a pair of Daniel Greene slippers. Belle Lynne Locke had also consumed several glasses of sherry. Iris noticed how Locke fumbled just a little with the little pink gloves. Genevieve had sold Iris two pair of Louboutin sling backs—in nude and black and a pair of white leather thong sandals. Iris was just as drunk, but with the wine of shoe buying. Shoes were the one purchase Iris preferred not to make over the internet. Here at J & G's Dolce Chasseurs, she knew no one else had ever put her foot in the shoes she'd purchased. The ladies paid for their shoes, hugged and gave both Jean Paul and Genevieve air kisses near their cheeks. They stepped out into the sunny sidewalk.

They walked next door to the café and had a light lunch, al fresco. Iris' lunch consisted of a Caesar salad, while Locke nibbled on chicken salad served on a bed of lettuce. As they chatted, Jackie cruised by in her red convertible. Her eyes fixated on Iris and Locke as she slowed while passing the cafe'.

"Alright. What's her story?" Iris asked peering over her sunglasses. Belle Lynne Locke looked back at Iris, and her lips curved into a teasing smile.

"Before we talk about Jacqueline, I want to talk about you."

"What about me?"

"I want to know whatever it is about you that has everyone whispering."

Iris knew it was going to come up sooner or later. She was glad for the opportunity to talk about it. She had been quiet for so long. She had hidden for so long. She might cry. Just thinking about Lloyd made her cry. She sighed and removed her sunglasses, smoothed her black cigarette pants over her thighs, and touched the diamond pendant resting at her neck.

"Well, what do you want to know, Belle?" Iris asked calmly.

Locke moved her chair over an inch or two, leaned in, and said quietly "whatever you want to tell me, but I'd prefer if you start at the beginning." She smiled and Iris relaxed a little. She had to tell someone. Right now, Locke was the only friend she had. So Iris sipped at her mimosa and started at the beginning…

CHAPTER 4: LLOYD

Iris took Lloyd Sutton's creative writing class as an undergraduate English major. She had read all of his books, and could hardly contain herself when he asked to see her after class. It was the end of the fall semester, and she had done well in the course. Dr. Sutton had plans for a new historical fiction novel and needed an assistant. His wife had usually assisted with his writing, but since their nasty divorce, he had taken a break from writing and people altogether. He had become impressed with the nineteen year old who sat at the front of his noon class. She was always early, always present, and always attentive. He offered her a job working as his assistant over the Christmas break, and she readily accepted until he explained she would live in his home for the duration of the break. Iris was uncomfortable at the news, but when he explained that Ruth, his middle aged housekeeper also lived there, she reluctantly agreed.

What was intended to be a holiday job of three weeks turned out to last for ten years-- the rest of Lloyd's life. Iris became Lloyd's research assistant, traveling companion, friend, dog-walker, and anything the eccentric little man needed. He was like a father or uncle to her. When he isolated himself to write, she was the only person he allowed to enter his solitary confinement.

Iris thought solitary confinement was harsh phrasing for a man who loved writing so much. Lloyd, however, informed Iris that he hated writing as much as he loved it, that often words were both his ailment and his antidote. Like the wheelchair in which he sat, Lloyd's writing got him where he wanted to be, even in his crippled state. His confinement helped him stay focused on the story and its characters. Brimming with shelves and shelves of books, solitary confinement was Lloyd's playground. It was a room that looked like fall year round, with piles of books from the floor to the arm of his overstuffed leather chair, where he read his chosen classics like, *The Catcher in the Rye*, *Lolita*, *The Sun Also Rises*, and *Sherlock Holmes*. The pile near the burnt orange upholstered chair consisted of *The Bluest Eye*, *Paradise Lost*, and *The*

Three Musketeers. When he read, Lloyd was always in one of the chairs. Often the piles of books would spill onto the floor when he was in a reading frenzy. They obstructed Lloyd's navigation; at these times Iris was allowed to come in and clear a path for Lloyd to move around and make his way, in his wheelchair, to the sleek MacBook Pro he liked to have positioned smack dab in the middle of the huge curved mahogany desk. The desk was as intimidating as it was inviting, with its curves and bends. Lloyd had it made special; now, Iris owned it--this gift from Lloyd that kept on giving even after he died. She situated the desk across from the fireplace in grandma Maggs', no her--Iris' study--just the way Lloyd had arranged it in his own study.

Other times, Iris would enter Lloyd's solitary confinement to bring him food, on a plain silver tray. He didn't ask for much: a turkey sandwich, dry, with water; almond butter on toast; Sun Chips. It was easy to see how others would think she was his glorified maid, or even an overpaid amanuensis; but Iris knew she was more than that to Lloyd. She had been his confidant, his muse, and always his second set of eyes. It was rumored that the unlikely pair—frail, temperamental writer confined to a wheelchair and a tall, curvy young student—were having an affair. Some even called Iris his "pet" or "Girl Friday." Once, she had mentioned the gossip to Lloyd, and he smiled and said, "Let them talk. They are simpletons who have never had anyone of any importance show any interest in them. Besides you do not work for free. You are invaluable to me, and I have compensated you well, but they need not know it. They are envious. That is all."

Lloyd had compensated Iris well. The work she did on campus was paid for through the school. For the work she did on the weekends and breaks, she was paid handsomely. After the two collaborated for a year, Lloyd began to pay her tuition and expenses. He called it a scholarship and never spoke of it again.

While Iris worked for Lloyd, he managed to write several books and sell the rights of three of them to movie producers. Iris, Ruth, and Manny—the driver—were Lloyd's family. Upon his death, Lloyd left his vacation home in Big Sur, Shakespeare (his Scottish terrier), and a sizeable nest egg to Ruth and Manny who had fallen in love during their employ. Lloyd had been an only child, his parents were deceased, and his failed marriage yielded no children. He willed the rest of his estate to Iris.

The death of Lloyd Sutton—the famous mystery writer—made national news. Ruth and Manny wed quietly and slipped off to start their lives together in Big Sur. Meanwhile, the tabloid reporters had a field day with Iris—calling her a gold digger, a child bride, and even a murder suspect. She would have left San Francisco, but she had nowhere else to go. She was just like Lloyd. That's why Lloyd took care of her. He had been a "college orphan" as he had put it. Iris' parents had divorced when she was a baby. Her mother was dead, and her father had moved to Italy with a girlfriend. The only family Iris had was her father's mother—Maggie Murphy-- who lived in Sweet Fields, Georgia. Iris located her grandmother and made a trip to Sweet Fields to visit her. Iris returned to San Francisco to take care of some business transactions and had planned a longer stay with her grandmother, but Maggie died before Iris could return. Maggie, having fallen in love with the granddaughter she hadn't seen since the girl was five, changed her will to include Iris as the sole beneficiary—not St. Andrew as she had originally intended.

"So," Iris sighed. "Here I am with no family, no friends, and more money and stuff than I know what to do with."

"That explains why there are so many whispers about you." Locke said gesturing to the server for another mimosa. "The pastor and the finance committee knew of Maggie's initial will, so you can imagine their surprise when they learned of the new one leaving YOU everything."

"I had no idea!" Iris gasped. "Should I give the church the money?"

"NO! Absolutely not! Not yet anyway. Just calm down and sit tight. You can help St. Andrew alright, but the timing has to be perfect. We have a number of things to do, you and I." Locke said in a loud whispered. "The first of which is getting rid of that Jackie Black."

"Get rid of? What do you mean?" Iris asked eyeing the plate of croissants the server had placed in the center of the table.

"There's something about that woman that disturbs me. She has the demeanor of some of the headhunters I've encountered on my travels. She's on a mission." Locke shivered,
"She's hunting for heads, and she has one candidate in her sights."

"You mean a fortune hunter?"

"I know what I said. She's a headhunter. She's looking for a husband. Not just any man will do. She's looking for a pastor, and right now, our own reverend is in her crosshairs." Iris opened her mouth and stared at Locke. "And don't ask me how I know. I just do. Pay special attention to her."

The pair left the café and rode in silence for a while through Sweet Fields.

"Why didn't you eat a croissant? You wanted to," Locke asked without looking at Iris.

"I try to limit my bread. I tend to have high glucose levels, and eating bread elevates it."

"Ah. I see. I would say you need some meat on your bones," Locke paused, "but I don't eat much meat myself. Anyway you have plenty of meat on your bones. Deacon Hughes noticed it. Especially the meat on your backside."

"Who? Noticed what?" Iris asked shocked.

"Deacon Hughes. He's the tallest man on the deacon's board. He's tall just like his daddy. His father, Big Hughes, was a good-looking tom cat in his day, but he married Edie who's almost as tall as him. William is their son; he is good looking like his father and clumsy like his mother. When you were at the front of the church, he couldn't take his eyes off you. He studied you from head to toe. He'll come 'round to your house this week, I suspect. Let me know when he does and what excuse he gives to call on you. You have to be careful of those long-legged Hughes men."

Iris said nothing. She had noticed the man Belle was talking about. She had made a mental note of how handsome he was, but she had missed the man's inspection of her. She hoped Locke was wrong about him coming to visit. She wasn't ready for romance. When Locke slowed to a stop in front of Maggie Murphy's former legendary Bed & Breakfast, Iris released her seat belt and reached for the door handle.

"Iris, we need to go to bible study on Wednesday night early. I need you to help me get rid of this Jackie Black creature. Now, will you be able to focus or are you already over the moon about William Hughes?"

"I'm not interested in William Hughes." Iris snapped.

"Good, but he's going to come sniffing around, as he is surely interested in you...or your money. Call me with any new developments. Especially if members of St. Andrew pay you a visit. Right now, you're a pretty pink piggy bank; the wrong people will be coming to smash you to bits and take what's inside. The genuine people, though, won't utter a word---because they won't know you from the girl at the Piggly Wiggly.

"Thanks, Locke. For everything."

"No, Iris. Thank you. Tetta!"

Later that day, Iris answered a ringing doorbell and found Jackie Black standing on her porch.

Iris opened the heavy oak door and spoke to Jackie from behind the screen door.

"What can I do for you?" Iris asked with a strained smile. Jackie was the last person she expected to see.

"I wanted to apologize for my behavior earlier today. You seem like a very sweet girl. We are both fairly new at St. Andrew. We could be good friends," she said smiling sweetly.

Iris was speechless. She wanted to tell the woman to get the hell off of her porch, but she needed to know if what Locke believed about her was true.

"Would you like some tea? We can sit on the porch." There was no way that woman was coming into her granny's house.

"Oh! I'd be delighted," she said moving to sit on the porch swing. Moments later Iris reappeared on the porch carrying two tall glasses of sweet tea.

"So how long have you been at St. Andrew?" Iris asked feigning interest.

"I moved here almost a year ago and opened a dance studio downtown. I became a member of St. Andrew, after my former pastor wrote me an excellent reference, and I joined the Deaconess Board right away." She sighed and took a sip of her tea.
Her eyes never left Iris.

"Wow. You jumped right in, didn't you?"

"Well," she gushed. "I also started the praise dance troupe. And I plan to work very closely on the St. Andrew Daycare project. Pastor Prentiss and I will be meeting this week to select the committee members. Would you like to be on the committee? I can make that happen since I am committee chair." Jackie tilted her head upward and stretched her neck slightly on the words, *committee chair.*

Horrified, Iris stopped the gentle swaying of the porch swing. "No. Absolutely not. I have way too much to do as it is."

"Oh, come on. What do you have to do? You're an heiress...twice over! You have nothing but time and money." She laughed loudly, touching Iris lightly on her arm. Apparently, she had heard the gossip. Iris figured everyone would know soon enough, but she did not appreciate Jackie's laughter. She did not like the sound of it; it was throaty. Stretched. Vulgar.

"Well, Jackie, speaking of time, I have to get back inside. I will think about the committee. When is your meeting with
Reverend?"

"We're meeting Wednesday afternoon at 4pm. I tried to have a dinner meeting, but he insisted we meet before bible study."

"Well, I need to think about it. If I decide to join your efforts, I will meet you at the church."
Iris watched Jackie smile and glide from her porch slowly.
Jackie folded herself into her Thunderbird and drove away.

Iris had to tell Locke what happened. She dialed Locke's number and pleaded aloud for her to pick up. She picked up on the third ring.

"What has happened, Iris?" Locke asked without so much as a greeting.

"Jackie Black just left my house. We had tea." Iris said excitedly. There was no response on the other end of the line for a while. Finally Locke spoke.

"How soon can you get here?" Locke's question came fast, like one word.

"Five minutes, I guess. You're what about 2, 3 blocks away?"

"One street behind you and three blocks down. Come around to the back gate. I don't want Harry seeing me accept company. He'll be dragging his sad sack of bones over to be nosy, and we have work to do. Well, come on!" And then she hung up.

Iris wasn't sure why she was excited, but she was. She grabbed her keys and ran out the back door. She unlocked the gate that led to the backyard and looked up to see Locke standing on a massive enclosed deck watching her from above. As Iris climbed the stairs to the deck, she thought of the stairs in Lloyd's Nob Hill mansion. She smiled. She looked through the glass and saw that Locke's eyes remained fixed on her with her mouth drawn into a tight line. Iris opened the glass door, and immediately Locke asked,
"did she touch you?"

"What? Touch me? Who?" Iris asked closing the door behind her.

"Did that Jackie creature touch you? Whilst you two were having tea?"

"As a matter of fact, she did. She touched me lightly on the arm." Iris touched her own arm lightly, as she followed Locke into a massive French country style kitchen.

Locke whipped around and faced Iris, "No. You wait here." Locke moved silently around the large island, pulled open a drawer, and gave a small bottle to Iris.

"Here. Put this on your hands and arms." It was a vial of sanitizer. "That's right. On up to your elbows." Iris did as she was told and waited for Locke to provide instruction. "Come over here. Let's get this thing together."

They settled around the round kitchen table where a crystal decanter and sherry glasses waited for them. A large wrought iron French-styled pendant light hung overhead. Locke slid over a small platter of tea cakes and noticed how Iris stared at them. Locke also noticed that Iris gave the slightest sniff, taking in the fragrance of the lemon and lavender flavored delights.

"Tell me what happened," Locke said quietly as she sipped from the dainty glass.

Iris relayed the details of Jackie's visit and waited for a response. Locke twirled her glass in her hand and turned the corners of her lips downward.

"Prentiss is planning a fundraiser for the daycare. This will be a gathering of who's who in Parish County. Everyone who is anyone of importance with more than a few dollars will be there. There will be some very influential people there from Atlanta, too. We've got to make sure this event goes off without a hitch. I've got my people working on it to make sure it is the most glamorous event since the mayor's daughter got married back in '99." Locke smiled and poured herself another glass of wine.

"You will join her committee and go to the meetings and report everything to me," she said after a long sip. "I need you to tell me every single thing that woman says and does," Locke said rising from the table. "I have some calls to make. I'll call you later."

Iris walked back home teeming with excitement. This reminded her of the days and nights she spent with Lloyd plotting the schemes of characters. This time, though, it wasn't in a book-it was real.

CHAPTER 5: THE EVENT

Iris remembered Locke saying that *her people* would make the gala more than aesthetically pleasing. Iris didn't know who Locke's *people* were, but they did a marvelous job. The place was dripping with elegance and sparkling with glamour all at once. Iris was fortunate enough to see the grand display in its completion, hours before guests began to arrive. Locke permitted this, because she liked the young woman. And while her tone with Iris was brisk at times, Locke felt a genuine kinship with Iris. She knew that Iris would appreciate the work put into making the gala an unforgettable event. And that, Locke's *people* did.

They had transformed the old Sweet Fields Armory into a wonderland of sleek black chairs, luxurious white linens, and lush flowers and foliage. White sheer drapes provided the backdrop of the two-storied space. Giant ferns sat atop twenty-foot columns that were aligned to section off the dance floor. Iris tried to keep her mouth closed, but she couldn't believe what she was seeing. How had the old armory been converted from an old musty warehouse to such an elegant venue? Iris thought that the room even smelled rich and decadent. The lux of the ballroom reminded Iris of the red-carpet events Lloyd would sometimes attend to celebrate his book and movie premieres. She was a long way from the red carpet and flashing lights of the paparazzi of Hollywood, but Locke had managed to bring Hollywood to Sweet
Fields.

She walked gingerly between the tables and saw the Steinway piano nestled between two columns at the edge of the white dance floor. She wanted to glide her fingers across the top, as she'd seen sultry singers on TV do, but resisted the urge, though it almost overwhelmed her. Between another set of columns was a bandstand. Iris imagined members of the band box would be arriving in the next few hours, but she was glad she could view the room without throngs of people bustling about. Iris thought about how the gala of the season was so different from her life of solitude with Lloyd. There were film screenings and viewing parties, but Lloyd required small intimate gatherings for events of that sort. This was totally different, and Iris would have to emerge from her cocoon of comfort. Locke was pushing Iris more than she was used to. Not only did she agree to be Locke's eyes and ears on the gala committee, but Locke had roped her into being a vital part of both its inner and outer workings. To top it off, Locke was holding a by-invitation-only nightcap after the gala. While the nightcap was more intimate, Iris knew nothing of the guest list, and her aversion for the unknown made her anxious.

This is why Iris decided it best to visit the venue before show time. She wanted to mark territories, so that when she returned by evening, her experience would not seem so foreign. She would also go by Locke's house before walking home to dress for the gala.

There were people at Locke's. She could see several silhouettes moving like dancing shadows behind the sheers at the window. Iris had always liked the big windows of the Victorian home. The vines creeping along the soft pink brick seemed to try to make their way inside through the long panes that were dressed in ivory sheers all around. On Locke's porch were two tiny women meticulously streaming copious strands of small clear lights along the front porch. Both women wore glasses on their noses, and they strung the lights with unflappable concentration. By the time Iris made it to the porch, Locke was meeting her at the front door. "Did you see it?" she asked briskly.

"Yes. It is beautiful and so tastefully done. How did you get it to make such a stark transformation?"

"I told you, Iris. I put my people on it. Don't look so shocked. Come on in."

"I will not be here too long. I just wanted--"

"I'm back here getting dressed. Do you need someone to dress you?" Locke's voice trailed off, but only because Iris was fascinated by the new look of Locke's home. The color scheme of black and white was reimagined in Locke's parlor and great room. There were tall bouquets of yellow tulips accenting two large round tables covered in crisp white tablecloths with a wide strip of ink black fabric dividing the whites of the cloth. Several people dressed in white scurried about, tugging here, pulling there, and smoothing elsewhere. There were taller bistro tables in the corners of the room with smatterings of soft yellow decor in the center. The ceiling was draped in antique white fabric, with the ends puddling in soft vanilla bunches on the dark hardwood floors. Iris could only imagine the ambience at nightfall with soft lighting and dainty white candles everywhere. "Come on! What are you waiting for?" Locke broke Iris' trance. As Iris followed Locke to her dressing room, she heard the silky low voice of a man. *A man?*

Iris thought. *In Locke's bedroom?*

"This is Antoine. He came to dress me." Antoine greeted Iris warmly, but spent very little time paying attention to her. He buzzed around Locke, pinning her hair, matching up accessories to a beautiful smoke gray dress hanging on her mirror, and fussing over an abundance of vials, canisters, and sprays. "So, do you think you're ready?"

"Ready for what?"

"Ready for your debut?" Locke gave Iris the once over. "Nope. You're not ready. Look at you now. You're as nervous as a humming bird. I've never seen anyone smoothing down skinny jeans. I don't think Maggs would even do that."

"Really, Locke. Must you make those kinds of assumptions? Have you no faith in me? At all? I'll be fine." Iris had not yet convinced herself of her own words.

"What are you wearing? I can send Antoine over to get you ready." At that statement, Antoine paused, turned toward Iris and raised his right eyebrow in slight objection.

"I can get myself ready. Besides, when did you become one to make such a fussy-fuss." Iris lifted her hand and flitted it around the room when she said the words *fussy-fuss*.

"I'm a little woman of few words, but it doesn't mean I don't know when to make a big deal. This, Maggs--I mean Iris--is a big deal.

Trust me. Now is the time to show Sweet Fields where your roots are."

"My roots are not here, Locke." Even as Iris said it, she had to admit, she was growing fond of Sweet Fields and St. Andrew. It felt like home to her.

"That's what your mouth says. But you wear that porch swing out every evening." Locke picked up a lemon teacake from a round silver tray Antoine had brought from the kitchen and into Locke's dressing closet. Her eyes slid up to see Iris glancing at the cookies. "You want some sweet tea? That's all I can offer you, since you don't eat anything breaded. You and those glucose levels."

Iris declined. "I have to get home and get dressed."

"I hope you wear the green one," Locke yelled from the dressing room as Iris left. "The green one says you have roots here."

Iris walked away smiling. She was excited. She hadn't felt excited in a while.

The men in tuxedos and women in black satin gowns were warming up their violins, cellos, basses, trumpets, bassoons, and clarinets. Iris noticed a rotund red-haired gentleman putting on his tuba. As she glanced at the array of orchestral instruments, she wondered *where did Locke get an orchestra?* She didn't know why she was surprised. Locke seemed to enjoy keeping her gala plans a secret from her...and everyone else. No one knew what to expect. The word on the street was if you wanted to see celebrities and be seen by celebrities, you should be there.

Iris had helped Locke strategically leak information about certain people on the guest list to boost ticket sales, and it had worked like a charm. Buzz about the gala was all over the airwaves, both AM and FM all the way to Atlanta. The handsome, recently divorced, TV judge Rick Carson, who most middle aged women thought to be the sexiest man alive was coming--alone. The adored news anchor for one of the most popular stations in the area was to emcee the program; Locke had smiled when she leaked that information to the deacon board. Even her devoted Clive had developed a small crush on Cindy

Sullivan. A few ladies from an Atlanta-based reality show were planning to attend as well. Sweet Fields was bursting at the seams with glamour, fanfare, and money, because Locke had personally invited CEOs of Fortune 500 companies, several of whom had RSVP'd.

The orchestra was no longer warming up and began playing in earnest, so Iris took that as a cue to slip into the ladies' room to check her makeup and hair. She gasped as she entered the room. Even the doors of the stalls were decorated with white satin and flower wreaths. Locke's people left no stone unturned. Iris was swiping her lips with gloss when the church organist, Maybelline Crowder, joined her in the mirror.

"Don't you look pretty?" Maybelline said a bit out of breath.

"Thank you. You look very pretty too" Iris returned with a curt nod. *When had she started nodding at people? Had she picked that up from Locke?*

"Do I really? I lost about 10 pounds trying to get into this dress." Iris looked at the dress--a satin concoction reminiscent of a block of Velveeta cheese. It was much too bright and shiny, but Maybelline seemed very proud of it. Iris looked at the winged sleeves that draped over Maybelline's rounded shoulders and fleshy upper arms; it reminded her of a small cape. The caplet fluttered about as Maybelline shimmied and jiggled uncomfortably in the dress. Iris watched as she smoothed the bodice, which was under much duress despite the layers of spandex underneath. Iris did not feel confident about Maybelline's dress and its durability.

"I hope it doesn't split open!" she panted.

"Are you okay?" Iris asked hoping Maybelline would say "yes" and leave.

"I'm as nervous as I can be. I'm playing a special medley of song tonight on the piano, and I'm afraid I'm going ruin it."

"I'm sure you've practiced and it will be fine." Iris said, hoping she sounded convincing.

"Yes. You're right. I have practiced long and hard. I can do this," she said smoothing the shiny material down over her ample hips and thighs. Iris couldn't help but think of the humiliation, should the thread on those seams give way.

Iris flashed her a rare high wattage smile and touched Maybelline's forearm lightly and said, "You'll be wonderful." She snapped her clutch closed and exited the ladies' room quickly.

As the bathroom door closed behind her, Iris took a deep breath and stepped into the flow of the evening. She'd taken Locke's advice and wore the green dress. It didn't make her feel any more rooted in the community. Iris had a hard time deciding which dress to wear. It was Locke who helped her narrow her purchase down to two contenders. Both were cut specifically for her curves, but the green dress was especially beautiful, because the Kelly green lace overlay featured beading that sparkled in the evenings lighting as Iris moved across the floor. Iris's dress was floor-length, which was an unusual find for her height. The long lace sleeves were snug and complimented her toned arms well. The sleeves fell just below her wrist bone and featured small Swarovski crystals that eliminated the need for jewelry. Tastefully fitted from the collarbone to knee, Iris's dress was its own accessory, and she wore it as if she knew it. She found her seat at the elaborately scaped round table and was met with Locke's mothering approving eyes. She was relieved to finally sit down. Instinctively, she reached for the tiny onyx spray vial of sanitizer that sat in the middle of the table. The warm vanilla and lavender scent of the mixture was heady and afforded her instant relaxation. "You're going to make it through this evening fabulously," Locked leaned over and said too loudly to Iris.

So far, Locke was pleased with the way the event was going. Promptly at 7 p.m. the who's who of Sweet Fields began to file in and fill up the round tables closest to the front and adjacent to the two long rectangular tables that sat the committee members. They were not advocates of being fashionably late, especially when they knew the guest list was chocked full of local and not-so-local celebrities. Sweet Fields wanted to be in their seats so that they could see the long parade of personalities saunter into the room.

"Have you seen that hideous Jackie Black?" Locke asked

Iris.

"Not yet," whispered Iris.

"I hope she doesn't drag in here and ruin everything. This benefit is important to Prentiss, and I will NOT have her turn it into the Jackie Circus Extravaganza."

"How could she ruin all of this, Locke? Really, this affair is beautiful. It rivals the ones I've attended with…" Iris's voice trailed off.

Locke patted Iris's hand with an elbow length lace gray glove. "Yes, I know. But it's just the two of us now. My Clive isn't here to keep me quiet, either. Still, we have to watch. Watch and pray." Locke winked.

Locke did not intend to upstage anyone with her gown, though it was almost impossible not to do so, and her nonchalance about just how impeccably she was dressed made her an even more intimidating figure. Her dress, too, was floor length, and designed especially for her by Antoine, her dresser. Every piece he designed for Locke was intended to mimic her personality, her steel gray demeanor that masked a large soft heart, her organic lifestyle, her non-fussy behaviors, her penchant for things of style and class, her complete disdain for germs, and her uncanny way of finding hidden diamonds in rough terrain. Locke wore a cascading gown with soft pleats above a cinched modestly jeweled waist and light fluid chiffon below. The color of the material was stainless steel, that's what Antoine called it. He said it was because he thought nothing living on earth could touch Locke, because she steeled herself from foolishness. Locke's hair was styled in a loose chignon at her neck and accentuated by a sapphire pin that glistened when she snapped her head around to listen to side conversations. Her only other accessory was a large sapphire ring set in platinum, which she wore on her right ring finger.

The band continued to play a jazzy version of "Great is Thy Faithfulness" as guests continued to arrive. The waiters, dressed in uninterrupted white, were dispatched and had begun to canvas the room to be sure their patrons were comfortable. The room bustled with energy as the sound of ice in glasses and the pouring of sweet tea and lemonade filled the room. The long awaited TV personality entered, and all women attendees 40 and older sat erect.

"Look at 'em," Locke quipped, "they are all a-puddle over this one."

"Who is it?" Iris asked.

"Somebody who is as annoying as a bee in a bonnet, but as gifted as a bootleg preacher when it comes to getting donations." Locke waved timidly as he came her way; however, before he could get to her table, Locke stood up and directed him to his assigned seat on the other side of the room. They air kissed and made their way, Locke floating, Carson strutting.

"So glad you could make it, Carson. You see how you've turned the women into 6th graders."

"I see, but you seem to be immune to my charms. When do you think I'll be able to have that effect on you?"

"Don't start that mess, Carson. I'm old enough to be your young mother. How well did we do in donations with the television promotion?"

"I think you'll be pleased," Rick Carson said, "you know, only you get my best work." Rick paused, he grabbed Locke's hand lightly and lifted it a few inches. "What, no spray?"

"You know better, Carson. I had my people rig up a light misting that triggers as soon as you cross the threshold. The guests think it's some kind of sweet smelling confetti." They both laughed as Rick Carson made it to his seat. "You need anything special before I go back to my seat?"

"As a matter of fact I do." Rick glanced toward Iris and smiled. "What about an introduction to that gorgeous girl in green sitting with you. You know I've heard about her. These old men in Sweet Fields don't know what to do with a woman like that. I'm so surprised you didn't do one of your famous hook ups when she came to town."

"Haven't you learned anything from the last mess you made of a woman's heart? Stick with television. Love is not what you do best." Locke nodded and floated back to her seat at the table.

Locke was gone just long enough for Deacon William Hughes to make his way over to Iris and perch in the empty space left by Locke. Iris was so busy observing that she didn't see him ease into the seat.

"Sister M-m-m-murphy," Hughes stuttered. William Hughes gathered himself and cleared his throat. "It's amazing how you can walk into a room fully clothed and make a more stunning impression than women who arrive half naked." Hughes tilted his head to the right as if he was using it to point at someone. She didn't look to see what Hughes was talking about, but only because she was so annoyed by his presence.

Hughes was a good-looking man. Tall. Dark. Handsome. Iris noticed that he stuttered a bit around her. Lloyd had stuttered...towards the end, and she didn't want to be reminded of Lloyd. Not right now. In addition, Deacon Hughes was a bit too admired by the women of St. Andrew. He owned a successful plumbing and home improvement business, and had gained quite a reputation for his ability to renovate the stately Victorian homes of Sweet Fields without compromising their character and integrity. Iris didn't want to deal with a man whose job it was to make house calls. Still, she heard he worked fast and was the consummate professional. He was always on time, and always finished a job before the end date he gave his clients. Hughes' prices were fair, and he didn't allow womanly charms to sway his bottom line.

Iris had heard all of these wonderful things about Deacon Hughes, and still she was not at all interested in him, at least not in that way. Truthfully, Grandma Maggs' house, though well kept, would need some work soon, so Iris entertained the Deacon a little while.

"Why thank you, Deacon Hu…"

"You don't have to be so f-f-f-ormal, Sister Murphy. Call me Will." Deacon Hughes placed his arm on the table as if to reach for Iris's hand. Iris looked at the deacon's arm and looked away. He was well dressed for the evening in a gray, modern and well-fitting tuxedo. He wore a deep cobalt blue tie with matching pocket square and a boutonniere the color of the bird of paradise flower. He had begun to grow a beard which was well trimmed and without one hint of gray.

The Hughes men were known for their grayless heads of hair. It was rumored that the oldest man in the Hughes clan didn't gray until he turned one hundred. This is what made the men of the Hughes family men of distinction, their coal black head of hair and their impeccable taste in clothes. In this area, William Hughes did not disappoint. He was consistently well groomed, well lined, and smelling good.

"I am not so sure about being so informal, Deacon Hughes. I wouldn't want anyone to think I was disrespecting your title as an upstanding member of the church and trusted cochairman of the board. You know how people talk."

"L-l-let them talk, Sister. They ain't talking about nothing they know for sure."

"I appreciate your wanting to calm my apprehensions. That's sweet of you, but remember, I am still the new kid on the block. I have to keep my nose clean. Anyway, I am quite sure half the women in Sweet Fields call you by your first name."

"Yeah, they call me by my first name, but I said that you could call me Will."

Locke was on the pair before either of them realized it. "Well, Deacon Will, I think I hear your seat at the table calling you right now. Get on up out my chair with all that foolishness."

William Hughes scooted the chair away from the table, and stood up. He was an impressive figure, and he towered over Locke. "Ms. Belle Lynne Locke," he said with a grin, "you're the prettiest old woman I've ever seen."

"Get yourself out of here, Hughes." Locke shooed him away and reached for the vial on the table to re-sanitize the soft seat covered in crisped white linen fabric. Right at that moment, there was the tap of a fork on crystal from the front of the room.

The band softened their music until everyone settled down.

"Welcome to the Benefit Gala for The Ava LeBeaux Early Learning Christian Academy and Daycare Center," Prentiss said. He wore a navy blue tuxedo accentuated with black at the collar and lapels. The outside pocket was trimmed with a band of black matte material. Underneath the jacket was a black vest. Iris noted that someone had tucked and dusted him. His black bowtie was frighteningly straight. The salt and pepper of Pastor LeBeaux's hair was complimented nicely by the suit's stately blue.

"This daycare center has been a dream of mine and my wife, God rest her soul, for quite some time. And I really thought New Orleans would be the place where this dream would come true. God saw fit to keep the dream alive, but just move it to another location." The guests laughed and clapped in a dignified manner. "Anyway, I'm glad you're here to help the dream become a reality and to put Sweet Fields on the map as one of the first Southern towns to offer quality Christian learning to our children early in their lives." There was more dignified clapping, and Pastor LeBeaux raised his hands to quiet the audience.

"God, when He led me here, gave me some unlikely people to have my back. This wouldn't be possible at all, had it not been for some good friends and beautiful people, a wonderful couple who supported this church and God's vision for it, even when the two became one less…" Pastor LeBeaux looked toward the table where Iris and Locke sat. Ever so slightly, Locke shook her head, no. One would have to be as close as Iris was to Locke to see the gesture. "Additionally, God sent a strong committee of planners, producers, protectors, providers, and just plain old good people my way to hold up my arms when the battle got a little too hard for me to fight." Pastor LeBeaux spread his arms out toward the audience, "Would the Benefit Gala Committee please join me out here on the dance floor. I promise I won't make you dance!"

Iris turned to Locke and stared at her like a deer caught in headlights. Locke nodded, "He called you up there. It's show time," she said.

Everyone had made it to the shiny dance floor except Iris and Jackie Black. As Iris made her way, the crowd quieted. Perhaps it was the flattering fit of the Kelly green lace dress (which became her signature color). Maybe it was the modest way she approached the dance floor as if she hadn't a care in the world, her long legs making effortless elegant strides across the room in spite of the unoffending

snugness of her dress. It could have been the simplicity of the thick coif of hair with its deep side part that smoothed into large horizontal bun at the nape of her neck. Then again, it may have been the intimidating 5'10" stature and the feet shod with red-bottomed matte gold strappy sandals. Whatever it was, the crowd was rendered speechless, and Iris had gained a place in Sweet Fields. The community was proud to own, claim, and adopt this beautiful specimen, and from that evening on, if anyone were to ask about Iris Murphy, every person present at the
Gala would say "Yes, I know her. She's from Sweet Fields."

Jackie Black, on the other hand, would never be acknowledged by the people of Sweet Fields as a member of the community. She was an enigmatic creature whose presence created dissonance in the hearts and minds of those who looked upon her. Jackie stood and walked slowly--too slowly-- to the dance floor.

Her dress was an amalgamation of geometric shapes and peacock feathers. It was the two-foot train of peacock feathers that the onlookers noticed first. Known for the beautiful display of colors, peacock feathers, when not on the peacock, presented a haunting bouquet of black eyes. These black eyes seemed to watch its onlookers as they made their way across the armory floor carried by Jackie Black.

Then, the crowd saw flesh. Above the unsightly clump of trembling peacock feathers, which ended at her knees, they could see Jackie Black's slender legs from the knee to the upper thigh through a black sheer veil. Women gasped as they feared they would see the woman's private parts. Men leered, hoping to see the same. Where the sheer blackness ended-just below where her thighs met her backside-black satin began, but it didn't last long. The scrap of material barely covered her derrière, for at the top of her buttocks, the fabric abruptly ended in the shape of a V. The bare flesh of her back --and some of her sides--was exposed all the way to the top of her shoulder blades. Two triangular pieces of fabric stretched across the very top of her back to hold the distasteful creation together. When she finally arrived at her place on the dance floor beside Iris, she whirled around dramatically. The peacock eyes stirred in their feathers. The onlookers who had been offended by her dorsal side were doubly offended by the front of her.

The boat neck of her dress was the only quiet part of her dress, for the bodice below it screamed with its severely molded breast cups accented by four raised black seams that ran from her bosom in a downward direction to her feminine center. The satin part of the dress ended in an arc dangerously close to the apex of her thighs, leaving the onlookers gaping at the front of her thighs and more peacock feathers that began at her knee.

"Do, Jesus!" the twins Luceal and Laura gasped aloud in unison. Setting their table afire with whispers and chuckles.

"What in blue blazes is she wearing?" someone whispered too loudly.

"Help your people, Jesus." Sister Washington said out loud casting a glance upwards.

Locke tightened her lips and sprayed a light mist from her vial. The sight of the woman dragging a collection of dead peacocks on the floor with the eyes of the feathers mocking the crowd was nearly Locke's undoing. She steadied her breathing and focused on Iris. Her Iris. *Maggs, you did good, girl*, she thought with a nod. She was bound and determined to not allow Jackie to ruin this event. She looked at Jackie's pageant smile and briefly felt sympathy for the wretched creature. Jackie was whirling with the idea that the gasps and whispers were because of the beauty of her dress. She beamed at Prentiss, who was still droning on into the microphone acknowledging each of the committee members. Because Locke's eyes were focused on Jackie, she knew the exact moment when Jackie realized everyone was smitten with Iris and not her.

Prentiss LeBeaux directed his attention to Iris and spoke, "To our own **very special** Iris Murphy, who has just recently made Sweet Fields home. I believe Sweet Fields is a great deal sweeter with this generous young woman in our community." The room erupted in applause. He continued, "because of Miss Murphy, the academy and daycare will have a state-of-the-art library complete with a technology wing." A second round of applause erupted and was louder than before. There. It was during the applause--both rounds-- that Jackie's countenance fell. Her face and sickening smile had faltered. Locke noted the tightening of Jackie's lips and twitch of the right eye--a tell tale sign. When Prentiss addressed Jackie's contributions, she lit up again like a twinkle light.

"Lastly, but not least, is Jacqueline Black. She, too, is new to Sweet Fields. Let's give her a hand," Prentiss said innocently. Jackie's eyes slid down the row of committee members and let her eyes rest on Iris. Her lips tightened again, and Locke knew there would be trouble soon.

As the introduction of the committee ended and the members were taking their seats, Locke noticed that Jackie did not return to her table. Instead, she stepped behind one of the 20-foot columns and disappeared. This bothered Locke. Jackie was angry, and crazy people aren't compliant when they're angry. She tried to put her eyes on Jackie but was interrupted when Rick Carson intercepted Iris' graceful glide back to her seat. Rick grabbed Iris' hand with his right one while his left hand went to her shoulder. He leaned in and whispered something in Iris' ear. Iris quite delicately tilted her head back and laughed, showing her perfect white teeth. This irritated Locke; she told Rick to stay away from Iris. She was even more incensed when Rick proceeded to take Iris' elbow and escort her back to her seat. When he pulled Iris' seat out, his eyes met with Locke's steeled ones. He winked. Locke was fit to be tied. She had lost sight of Jackie and Rick was trying to force himself in a match with Iris. She slid the ornate vial over to Iris and nodded for her to use it.

Meanwhile, Prentiss was enjoying his time at the microphone. He was gushing over his beloved Ava. Eventually, he announced a special musical selection to be played by the Sweet Georgia Orchestra with guest pianist, Maybelline Crowder.

Maybelline strutted out to the piano and seated herself comfortably at the Steinway. She waited for the applause to completely die before beginning. She watched the conductor and began on his cue, starting the medley of the late Ava's favorite classical pieces. The orchestra would join her here and there. The medley went from

Moonlight Sonata to *Hungarian Dance No 5* to *For Elise*. It finally ended with *Flight of the Bumblebee* with the spotlight from the rafters on Maybelline. The congregants of St. Andrew who were in attendance were shocked, as no one knew she was such an accomplished pianist. With her head down, cheeks puffed with air, and sweat beading at her brow, Maybelline played her heart out. The jumbotron at the front of the room panned the audience and orchestra, but stopped on Maybelline. It zoomed in on her pleasant, round face and then moved to her fingers that were flying with confidence and finesse across the keys of the Steinway. The audience was in silent awe as Maybelline's fingers moved over the keys with lightning speed. When she struck the final chord of the piece, the audience erupted into thunderous applause. She stood from the piano bench and walked around to the front of the piano, as she had practiced, and curtsied. She gestured to the conductor and orchestra, as applause continued to rip through the building.

Locke and Iris exchanged glances and sighed in relief. Maybelline had earned her moment in the spotlight. She had played beautifully, even though her dress was its own spotlight. Cindy Sullivan announced that after the upcoming video presentation, the audience would have another chance to hear Maybelline Crowder play during the appeal for the attendees to donate to the center. The voice directed their attention to the jumbotron for a video presentation of donors and supporters of the Ava Center. Various CEOs, television personalities, and other celebrities (all of whom Locke knew personally) shared the amounts of their contributions. While waiters prepared to distribute linen envelopes for the contributions, Maybelline returned to the Steinway for some "giving music" as Prentiss had called it.

Maybelline, still basking in her crowning moment, happily moved to the beat of "The Second Line," as she pounded it out on the keys. Her enthusiasm was contagious, and the crowd clapped along; some tapped their feet; others swayed in their seats with their white linen napkins raised, but all were shy about moving to the dance floor. The music stopped suddenly. There was the uncomfortable sound of splitting wood, and a "Whooo" sent up in a wave from the audience. Maybelline, who before had been bouncing gleefully on the piano bench, was on the floor! The orchestral musicians tried to recover Maybelline's topple with their own rendition of the tune, but they needed her to set the tempo. Maybelline struggled to get up. Two gentlemen went to her aid. Though back on her feet, she was still too flustered and upset to resume the music. She started towards the ladies' room to gather herself.

As she walked past a smiling Jackie and her dress of eyeballs and feathers, Maybelline heard a loud tear and felt a faint cool breeze where the satiny material of her dress had slipped away. Time stood still and all other sounds ceased. The entire room seemed to hear the rip of the fabric. When she looked down, Maybelline saw a puddle of cheese-colored satin at her feet. The lower half of her gown was on the floor. In a matter of seconds, the joyful second line music had ended. There Maybelline stood, on the ballroom floor in a puddle of Velveeta cheese satin, covered only by black knee-length Spanx. Sister Washington, the church nurse, jumped to her aid quickly, because she had seen this kind of disaster before (wardrobe malfunctions happened sometimes when churchgoers got happy in the spirit). Jackie swooped in and lit onto the piano, picking up where Maybelline had left off. There were whispers and craning necks, but the Second Line party music proved to be an effective distraction.

The money didn't stop flowing either. The white satin boxes containing the donations were filled to the brim, and had to be changed repeatedly to make room for more. Champagne was flowing at every table, and Jackie--having saved the evening--was bouncing merrily at the piano while acknowledging Prentiss' approving and grateful eyes.

The night of merriment and charitable giving ended on a high note. The five-course meal had been exquisite--lamb, beef, and chicken with gourmet side dishes and crème brulèe for dessert. There had been swag bags for everyone containing products thoughtfully donated by local businesses. And the celebrities in attendance tarried a while to chat with fans and sign programs. Yes. The night had been an affair to remember. Locke's people and their people set about breaking down the staging and decorations while the wait staff began cleaning the industrial kitchen. The well-dressed throngs thinned, and the parking lot was lit up with headlights.

Only Prentiss LeBeaux waited until the end. He thanked people for coming as they left. Jacqueline lurked about pretending to help clean up. While she was trying to give instructions to the decorators, Prentiss said his final goodbye and started to his car. Jacqueline spotted him just in time to stuff her feather-bedecked self into her Thunderbird and follow him across town.

CHAPTER 6: CELEBRATION SUNDAY

Iris, completely wrung out from Saturday night's festivities, managed to look as fresh and fabulous as she usually did the next day for Sunday service. Antoine insisted Kelly green was her color and convinced her to wear it again. Iris slipped into her Kelly green pencil dress with a smug smile. She fastened her skinny black patent leather belt and looked at herself in her granny's floor-length mirror. She had always known she was attractive, but last night, she *owned* it. She patted her messy bun of curls, straightened the black jeweled brooch at her neck, and slipped her bare feet into her favorite pair of black patent leather Louboutins.

While Iris was home dressing for church, most of the men who comprised the deacon board of St. Andrew had already congregated at their favorite gab corner near the back of the church. The renovations that took place at St. Andrew afforded them a tricked out, but still appropriately sanctimonious, den to count money and handle petty church disputes. Most of the time, the men used the church's version of a man cave to sit, drink coffee, and gossip.

There was much to be said, because Hughes had managed to gain a brief audience with Iris. The men were anxious to see how the conversation went. And Hughes was anxious to embellish the conversation to engage their curiosities. "Yeah, I sat and talked with her. And you know how some women are real pretty until you get up on them? Not this one, brethren. Her pretty held its ground. It didn't lie."

"I'm surprised you said anything to her, Hughes. You know how you get to stut-stut-stuttering when you get around a woman." Deacon Clemson Callahan delivered the low blow. And he got away with it, because he was chairman of the deacon board, a position that Hughes hoped to have; he was, after all, next in line. Hughes figured Clemson would be around a while. No one really knew how old he was, because he had more energy than a hummingbird. Unlike the hummingbird though, Clemson was not a man who'd live a short life.

He probably would never die. Hughes thought it was because of all that juicing he did. He called it holistic living. To William Hughes, a meat and potatoes man, the clean eating Clemson was always blabbing about was probably nothing more than another passing fad.

Clemson continued, "but I understand when you get around a pretty woman, like my Judith. It throws you off a bit." Callahan was standing over Hughes, who had sat in one of the wing chairs near the large flat screen TV mounted on the longest wall above the faux fireplace. Clemson propped his foot up on a small stool upholstered in rich burgundy tapestry. His shoes were so shiny, that Hughes could see the reflection of his own jet black hair in them. Clemson's shoes were the kind that laced up to the ankle, black with a shiny round toe that was accessorized by a meticulously stitched double seam across the top. This was the only telltale sign that Clemson may have been up in age. "Well, tell us what she said, Hughes! We don't have but twenty minutes before church starts. Maybelline will be tickling those keys right on time."

"Well at first she was kind of shy, but then, she said she heard that I did good work on, well, pipes and such. She invited me over to check on hers. Said, she'd like for me to look at a coupla things around the house." The other men of the board drew closer to Hughes, interested. Hughes leaned back in the chair and kicked Clemson's foot from the stool to replace it with his own. "Yep, that's what she said."

Clemson squinted. Hughes knew of his own hyperbolic tendencies, but sometimes he couldn't help coloring the story, just a little--especially when there was a captive audience. He waited for Clemson's response. He knew the older man would call his hand. "Hughes, don't go getting any ideas off of a two sentence conversation. You probably couldn't hear her over that band sitting up in that box at the gala. Maggs' house needs work, bottom line. Maggs hadn't hired a man to fix up around that house for years before she died. There's sure to be some problems. Sister Murphy ain't stud'n you."

"Sister Murphy hadn't had a working man around her either, unless you count that piece of man she helped write all those books. What kind of job is writing anyway for a real man? She needs to know better. I can make her know better," Hughes chuckled his last sentence out with confidence.

"You can hardly make a sentence, doc," said another deacon said with a guffaw.

"You have to get her to sit long enough to wait for you to get your words out first," one of the deacons muttered from the back of the room.

"What you really have to worry about," Clemson said as he ran his fingers through the hair he still processed after 40 years. He peered into the blank screen of the TV for stray strands, "is Locke. It's like she's got a padlock on the woman. She's just like her husband, God rest his soul. She puts a lock on anything that has to do with money."

Hughes stood up and straightened his suit jacket. He pinched at the crease of his pant leg and drew his fingers all the way down each side. "I can handle Belle Lynne Locke," he said with a fond smile, "she's as cold as steel, but she still has the warm softness of a woman down in there somewhere." This was something Hughes knew for sure, because he'd seen it for himself when his mother died. Locke showed him kindness and compassion that had surprised him.

"Well, it sure was some kind of night to remember. Judith and I were so worked up over all that classy dancing we did, that we couldn't keep our hand off of each other in the car. We drove up to Process Point and…"

"Aaaaaaaaaah, naw brother," the other deacons wouldn't let Clemson finish his sentence. They knew where it was going, and they didn't want to join the ride.

Iris arrived at St. Andrew just in time to see the fraternal exchange of the well-dressed deacon board walking from the back of the church and to watch Locke, dressed in a flowing linen dress that was unmistakably one of Antoine's designs, consecrate her seat. She caught Locke's eye, nodded and seated herself in her own consecrated space. The church was buzzing. People were still excited about the night before. Some women had slept "pretty" so they could show off their elegant hairstyles, while one or two ladies opted to wear their dresses again so those who didn't attend the gala could see how beautiful they had been the night before.

The deacons filed in, followed by the deaconesses. Some organ music had started, but Maybelline was not the musician. Poor Maybelline. Iris wondered if someone had gone to check on her last night. She doubted anyone did. When the pianist began to sing, Iris' head snapped in the direction of Locke. Locke, recognizing the singer as Jackie Black, tightened her lips and narrowed her eyes.

"She sounds terrible," Antoine whispered. "Crying and screaming always makes people look and sound like jackasses."

"Shhh. You can't say that in church!" Iris whispered after letting an audible laugh escape her lips.

"I can't say she sounds like a jackass? Why not? It's the truth. Ye shall know the truth, and the truth shall set you free." Antoine said sucking his teeth and rolling his eyes. "Anyway. Jackass is in the Bible. In fact, Jesus rode a jackass, so I can say it in church." Iris giggled. It had been a while since she had giggled-well, she had giggled last night. She had actually laughed out loud-at both that handsome devil Rick Carson and at Jackie Black. Jacqueline Black made laughter much too easy for Iris. Her behavior at Locke's nightcap, though no laughing matter, was laughable, to say the least. Iris could not get the scene of the night's fiasco out of her head.

After the gala, Locke had invited twelve of her most special guests to her home for a nightcap. Some of them knew each other, and some met for the first time. A convoy of limousines and luxury sedans made their way slowly through the quiet streets of Sweet Fields and lined Superior Street in front of Locke's brick home. Her home, dressed in the same colors as the armory-- polished blacks, creamy whites, and pale golds-welcomed the guests. There were three waiters still dressed in white at the ready. One tended the finger foods, another made specialty drinks in the oversized French country kitchen, while the third circulated among the guests tending to their drink requests. The lady Iris spotted earlier hanging decorations stood guard at the door. The last guest to arrive had been Prentiss; this was no surprise, as he assumed his traditional pastoral duties at the door thanking guests for their support.

Prentiss had come in and settled into a large chair next to Locke in the grand parlor. All seats--occasional chairs, sofas, and settees were comfortably occupied. Iris was sitting in front of the picture window on a loveseat with Antoine, the fashion designer whom Locke had discovered making costumes for female impersonators in New York. They'd become fast friends at the gala. He, too, was mesmerized by Iris in her Kelly green.

Jean Paul, a Frenchman, whose gambling had cost him and his sister, Genevieve their shoe store in France, occupied a settee near the fireplace. Because of Jean Paul's gambling debts, the bookies had assaulted and tortured Genevieve--she had not spoken a word since.

Celeste was the daughter of friends of the Lockes. After hearing her sing, Clive and Locke paid for her voice lessons and her trip to an American Idol audition. The famous singer was curled in an occasional chair with Kofi perched in a window seat nearby. Clive had found Kofi on a trip to Africa, took him off the streets, and placed him in a home with some friends in America.
He was now a bodyguard for Celeste.

Ethan and Patricia were sitting with Jackson Reed on an oversized sofa chatting quietly about money. Ethan Stone was Clive's nephew who had traveled to Italy to become a chef. He owned one of hottest restaurants in Atlanta. Patricia was a single mother/business student who had been waiting tables at one of the Locke's favorite eateries when the two met. Locke, after getting to know Patricia, had insisted that she and Clive invest in her business, a daycare center. That had been ten years ago. Patricia's business idea had blossomed into a chain of daycares for single mothers. Jackson's father and Clive had been boyhood friends. Clive convinced Locke to attend a political fundraiser for Jackson Reed's mayoral campaign, and she had been smitten with the dapper wordsmith ever since.

Anita and Tony were huddled together on another sofa.
Anita was a playwright who had wowed the Lockes with an offBroadway show. The Lockes, impressed with her refreshing and

pure talent, invested in her theatre troupe. Tony was a brilliant mathematician whose mother, during his senior year of high school, was raped and killed. Locke couldn't help but reach out to the hurting teen. She and Clive had paid for his college education.

Locke, like a queen mother, sat near the doorway in a navy velvet wingback chair with brass tacks around the edge. The merriment overflowed much like the sherry and champagne until it was interrupted by the ring of the doorbell.

Locke looked to the front door with a snap. Ruth, the doorkeeper for the evening, answered, "Good evening. May I help you?"

Jackie Black's voice cut through the merriment like a switchblade. She threw her head back and retorted, "Yes. I'd like to come in."

"Your name, please?" Ruth asked looking over her blackrimmed glasses.

Jackie laughed. She thought the pomp and circumstance of having a doorkeeper was a joke. Surely they expected her, especially with Prentiss there. "Why, Jacqueline O'Shelle Black." she said with a deep curtsy. The feathers of her dress shimmied and rustled as she slid up from the curtsy.

"Please wait here," Ruth said and closed the door gently in Jackie's face. While Ruth conferred with the mistress of the house, Jackie took the opportunity to enter--on her own, uninvited. Ruth was still with Locke when Jackie made her presence known.

"Good evening, everyone." She said standing in the doorway wearing a hideous peacock feather-trimmed shawl about her shoulders. Jackie's priceless pageant smile was plastered across her face. She was posed, as if everyone had been waiting for her. She stood in classic fifth position, and if the guests looked closely enough, they would have seen an iridescent purple peep toe pump with one lone feather draping the arch of Jackie's right foot, the wicked eye of the feather looking up into the faces of Locke's gifted band of twelve. The hush that came across the room was only interrupted by the hiss and swish of the feathers settling around Jackie's lower body. Sentences and glasses of champagne hung silently in the air, unfinished.

"Jacqueline. This engagement is invitation only. We will see you tomorrow at church." Locke maintained a sickening sweet tone while looking into Jackie's faux gray eyes. Kofi moved stealthily in the background and was beside Jackie before she could end her dramatic gasp. He placed one hand at the small of her bare back while the other took charge of her elbow and guided her out.

"Pastor LeBeaux, are we not meeting tonight?" she asked over her shoulder. Her voice, the question, was barely a whisper and was carried by a desperate tremor. Prentiss did not answer. Jackie, in response to his silence, spun around to see Prentiss engaged in conversation with Iris. They were laughing! "Prentiss!" she cried.

"Oh! Jackie. Are you leaving already?" he asked when he snapped out of his laughter with Iris. "Of course, you must be tired after all the excitement of the gala. Having to fill in for Maybelline at the last minute must have drained you. Let's talk after church tomorrow. Goodnight." he said pleasantly, completely unaware she was being thrown out of the party.

Locke said nothing. She watched the situation unfold with a pleasant smile. She nodded as she watched Kofi escort Jackie out onto the front lawn. He locked the door upon his return. Kofi perched in the window seat near Celeste who was talking with Antoine about dressing her for the upcoming red carpet season. The server with the finger foods made a round as did the server with more glasses of sherry, wine, and champagne. As Iris stood to join Antoine and Celeste in their conversation about fashion, she heard a loud wail. She looked out of the picture window behind her just in time to see Jackie Black standing on the grassy lawn stomping her feet and shouting in what sounded like French. She continued to stomp away, until the feather flew from one of her awkward purple shoes.

"What is she saying, Jean Paul?" Antoine asked. Jean Paul stood with his glass of wine and joined Iris at the window. After listening for a few seconds, Jean Paul dragged his hand through his curly white hair and stroked his fluffy beard.

"*Je suis plus digne d'une invitation a cette bande de marginaux.*"

"I don't want to say in the company of women, monsieur. It is not very good French, but I get her point."

"*Ce petit lutin rétréci d'une femme ne sera pas me tenir loin de lui. Je vais avoir mon jour*!" She yelled louder.

"Which is?" Antoine asked arching a perfectly shaped brow.

"Nothing. Her point is moot, whatever it is." Locke said raising her glass. "A toast!"

Prentiss who was then talking to Jackson Reed, raised his glass and said "To generous friends!"

They raised their glasses and yelled a rousing "Salut," as Jackie shouted something else in French. She whirled around and around, causing the tail of her dress to take to the air around her like wings. One by one feathers began to disassemble from the bottom of the dress. Jackie stopped mid spin, recognizing that she was losing herself and her accoutrements. Frantically, she scoured and scraped the ground in search of her precious peacock feathers.
All the while, she continued to rant in French.

"*Je ne vais pas être en reste par une femme orpheline curieux qui se habille comme Poison Ivy. Iris, vous ne avez pas entendu le dernier de moi.*" Iris recognized her name in the verbal outburst. While the others drank merrily, Iris sat down her glass and left the grand parlor quietly with her cell phone in her palm. She said nothing to the others, but Kofi followed her to the door.

"Let me, Iris." He said in a deep baritone voice.

"No. She called me out. I shall answer." Iris said. Iris was tired of people calling her name for no good reason. She had abided all the chiding and harassment she was going to--tabloid reporters were one thing, but a desperate troublemaker was another. It was going to end. Tonight. She glided carefully down the brick steps and walked the footpath to the lawn where Jackie was then squatting with her feathered train all around her. "Jackie, what do you want?" "Why wasn't **I** invited?"

"This gathering is for Locke's very dear friends. That's why."

"But Prentiss was invited." She said pouting.

"That's because Prentiss is a very dear friend." Iris was perplexed by Jackie's child-like behavior.

"Prentiss is my dear friend, too," she whined, "we should have been invited together."

"Listen to yourself Jackie. You make absolutely no sense. Now, if you really want Prentiss to see you tonight, I can call Officer Martinez to come and cart you off to jail for trespassing, and maybe Pastor LeBeaux will add you to his list of sick and shut in. He will be sure to come visit you then. Is that what you want?"

"Out of my face, Iris!" she swooshed her hand through the night air as if it held a magic wand. "I was here before you!"

"And I'll be here after you, " Iris said taking one step closer to Jackie who had started pulling the peacock feathers from her shawl and dress in a fit of anger. "Get your rumpled, ruffled, raggedy feathers together and get off this lawn, or so help me, you'll be a very popular bird in the county jail," Iris said with her eyes narrowed into slits.

Jackie said nothing, but screeched in agony. Defeated agony. She threw off her shawl and plucked the feathers from her dress while tears streamed down her face. Iris's boldness didn't dissipate. She drew even closer to Jackie Black and whispered, "and do NOT pick off another feather from that dress. I won't have Locke's lawn littered with the feathers of a naked bird." Iris returned to the grand parlor and closed the blinds overlooking the lawn that was the stage for Jackie Black's tantrum. She rejoined the conversations and found Locke talking to Prentiss but looking directly at her. The dialogue between the two looked very official. Prentiss's eyes never left Locke's face, and therefore, he knew nothing of Jackie Black's obsessive fit of the evening.

And now, on the Sunday after the gala event of the season (with all of its drama), Jackie was sitting on the organ trying desperately to sing "How Great Thou Art" with a raw throat and red eyes. Pastor Prentiss LeBeaux sang excitedly unaware of the instability that sat so close.

Pastor Prentiss LeBeaux was full. He was overwhelmed with gratitude to his parishioners and the community of Sweet Fields. He was especially grateful for Locke's friends who had given so generously just because she was affiliated with St. Andrew. His sermon was much shorter than usual, because he was overcome with emotion.

St. Andrew, y'all really outdid yourselves last night! You really made me proud. I have never seen such generous people give as freely as you did to help get this academy and daycare built. As I reflected on this grand occasion, I thought about Paul's letter to the Ephesians. Turn with me to Ephesians 6:8; it reads: [8] Knowing that whatsoever good thing any man doeth, the same shall he receive of the Lord, whether he be bond or free. [9] And, ye masters, do the same things unto them, forbearing threatening knowing that your Master also is in heaven; neither is there respect of persons with him.

St. Andrew Family, I'd like to share with you with this thought: What you make happen for others, God will make happen for you. You have been there for me in my darkest hour. You have held me up in prayer. You have rejoiced with me. You have loved me. Supported me. Fed me. Last night, you all gave your all--not just to me on behalf of my sweet Ava, but to the entire community. Many of you gave your hard-earned money, several gave of your time and talents, and a few special people gave themselves. For those of you who gave to this ministry until it hurt, I love you and appreciate you. I want you to remember that what you make happen for others, God will make happen for you. God will never leave you alone--unavenged, uncared for, or unconnected. He will never leave his children abandoned, all alone out in the wilderness. But when he brings you out, He wants you to do the same for someone else. Turn to your neighbor and say "what I make happen for someone else, God will make happen for me!" Because you all have made so much happen for me, I want to return the love, the kindness, and gratitude.

CHAPTER 7: JACKIE'S DECLARATION

Pastor Prentiss' sermon had struck a nerve...or two with Jackie. She had left the church and driven to her dance studio. As soon as she had locked the door behind her, she began peeling off her clothes.

"I cannot believe how I came from the big city to this simple little town only to be shunned and shut out! How dare they? How long will they grieve for Ava? When will they move on? Prentiss is a young man. A handsome, virile man who needs a woman's touch. He needs me. He's so sad, but I can bring him back to life! If I don't do something, that little old woman will have him dry right up all by himself! Well I won't have it!" she said almost shouting. She had taken off her black chiffon duster and wore nothing but black leotards. She moved to the small bathroom and looked at herself in the mirror.

"I am beautiful. I am sexy. I am a woman. I am a lover. I can be anything--anyone I wish to be, and I want to be Mrs. Prentiss LeBeaux. I SHALL be his wife, and no one will stop me. Not that Poison Iris with her money and her pretty white teeth. Prentiss thinks she is so pretty and so generous and so sophisticated, but I'll show her! Pretty is for girls. I am a woman. I wanted to be her friend, but she wouldn't even let me in her house! Why?" A tear sat on the edge of her eyelid.

"It's just like what happened the last time in Atlanta. Everyone always shuts me out!" she screamed. She grabbed a towel and scrubbed at her makeup violently. The tears continued to flow. "But Pastor Prentiss told ME, with his own mouth, that whatever I made happen for others, God will make happen for me." She wiped her eyes with the backs of her hands and ran her palm over her short blond hair.

"I have saved the day for Prentiss. I have carried the load for Prentiss. I have played beautiful music for Prentiss. I have loved Prentiss. God, I know you will make those things happen for me. I have sown. I will soon reap. Amen." Jackie opened her eyes. She did not realize she had whispered a small prayer until she said "amen." She felt her random lapse into prayer was a sign from God. That he had sanctioned her to show everyone at St. Andrew that her purpose in Pastor Prentiss' life would not be denied.

"I'll teach them to shut me--Jacqueline O'Shelle Black-out! I will destroy all of them. Prentiss will hate them all, and I'll be there waiting to console him. Comfort him. Hold him. Love him." she smiled as she left the bathroom. "That gorgeous man and St. Andrew will belong to me. Everyone will forget about Ava and love me!"

She pressed a button on her bookcase stereo and Jennifer Hudson began belting out "*And I Am Telling You.*" Jackie began to spin around, kicking up her legs in rhythm. She dipped her head and shoulders low to ground before throwing her body into the air. She leapt and spun and bowed. Her arms flailed to and fro as tears streamed down her eyes and cries tore from her already raw throat. At the dramatic end of the song, Jackie whirled around and landed on the floor with a loud thud. She lay there on the floor, spent and sobbing loudly. After several minutes of crying out in her raw love for Prentiss LeBeaux, she wiped away tears and sweat and pulled her long legs into her chest, rocking gently to and fro, mumbling.

"Iris and Locke left me alone on the lawn, uncared for, and unconnected. Poor Prentiss is under their spell, for if he had known I was outside and uninvited in, he would have spoken up for me. They distracted Prentiss so he wouldn't see me. But they will soon see me, in all my glory, standing proudly as Mrs. Jacqueline O'Shelle Black-LeBeaux. And heaven help me, if they don't see. St. Andrew and Sweet Fields will love me." She stood, ran her hands over her damp, closely cropped curls, and bent deeply at the waist, stretching.

Jackie was too engrossed in her monologue to realize that Locke had just slid by her studio in the sleek navy Cadillac. Locke was on her way to see Maybelline. "That poor woman," she said out loud as she pulled her car into Maybelline's driveway. Maybelline's gold Camry was not in the garage. Locke noticed that it sat in the driveway, askew, as if parked by a bank robber on the run. She stepped out of the car and took note of the clusters of Black Eyed Susans Maybelline had in cobalt blue pots on either side of her yellow door. Locke pressed the doorbell with her gloved hand. She heard stirring inside.

"Maybelline. Don't be silly. I won't stand out here all afternoon." Nothing. Locke followed a stone footpath to the back deck. Maybelline often sat out back drinking sweet tea. But no one was there. As she made her way back to the front she caught Maybelline peeping through one of the panes at the bay window.

"Come on out here, Lena, and open this door." Locke knew that Maybelline would understand she meant business, when she called her Lena. Locke hadn't called her Lena since she was a child.

By the time Locke made her way around, the yellow door was open and the entryway unoccupied. Maybelline, however, had disappeared to her bedroom. Locke took inventory of Maybelline's living room. There were beautiful little trinkets along her fireplace mantle. Her overstuffed sofa was red and decorated with purple and green pillows. The oversized loveseat was also red and draped with a chenille blanket of the same hue. A denim and white chevron pillow sat neatly in the chair. There were things everywhere in Maybelline's living room, and yet every single item had a proper and perfect place. Maybelline's house invited guests to visit and never leave. And, if there was one thing Maybelline did well other than playing piano, it was keeping an immaculate house. Even though she made a handsome salary working at PC&G Manufacturing Companies as the managing engineer for all sustainable bottle cap design engineers, Maybelline was content to live quietly in her sage stoned cottage with vines of ivy creeping up the sides.

Maybelline's house smelled of eucalyptus and mint. Locke liked the cleanliness of the smell. She did not spray.

"Ms. Belle, please don't lecture me right now," Maybelline mumbled from the bedroom.

"The hell you say, Lena! Your dress drops around your ankles one time, and you want to go hole yourself up. You didn't even come to church today. That horrible bird woman, Jackie Black, tried to play like you. She sang like a sick cat." By now, Locke had made her way to Maybelline's room, a large queenly space outfitted with an ornate Paul Bunyan bed. Maybelline's bedding was bright yellow, accented with navy and white. Her bright white sheets were crumpled in the middle of her bed where Maybelline sat wearing a white PC&G T-shirt, very short denim shorts and a head full of the biggest rollers Locke had ever seen in her life.

"That's easy for you to say, Ms. Belle. All of St. Andrew didn't see your rump as you walked across the dance floor at the biggest gala of the last 10 years. I've never been so embarrassed in my life." Maybelline crumpled up the sheets even more and wiped at her wet face. She rocked slowly, back and forth.

"Yes, Lena. You have been more embarrassed. Remember the time when you were getting on the church bus to go to the Youth Rally down in Rayton County, and your slip fell down to your ankles? Remember that? Didn't you keep on living after that? Became an accomplished pianist? Got a scholarship to MIT? Making more money than most folk can shake a stick at, down at PC&G? You're the only woman manager in that place. So what, they saw a little Spanx last night! It's about time you did something daring."

"Ms. Belle, none of those things matter when you're made a fool of by someone you hardly know. I don't know why she…" "She who? What are you babbling about Maybelline? Get yourself together so I can hear you right!"

"That Jackie Black!" Maybelline vomited her name out of mouth, almost choking on the k's in her name.

"Wait a minute, Maybelline. What has Jackie the buzzard to do with all this?"

"She stepped on my dress, Ms. Belle. She stepped on my dress and smiled while she did it."

"Now, Maybelline. Your dress was tight. It was hugging you like the skin on summer sausage. You sure it wasn't a wardrobe malfunction, like Janet Jackson had? Do you know I was there the night that happened? I told my Clive…"

"Ms. Belle. It was Jackie Black. While Nurse Washington was helping me get myself together, Jackie, walked past me and whispered, "*thank goodness you're not the only one who can play piano in this room.*" Maybelline broke down after that and flopped back onto the bed. She stretched her arms out and cried. "I've never done anything to that woman. Why does she insist on vexing me so?"

"Have you eaten today?" Locke asked Maybelline. Her eyebrows were furrowed.

Maybelline sat up quickly. "Do I look like I need something to eat?" She cried even more.

"Yes. Yes you do. You look a mess. I brought some of my lavender and lime teacakes. They are out in the car. I'm going over to my house and fix you something fresh from my garden.
The teacakes will hold you until I get back."

Locke gathered her dress and started toward the front door to her car. She retrieved the teacakes, which were in a dainty silver tin tied with a purple bow. "Now you eat a few of these, the lavender will calm you down. I'll be back shortly with something more hearty, filling, healthy. Then you can play me something on that Baby Grande when we're done."

"Thank you, Ms. Belle," Maybelline sniffled. "I appreciate you for stopping by."

Locke threw her black-gloved hand up in the air as if agitated with Maybelline. "You go in there and pull yourself together."
Locke thought about Maybelline and the dress and Jackie Black and the embarrassing production she rendered outside on Locke's lawn the night before. Ever since Sister Jackie Black arrived, things at St. Andrew had been a little off. Now she was messing with Maybelline, who really never bothered anyone. She knew what Maybelline said about Jackie sabotaging the dress was true, even though she didn't see it herself. What she didn't know yet was what she was going to do about it. Something would be done, and Iris would have to help her do it, before Jackie struck again.

NOVELLA II: LOVE YE ONE ANOTHER

CHAPTER 8: SUNDAY

All Maybelline could see from her spot in the pew were the long brown Senegalese twists Jackie Black now wore. They were swaying to the beat of Jackie's playing on the organ. Maybelline detested the sight. It had been a long time since she rested her fingers on the keys of the organ at St. Andrew, and she missed it, terribly. All of the encouragement in the world couldn't get her to reclaim her spot as St. Andrew's minister of music.

Jackie Black was now murdering Richard Smallwood's "Anthem of Praise," and evidence of her inexperience as a music director was in the choir's singing. From the choir loft, several sopranos gave Maybelline the death stare as if to say, *would you please come back and save us from this racket?* The tenors were not so kind. After each set, they would sit in their seats, lean forward and beckon, furiously, for Maybelline to take the bench. Maybelline slowly shook her head, no, and her heavy burgundy black curls seemed as lifeless and limp as she was sitting on the pew.

Each time Maybelline thought about recovering her seat at the instrument, memories of the wardrobe malfunction arrested her, and she would stop shy and rest in a nearby seat. Each Sunday, Jackie Black would arrive several minutes early, glance over at Maybelline with raised eyebrows, shrug her shoulders, and sashay up the aisle to begin her incessant banging.

"Maybelline," Deaconess Luceal hissed, "things just aren't the same since you stopped playing and singing solos here. Won't you come on back?"

Luceal's twin, Laura, followed up with, "Come on, sugar. Jackie can't play worth a quarter. My posture of worship is interrupted every time she moves her fingers 'cross the keyboard." Of course, not everyone had seen the wardrobe malfunction, but Jackie Black made sure everyone heard about it.

"Brothers and Sisters," she had said from her position beside the organ during the Wednesday night Bible Study following the charity event. "I have an announcement to make regarding choir rehearsal on Thursday night. Because of Sister Maybelline's misfortune at the gala, God has impressed it upon my heart to act as minister of music until our sister's heart is healed from the embarrassment of her dress busting and falling completely off of her." At that statement, Jackie Black paused and bowed her neck dramatically and shook her head vigorously from side to side causing the curtain of Senegalese twists to wave and ripple heavily on either side of her face. She then snapped her head up and continued. "Most of you are unaware of the pain and suffering she's experiencing. But the Bible admonishes us to rejoice when others have victories and to mourn when others mourn. Today, I mourn, and I will *stand* in the gap until our sister is ready to resume her position." On that night, both Luceal and Laura supported Jackie's announcement with hearty amens they'd soon regret.

Other than the amens of the twins, after Jackie's announcement, no one else said a word. The air was still, save for a faint wafting scent of cocoa butter. Pastor LeBeaux stared at Jackie in confusion, but shook off his dumbfounded look soon enough to say, "Thank you Jackie for being proactive. See saints, this is what being in the body of Christ is all about. Bringing our divers gifts and talents together to build up the kingdom." Jackie beamed and dramatically swung the long twists across her left shoulder.

Maybelline tipped out of bible class, went home, placed the remnants of her ball gown into the fireplace and burned them. It was only a phone call from Locke, not thirty minutes later, that lifted her spirits enough to return to church two Sundays later.

"Why'd you leave, Maybelline?" Locke asked her loudly.

"It's too embarrassing, Ms. Belle," Maybelline whined, "I can't go back there."

"Yes, you can, and I'll tell you why." Locke paused weighing her words carefully. "You weren't the only one to have a wardrobe malfunction on the night of the big event. Jackie AND her wardrobe malfunctioned that night," Locke laughed, "and I got the feathers to prove it!"

Locke told Maybelline the entire story of what she called, *The Flight of the Peacock.* "That 'Flight of the Bumblebee' you played was nothing compared to the show Jacqueline Black gave in my front yard after the gala."

"You don't have to lie to make me feel better, Ms. Belle, but I have to say, that is sure a funny story. I can see it now, Jackie flapping around. Peacock feathers flying everywhere!"

"You may not have to picture it. I may be able to do you one better. Anyway, Maybelline, when have you ever known me to make up funny stories? I've been too many places on this planet to make up stuff. I've almost seen all there is to see."

"I know, but why would Jackie air my dirty laundry, when she has dirty laundry of her own?"

"Because she's crazy, Maybelline. She's as crazy as a road lizard, and don't you dare let a road lizard take away the beauty God gave you. She's not worth it."

She's not worth it, is what Maybelline had to keep saying to herself to each time she sloughed herself away from the bed to get dressed for church on Sunday Morning, and this Sunday was no different.

The blood still washes,
The blood still cleanses,
After all these years,
The blood still has mir-rack-you-luss pow'r!

Jackie sang in an inconsistent and raggedy soprano. She snapped her head around on the word *miraculous*, defaming its true meaning. The choir members shook their heads slowly as they came in on the verse, "It stiiiiilllll washes; it still cleanses."

Maybelline swayed back and forth with her eyes closed, thankful she was able to feel the sentiment of the words, even though the music was lacking. When she opened her eyes, she saw that Pastor Prentiss seemed more interested in her than the worship music.

Was he that disappointed, because she'd stopped playing? Was he angry?

No, the look wasn't anger. It was… Maybelline shook her head. Maybe she didn't see what she thought she saw. She continued to concentrate on the words.

Locke had a harder time enjoying service ever since Jackie Black took possession of the minister of music post. A creature of habit, Locke was used to being able to time exactly how long devotion, offering, and worship singing would last, and was correct down to the minute of the time Pastor LeBeaux would take his text. With Jackie on the keys, there was no telling when the sermon would commence. Locke did not like this. Locke did not like Jackie, and it had become Locke's purpose to shut down every takeover Jackie was staging.

Locke had been talking to Maybelline for weeks about playing again, but Maybelline wouldn't budge. She knew that if she didn't convince Maybelline to begin playing for the church again soon, Maybelline may do something drastic. Locke had seen what happened to people when they were not given the opportunity to express their gifts fully and do what they loved the most. It was like suicide.

Locke continued to scan the church for signs of unrest Jackie may have caused. She thought sure she caught Pastor LeBeaux watching Maybelline with affection, but didn't spend enough time on the body language to make a good assessment. She was most concerned about Jackie's attempt at a silent coup. William Hughes' eyes rested on Iris, of course; however, Iris didn't seem to notice. Like Locke, she too, was on guard for some of Jackie Black's small productions. This Sunday, everyone, except Jackie and Maybelline, was tucked in place--but things were amiss, Locke could feel it.

When Jackie finished her musical numbers, she slid dramatically from the piano stool and walked to her spot, near where the deaconesses sat. She did not, however, sit in her original seat. She sat one pew ahead of the ladies. Locke watched as some of the sisters bent their heads toward one another in wonderment of what Jackie was up to, but it was obvious that they did not take her position seriously enough to warrant tapping her on the shoulder and redirecting her to her place with the rest of her deaconess sisters. That was it--Jackie's thing for this week.

Subtle enough, Locke thought.

As subtle as the change in seat was for Jackie, it was evident that Jackie had been "doing things" every week to cause unrest. One week, she replaced the floral arrangements on the pulpit with gladiolas. Sister Katie Caldwell, Sweet Fields' florist, who was lauded and awarded year after year during Atlanta's "Fabulous Flowers" competition for her unique and elaborate flower arrangements, was outraged. She maintained the floral arrangements for the church as a donation from her business. Another week, Jackie had added a tablecloth to the communion table. The oldest and most respected deaconess, Mother Emmadine Walker, removed it after the whispering from the congregation interrupted the service, for everyone knew nothing was to be placed on the sacred table. Another Sunday, Jackie took it upon herself to personally greet first time visitors when they were asked to stand. While the ushers were giving them church literature, welcome cards, and such, Jackie greeted each one with a hug, slipping each her business card. This disrupted the service, as there were a dozen visitors scattered throughout the massive sanctuary. Finally, during Sunday School she had taken over one of the children's' classes because the teacher was running five minutes late.

"I'm sorry little ones. I ran over a nail this morning, so my tire was flat. But I'm here now." The teacher was cheerful in spite of the hiccup in her morning, and the 8-year-olds stood up and cheered when she walked into the classroom. She turned to Jackie Black, "Thank you so much, Deaconess Black. I think I can handle it from here."

"No need, Sister Berry, I'm here now. We shouldn't disrupt the order we already have in place. The children need to see that timeliness is next to Godliness. God is *always* on time," Jackie said dramatically.

"Yes I understand, but it was an accident; it was beyond my control. Usually I am early for church school. I'm always on time."

"Well, you weren't on time today," Jackie grinned out the words. She turned toward the children, who were very anxious to have their teacher back, "and children, tardiness is not of God."

Thread by thread, Jacqueline O'Shelle Black pulled at the fabric of St. Andrew. Her actions on the surface were trifles, small things most of the membership of St. Andrew did not take seriously or even notice for that matter.

"She means well," some of the women's ministry surmised.

"Sister Black's spirit of excellence, always compels her to keep working for the Lord," some of the deacons asserted.

"She has a zeal of God that causes her to keep pressing toward the mark of a higher calling in Christ," quoted some of the mothers.

"She's so helpful," said the youth director, "I love that she always wants to be found doing the work of the kingdom."

Others thought she was doing things on purpose. What they didn't know was WHY she was doing these little aggravating things. What purpose did they serve?

Locke returned her attention to the pulpit where she saw the associate pastor, Rev. Charles Edwards standing at the podium. Locke liked Rev. Edwards. He was a pecan-colored man with fine hair, straight teeth, and a thin mustache. He was tall with broad shoulders, and he was always impeccably dressed. Everything about Rev. Edwards said "order," from his fresh haircut to his spit-shined shoes, which gleamed so that anyone who got close enough could see his reflection. His hands were the right texture-not soft like a woman's, but not hard and dry as if he didn't take care of himself.

Locke remembered his interview for the position of associate pastor. He had gotten her vote simply because of his attention to detail. He knew the entire history of St. Andrew's by memory. He knew all of the trustees, founding families, and key members on sight. And most importantly, he knew the word and how to apply it to everything else he knew about Sweet Fields and St. Andrew Church.

When asked about how he views and handles conflict in the church, Charles Edward Jr. stated in an authoritative voice, "The word of God says that all things work together for the good of the people who serve Him, and those who are called to His purpose, so conflict, well it works for our good. But it doesn't mean that it should go unaddressed. The Bible says we should mark them that sow discord among the brethren. I am a military and spiritually trained marksman."

That's what Locke liked most about Rev. Charles Edwards, Jr. He said what he needed to say without extra words or unnecessary explanations. Rev. Edwards was quite capable of running the church and did so without fuss or fanfare. On Sundays, he blessed the offering and ended the service with the benediction. On Wednesdays at noon, he conducted prayer and bible study. During the week, he visited the sick and shut in.

He and his wife, Karen, were faithful people. Karen was so quiet that Locke sometimes--most times--forgot she existed, but Karen ran the nursery on Sundays and Wednesdays like a welloiled machine. Karen Edwards, more than anyone else at St. Andrew's, was excited about the daycare. In fact, Karen was so good with the babies that many a working mother tried to hire Karen full-time to watch their precious ones. Locke snapped out of her streaming thoughts and refocused on the pulpit. Rev. Edwards was announcing something.

"St. Andrew family, I want to acknowledge a special visitor--my father. He recently retired and made visiting us his first order of business. He will be with us for a week or so. I trust you all will make him feel right at home here in Sweet Fields." The audience applauded. Locke noticed a giant of a man near the deacon's section. He stood ramrod straight and bowed his head slightly. Charles Edwards, Sr. caught Locke's eye in more ways than one.

Iris decided that if she was going to stay in Sweet Fields, there had to be some changes to the Murphy Inn, as it had been known during its tenure as one of the state's premier bed and breakfast inns. While the woodwork was still gorgeous, it required some updating. She thought about making it a bed and breakfast again, but she wasn't sure if she liked strangers being in her home. At the same time, the house was ridiculously large for one person to rattle around in. At any rate, giving the Murphy Inn a facelift would begin with the kitchen and bathrooms.

She wanted to gut the kitchen completely and rearrange it. The sink could remain where it was, but a dishwasher was of the utmost importance. All four of the full bathrooms were spacious but tiled in wretched pinks, reds, blues, and yellows. She wanted warm and neutral colors, claw foot tubs, and walk-in showers in the bathrooms. The bathrooms would definitely have to be gutted and re-arranged. After church, Deacon Hughes approached her with a hearty handshake. She returned the gesture with a beaming smile.

"Deacon Hughes! I'm glad to see you."

"Well, that's good to know, Sister Murphy. That's good to know."

"I'm thinking of remodeling the Murphy Inn, and…"

"Whew. I haven't heard that name in long while. The Murphy Inn," he said rolling the name around on his lips. "You gonna run it as a B & B again, Sister Murphy?"

"Oh. I'm not sure about that. I do, however, want to update the kitchen and bathrooms. I wonder if you could come take a look for me." Hughes' eyes lit up with glee.

"Of course I'll come around. What day?"

"Oh, whenever you have time. I want you to schedule me just like you would anyone else. Maybe I should have just called your office number rather than bothering you about business on a Sunday."

"Oh no. You call whenever you want. I can come tomorrow afternoon. I'm doing some work at a house a couple of blocks from you. Is about 4pm okay?"

"Yes, that's fine, Deacon," Iris said barely touching him on his sleeved forearm. "I'll see you tomorrow evening." she said before starting down the church steps.

William Hughes resisted the urge to slide his hand across his sleeve. *Iris Murphy had touched him; now if that don't beat all*, he thought. He turned slightly to get a final glance at Iris as she walked away. He pretended to jot down something in one of the small black notebooks he kept in the inside pocket of all of his suits. He looked down at the empty white sheet seriously, feigning a business like demeanor, but in his heart he was calculating his next step with Iris Murphy. In his head, he was calculating the story he would spin for the brethren in the deacon's den on next Sunday morning before worship service.

Locke was already walking across the church parking lot toward Pendleton Park by the time Iris and Deacon Hughes were finished with their conversation. Iris saw one of the guests from church services making his way with long strides toward Belle. It was the Assistant Pastor's father, Charles Edwards, Sr. He finally caught up with Locke, and Iris slipped on her sunglasses and watched as Locke, with a femininity she hadn't seen in her before, lifted her sunglasses and sat them daintily atop her locs. Iris, waved in Locke's direction and pointed toward her house, to signify she was headed home. Locke nodded and turned her attentions to Charles Edwards, Sr.

"Mrs. Locke, you have some stride in you to be such a dainty lady," said Charles Edward, Sr. once he'd caught up with her.

"Hi, I'm Belle Lynne Locke. I prefer introducing myself. It's uncomfortable for me to speak with someone who knows me when I don't know him." Locke extended a gray gloved hand to him. "But if you get this introduction right, you may be able to call me Belle Lynne." Locke smiled, and for Sweet Fields, Locke's smile was the smile seen across Georgia. Worshippers at St. Andrew who were still spilling out of the church's door could see the beautiful grin. Some of the parishioners, who were getting into their cars, caught sight of it as they looked past the deacons who were inspecting Sister Berry's tire. They glanced up in time enough to feel and see the warm sensation of Locke blushing. The sleepy town of Sweet Fields took note of the man who solicited this response from Belle Lynne Locke, and it was the talk of Sunday dinner that day.

"I'm sorry, Mrs. Locke," Charles laughed. It was a big wide laugh, one that came from the belly. It was the laugh of a happy person, a person who had let go of something. "Let me begin again. Hi, I'm Charles Edward, Sr. Your Assistant Pastor is my son. Just to keep down confusion while I'm here, I've been asking the members to call me Eddie. I saw you walking toward the park, and thought I'd try to catch up and walk with you. I've always enjoyed a nice Sunday afternoon stroll."

"I'm pleased to meet you, Mr. Edwards. I think your son is a good young man, well able to serve St. Andrew. I too enjoy a nice Sunday afternoon stroll, but I usually do it alone." Locke had begun to steel herself against Eddie as soon as she heard him laugh. His laugh, like her Clive's, filled every bit of the air around her, and this fact alone made Locke feel as if Eddie was an intruder. In a matter of seconds, Eddie had managed to pour his laugh into the crevices that Locke thought she'd patched up after Clive died.

"There's a first time for everything, Mrs. Locke, but I can tell you're a lady who doesn't like to be caught off guard. I understand. I'll be here all week, and if you're a walker, like I think you are, then I'm sure we'll walk into each other along one of these tree-lined avenues." With that, Eddie performed a stiff military turn to commence his walk.

Locke plopped the sunglasses over her eyes and rifled in her bag for a handkerchief. The few items she carried in purse seemed so noisy as she searched for something to wipe her eyes. Little vials of sanitizer and metallic tubes of lipsticks and glosses clucked against each other while she dug feverishly for the handkerchief. Charles Edward, Sr. turned around once more to take a look at the small striking woman he'd asked for a walk. He wondered to himself, *what is she looking for in that purse? I hope she hasn't lost her house keys.* In a small sliver of time, Eddie thought about going back to help Belle Lynne Locke retrieve the lost item-whatever it was--but something told him to leave it alone. He turned and continued his walk.

There were three people left in the church. Everyone else was in cars and well on the way to a local eatery or someone's grandmother's or aunt's house for a big Sunday dinner and then a quick nap to sleep off all of the heavy entrees, cakes, and pies.

Maybelline was usually one of the last in line to greet the pastor after church services. She moved dispassionately down the center aisle. Two armor bearers were behind her, signifying to the few stragglers chatting in the sanctuary that Pastor LeBeaux was finished receiving members.

"That was a wonderful sermon you preached today, Pastor. Sometimes we need a word of encouragement to get us through the week. I was definitely encouraged this morning." Maybelline spoke barely above a whisper.

"Well, to God be the glory, Maybelline. I'm glad God was able to use me to speak to your heart, but you don't sound too encouraged." Pastor LeBeaux bent down just a little to align his eyes with Maybelline's, whose head was lowered, the heavy bangs falling into her eyes. "But I think it's time we talk about how we can get you to reconnect with the choir. It's been a while."

"Yes, Pastor." Maybelline lifted her head slowly to meet Pastor LeBeaux's eyes. "It has. But there are circumstances that I just can't get past keeping me from my post."

Pastor LeBeaux signaled for the armor bearers to leave. He turned to look for Francis, who had blended into the background. "Francis, will you come on in the study while I talk with Sister Maybelline?" Prentiss turned to Maybelline, "Have you got a few minutes?"

"I do."

The three walked toward the Pastor's study. Jackie Black was sitting in her car waiting for Pastor LeBeaux to exit the church. She was sure that he would be hungry by now. But his car was still in its assigned space, and Maybelline's car was still on the lot as well. She hadn't seen Francis the Secretary exit either, but she often walked home, plus Francis was so quiet, Jackie could have missed her. Jackie Black got out of her Thunderbird and reentered the church. She walked up the center aisle slowly and took a left at the front of the church. There she saw the seat of memorium for Prentiss' dear sweet Ava. Jackie sat there. She crossed her legs, straightened her back, and stretched her neck. Lifting her head up high, Jackie extended her right thin manicured hand to an imaginary guest, "Ah yes," she whispered, "I'm the first lady of St. Andrew, Jackie O'Shelle Black LeBeaux. This seat is fine." Jackie grinned and preened imagining what her new life as First Lady LeBeaux would be like. She was slowly beginning to gain the respect and even love of most of the members by trying to make minor improvements here and there. The others would soon see her value and follow suit. Eventually, Jackie Black thought, she would make her way into the first lady's seat, and everything at St. Andrew's would be perfect. Jackie continued to wait for Pastor Prentiss to emerge from his study.

Pastor Prentiss offered Maybelline a seat in his office in front of his desk. As he made his way around it, he signaled for Francis the Secretary to sit opposite Maybelline.

"Now Maybelline, you know how we miss you and the way you tickle the ivories every Sunday morning. What's it going to take for you to come back? Money? You need a raise? You know we're working on ordering new choir robes. We just have to get the choir members to agree on a color."

"Well Pastor, to be honest, I really don't know." Maybelline leaned back in the chair, tilting her head slightly as if she was thinking about what to say next. "It's just that. It's just that, things aren't the same here. I feel as if I don't belong and that feeling has been stronger since...well, since…"

"Okay, I know that was embarrassing for you. But it was an accident. And really, I don't think the congregation even remembers the incident. What they do remember is the way your anointing ministered to their hearts while they sit out there in those pews. Maybelline, you know that the accident at the gala was just a trick of the enemy to keep you from your work in the kingdom. He formed a weapon against you, but the bible says that the weapon will not prosper. It looks like you're willing to let it prosper, Maybelline. Don't let that happen, because I miss…" Prentiss caught himself and gave a quick glance to Francis the Secretary to see if she had heard him. Francis didn't look up, but continued to scratch on the yellow steno pad with her pencil.

"The members miss you."

"That's really sweet of you, Pastor. And you know, I know all about weapons and prospering, but that really doesn't do much for me when I've been publicly embarrassed like I was a few weeks ago. I just keep thinking that every time I get up on the organ stool, all people will see or remember is an image of me with nothing on but my underwear."

"That's not true Maybelline. We've all been in an embarrassing position before. Accidents happen…"

"Pastor LeBeaux. I wish you'd stop saying accident. It wasn't an accident." Maybelline's breathing became labored, and she felt herself getting angry. She was hot all over. She wanted to stop herself from talking, but she couldn't. "It wasn't an accident. It was Sister Jacqueline Black. She stepped on the train of my dress and tore my dress off!" Maybelline stopped talking and let out a loud sigh. "And Pastor, I could have lived with that, because most of the people at the gala didn't see, but then she announced it at Bible Study, and now everyone knows, even though they didn't see. I can see the 'poor Maybelline' look in their eyes when they greet me. The twins can't keep their snickers back when I walk by. Tell me now, Pastor. How would YOU recover from that? What could help YOU forget? Especially when everything around you won't let you forget. Every Sunday I drag myself into this church, a church where I grew up and played for years, and see a reminder of what happened sitting on the organ stool. What can you say about weapons now?"

Pastor LeBeaux looked up at Francis the Secretary again. Francis gave him a curt nod, verifying that all Maybelline said was in fact true. "I'm sorry. I didn't know. You didn't tell me. If you would have just told me…"

"Then what, Pastor? You would have called us in for a conference, right? She would have said it was an accident. That it could've been anyone who stepped on my dress, what with all of the people in the room. You would've talked about forgiveness. She would have flitted out of here as if she'd done nothing wrong." The words kept coming. "You don't see anything Pastor Prentiss." She said the words slow. "You only see what you *think* is good. You only see your Ava's daycare. You only see a woman busy and on fire for the Lord. You don't see how she does… she does… things. Things around here that look like the work of the church, but it's really the wiles of the devil. And I won't be the only one she hurts if you don't open your eyes."

"Listen Maybelline, I know you're upset. You're emotional. You've been hurt. But that doesn't mean you aren't a vital part of the kingdom. God can wipe all of those tears away if you give that pain over to Him. Remember, God can give you joy in the morning."

"So, Pastor. You're going to let Sister Black tear up the church all night while you wait on your morning joy?"

"That's not what I mean…"

"I've decided how to deal with it, Pastor. And this conversation has helped me put everything into perspective. I can't continue to subject myself to St. Andrew and how it's being sifted by Satan. I can leave, and I believe God has given me a way out. My job has offered me an opportunity to establish a plant and corporate office in Beijing. I've been afraid to take the position, wondering if that's where God wants me to be. But like you, I'm a student of scripture too, and right today, I've realized that the spirit of fear is not of God. The fear and anxiety that arrests me here at St. Andrew is not of God. I'm going to make a power move and take the position in Beijing." Maybelline stood up and wiggled down her black pencil skirt. She pulled the long thick bangs of her hair away from her face and behind her left ear. She couldn't moved fast enough to keep Prentiss from seeing the tear rolling down her smooth chubby face, but she slipped her sunglasses to cover her eyes anyway. "Pastor. You pray my strength in the Lord."

Prentiss LeBeaux stood up. "Maybelline, let's not leave it here. Let's go get some lunch and you can tell me more about your new position. You know, when you're leaving. When you're coming back."

Maybelline's face lit up. She removed her sunglasses and squinted her eyes, which were still wet with tears. "Sure, Pastor. But let me warn you, I've cried so much over the past few weeks, I can't even see straight. And I know you wouldn't want to eat with a woman who looks like a raccoon by the face." Maybelline giggled. She hadn't giggled in a long time.

"Oh, I don't mind at all, you can cry with me whenever you need to. That's what I'm here for." Pastor LeBeaux smiled at Maybelline, because he meant exactly what he said. He scanned his desk for lingering tasks, "I have some things to finish up here, and I'll swing by to pick you up as soon as I'm done."

Maybelline left through the Pastor's study door at the back of the church. She was a good four blocks down the avenue by the time Jackie Black had grown bored with her daydreaming in the sanctuary and went outside to see if Maybelline's car was still in the parking lot. It was gone, but Pastor LeBeaux's car was still in the same spot. Jackie walked down the hall to the study to see if there was anything she could get Pastor Prentiss while he labored in the word.

"Francis, is Pastor busy right now?"

Francis looked up from her desk and placed her pencil down on the steno-pad. "Yes, he's busy, Sister Black. He has a few things to finish up before he leaves for the afternoon."

Jackie took a seat. "That's okay. I'll wait for him."

"You shouldn't wait. Pastor LeBeaux has an afternoon appointment off campus. After that he won't be coming back to the church. I'll have him to call you."

"Well, if you could just buzz me back, I just wanted to see if he needed anything before…"

"I'm sure if he needs something, he'd let his secretary know. He made it clear that he didn't want to be disturbed. I can't buzz you in right now. I'll have him to call you. Good afternoon, Sister Black.

"Good afternoon, Francis," Jackie said curtly, and left, taking long swift strides to her car. She folded herself into her Thunderbird, slammed the door, and sped away.

CHAPTER 9: MONDAY

Jackie Black woke up on her full-size bed shoved into the corner of the backroom of her dance studio. She had tossed and turned all night; she couldn't sleep for thinking of Prentiss and how he had slipped by her on Sunday afternoon. She needed him to understand how much she wanted to care for him.

"I can't seem to get his attention. He works hard for those people at that church, and they do nothing for him," she said aloud as she performed her morning stretches. "That's alright, Pastor Prentiss. I see how hard you work, and I will be your help meet." She smiled and devised a plan. God had sent her to be Prentiss' angel, and she would not let her job go undone.

Jackie dressed quickly in white leggings, a white embroidered knee-length tunic, and white ballet flats. She adorned her epic twists with a white scarf wrapped around her forehead several times as a headband.

It was still very early on Prentiss' street. Lawn sprinklers were the only movement and noise she heard as she climbed out of her car and stealthily made her way to the pastor's front porch. The church had acquired the parsonage some twenty years earlier and remodeled the large craftsman style home for the pastor and his family. In the past, the Young Men's Ministry maintained the lawn of the parsonage, but Prentiss had insisted on cutting his own lawn and trimming his own hedges. Jackie was in too big of a rush to notice or appreciate the neatness of the premises. She was looking for his laundry bag that he left for local cleaners to pick up. She scanned the porch and found a canvas bag near the front door. She stooped to pick it up and tried to remain calm as she hurried back to her car. Once she was down the street and around the corner, she pulled over to gather herself and her thoughts. Her heart was beating fast, but God had answered her prayer for courage to do His work.

She reached down to open the laundry bag and grabbed a handful of dress shirts. Hints of cypress, jasmine, and patchouli engulfed her nose, and she relished in the scents. It was his signature cologne. She smelled it every Sunday when she greeted him at the back of the sanctuary. She pulled out each shirt, fingering the buttons. Once she had inspected each sufficiently, she returned the seven shirts to the canvas bag and proceeded to the cleaners on Harrison Street--not Christmas Cleaners--where Prentiss usually did business. It was only 6:30 am, so Jackie was early enough to get the one-hour special. She requested heavy starch. While she waited for the pastor's clothes to be cleaned, she went across town to her favorite bakery. She order two muffins, two scones, and two mini breakfast quiches. She topped off her order with sample bags of specialty coffee. She assembled her purchases in a gift bag and printed very carefully:

I have given myself to God to be used for His glory, and God has positioned me to be of help to you. Enjoy your day. With the Love of God, Jackie B.

Jackie returned to Harrison Street to pick up Prentiss' clothes, and then she returned to his home which sat four houses down from the church. This time, confident that she had done the will of God, she emerged from her car, retrieved her gift bag and his clothes and paraded proudly to the front door. She hung his heavily starched shirts on the hook near the door and hung the gift bag carefully on the doorknob. She lingered on the porch a while, hoping that Prentiss would hear or see her on his porch and invite her in. She inspected the potted plants and then dragged her hand along the arms of the porch rocking chairs. She imagined that she and Prentiss would have their coffee in the mornings and a glass of tea in the evenings in these very chairs. "All in due time" she whispered. "All in God's time," she corrected herself.

When 9 am rolled around, Prentiss was jolted from his sleep by a phone call from Christmas Cleaners. It was Harry Christmas, the owner.

"Rev, I hope I didn't wake you. I just wanted see if you forgot to set your clothes out this morning for pickup. I can send Ray back by there if you did. He's over on the next street."

"Mr. Harry, I sat my clothes out last evening before I headed to bed. Now, I hope no one took my clothes." Prentiss was starting to get a little vexed. Things had always been quiet in his part of Sweet Fields. He slipped his feet into his leather slippers and stuck his head out of the front door. He saw seven white shirts and two pair of dress slacks hanging from the hook beside the door. He also saw a large white gift bag knocking against the outer doorknob.

"Mr. Harry. I think someone had my clothes done for me-you know, as a gift. I appreciate your calling."

"Must be nice to have such thoughtful congregants, " Harry laughed in one part because he was one of those thoughtful congregants. The Christmas name was etched into the cornerstone of the church's foundation. The other reason he laughed was because everyone knew he cleaned the pastor's clothes just as his father did for the pastors before Prentiss. Only a newcomer wouldn't know that.

Prentiss ended the call with Harry Christmas and snatched the bag off the knob and clothes off the hook. He read the card and shook his head. The writing on the card left him more confused than grateful, especially after the news Maybelline shared with him on yesterday after church. Sure, he'd dealt with church conflict before, but it had seemed that everything Sister Black had done for the church was in an effort to build up the kingdom.

Kingdom building couldn't cause conflict, could it?

Sister Black had been one of the biggest champions of the new daycare, next to Karen Edwards, of course. She could be a bit of a zealot, this Prentiss LeBeaux knew, but this was common behavior for a new member trying to prove herself and show others she could be a vital part of the body of Christ, that she was willing to commit her giftedness to the cause of Christ. The news of Sister Black being deliberately mean perplexed him.

What niggled at the back of Prentiss LeBeaux's mind was the fact that a treacherous act attributed to Sister Black would be the very one to take his faithful minister of music away. He enjoyed seeing Maybelline Crowder on the organ, seeing her smile at the choir members when their voices blended perfectly. Seeing her giggle when one of the sopranos fell into a part when she wasn't supposed to. Seeing her raise her left eyebrow when someone was off key, and seeing the thick curls fall over her eyes and then seeing her pull all of that hair into a long ponytail at the nape of her neck. Pastor LeBeaux enjoyed just seeing her. Her heart-shaped face was full and clear. The skin did not pull taut around the bones like a skeleton. No, she didn't look emaciated and starved. She was healthy (that's what his mother used to call it). Like Ava, she was curvy and soft. She kept herself looking good, smelling good. And her hair. Prentiss didn't quite understand why she never combed her curls out, but left the hair in neat parts, as if she'd just taken the rollers out. Prentiss LeBeaux smiled to himself. He chuckled too, as he remembered some of his college buddies teasing him, because he *liked 'em thick*. Yes, Maybelline was the kind of woman he enjoyed seeing. "Oh Lord," he said aloud. He enjoyed seeing her.

Prentiss LeBeaux dropped the gift bag onto one of the stools at his breakfast counter. He hefted the clothes into his closet, closer to the back. They were heavy with starch, and it irritated Prentiss LeBeaux that he would have to be scratchy throughout service the next Sunday. The heavy starch chafed, especially at his forearms, and if he sweated, even a little, he itched to high heaven. It was all he could do to keep a stiff shirt on his body while he was in the pulpit.

If Maybelline was correct about Sister Black, and he was sure she was, Francis his trusted secretary confirmed it, he would have to do something. God knows Prentiss LeBeaux hated conflict. He hated being the one to speak to his congregants about being the source of discord, but if Jacqueline Black could run Maybelline off, she could surely sow discord among the rest of the flock, and discord was exactly what St. Andrew did not need. They had just healed from an ugly split, they were just coming together as a united body and were just moving toward expanding the church to accommodate a daycare and learning center. Pastor LeBeaux walked to his bed. He sat down heavily, as if he were tired from a long day's work, even though he'd just woken up. He stood up, turned toward the foot of his bed and kneeled to pray.

"God you've always been there for me, and I appreciate the tenderness you've shown toward me all of these years. Had it not been for you, I couldn't even bend my knee to talk to you and lend my ear to hear your sweet voice. Thank you.

You've given me a good congregation. You've allowed me to lead this flock over the last few years without incident. You've sent faithful workers, faithful tithers, men and women of divers, gifts, and children to keep the church growing and going. I couldn't ask for a better group of people. Thank you for them. I pray their strength in the Lord and ask you to keep a shield of protection all around them.

Now Lord, I've found myself in an uncomfortable place. You know my weakness. You know my compassion for people is a blessing and a curse. You know how I get tunnel vision when it comes to carrying out your vision, and this vision, since it meant so much to Ava, this vision, I confess has blinded me. I think. I think, Jesus that I've even been blind to matters of my own heart. Maybelline. Maybelline... just guide her in the right way… even if it's not my way. Give me the words to say to her. I'm her pastor, and I want to do right by her. I want her to be whole. And grant her some peace, Lord. Rock her in the cradle of your arms and sit her in your lap of love, to be caressed by your soothing spirit and healed by your balm of loving kindness.

I admit I've missed some other things that have gone on. I ask you to help me discern what's happening in St. Andrew, and pray that if there is anything that's not of you, I have the strength to handle it with the sword of the word; to root it out and cut it off with your divine strength and power. Stand up in me. Don't let my compassion become a perversion. Show me what I need to see, and let me see and hear the signs you set before me. I know you can, and I believe you will, and I thank you that you've already done what needs to be done, that you've set those wheels in motion. In your darling son, Jesus' name I do offer these prayers. Amen"

Prentiss LeBeaux got up from his kneeling position slowly. His heart was still heavy, but not with the heaviness that came with Jackie Black. Maybelline was in his heart, and it hurt him that she was there, especially since Ava was there too. For years he'd grieved so hard for his wife, he didn't really think of finding companionship in anyone else, and so he didn't try. Somehow, in a way that Prentiss LeBeaux wasn't even aware of, Maybelline crept in. And each time he saw her, she made her way in further.

During lunch the day before, Maybelline and Prentiss had laughed so much together that he was sure they'd be put out of the little mom and pop diner that sold the best cornbread dressing he'd ever tasted. Maybelline wasn't as impressed with the cornbread dressing as she was with the lemon icebox pie.

"Pastor, this cornbread dressing pales in comparison to my cornbread dressing." She had tapped the last bit of dressing off of her fork onto the side of her plate and was now picking over the bits of turkey that were mixed in.

"Dressing is an art that few master," Pastor LeBeaux said. "I've tasted a lot of dressing and can say only two have been good. This dressing right here, and my mama's dressing."

"Okay. Okay. That's what all men say. Every man in the universe, even on Mars, up there on Jupiter, thinks his mom is the best cook. But I can burn, Pastor."

"Aw Maybelline, I don't believe you. You're one of those modern women. A feminist. You do that new-fangled cooking where you don't need nothing but a microwave. You don't know what you're doing in the kitchen. All you know how to do is sit at a computer and boss people around. Yeah, I heard how you run things up at the plant. You don't fool me with that shy act."

"Wait, I thought we were talking about cooking. I try to keep that part of my personality separate from my church life. But every now and then, it creeps up on me." Maybelline looked at Prentiss knowingly and after a short pause, they both laughed.
"Anyway, when you think about it, cooking and engineering are a lot alike. It's all about getting the right pieces in the right places. Getting the right people to do the right job. It's about using resources to create something beautiful. That's how I approach my cooking. And I'm going to show you before I leave here for Beijing. I have to eat good before I leave, because I'll probably starve when I get there."

The mention of Beijing set Pastor LeBeaux on edge. He scratched at the top of his head, as was his way when he got nervous. "So when do you leave for Beijing, Sister?" All of a sudden his tone was formal.

"I leave on Tuesday. It's a temporary assignment--well, it's temporary if I so choose. I'll be there for a few months, with an option to stay on permanently if I like. It depends."

"Well, it's a great opportunity. It's good to see members doing great things in the world. I'm proud of you."

"Thank you, Pastor. And I need to tell you that I'm sorry about how I acted when you tried to talk to me in your office. My managerial side kicks in quick when I get nervous and stressed. It helps me maintain some level of control. I didn't mean to disrespect you at all. You know I've always esteemed you highly. I never meant to disrespect the memory and vision of your wife. Do you forgive me?" Maybelline shook her hair back out of her eyes. They were bright as they stared into Pastor LeBeaux's. There was a sincerity there that put a crack in the grief that he had been carrying for Ava for so long.

"Maybelline, please don't worry about that. I understand that things have been difficult for you lately, both personally and professionally. Your feelings are valid because they are yours. And frankly, I needed a little kick in the pants. I've had it pretty easy since I've been at St. Andrew. I must admit it; I've been coasting along. I needed to be shaken up. You brought in reality, a reality that most members try their best try to shield me from. I appreciate your honesty, and I accept your apology." It was all Pastor Prentiss could do to not drop his fork and reach for
Maybelline's hand. He resisted. "Now, let's talk about all this cooking you can do. I'm not going to let you leave Sweet Fields without proving your claims. So when's lunch?"

"Pastor, you can have lunch every day this week. I'm off all week, and I plan to cook everything left in my refrigerator AND deep freezer before I leave. I can't eat all of that by myself, so you have a standing appointment for lunch every day. I'll show you that there's more to me than Bach and business suits."

"Well, it's a deal."

Maybelline reached over the table and shook Pastor LeBeaux's hand. And that is how it all started, before it all ended.

On Monday morning, Pastor LeBeaux woke musing about how much he enjoyed Maybelline's company and looking forward to noon when he'd see her again. He thought about what he would say to her today and from where he'd pull up topics of conversation. He prayed for her.

Glancing back at the gift bag, Pastor Prentiss LeBeaux realized that Maybelline was not the only parishioner who should get his attention. Eventually, he would have to deal with Jackie Black, and as he looked back on all of she'd done, he realized that the conversation would have to be something serious.

Monday evening at 4:30pm, Deacon William Hughes rang the doorbell of the Murphy Inn. Iris ran down the stairs in black Lululemon capri leggings, a pink Nike tee, and bright pink and orange colored sneakers. Her hair was pulled back in a large curly puff.

"Hello, Deacon Hughes!" she said with a warm smile and a lilt in her voice.

"I'm s-s-s-so sorry I'm late. I'm never late, but Mother Stewart and her daughter Eliza got to talking to me and I just c-cc-couldn't seem to get out!" he was flustered. He couldn't stop staring at her hips in those leggings.

"I understand, Deacon Hughes. It's not a problem at all. Come on in." she stood aside and gestured for him to enter.

Even while working, William Hughes, was well put together. His dark blue Dickies were severely starched; the short sleeve shirt was pulled tightly over his flat stomach into a perfect military tuck. Iris had never seen much of Deacon Hughes' skin, but she couldn't help but notice his muscular forearms were the color of milk chocolate. As he walked past her to enter, the pleasant scent of a woodsy aroma with a hint of musk teased her nose.

"Let's look at the kitchen first, shall we?" Iris said sidestepping the tall man and leading him into the kitchen. "I plan to redo everything in here, but most importantly, I want a larger sink and a dishwasher right over here," she moved to where she wanted the sink and dishwasher. When she looked at Deacon Hughes, he was smiling and nodding.

"I see. I can do that. Lemme take a look under this sink here." He stooped down and opened the cabinet door beneath the sink and shined his flashlight. Iris was pleased the Deacon had thought enough of himself and her to not show butt crack. She found it distasteful and never got used to the sight, even though it was generally expected. His shirt remained neatly tucked, and the bend of his knee revealed the slightest outline of a very muscular thigh. *This is so much better than butt crack*, Iris thought.

Hughes looked around for a while before standing up again. He noted mentally how clean everything was. Even the corners and crevices were spotless. He thought about how his mother always said nasty women were from the devil. He turned on the faucet and appeared to be listening for something. "Your water pressure is fading a bit. Looks like you want to move the sink over a few feet. You want the dishwasher about a foot to the left or right?"

"To the left." she said picturing her dream kitchen.

"I can do that. What's next?"

She pointed out the bathrooms and explained that she wanted to change out bathtubs and install walk-in showers in each.
Her phone rang, so she left Deacon Hughes to inspect the carefully cleaned bathrooms.

"Hello," Iris answered with a bit of agitation.

"Is that Hughes' van at your house?" It was Locke. Over the past few months, Iris had learned how to *see* and hear Locke's voice. On this occasion, she heard an impish smile.

"My goodness Locke, how do you know *everything* going on in this neighborhood?" Iris giggled when she asked the question.

"Well, you told me last Sunday, you were running off to catch up with Hughes, so he could take a look at the house. I'm glad he's over there. Maybe you'll get serious about reopening the B & B. Do something with yourself instead of hanging out with old ladies all the time," Locke chuckled. "Anyway, you know Mother Stewart and Daughter Liza can't hold water in a glass. Liza called me right after

Hughes left. She was fussing. She wanted to have closing prayer with him, but Hughes was rushing the job because he was trying to hightail it over to your house."

"I'm sure that duo will have some choice glances and side eyes for me on Sunday."

"Don't worry about them. They like looking at men, especially Hughes. He probably reminds them of his daddy, Big Hughes. You know Liza used to cat around with him, back in her younger days. Anyway, get on back to Hughes. I'm sure he's in your kitchen making up stories to tell the other deacons about how you got a crush on him and what not. You can't leave him to his own devices too long. Go break his train of thought."

Iris certainly didn't want Hughes' imagination running away with him. She'd had enough with the one awkward encounter with him during Sweet Fields' event of the season, the charity ball for the church's new daycare and center for academic excellence. "I will come by and chat with you later, Locke."

When Iris got back to her kitchen, she found Hughes standing up straight with a small black pad in his hand. What struck her most was that Hughes wasn't writing. He looked as if, she wasn't sure, but he looked as if he was daydreaming. "Is my situation that hopeless?" Iris inquired.

"Aw. N-n-n-no. No. Nooooo. I can take care of it." Hughes slapped the notebook shut. "What else you got? I'm up for the challenge."

"Well, I wanted to put a laundry room in the basement," she said as she walked toward the basement stairs. "I hate coming down here. It's kinda scary" Iris said opening the door to the basement and creeping down a few stairs after William. "Aw now, Sister Murphy. I can fix it so you won't be scared to come down here by yourself anymore. All you need is some strategic lighting in your life. But, surely you're not scared with me here with you."

"No. I suppose not. I want to finish the basement with a half bath and a laundry room. Is that possible?"

"Well, I'll need to take a look around. I might be a while." he said descending the creaky stairs while she stayed on the second step.

"Okay. I'll leave the door open. Take your time." Iris said, glad to get out of the dark space.

It was after 6pm when Deacon William Hughes, the only real plumber in Sweet Fields, joined her in the kitchen again. "Well, Sister Murphy, I'm all done. Do you have a few minutes to talk?"

"Sure. Come have a seat. Would you like some tea or coffee?"

"Coffee sounds nice," he said with a smile. "I take mine black. No sugar."

Iris took out the tin of lemon scones Locke had given her earlier that day.

"Would you like a scone? Please help yourself. I can't eat all of these," she said taking out a bottle of hand sanitizer, a small teal plate, and a cloth napkin for him. When his coffee was ready, she poured the strong black liquid into a matching coffee mug and sat it near him on the counter.

He ate at the scone and gulped his coffee while she went to find the pictures of the kitchen she wanted. They talked about the design, the fixtures, and the pipework the house needed for almost an hour. He explained that the work would be rather extensive in the basement and approached the topic of fees rather tentatively. When he gave her a ballpark figure, she didn't balk as he thought she would. Instead, she smiled pleasantly and offered him another cup of coffee.

"Thank you, but I shouldn't. It's much too late. I need to get going. You just let me know when you're ready for me to start working on the house," he said placing his coffee cup in the center of his saucer, standing up and replacing the bar stool to its original position. Before he turned from the counter, he dusted at the slightest crumbs he'd dropped while enjoying the scones. He walked over to the stainless steel trash can, tapped it open with his steel toe boots and dusted the crumbs into it. This made Iris smile. She liked that he straightened up behind himself.

She walked him through the house turning on lamps as she went. She hadn't realized it was so late. She lit up the dusk of the evening by turning on her porch light. William slipped her his business card. It was navy with white block writing: Hughes Plumbing and Home Improvement. Beneath the text, also written in white but smaller, was Hughes' office phone number and website address. *Not a lot of fuss*, Iris thought. She did not like too much fuss.

"If you need me, call my cell phone. It's on the back, there. You can get me quicker on the cell than you can calling the office. Goodnight, Sister Murphy," he said walking down the porch steps with a big grin on his lips.

Iris had to admit she enjoyed the sound of company, the heavy steps of Williams' work boots making their way down. It may be time for some life in the house. She stepped back inside the screen door and watched Hughes climb into his shiny black Chevrolet service van. Hughes shoved a navy baseball cap onto his signature jet black hair, tipped the cap at Iris, and drove away. Iris did not see the big grin William Hughes had on his face, nor did she surmise that her hospitable gesture of offering Hughes scones, (the ones that Locke made, that she wasn't going to eat anyway), had affected him deeply. Hughes now considered himself a strong contender for Iris's heart. He remembered his mother saying, before she died, that one way to a man's heart was through his stomach. Hughes had only visited Iris once, and already she had begun making her way to his heart through his belly. The scones were delicious and tasted fresh, like the lemons had come right from her backyard. Hughes' only regret was his inability to say no to the little old ladies who had thrown him late to get to Iris Murphy's home.

The pair were mother and daughter-in-law, and one could not leave the other alone. Carrie Stewart, the mother, was 98 and on the precipice of dementia brought on by Alzheimer's; she'd begun asking the same questions over and over again. She'd also taken to entertaining imaginary teen-agers in the parlor in an effort to distract them from taking her money bags. Though her mind was drifting, slowly, she was physically in tip top shape. She did her crossword puzzles each morning. She walked on the treadmill in her basement for 20 minutes, (sometimes 40, sometimes 60 if no one was there to make her remember she'd already walked) right before her lunch. And she could still give a tongue lashing that required emergency room stitches--cussed worse than a sailor. William obliged her. He cherished the company of the old woman, as she reminded him of his own grandmother.

The daughter-in-law, Eliza Stewart, was 70 and sassy. She wore too much rouge, and never missed an appointment at Miss Pretty's Palace. It was rumored that William's father and Ms.
Eliza courted from 4th grade on up until Ms. Eliza and Big Hughes (Williams' father) parted ways for college. The relationship didn't weather the distance, and both parties went their separate ways. Ms. Eliza married Mother Stewart's son, Renard, who was 10 years Eliza's senior.

The 10-year gap in age was the big scandal of 1965, and the fact that both Renard and Eliza wore huge afros and black turtlenecks on their wedding day. The marriage lasted 40 years, just long enough for Eliza and Carrie to become best friends.
Eliza was president of the prayer band, and she proved her prayer prowess by randomly breaking out in bouts of prayer in prostrate.
Anytime. Anyplace.

Eliza was led to pray right before Hughes was leaving for Iris'. Daughter Eliza said she wanted to pray for Hughes' safe travel, that was only two or three blocks away. She said the spirit had told her that there may be danger if he left right then. Daughter Eliza prayed lying flat on her belly with her arms outstretched for eleven straight minutes. It took Deacon Hughes 11 additional minutes to get her up and off the floor. All in all, the comedy was worthy of the extra 22 minutes, and Hughes wouldn't change that experience for anything.

CHAPTER 10: TUESDAY

Prentiss LeBeaux woke earlier than he usually did. He stood in the picture window that looked onto the porch and sipped his coffee. All was quiet on the block. After his customary cup of morning coffee--black with sugar--he dressed in dark blue slacks, white collared French blue shirt, and navy oxfords. He grabbed his briefcase and decided to walk the short distance to the church as he often did. As he got settled into his office and ready to take on the tasks for the day, Francis arrived.

"Good morning, Pastor," she said standing in the doorway of his office. "Do you need your list for today?" "Good morning, Francis. I have the list. I have a conference call with the architect in a few minutes and mustn't be disturbed."

"Alright," Francis said with a nod. "Would you like a cup of coffee?"

"Yes, thank you." Francis slipped out of the office and closed the door. She started the coffee maker and settled into her own tasks. When the coffee was ready, Francis took Pastor LeBeaux a mug of black coffee with five sugars. He was on the phone when she entered. He nodded and mouthed the words "thank you." Francis appreciated that Pastor always said "thank you." As she exited his office, she heard a familiar voice.

"Yoo hoo, Francis! Good morning!" Jackie shouted halfway up the stairs. Francis sighed heavily as she quickly pulled the door closed behind her.

"How may I help you, Sister Black?"

"I would like to see Pastor if he's in. I brought him breakfast." Jackie carried a picnic basket in her too slender hands. "I'm sorry, Sister Black. He's on conference call and is not to be disturbed. You may leave the basket if you like. I'll see that you get it back," Francis said from a blank face. Jackie was disappointed and sighed heavily.

"Oh, but I need to *speak* with him, Francis. Can't I wait?"

"You may do as you wish, but the call is usually a lengthy conversation. He specifically asked not to be disturbed until lunch."

"Maybe I can speak with him then?" Jackie eyes opened wide.

"I'm afraid he has a lunch appointment; thus, the permitted interruption. I am sorry, Sister Black. I will see if I can slip in your basket of...uh...your basket in between calls. Please," Francis gestured to a space on a nearby table, "put it here. I'll give it to him." Jackie looked dejected as she slid the basket on the table.

"Thank you, Francis." Jackie said sadly turning to the stairs. Her green broomstick skirt dragged the steps as she descended. Francis looked in the basket and wrinkled her nose. She could smell the diner grease through the Styrofoam containers. The basket contained grits, bacon, sausage, waffles, eggs, and hash browns from Patsy's Diner. Francis shook her head. Pastor Prentiss didn't like Patsy's Diner. Likewise, Pastor Prentiss didn't eat pork in the morning. He complained that the food sat on his chest. She closed the basket and returned to her task of entering tithes and offering information into her data collection system.

A few hours had passed, and Francis was near the end of a stack of envelopes when she heard the door open.

"Hello, Francis," Maybelline called out as she came up the stairs. She didn't shout like Jackie, Francis noted. Then Francis remembered the basket of greasy breakfast food! She grabbed the basket and shoved it under her desk just as Maybelline entered the room.

"Hello, Sister Maybelline. Have a seat. He may still be on the phone." Francis stuck her head in briefly and came right back out. "He's ready for you, Sister Maybelline."

Maybelline offered a warm smile to Francis and carried her large thermal bags into Pastor LeBeaux's office. He could smell the rich marinara sauce from outside the door, and his stomach turned with delight in anticipation of Tuesday's offerings from Maybelline's oven.

Maybelline placed the thermal bag onto Pastor LeBeaux's desk, where he had already made a space for her to put down the food. She

lifted a large carryout from the top and took it out to the reception area. "Here you are Francis. I hope you enjoy it." Prentiss LeBeaux spoke loudly from his office, "Sister
Crowder, tell Francis to come in and sup with us this afternoon."

Francis looked up at Maybelline shyly. "No thank you, Sister Crowder. You all go on. Enjoy yourselves."

"Are you sure, Sister Secretary?" Maybelline smiled at Francis sweetly, "There's plenty of jesting and jiving to go around."

"Yes, I'm sure. Go on and eat your lunch before it grows cold."

"Alright, Francis. I'll let you slide this time." Maybelline turned to go into Pastor LeBeaux's office. "You'll never eat another meatball sandwich from Subway after this, Pastor."

"You *didn't*," Pastor LeBeaux said dramatically, "not a HOMEMADE meatball sandwich."

"Oh yes I did, with sweet potato fries. I'm telling you, you can't put a price on Maybelline's meals."

Prentiss LeBeaux was already busy taking the top off the steaming dish of fries. "What's this on top of it?" He said while still chewing.

"I just sprinkled them with some raw sugar, brown sugar and cinnamon. That's all."

"Ketchup?"

"Ketchup?" Maybelline balked, "Pastor, what's wrong with you, man? You have to dip these delectables in my special sauce." Maybelline took out a small container of dip made with honey, paprika, Sriracha and spicy mayo. It was a soft coral color. "This is what you use for sweet potato fries right here."

Pastor LeBeaux dipped three of the fries in the sauce. He closed his eyes. "Mmmm. Mm. That's good. Maybelline you can't tell me you had this kind of stuff left in your refrigerator."

"Pastor, I have more food than I know what to do with. I have to admit that the meatballs came from Piggly Wiggly. I keep a package of meatballs in my freezer for hard times, but that marinara sauce, now that is scratch cooking right there. I put just a little on your sandwich, and some on the side, in that little container right there." Maybelline pointed to another small container beside the telephone. "And get some napkins, because if it's good to you, I know it's going to be messy."

Maybelline's navy and white maxi dress rustled and landed softly with every move, as she continued to pull the warm dishes from the bag and arrange them across the desk. The flip flop of her gold sandals added hominess to the office space, and even Francis the Secretary felt her shoulders relax in response to the movement and flow of Maybelline's presence, as Jackie Black's presence had placed Francis the Secretary's otherwise calm demeanor on edge.

Prentiss LeBeaux was euphoric with the bursting tastes in Maybelline's food and the warming scent of the musky perfume she wore. Finally, after unveiling what she called the piece de resistance, her homemade pumpkin bread complete with crumble topping, Maybelline sat down with Pastor LeBeaux (who had already gotten full tasting everything) and had lunch.

After Maybelline had packed up her thermal bags and left, Francis went into Pastor's office.

"Pastor, I didn't have a chance to tell you that Sister Jackie Black brought you breakfast this morning...breakfast from Patsy's Diner. I know that food doesn't agree with your constitution, and you were going to eat with Sister Maybelline..."

"Thank you, Francis. Will you dispose of it for me? Patsy's Diner makes me sick to my stomach. The last time I had something from there, I thought I was having a heart attack!" "Yes, sir. I remember. What should I tell her if she asks about it?" Prentiss sighed.

"Tell her I appreciated her thoughtfulness." he shook his head. Before he could elaborate, his cell phone rang and Francis disappeared without a sound.

Francis took the basket down to the fellowship hall and emptied its contents into a garbage bag, which she then threw into a dumpster behind the church. She hated to throw the woman's "gift" out like that, but that greasy smell would just get worse as the day went on. Francis finished the chore and returned to her desk just in time to take a call from Jackie.

"St. Andrew Church. How may I help you?" Francis said.

"It's Jackie, Francis. Did you give Pastor the breakfast?"

"Yes, I did. He was thankful for your thoughtfulness, Sister Black."

"Oh! Wonderful! I'm glad he enjoyed a hearty breakfast." Jackie sounded overjoyed.

"I'll have your basket at bible study if you wish to retrieve it then. Have a good day, Sister Jackie." Francis said before hanging up.

After talking with Deacon Hughes about her remodeling plans on Monday, Iris was so excited that on Tuesday, she spent the day at the local home improvement superstore looking at paint chips, kitchen and bathroom fixtures, and window treatments. As she eased her ibis white Audi RS 5 down the quiet streets of her neighborhood, she noticed an unfamiliar car parked on the street near her block. Sweet Field residents, as a rule, did not park on the street in front of their homes. Cars littering the sides of the streets were thought to disrupt the tranquil beauty of the homes and lawns, so only visitors parked on the street. As she got closer, she realized the black Mercedes-Benz McLaren was parked in front of her home...and it bore vanity plates that spelled "RICK." She sucked in a breath and eased by the car to turn into her driveway.

She gathered her bag of paint, tile, and carpet samples from the passenger seat, and smoothed down her tan maxi sundress and proceeded to her front porch.

Her heart skipped a beat when she saw him swaying back and forth on the swing. While she was sure her pupils dilated a bit at the sight of his swarthy facial hair and wicked smile, she narrowed her eyes in frustration. *How dare he stop by unannounced?*

Why didn't he help out, get up, stand up as she approached? Better yet, didn't he see her drive by and hear her park? Why didn't he meet her at the car? She sighed. Rick Carson's celebrity status made him accustomed to women throwing themselves at him, and immune to being genteel toward women who did not. He didn't have to work for a woman's affections, but as she looked at him smiling at her, Iris decided that he would work for hers. Hard.

"Hello, Iris. I was beginning to think I'd have to wait all day for you," he said speaking loudly from the porch and pulling his sunglasses over his head.

"Well, Rick. It would have served you right. Since you didn't call first." Iris was nimble with the packages, but the unbalanced weight of the swatch books and decorating magazines slowed down her gait noticeably as she ascended her porch steps. "Ah, yes. It seems that the south has a way of convincing women that they should waste time with formalities. It's 2014, Iris. I pegged you for a modern, strong woman who abhors such conventions, and for the record, I do not have your phone number."

"But you managed to procure my address." Iris shifted the weight of her shopping bag in her arms. Rick Carson, however, did not move from the porch swing. She put the bags down onto the white washed wood of the porch and sat down in her grandmother's rocking chair. The chair faced the swing, where
Rick Carson was in her direct line of vision. This was not the way Iris had arranged things. Rick Carson had changed the porch seating. *The nerve*, Iris thought.

"Well, you got me on that one. But seriously, it's not hard to find people in Sweet Fields. I was in the area anyway, dropping off some late donations to Belle, and I thought I'd stop by to see my new friend," he said smiling. "So, Iris. How are you?" "I am very well, Rick," Iris said taking in details about his attire. He wore flat front khaki pants, a dark blue retro-style polo, and leather driving moccasins. She liked his casual, carefree ensemble, but then, she had a special attachment to men's' fashion; she dressed all of Lloyd's male characters and sometimes picked out clothes for Lloyd too.

"And what about you? How are you?" Iris asked looking away from his intense gaze. There was something that bothered her about his pencil mustache and soul patch under his lip. It made him look like a pirate.

"I'm better, now that I've laid eyes on you again," he said as if he were undressing her.

"Well, I'm glad you're better," she said with a hint of sarcasm. Iris stood up from the rocking chair and moved it back to where it had been originally. "If you'll excuse me, Rick, I have some work to do."

"Is it something I can help with?"

"Not at all. Thank you for offering." Iris had reclaimed her shopping bag and stood between the screen and the heavy oak door.

"Iris, would you have dinner with me tonight? I hear that Argentine Steakhouse is really good." He had moved from the porch swing and was holding the screen door for her. He saw the hesitation in her eyes and continued.

"Just one date. Dinner and that's it. I've got to be back in Atlanta early tomorrow for a special taping of my show. One quick dinner, and I promise I'll call next time," he said with a wink.

Iris stood looking disinterested in the offer for more than a few seconds. "It's four o'clock now, so come back at 7pm." she said with tight lips.

"Seven is pretty late, but…"

"It's either 7 p.m. or not at all," Iris said with a devilish smile. "I told you, Rick, I have things to do and you DID drop in without calling first. Seven is the best I can do for you." She fished her keys from her handbag, her back turned to Rick.

"I will be back at 7 p.m. sharp, Iris. Until then," Rick leaned into Iris' personal space for a kiss when Iris opened the door and entered. The screen door closed with a loud thwack. Rick Carson almost lost his pucker as it closed. Then, the heavy oak door thudded closed in his face.

Rick Carson had never been given an ultimatum from a woman. Never. That was usually his job. He made the demands and the love-struck women acquiesced, but Iris had quickly turned the tables on his run of the mill romantic encounters. He stood there looking at the elaborate oak door through the old-fashioned screen.

The longer he stood, the more insolent he became. Did she even realize who he was? He was Rick "The Ruler" Carson! He had won Emmy Awards for his reality courtroom show! She should be kicking up her heels to go to dinner with him. Iris Murphy clearly wasn't in the know, but he would rectify that tonight.

He left her porch aggravated that he had three hours to kill. He had assumed that she would be elated to see him, make him dinner, insist that he not drive back to Atlanta so late especially after drinking so much wine, and he would take it from there. But, no. Now he, Rick Carson of daytime television, had to bide three hours of time for a woman who'd slammed a heavy wooden door in his face. He really hoped she was worth it.

Rick Carson's black McLaren crept through Sweet Fields drawing attention from drivers and pedestrians. Behind his tinted windows, Rick smiled smugly. He took his time sightseeing the sleepy town, all the while, purposely piquing the town's interest in him. As he slowed at a stop sign, he noticed a cathedral on the corner across from a park. It was a beautiful sight. The church. The park. The quiet town. It was all quite picturesque. The sign in front of the church read *St. Andrew Church. Prentiss LeBeaux, Pastor.* Rick laughed out loud at his luck and turned his car into the parking lot. He noticed a car in the parking spot reserved for the pastor and decided to stop in for a chat with the right Rev. LeBeaux. Francis the Secretary greeted him as warmly as she could and asked him to wait in the lobby until Pastor LeBeaux was off the phone. Rick, again, was aggravated that no one showed any urgency in attending to his needs. He sat in the tan wingback chair and watched Francis the Secretary continue her bookkeeping.

Rick did not like watching Francis the Secretary. She was not an ugly woman, nor did she have some infirmity that made her uncomfortable to look at. That is not what made Rick Carson, people, uncomfortable with Francis the Secretary. Francis had a way. She had a way of standing right in front of a person, and making that person forget she was there. Like an apparition or ghost, she came and went, but not really. She was brown, the kind of brown that blended into every other color of the rainbow, the kind of brown used for carpet in poorly built apartment complexes, the kind of brown that was the color of untreated wood. Bark brown.

Her chameleon-like way worked mostly to her advantage and always to the disadvantage of others. When around Francis-her wardrobe of brown suits and blouses and oxford shoes, her limp, bobbed hair that stopped at her jawbone with its part not-sostraight down the middle, her round tortoise shell glasses that blended right into her face, and her almost indistinguishable smell of cocoa butter (or Chantilly on Sundays)--people became uninhibited and loose-lipped. Folks would say things they shouldn't. They would make faces at people they hated and spit on the ground in response to things they didn't want to hear. You would even behave inappropriately, perhaps pick your nose or examine wax just procured from your ears, around Francis the Secretary. This is exactly what Rick Carson did as he sat waiting for Pastor LeBeaux.

It wasn't until Francis shifted in her seat at the desk, that Carson smelled the faint scent of cocoa butter and heard the scratch of her pencil against the paper upon which she was writing.

He quickly removed a handkerchief from his back pocket, whisked the tiny blob of sticky brown wax from his pinky, and sat forward with his elbows on his knees, waiting for Pastor Prentiss LeBeaux to get off the phone.

"I've buzzed you in," Francis said. As Rick Carson's stride reached the end of Francis' desk, she plopped a small bottle of Dollar Store sanitizer on the desk in front of him. He obeyed the silent command and entered LeBeaux's office. And as is common to most people who meet Francis the Secretary, she was completely forgotten about by Rick Carson once she left eyesight. "Pastor LeBeaux," Rick Carson extended his hand to Prentiss, who stood up to receive him.

"My brother," Pastor LeBeaux sat down behind his curved desk. Towering behind him were two large overfilled bookshelves. Beside each bookshelf were two floor-to-ceiling windows that Francis the Secretary kept remarkably clean. The sheers were open and let in the afternoon sun. "I never thought I'd see you in this place. What brings you my way?"

"I had a few late donations for the center, so I dropped them by Locke's house to give to you. I didn't know the church was so near her home. I could've have brought them to you instead."

"Don't worry about that, Rick. Those donations are in good hands. If God gifted Belle Lynne Locke with one thing, it was with the gift of multiplication. She can multiply some money, like the man in the Bible with the talents. She does NOT go and bury what she gets; she doubles, triples, quadruples it." Both men laughed, even though Rick knew nothing about men with talents and multiplication and the Bible.

They were an interesting pair in the office. Rick, with his glamour boy persona, navy driving shoes, Ray Bans, and expertly lined hair cut, and Prentiss in his black dress slacks, button down shirt, brown lace ups, blue tie and cufflinks. It didn't look as if the two would have much to talk about. It didn't seem fair that the pair was so unevenly matched. Rick looking for clues. Pastor Prentiss LeBeaux, clueless.

"Listen, Rev," Rick leaned back in the wing backed chair, twin to the one posted near Francis's desk. "This Iris Murphy.
She's a member here, right?"

"Yes. Yes she is. She is a fairly new member. Kind of shy, but consistent, dedicated, and loyal. Maggie Murphy was her grandmother. She used to own a Bed and Breakfast down the street."

"That's her. She's fine too. Not all emaciated and chopped up like those mannequins I see around downtown Atlanta," Rick Carson said licking his lips.

"Well if that's what you like."

"Yeah, it's what I like. But I want to get this one right. It seems like her heart is with St. Andrew. You said she was a consistent member, right?"

"She sure is. And she doesn't keep up a lot of mess. She spends a lot of time with Sister Locke. It's good that she's found a friend in her."

"I noticed Iris was one of your biggest donors at the charity event. She donated the technology wing. She looks too young to have pockets that deep."

"Looks can be deceiving Mr. Carson. If you'd done your homework, you'd know that Iris is a double heiress. One by way of Maggie, and the other by Lloyd Sutton."

"The writer? Last month the movie based on his book, 'Don't You Ever Wander,' came in first at the box office. That dude is still making money in the grave!" It took a lot for Carson to shield his excitement. This information made Iris a little more worth the three hour chase he was on. "So SHE was his 'Girl
Friday'. I knew she'd moved here, but had no idea."

"Well, I wouldn't say Girl Friday, but…"

"Say, Doc. So how do I get in with her?"

"I'm not sure I'm the one to answer…"

"What time does service start on Sunday morning?" "That's a long way to drive for church. Shouldn't you perhaps look for a flock closer to…"

"My grandmother use to tell me, Pastor, that the way to a woman's heart is through her church. Now isn't that right?"

"Well, I guess, but the church is not a …"

"I'll see you Sunday morning, Pastor. I'll get the times off the announcement board outside." Rick Carson stood to shake Prentiss' hand. Prentiss was still reeling from the conversation, or lack thereof, he'd had with Rick Carson. He stood anyway and shook his hand.

"It will be good to have a new sheep in the flock, Mr. Carson."

"By the way Pastor, what are the monthly membership dues for St. Andrew? Aw, it doesn't matter. Do you have a secretary? Just have her draft it out of my account." With that, Rick Carson was out of the door before Pastor LeBeaux could respond. Carson's faith in fame and fortune had been renewed and that renewal could come to pass with his new pet project, Iris Murphy, *his* new Girl Friday--and connection to Hollywood.

By the time he finished his automatic draft paperwork for his monthly "dues" to the church, he had just enough time to freshen up before returning to the Murphy Inn. He drove back the way he came and stopped in front of the majestic Victorian house and waited a few minutes before exiting the car. During those few minutes, he sprayed a breath spray, ran a brush over his waves, and grabbed a sport coat from his backseat. He took his time getting to the front door, giving the neighbors ample time to recognize him. He didn't know that since it was dusk dark, the neighbors wouldn't be able to see him anyway with their failing eyesight. He rang the doorbell, and after a short while, Iris answered the door wearing a crisp white collared blouse with quarter-length sleeves paired with a khaki-colored high-waist pencil skirt. Thin gold hoops hung from her ears, and a delicate gold necklace laid at her throat. The cognac-colored satchel that rested in the crook of her arm matched her wide belt and sandal heels.

"I'm ready." Iris said stepping out of the door and closing it quickly behind her.

"I like your hair. You look amazing," Rick said in a lowered voice as she started down the porch steps. "Thank you." Iris said running a hand lightly over her cloud of curls that hung loose about her neck. The walk to the car seemed to take forever because Iris slowed her stride so Rick could get to the car and open the door, but Rick seemed determined to walk behind her to gawk at her backside. When Rick finally opened the car door for Iris, he leaned in and took a conspicuous whiff of her perfume.

"You smell good enough to eat," he said before closing her door. While he walked around the front of the car, his eyes never left Iris. This made her uncomfortable. She wanted to get out of his low-slung car, curl up in her granny's bed, eat leftover Chinese and flip through home improvement lookbooks.

"You know, there was a time that I couldn't dream of being this successful," Carson stroked at the tuft of hair tucked beneath his bottom lip, "but my mom always told me I was gonna be something special. And by the time I started junior high, I believed her."

Iris looked out of the window at the warmly lit houses along the streets. "A mother knows," she said, her voice trailing off in disinterest.

"My mother told me I was the best looking baby she'd ever seen. She said that she'd feel sorry for the other mothers in her civic club, because their babies weren't as handsome as I was." Rick chuckled. "I was her late-in-life baby. After years of trying, she finally got her first and only boy. Me. Rick 'The Ruler'
Carson."

Iris scoffed, "The Ruler? Ruler of what?"

Rick continued on as if he hadn't heard her. "My sisters were so jealous of me. I have five of them, you know. They said I could get Mama to do anything. They were right. My sisters and my mom? They taught me everything I know about women." Rick glanced over at Iris. "That's the start of how I became the man I am today."

"And what kind of man is that, Rick?" Iris asked sarcastically.

"A man on the move, Iris." Rick placed his arm on the back of Iris's seat. "I never stop moving. You see, this judge show, that's not all I have in mind for my life. I mean it's good and everything, but I don't want to be restricted by that judge's bench. Eventually I'd like to get into movies. Of course, I know I'd probably have to start with one of the major series, just to get my name out there in the Hollywood circles. But I've always felt this face," Rick glanced into the rearview mirror, "was made for the big screen. And I'm going to get there, too." Rick continued yammering on about himself until they pulled up at the restaurant.

Iris was relieved when they finally arrived. She opened the car door and got out herself just so Rick wouldn't have an opportunity to get close to her again. They entered the Argentine Steakhouse and were greeted by an attractive dark-haired man whose nametag read "Jorge." Jorge flashed Iris an ear-to-ear smile.

"A table for two will be just a moment. Please. Have a seat." He gestured to an oversize brown leather sofa nestled in a corner with a glowing lamp nearby. Before they could sit, Rick threw an arm around Iris' shoulder.

"Sweetheart, I'll be right back." He started down a nearby hallway towards the restrooms. *Sweetheart? He called her sweetheart?* Iris had begun to run down Rick's list of offenses when the dark-haired greeter approached.

"Your table is ready," Jorge said with a wide grin. "I am so sorry for the wait. I wanted to prepare the most romantic table for you," he said with a wink. "Follow me."

Iris liked Jorge's warm smile, but she did not like the idea of romantic table with Rick. As she followed Jorge to the "romantic table," she wondered if she should have waited for Rick. She shrugged and enjoyed the few minutes she had away from him. Jorge pulled out her chair and she flashed him a genuine smile. The table provided a calming view of a landscaped lawn complete with a large fountain. She looked around to see if Rick was looking for her, but found him at a table signing autographs. She looked at the size of his smile and listened to the joy in his laugh and realized the man really enjoyed being a celebrity. Rick "The Ruler" Carson wasn't a TV persona; it was who Rick really was. He loved the attention. He needed it. As she decided that Rick had forgotten that he was on a date, she heard a familiar voice above her.

"Now, Sister Murphy, it doesn't make sense for both of us to eat alone," William Hughes said. Iris was surprised to see him and craned her neck up to look at him while she told him so.

"Deacon Hughes! It's so good to see you!" Iris couldn't explain just how much she meant those words. She finally decided to go on a date, and her date was spending the evening talking about himself and signing autographs. "I'm not alone exactly, but why don't you have a seat for the time being?"

William Hughes looked surprised to be invited to sit with Iris. He pulled out the chair in front of Iris and settled in it.

" I don't want to interrupt anything."

"You're not interrupting. I've never eaten here before. What would you suggest, Deacon?"

"Try the empanadas for an appetizer. If you like garlic, try the steak with chimichurri sauce. Those are my favorites. And Sister Murphy, please call me Will," he said leaning over the small candle at the center of the table.

"Garlic, huh? Good thing I have breath mints," she joked and they both laughed. William enjoyed Iris' laugh. She threw her head back just a hair like she did at the gala when that Rick Carson said something funny to her.

"Now, I don't care for the dulce le leche much. Too much milk for me. I like a good cake or pie."

"Don't we all like cakes and pies?" Rick said walking to Iris' side of the table and resting his hand on her shoulder, pulling her into his thigh slightly.

"Rick, this is Deacon William Hughes. William, this is Rick Carson." William noticed how she pronounced his first name and liked it. He looked up at Rick and nodded a greeting.

"Nice to meet you, Carson." He knew he should have stood and let the man have the seat, but he couldn't. What man in his right mind left a woman as beautiful as Iris Murphy sitting alone in a restaurant? Carson didn't deserve to be on date with Iris.
And William had a mind to say so.

"Well, Deacon, it's a pleasure to meet you. Now, if you don't mind, I'd like to finish my date with this lovely lady." Rick said dropping his voice a bit like he did on his show when he really meant business.

"Ah, I see. I was wondering who would leave a beautiful woman like Iris sitting in an ambient restaurant all by her lonesome. A wiser man wouldn't leave her side," William said straightening the utensils he had moved.

"Yes, but a bigger man would step aside and not interrupt a man's date," Rick ground out through a fake smile. Iris, uncomfortable by the exchange, reached out to touch William's hand, but William paid no mind.

"A bigger man, you say?" with that question, William Hughes slowly stood to his full height, which was much taller than the medium-sized Rick. Iris gasped. She had never noticed William the way she was noticing him now. As he rose slowly from the coveted chair, she lingered on the firmness of his chest in the starched white shirt opened at the neck, the flatness of his belly encircled by a black leather belt, and the muscular thighs under the black gabardine slacks. By the time Iris had taken in the physical glory of William Hughes and looked at his face, his mouth was in a tight line and his eyes were narrowed slits.

She looked at Rick, who was standing too close to her. He had taken his hand off her shoulder and the other out of his pocket and curled them at his sides. His lips were tucked, making the soul patch that Iris disliked visible. Iris stood and moved between the two gentlemen. She put a hand on each man's arm. "William, I am so glad you came over to say hello. I really appreciate the suggestions for dinner," Iris said rubbing his forearm lightly. He turned and looked down at her and smiled. He held her gaze for what seemed to be an eternity. Finally, he covered her hand with his large one.

"It was good to see you, Sister Murphy. Let me know if you like my suggestions," he said releasing her hand. "Carson," he said curtly with a nod. Iris unashamedly watched William leave the dining room.

"Sweetheart, let's eat. I'm starved," Rick said seating himself and waiting for Iris to sit down. "I'll order for us both," he said taking her menu.

Iris had a good mind to walk right out and call a cab, but she didn't. She eased back into her chair and tried to regain her composure.

"Rick," she said sweetly. "Do not call me sweetheart. My name is Iris. You may call me Iris."

"Oh, I just--"

"And you will not order for me. I will order for myself." Iris slid the menu from between Rick Carson's fingers. There would be no Rick ruling on this date.

"Well, Iris, I didn't mean anything by it. Some ladies like for a man to take charge now and again."

"If you do it **now**, there won't be an **again**." Iris said beckoning ever so slightly for the server. When the server arrived, Iris ordered first.

"I'll have the empanadas and steak--well done--with chimichurri sauce, please." she said speaking directly to the server.

"I'll have the short ribs," Rick said never looking at the server. The server took Rick's drink order and brought back warm rolls and gold-wrapped pats of butter. Just as Iris decided to give a pleasant conversation a try, two ladies approached the table and asked Rick for autographs. They gushed, and he blushed. He laughed and flirted with them.

"I knew it was you! I'd know that mustache anywhere. You're so sexy in person!" one lady squealed. Rick laughed out loud and rubbed his mustache.

"Sweetheart, you just made my day. Both of you," he said with a wink.

"YOU have made our day too, Mr. Carson. Can we take a picture with you?"

"Of course, sweetheart. Of course." Rick said. He never even looked in Iris' direction and neither did the women. Iris decided that the date was officially over, but she let him finish. Just as the trio finished taking pictures, more diners recognized Rick and meandered over for some celebrity attention too. Iris slipped her phone out of her purse and noticed she had a missed call and a text.

The missed call was from Locke; she had not left a message. The text message was also from Locke. It read:

Cut date short. Come home ASAP. --B.L.L.

Iris panicked. She texted back:

Is everything okay?

She looked at Rick who was surrounded by all the women in their dining room. He had forgotten all about her. Another message had come through:

Yes. End the date. Go straight home. --B.L.L.

Iris wasn't sure what Locke was up to, but she was glad for an excuse to cut the date short. She caught the eye of Jorge who was walking through the dining room and explained that she would like her meal packaged to go. Jorge winked again and set about his new task. When the impromptu photo shoot was done and Rick returned to the table, he found Iris sitting in her chair with her purse in her lap and her meal packaged neatly in a carryout bag.

"Rick, I'm so sorry. I just got a disturbing text. I really must get home. You don't mind, do you?"

"Is there something wrong?" He asked looking a bit frustrated.

"I believe so, though the message was a bit vague. I really need to get home and see what's going on. If you'd rather stay, I can call a cab."

"No. We can go. Let me settle the check."

"I've already taken care of it. Let's go, please."

The two left the restaurant quickly with Iris leading the way. Rick was still waving goodbye to his fans in the dining room.

The ride home was short and silent. He did not take the scenic route as he had done on the way to the restaurant. Nor did he talk about himself or anything that had happened. Iris rode in silence looking out of the passenger side window. When they arrived at her home, Iris hopped out with her handbag and her carryout package and very nearly ran up the porch steps. Rick followed her with his confident saunter. It took a moment for Locke's presence on her porch swing to register. Before Iris could acknowledge Locke, Carson stepped onto the porch and walked right into a loud crack across his cheek.

"What tha?" the shocked and startled Rick cried out.

"You are a selfish, self-centered, superficial, skirt hound who needs his back cut with a whip! How dare you nosey around in business that is not yours? How dare you make designs on someone else's money? How dare you cause a scene in public with a man who has more honor and respect in his pinky toe than you in the whole of your existence? I am disappointed in you, Carson. You tried to join a church the way one joins a country club so you can make some Hollywood connections. Your mother Roselynn, God rest her soul, would spin in her grave to know what you've become. You get off this porch!" Locke raised her voice and pointed to the street.

"Ms. Belle, this is not your porch," he chuckled. "And Iris is not your daughter. She's a grown woman, and if you wanted someone to boss around, you should have had some children of your---"

CRACK! The hand connected with Rick's face. Again. Louder. Harder. Painfully--for both the giver and the receiver. "Carson, I helped take care of you when your mama was on her deathbed. I cared for you while your sisters were too busy living their lives to come and see about you or their dying mama. Don't mess with me. I will rain down a wrath from which you nor your so-called career will never recover. I know things. Things that will ruin you. You go play your games elsewhere, but not here. Not here in Sweet Fields. Go on." Locke was standing on the edge of the porch, and Rick "The Ruler" Carson laughed, dramatically bade them both a good evening, and walked confidently to his car. He even tooted his horn as he drove away. He put on a brave face, but when he got behind the tinted windows of his beloved

Mercedes, he was hurt and angry. *Ms. Belle didn't have to say all of that in front of Iris. My sisters love me. And Mama's death was a painful ordeal. She didn't have to bring that up. Not in front of Iris.* He drove like a bat out of Hades. When he got out of the Sweet Fields city limits, he felt better and decided that Belle Lynne Locke was just like the rest of the women he knew. Emotional and over reactive. He'd give her a few days and then, he'd send some flowers. Flowers always worked. He'd call and everything would be alright.

Iris stood near the door, never having left her spot. Locke was upset. She had raised her voice and had slapped Rick--not once, but twice. Iris wanted to hug her, but had second thoughts. Instead, she took out one of the small vials of hand sanitizer that Locke had given her, and handed it to her.

"Locke, come on in. I have some wine."

"I brought my own," she snapped grabbing a tote bag from the porch swing.

The two ladies entered the Murphy Inn, as some people still called it. Locke had not been inside Maggie's home since Maggie died. When she visited with Iris, she had either sat on the porch or invited Iris to her home. Locke looked up the staircase that greeted her at the front door with a sad smile. She glanced to the left and saw the French doors closed to the formal living room. Iris had pointed to the room on the right of the staircase.

"Let's sit in here," she said sitting her leftovers on the mahogany coffee table. I'll get the glasses." Locke looked all around the room with a wistful smile on her lips. She reached inside the deep pocket of her light blue linen dress and retrieved a handkerchief and dabbed at the corner of her eyes. She ran her fingers along the fireplace mantle, lingered at the bay window, and eventually sat on the edge of Maggie's chair. It was a large French Victorian armchair made of rosewood.

"I don't mind if you sit in her chair. Make yourself comfortable," Iris said as she placed a crystal wine glass in front of Locke. As Locke poured the wine, Iris curled her socked feet under her on the overstuffed sofa. "You know, I've never invited anyone here? Well, except for William to look at the kitchen and bathrooms."

"I know. This is my first time since she passed. I couldn't bring myself to come in here. Too many memories."

"You and Granny were close?"

"Close doesn't even begin to describe it. Maggie has a lot of my secrets in that grave with her, and I've got plenty of hers to take with me. I'll tell you about some of our adventures one day, but not today. Today, we have to talk about that scoundrel Rick Carson and this date." Iris didn't like the way Locke spat out the word **date**. "How did you end up going somewhere with him?"

Iris sipped the wine Locke had given her. "Well, I had been out at the Home Store and when I came back, he was sitting on my porch. We talked briefly before he asked me to go to dinner with him. I agreed but made him wait until 7p.m."

"Made him wait? Whatever for?"

"I didn't like that he just showed up unannounced and moved my rocking chair! I figured he thought I would drop everything for him, so I did not. I told him he had to come back at 7pm--take it or leave it." Iris, after hearing herself say this out loud thought she had been petty, but Locke threw her head back on the carved wood of the chair and laughed heartily.

"You are more like your granny than you even know!" Locke said in between ripples of laughter. "Go on, Iris. Tell me the rest."

"Well," she said opening the bag of leftovers. "He left and came back. I listened to him talk about how beautiful he was as a baby all the way to the restaurant." She rolled her eyes. "When we got there, he went to the restroom, I sat at the table, and then Deacon Hughes sat down at my table."

"Hughes is starting to make a habit of that--sitting in people's chairs. Go on."

"No. He came over to say hello, and I invited him to sit down because Rick was at the front of the restaurant signing autographs and taking pictures." Iris bit into an empanada. "We chatted about the restaurant and what I should order. Then Rick walked up. That's when it all began."

"I need to know exactly who said what," Locke said pulling out a round tin of teacakes from her tote. "What is that you're eating?"

"An empanada. Have one. It has veggies in it," Iris said holding out the container of the meat pastries.

"Meat?" Locke asked with a wrinkle in her nose.

"Yes," Iris replied.

"No. Thank you. Continue with the story." Locke leaned back in Maggie's chair and propped her feet on the embroidered footstool nearby.

Iris recounted the entire conversation almost verbatim while nibbling on her empanada and sipping her wine. Locke sipped on her wine and nibbled at her teacakes.

"So, William said 'bigger man?' and stood up slowly like he was gonna handle some business?" Locke giggled.

"Yes. He was so angry, that he didn't even notice when I touched his hand. Eventually, I got in between them and diffused the situation."

"What was Rick doing?"

"Nothing, really. His hands were quivering a bit, and his lips were folded in. He just stood there and tried not to look up at William. I was so embarrassed. I just wanted to go home after that. Then some women came to our table asking for pictures and autographs, and Rick acted like I wasn't even sitting there. That's when I saw your text, cancelled his order, paid for my food, and told him I needed to leave."

Locke was giggling again. "You cancelled his order?"

"Yes. It was petty, wasn't it? To cancel his order. Oh well. He had been such a pain in the neck, so I decided he didn't need to eat." Iris shrugged and laughed when she saw that Locke was surprised and amused.

"I knew you had a mean streak in you. It's a little thinner than Maggs' but it's there just the same." She held the large round pink tin to Iris offering her the teacakes. She didn't say a word when Iris took two of them.

"So what was the text about? Why did you tell me to come home?"

"You're gonna want some more wine for this," Locke said pouring the last of the wine in Iris' glass. "First, Pastor LeBeaux came 'round to pick up his tin of teacakes I made for him. I make him some every week. He told me that Rick Carson had been by to see him at the church and that he had asked mainly about you. I asked Prentiss, 'what did you tell him?' and Prentiss told him what little he knows. You moved here from the west coast, had worked with that famous writer, inherited Maggie's estate, and was single. That's it in a nutshell."

"Okay…"

"Rick showed interest, but not in you, Iris. I know him. He wants to get into movies and is hoping that you can help him make some connections in Hollywood. He even joined the church! Prentiss said Rick laughed about reaching you through the church." Locke paused to watch Iris' reaction to this. Iris threw the rest of the wine into her mouth and reached for the second bottle that Locke had produced.

"A little while later, I got a call from Big Hughes."

"Who is Big Hughes?" Iris asked reaching for a second empanada.

"William's daddy. He called me because William had stopped by to see him. And apparently, Junior was beyond angry. Big Hughes said he hadn't seen his son that angry since William busted a boy's jaw for talking about his mama. I remember that. William tore that boy's jaw almost clean from his face. The boy had said something nasty about Edith's long legs, you know she was as tall as he is, and William hit the boy's jaw while his mouth was open and dislocated the mandible."

"How old was he when he did that?"

"High school, I think. Anyway, Big Hughes wanted to know who was behind his son being so upset. He said it took him a while--and a couple of brandies to calm him down. So I put two and two together. Rick had you out trying to get next to you and he was marking his territory with William. I knew nothing good could come of this **date**."

"Well, something good *did* come from the date. I got to see a side of William that I rather like." Iris said shifting on the couch and grabbing another teacake.

"I see." Locke said leaning back and shifting her weight onto her side. "Well, Iris. I like William. I give him a hard time here and there, but he's a good man and a gorgeous sight if you like 'em long and lean." Locke's lips had curled into a mischievous grin.

"Speaking of gorgeous sights...I saw you and the reverend's father chatting after church. What did he say to have you grinning like a school girl?"

"Well, he didn't say much of anything. I didn't let him."

"What do you mean you didn't let him? He's a fine looking old man. You should've let the man talk to you."

"Well he came running at me so fast, asking me if he could walk with me. He called my name like he knew me. That threw me off."

"Well, I understand that, but you should be flattered. Flattered that he did his homework so fast and came after you. There's no harm in that. Is it?

"I guess not." Belle tapped the crumbs away from her teacake onto her napkin. "But he did something that shook me up a bit."

"Oh yeah," Iris leaned in and smiled at Locke. "What'd he do?" Iris knew Locke was affected by the wine because her words slurred together.

"He laughed," Belle said flatly. She took a sip of the wine. She put the glass down and then picked it up and took another sip.

"Laughed?"

"Yes, Iris. He laughed. And I promise, my heart fell down to my Shandals when I heard that man laugh. Sounded so much like my Clive. Then I looked up at him, and he wasn't my Clive." Locke leaned back in the chair and closed her eyes. "I felt bad that his laugh made me feel so good."

"I can understand that. But it's okay, Belle. You're a gorgeous woman, and that Charles Edward, Sr., he's ALL man.
Clive would want that for you."

"I know he would, but I felt like I was cheating on him. I'm not sure if I even should have felt all that, you know down in my *belly*. You know that's the way Pastor LeBeaux says, *belly*. Like he's straining and about to choke on the word--*belly*." Both ladies laughed hard. "I felt that man's laugh in my...*belly*." They laughed again.

"So what are you going to do about it?"

"I'm going to take a walk, Iris. That's what I'm going to do."

By the end of the night, Locke and Iris had eaten all of the teacakes and polished off two bottles of wine. Locke offered to clean up, but Iris declined. Iris offered to drive Locke home, but Locke declined.

"I'll walk you home, then." Iris said looking for her shoes.

"No. Who's gonna walk you back home? Besides, I have my two friends with me."

"Who?" Iris asked. Locke slid her small hand inside an interior pocket of the tote she was carrying and brought out a small gun.

"Gun and Shot have never let me down, and I suspect they won't start tonight." She opened the wide oak door and stepped into the night air and inhaled deeply. "You go on and call William. Come 'round tomorrow and tell me what he had to say for himself."

"Okay. Call me when you get home." Iris said from the porch.

"Goodnight, little girl." Locke said moving quickly down the sidewalk. Iris stood on the porch and watched Locke's small figure slip into the shadows.

Iris was going to call William Hughes. She was going to apologize for Rick's behavior and offer to make it up to him. She hadn't been nervous to talk to him before, so why was she nervous now? She thought of what she would say in the shower and throughout her entire nighttime ablutions. Once she was settled in the cozy occasional chair next to her bed, she dialed William's cell phone number. She looked at the clock and realized how late it was, but it was too late to hang up.

"Hello?" William's deep voice didn't sound laced with sleep. Perhaps he hadn't gone to bed yet.

"William, it's Iris. I hope I didn't wake you."

"Oh! Sister Murphy! No. You didn't wake me. I was watching the news. How are you?" He didn't sound angry, and Iris was relieved.

"I'm okay. I just wanted to apologize for tonight. For Rick's behavior. I'm really sorry."

"No. I owe you an apology. I lost my temper a bit. I'm sorry if I embarrassed you." His voice was lowered. Sexy.

"No. I wasn't embarrassed because of you. Rick had been terrible most of the evening."

"Well, what were you doing with him anyway? He apparently doesn't know how to treat a lady," he sounded a little aggravated.

"Well, it's a long story, but I wanted to thank you for coming over and saying hello. It made things a lot better. I don't want to hold you up."

"No. No. I'm just watching the news--the same news I watched at 5. What did you order for dinner?"

"I ordered the empanadas and the steak you suggested. I ate the empanadas when I got home. I haven't touched the steak yet. I think I'll have it and some eggs for breakfast."

"You didn't eat at the restaurant?"

"No. While Rick was off taking pictures and signing autographs, I had it packaged to go. I didn't eat until I got home."

"Well, I'll be! That's a poor way to experience the Argentine Steakhouse! You'll have to go again--with someone a little more pleasant, perhaps." His voice made the statement sound like a question.

"So you go there often?" Iris knew he was skirting around asking her out, but she didn't want to address the hint.

"Yep. I have my dinner there every Tuesday. I try something new on the menu each week. It's my one splurge."

"You don't mind eating alone?"

"I did at first, but it's better than eating at home alone. Who wants to sit at a dining table all by themselves?"

"Wait. When you eat at home, you eat at your dining table?" Iris almost laughed out loud.

"Yes. Where do you eat? On the couch?" He laughed. It was a hearty, masculine laugh. She liked it. "No. Don't tell me, you eat in front of the TV."

"Well…"

"No, Sister Murphy…"

"Call me Iris. If I'm calling you William, you can call me Iris." His laughter stopped cold.

"Iris." There it was. He did that thing with his voice. "If you are eating on the sofa in front of the TV or God forbid, in bed while watching TV, or heaven help us if you're standing over the sink…" He starting laughing again.

"Well, when the weather is nice, I eat on the balcony off my bedroom or on the porch. I usually have dinner in the sitting room while watching TV. This is a big house. I pretty much just live in the master bedroom."

"I understand. My house is too big for one person, too. My parents raised me eating at a dining table, so it's a habit. I read the paper while I eat. Then, I take my coffee and a slice of cake and watch the news or a game." Iris could tell he was smiling. "Now, if you ever want to join me for dinner, you're more than welcome to do so."

"William Hughes, are you asking me out?" she asked trying to be playful.

"I should probably let you get over the date you've had tonight before mentioning going on another one, but I am. I am asking you to join me for dinner...whenever you're ready."

"Thank you. I accept. Can I join you at Argentine's on your next visit?"

"Of course. I'm sure Jorge will be happy to see you again," he chuckled. When Iris didn't say anything, William said, "I'm just kidding." Jorge had said to William "Senor, if a man has to fight over a woman, she should look like her" and jerked his head in Iris' direction.

"And I'll be happy to dine with *you*." Iris said smiling at her ability to think on her feet after so much wine. "I should let you get to bed. Good night, Will."

"Good night, Iris." She liked how he said her name. She threw herself on the bed and laughed out loud. William Hughes was going to be something else.

CHAPTER 11: WEDNESDAY

At 6:15 a.m., Belle Lynne Locke sat in one of her front porch rocking chairs enjoying the cool dewy breeze of the morning. She wore a sage colored running sweater, which hid a crisp white tank under its zipper. Her yoga pants were gray and just snug enough to reveal the toned results of her early morning walks. On a small stone table sat a cup of chamomile tea, the chamomile was fresh, right out of her back yard. It fragranced the space around her and soothed her as she prepared her mind for meditation.

Belle Lynne Locke was feeling daring this morning. Snuggled near her outer right thigh was a pair of knit gray gloves, the kind with the fingers cut out. She picked them up, examined them closely and said out loud, "I've gotten too old to wear foolishness like this." Even so, she slipped one onto her hands, closed her eyes for a brief moment and waited. She heard the syncopated rhythm of running, and looked up to find Charles "call me Eddie" Edwards, Sr. running up the path to her porch. "I told you we'd have a chance meeting with each other again, Mrs. Locke." He jogged in place for a few minutes and grinned waiting for a response.

"I'm not sure it's called a chance meeting when you just show up at my porch steps like this." She slipped on the other fingerless gray glove. "The young folks call it stalking, Mr. Charles Edward, Sr."

"Please, it's Eddie. We don't have much time left in our lives; let's not waste it calling each other by our full names."

"Well since you put it that way, I'll let you call me, Belle."

"I've been waiting to hear you say that since I met you on Sunday. You look like you're ready for a run. Come on down, and let's blaze a trail."

"More like a promenade. I don't run. Not much anymore. But I can walk pretty fast. If you don't mind slowing down, I'd be happy to join you."

"It'd be my pleasure." Eddie held out his hand in a gentlemanly gesture to assist Locke down her stairs, stairs she'd been coming down alone for many months. Locke hesitated and felt a tinge of embarrassment. The ridiculous gloves. She reached for Eddie's hand and allowed him to escort her down the stairs. He lifted her hand, gently. "I wanted to say to you on Sunday, that it's been a long time since I've seen gloves on a woman. Those are the types of nuances that make a woman a lady to me. Now I see you have on a racy pair today. What is it? You have gloves for every occasion?"

"Not EVERY occasion. I have gloves for every obsession. That answer would be more appropriate."

Something in Belle's voice let Eddie know that he shouldn't press the issue, he knew she'd come back around to it when she was comfortable with him, when she was ready. He was serious about liking the gloves. They were sexy. He'd always thought that as time went by, the less clothes women wore, the less sexy they became. To him, Locke's small stature, her tiny hands, the neatness of her locs, the way the light airy clothes she wore waved when she moved were the sexy things he observed about her at St. Andrew when she walked toward the front to lay an offering in the collection basket. His first order of business, once the benediction was given, was to find out from his son who she was.

"I am retired military. I know all about obsessions. I have a few of my own, but I never share them unless I've walked more than one mile with someone."

"That's a good policy. Anyway, I like to keep people guessing about why I do what I do. My gloves. My locs. All the linen that never stays pressed. It adds up to something, but sometimes I don't even know what all."

"I don't know either, but I knew I liked it when I saw it."

"Well aren't you the fast talker? And it hasn't been a mile, yet. I have to leave some of my virtue for the walk back to my porch. Slow down a little. So how long will you be in our Sweet Fields?"

"Well, Belle, I had an agenda before I left to get on back to North Carolina after church Sunday. But it's a funny thing, as soon as you make a plan, you find out how quickly your plans are subject to change. My plans aren't always God's plans, I see."

"You haven't answered my question yet."

"I'm trying to flirt with you, Belle. I guess I'll have to tell you straight out. It all depends on how this little walk goes. I'll make my decision after that."

"That's a strange way to plan your time, Eddie, around a walk and a woman you don't know who wears gloves with the finger holes cut out. I wouldn't advise you to live your life like that. You don't know a thing about me. Who's to say I don't have a man half my age waiting at home for me? He could be on my porch right now, ready to take you out when you walk me home."

"He may try, but he wouldn't succeed. Besides, I've done my homework. I know what kind of woman I'm dealing with.
Anything else I need to know, I'll ask you myself."

"So ask."

"What do you miss most about your husband?"

"I miss his laugh." Belle was surprised at how quickly she answered the question, how easily the words came out, and how at ease she felt with Eddie. "One thing Clive had was a great laugh. He always laughed. His laughter was good for my soul."

"What else?"

"Well, he spoiled me, but not in the way that he thought I was fragile, like I couldn't do anything for myself. Clive loved me and he gave me everything he could carry, because he loved me so much. You know that kind of love makes you think everyone loved like that. I was always disappointed when I found out differently. Always. But it was good to know that that kind of love, Clive's kind of love, was here for me. I didn't see that with my own family, what with my daddy going off the rails, and my mama running herself crazy to keep him on the rails, there wasn't much time for me to see anything but a life of tip toeing around so I wouldn't upset anyone. I grew afraid of whether or not any little thing I did would send my daddy off." Belle laughed. "And I do mean off. He was as crazy as a road lizard."

"I don't believe you, especially with you always looking so calm, reserved, and in control." He slowed his pace, touched Locke's elbow, and gently turned her toward him. "How can a crazy road lizard make something as regal and classy as you?" Locke held up her half-gloved hands, she had to tip-toe just a little bit to place them right in Eddie's face. "You see these, don't you? They're not too classy. You asked me about the gloves. Well they come from living with a man like my daddy." She turned again and began to walk. Eddie fell in. "My father wasn't always the way he became in the end. But by the time I was 8 or 9 years old, he'd begun to stay in his room and only come out for meals. He had Mother go out and buy him some black paint so it'd always be dark in the room where he spent most of his time. When he did come out, he came out guns a-blazing. Nothing was ever clean enough, the utensils in the drawer were never lined up just so. All his shirt collars weren't turned down the same way in the closet. His food was touching just a teeny tiny bit.

When Mother discovered she couldn't keep up with his little quirks, she solicited me in helping her keep him quiet. I went to school smelling like Clorox and Lysol everyday. My hands were blistered and always dry. That's what started the gloves. When I got old enough to work and buy my own personals, I'd slather Vaseline all over my hands and stick them in gloves to keep them from drying, cracking, and bleeding. By the time I got married, I'd gotten so use to wearing them, and my mind had been warped into believing that there were germs everywhere. I couldn't go many places without them." Locke threw her head back and laughed loud and long. "Eddie, I was so glad when they came out with hand sanitizer, I went to a chemist I knew and had him make a special moisturizing formula just for me. I still can't shake the gloves, though. I expect I'll be wearing them off and on until I go to glory."

"That makes perfect sense to me. And no, I don't think you're crazy. I got more crazy than you, I promise."

Locke continued, as if she couldn't stop unless she gotten it all out. She hadn't told the story in years, mostly because no one, but Clive of course, believed or understood her. And just a tiny bit of her, even at 61 years old, was embarrassed. "My father eventually drove Mother crazy. If she could've lifted herself and smoothed every wrinkle out of that dress she was wearing on her cooling board, Mother would have. Even with my father dead-and he died clean-- she was always peeking around corners to tidy up things that weren't dirty. You know how when old people pass on, they leave a house full of clutter and papers and stacks and smelly clothes and I don't know what all?"

"Yeah, that's how it was with my dad. We couldn't even have the repast at the house, because it was packed to the ceiling with old newspapers."

"Well, it was the complete opposite for me. It wasn't like it was on TV, where you go through their old things and personals and get all nostalgic. Mother had cleaned the closet out so well, I could take a nap on the floor in there. No old clothes and papers to brood over for memories. No two-hour crying marathons over old letters and recipes. I just walked right out of the door and closed it behind me, me and my gloves."

"Locke, your gloves are fine with me. And with that treatment of Vaseline on your hands, I'm sure that they are softer than a baby's rump. Let me see 'em."

"No!" She giggled nervously, "I can't let you do that!"

"Let me just see 'em Belle. You're guarding them like they are made of platinum."

"Charles Edward, Sr., I'm trying to help you out! Once you see these hands, you're going to have a hard time staying away. I don't think you're ready for that. Anyway, this is where I turn around, and this is where I ask you about the sordid details of your life."

"I don't mind sharing, but I plan on holding that beautiful hand before we get to your front porch, and you're going to let me."

"When Hades becomes heaven I will. Now, your turn.
Tell me a story."

"Okay, well. There once was a young man who had a promising future. High school basketball. Dating best looking Senior Girl at Newton High School, and the promise of a full scholarship to college. Then, the best looking Senior Girl missed her monthly meeting. Then she missed another one. And I became a father first and a husband four weeks later. My oldest daughter, Valerie, came six and a half months after the wedding."

"Hush your mouth!"

"I wish I could. Out the window went the scholarship. I went to the Army and took my wife on with me. Just like basketball, I took my Army career seriously, serious enough to leave my wife at home for long stretches of time. Coming home just in time to make another baby. Lexine was next. Then finally came my boy, Charles Edward, Jr." Eddie let a proud smile ease across his face. "I wasn't a good husband, Locke."

"Yes. You were; you took care of your family and your children."

"I guess you're right. But I didn't take care of my wife's heart. She stuck it out a long time. Sixteen years. I came back from a two year tour of duty, and she had packed up and left. She left and the papers came. I didn't even hesitate, because I knew she wasn't happy. I think that is when my ex-wife fell in love with me. It was the weirdest thing. But the weight that lifted off of me after I signed those papers wouldn't let me go after her. I've been single since. And on last Sunday morning and today, I discovered what you're supposed to feel like when you're really into someone. Here I am, pushing sixty and just now discovering how people are supposed to enjoy one another."

"You mean I'm older than you?" Locke scoffed. She quickened her pace in a failed attempt to walk ahead of Eddie. It would only take one good step for Eddie to catch up, but he played along. "Little boy, get on away from me. The cops are going to arrest me for robbing the cradle!" Locke had picked up her walk to a slow trot. Eddie caught up with her with no effort at all.

They walked in silence for a few minutes. This time, Locke placed her hand on Eddie's forearm to slow him down to a stop. "You know there is absolutely nothing wrong with my hands. They're no different from any other woman. I'm just a little messed up in the head with these gloves."

Eddie looked down and Belle. His brown eyes looked serious, and his forehead was furrowed just a little. He tilted his head to the side and said, "I told you that you don't have to worry about that. I heard your story, and I understand what those gloves mean to you. I won't take that away from you. That's not for me to do. I'm just glad you opened up to me like you did." "Yeah. That made me feel better, talking to someone like you. There's something about you, your eyes that makes me want to tell you all my business. I don't usually do that."

"I'm glad you did."

"And I'm going to show you my hands," she said pulling off her glove, "let's go on and get this over with, so you won't be making a fuss over it like you've been doing." Locke knew she had beautiful hands. She spoiled herself with manicures and paraffin peels. She got sugar and salt scrubs, mud treatments, and seaweed soaks. She used raw shea butter mixed with coconut oil and a dollop of sweet almond oil to make them glisten. She had pretty hands and during the walk she decided to let Eddie see them.

Eddie looked at Locke's hands a long time, turning them over in his own hands. He brushed his own fingers over each one of hers. He was only joking when he said they should be soft as a baby's bottom, but then he felt them. "They are soft as a baby's bottom. How is it that you're in your 60's and you got the hands of a 21 year old woman who's never worked a day in her life?" Belle Lynne Locke smiled. "Belle, you better put those gloves back on. You got the kind of hands that'll make a grown man cry. That's why you keep 'em covered, because if you didn't, these men folk here in Sweet Fields would be lined up at your door all the way around the block." They both laughed and walked on to Belle's house.

"I told you," she said as they walked up the steps to her porch. Eddie sat outside with Belle most of the morning. She pressed him some fresh green juice with her juicer: kale, apple, pineapple, ginger and lime. She poured the juice into two mason jars and put a straw in each. Belle was happy. Sitting on the porch talking with Eddie revitalized her, and she knew that she'd want to keep company with him again.

On Wednesday mornings, Jackie had dance pupils. A local private school hired Jackie to teach a dance class. She had 10 girls in the class aged 5-8. Even though she was busy, she was determined to let Prentiss know she was thinking of him. She considered her schedule and his and decided to leave a *Thinking of You* card for him in the church mail slot. The card had swirling ribbons and flowers on the front. Jackie had written on the inside: *I know Wednesdays are your busy days, but I just wanted you to know that I am always thinking of and praying for you. I am here to help should you need me. With Love, Jackie B.* The card had been sprayed with White Diamonds perfume, envelope sealed, and slipped into the mail slot. Francis retrieved it and recognized the handwriting immediately. She placed it on top of the mail she gave to Pastor LeBeaux when he arrived. He smelled it before he even opened it. "Francis, has this card been soaked in perfume? Who sent such a thing?" he fussed as he opened the envelope. When he saw the signature, he became irate. "Francis, will you put this in a file folder somewhere? Don't throw it away, but I need it out of here." Prentiss said wrinkling his nose. His displeasure for Jackie was growing like a wildfire; she had embarrassed Maybelline, put heavy starch on his shirts, brought him Patsy's greasy food, and sent inappropriate cards. He did not want to talk to her whilst he was angry, but something would have to be done about Jackie Black. While he sipped his coffee that Francis had slipped onto his desk, he decided he would talk to Jackie after the picnic. He didn't want any retaliatory shenanigans at the picnic.

Iris woke late with her head spinning a bit. The wine. The teacakes. She took a couple of aspirin with her orange juice and warmed up her steak from the night before. The women of St. Andrew were planning what they would cook for the picnic, but Iris didn't want to cook any of the dishes she knew how to make. They weren't southern. She decided to contribute financially to the picnic, instead, but she wasn't sure how to do it discreetly. As she had a chunk of her leftover steak and some eggs she scrambled, she thought of Francis. Francis the Secretary was the soul of discretion. She decided she would take a brisk walk to the church and give Francis the money to pass along to the committee.

According to Locke, the food had not yet been purchased. The meat had been ordered from a butcher in the next town, but payment was on delivery. She wanted to be helpful, and she didn't want to cook---not really. Besides, she had never cooked soul food. Latin food was a different story. Ruth had taught her to cook all kinds of food, and Lloyd loved the spiciness of Latin cuisine. She would prepare something for herself, but not for the masses.
They'd laugh at her most likely.

Iris had noticed Francis the Secretary and her eerie ways of moving about. *She could have been a ninja*, Iris thought. After breakfast, Iris pulled her hair up in a high bun and slipped into a tee shirt, some wide-leg yoga pants, and her favorite neon pink and orange sneakers. She stepped off the porch and into the sunshine and sighed. Despite the date she'd had the night before, she was actually happy. Most times, she was bored and restless, but not today. Today, she had a purpose and a plan for her day.

"Good morning, Francis." she said brightly.

"Good morning, Sister Murphy. What can I do for you?"

"Well, I wanted to leave something with you for you to pass along to the picnic committee. I prefer you kept it confidential." Iris slid a lilac colored envelope to Francis; the envelope contained a money order made out to St. Andrew Church with a memo in the corner: *Annual Picnic.* Francis looked up at Iris and nodded.

"I will make the committee chair aware of their funds momentarily. It will be an anonymous donation." Francis nodded again and managed a small smile.

As Iris turned to leave the office, she met Melvin Collier, the serious usher, coming into the room. He seemed surprised to see her, and held in his right hand a small brown paper bag. In perfect script across the front were written two words, *For Francis.* In his left hand was a Starbucks cup. A small stream of smoke ascended from the opening. It didn't smell like coffee. The scent was very faint. It was tea, chai tea.

"Hi Sister Murphy," Melvin Collier said in an official voice. He wore starched khaki pants with very sharp creases, and a light blue polo shirt sharply creased down the sleeves. He looked as if he were wearing a uniform for his first day of school.

Iris looked up into Melvin Collier's long thin face. She smiled. "Hi, Mr. Collier. How are you?"

"I am fine." He nodded toward Francis the Secretary and side-stepped Iris to get to her as if Iris had a sign on her that said *wet paint.* Iris watched as Melvin placed the bag on Francis the Secretary's desk quietly, so quiet that the bag did not make a sound. He said softly, "It's chai with soy, just like you like it." Then Francis did the strangest thing. She looked away from her steno pad, took off the round tortoise shell glasses, lifted her eyes to look at Melvin Collier and smiled ever so sweetly, revealing a perfect set of teeth, and the longest eyelashes Iris had ever seen.

"Thank you, Brother Collier," Francis the Secretary answered. It was only when Francis swept her glance toward the door where Iris stood, that Iris realized she'd been staring at the pair. Iris closed her mouth, which was held agape, and lowered her eyes. Just as quickly as Francis the Secretary's smile came, it went. "Thank you, Sister Murphy. You can be sure this will be handled sufficiently." And just as soon as the words left Francis the Secretary's lips, she blended into the walls of St. Andrew.

When Iris left, Francis the Secretary took the bag Melvin Collier brought for her and put it in a small compartment to the left of her desk. She took a sip of the tea, closing her eyes as she slurped the foam from the top. "This is very good, Brother Collier."

"I'm glad you like it, Sister Francis."

"I do like it. Chai Tea is my favorite."

"Yes, I know. And I know how milk messes with your stomach. That's why I got you soy."

"Thank you, Brother Collier."

"You're very welcome, Sister Francis. Mind if I sit with you for a few minutes?"

"Please. Do sit."

This is the way the conversation went every Wednesday with Francis the Secretary and Melvin Collier, St. Andrew's head usher. Each week he brought her an almond butter and mayhaw jelly sandwich on rye, a granny smith apple, a bottle of water, and a venti Chai tea with soy from Starbucks. And each Wednesday Francis the Secretary began her conversation with Melvin Collier with, "This is very good, Brother Collier."

Francis the Secretary had been in love with Melvin Collier for a year before she ever uttered a word to him. They'd gone to church together for several years, passing each other in the aisle during offering, stealing glances after they drank from their cups of sacrament, and whizzing by each other in the parking lot.

Melvin was passionately predictable; that's what Francis the Secretary loved about him. He was the mailman for Sweet Fields, and each day (except Wednesday, which was his off day, and Sunday, of course), promptly at 2:40 p.m., Melvin was delivering mail to the church office. On Sunday mornings he arrived at church exactly 15 minutes early. At precisely 11:00 on Sunday, he was at his post, holding the door as people gathered in the vestibule and tugged at the door softly to enter the sanctuary where church had already started. Melvin did not leave the church until all parishioners had filed out and all abandoned bulletins, candy wrappers, communion cups and unleavened breadcrumbs were collected and trashed.

In the little yellow steno pad, Francis the Secretary kept notes on Melvin Collier. She was trying to find a time, or moment when he was not so predictable. Then she would know he was not a man upon whom she should waste words. She noted when Melvin Collier found the perfect seating for visitors. She noted how he was able to direct young mothers to the quiet room to hush irritable babies without embarrassing them. She noted how he held the door firmly during prayer, scripture reading, and the call to discipleship. She even wrote a note to God, explaining that as soon as Melvin Collier was late for his mail delivery, uncreased in his clothing, or faltering with his signals to his fellow ushers, she would not make more notes on him. God made Melvin Collier even more consistent. The creases in his pants kept time and continued in earnest with their 2:40 deliveries. And so Francis the Secretary noted and noted until she finally got up the guts to talk to him. One Tuesday at 2:40, when Melvin Collier showed up to deliver the mail, Francis the Secretary spoke.

"Do you have off days, Brother Collier?

"Yes, I do, Sister Francis."

"Do you eat on those off days, Brother Collier?"

"Yes, I do, Sister Francis."

Francis the Secretary ran out of words. There was silence until Melvin Collier picked up the conversation.

"Francis, I'd like to eat lunch with you on my off days. I am off on Wednesdays. I can bring you whatever you like at 10:30. We can eat lunch at 11:00 until 12:00."

"What will you do from 10:30 to 11:00, Brother Collier?"

"I'll be fine watching you. I'll be fine watching you."

They worked out the particulars of lunch. Francis the Secretary wasn't choosy, but she did love mayhaw jelly. When she told Melvin Collier that she loved mayhaw jelly, he didn't flinch. He knew exactly where to find it. He knew it was a Georgian delicacy, and he knew he wanted to be the man to fetch Francis' mayhaw jelly and almond butter sandwiches for the rest of his life.

Iris bounded down the steps toward Pendleton Park, excited about her day and how it had just now offered her a wonderful surprise. She didn't know what to do with what she saw, but she did know to see Francis the Secretary smile made her happy. Her smile was contagious, and even though Francis the Secretary didn't smile for Iris, Iris felt that she should thank her for it. She made a mental note of the thought before it escaped her and started her search for all things Bed and Breakfast.

Iris ended her day of researching Bed and Breakfast Inns with a turn in the kitchen. She had gotten in the mood for something spicy and decided to make her favorite--Latin burgers with caramelized onion and jalapeno relish. This was the first meal Ruth had taught her to make. Eating Locke's teacakes the night before had awakened her sweet tooth, as she knew it would. She knew if she made her favorite dessert, Mexican chocolate cake, she would eat it all, and she definitely could not do that. As she started pulling out the ingredients for the cake, the phone rang.

"Hello."

"Uh, hello, Iris," William Hughes said. "How are you?"

"I'm fine, William. How are you?" She was glad he called but didn't want to seem too excited.

"Oh. I can't complain. Didn't I see you in the park this morning?"

"Maybe. I did walk through there today. What did I have on?" Iris teased.

"What? You forgot what you were wearing?" He laughed. "You had on a light colored shirt, black pants, and the loudest running shoes ever made."

"Yep. You saw me."

"EVERYONE saw you. How can anyone miss those shoes?" He was still laughing. *So he liked to joke around*, she thought.

"Well, William, that's the point. I can't have plumbers with ball caps pulled low over their eyes running me over, can I?"

"No. We most certainly cannot have that. Had I not been on my way to a job, I would have stopped and chatted with you a while."

"That would have been nice. Did you have a busy day?" she asked not sure why.

"I was so busy that I haven't eaten all day. I managed to grab a protein bar between jobs, but that's it."

"Do you like spicy food?"

"Sure. I like a little kick now and then. Why'd you ask?"

"I made some burgers, and I'm putting a cake in the oven in a few minutes. If you want---"

"Wait." He sounded serious. "What's spicy? The burgers or the cake?"

"The cake, of course," Iris said trying not to giggle. But when William remained silent, she broke. "I'm joking. I made Latin burgers and **they** are spicy."

"That sounds good. I'll be there in about an hour."

"Okay. Bye." Iris quickly mixed the cake and slid it into the oven. Forty-five minutes later, William rang the bell.

Iris had seen William in suits, a tuxedo, dress slacks and shirt, and his navy Dickies, but she was not ready to see him in chinos. All six feet and five inches of William filled up her doorway. He wore a pair of chinos, a white polo-style shirt and brown deck shoes.

"You didn't have to change clothes," she said nervously as he walked into the house.

"Yes, I did. Besides, you changed clothes," he said following her through the house into the kitchen. He appreciated the way her gray maxi dress fell softly onto her curves.

"Well, I was sweaty after my walk."

"And so was I." He smiled and sat at the breakfast bar. "Something smells delicious."

"I hope you like it. I thought we could eat on the deck," she said grabbing two covered plates that held juicy burgers on thick buns and potato chips. William opened the door that led to the deck and took the plates from her. She grabbed a pitcher of sweet tea and two glasses and joined William on the deck of her grandmother's house. She had never eaten on the deck before. It overlooked the large, well-kept backyard and sat adjacent to a glass-enclosed room that her grandmother had used as guest dining room.

As she approached her seat, she was pleasantly surprised when William stood and pulled her chair out for her. He was such a gentleman. William bowed his head and said a quick grace and dug right into his burger. They laughed and talked about his clients, her food, and the Murphy Inn. It was over Mexican chocolate cake and coffee, that they realized that it was Wednesday and that they had missed bible study. Iris had started going, but she wasn't a regular attendee like William.

"They may send a search party for you, William."

"Nah. They'll think I'm working late or something," he shrugged. Then he stood up (and Iris' eyes couldn't help but follow) and gathered their plates and glasses. Iris said nothing, but watched him clear the table and take the dishes into the kitchen. When he didn't come back right away, she followed him inside and found him rinsing out the plates and stacking them on the left side of the sink. She sat at the breakfast bar and watched him. She had not noticed how broad his back and shoulders were. Nor had she noticed how his legs were slightly bowed. She had to concentrate on being quiet, for a grunt of approval was bubbling in her throat.

"William, what are you doing? You don't have to wash the dishes. Just leave them in the sink."

"I knew you were gonna say that. You cooked. I could at least rinse the dishes. Besides, it's a habit. I rinse my dishes, put them on the left side until I get enough for a full load for the dishwasher."

"But I don't have a dishwasher."

"And I'm gonna take care of that for you," he said drying his hands off on a clean towel.

"It's getting late, and I don't want to give old man Bennett too much to talk about."

"Bennett? Who's that?"

"The old guy across the street. You've probably seen him looking out of his window. He doesn't talk to people he doesn't already know, but he can talk up a storm when he gets to know you. If I know Bennett, he's got your schedule pegged--if you have one. He logs everything that happens within his view. He went to Vietnam and came back a little off kilter. I'm sure both of my visits have already made it into the Bennett files," he chuckled.

"Here," Iris said jumping off the barstool. "Take some of this cake home with you." She expected to hear him decline, but he did not.

"That's gonna make a nice reminder of tonight on tomorrow's lunch break. I've got a busy day tomorrow too," he said watching Iris deftly cut the remainder of the cake into generous slices and place them in a large Tupperware container.

Around the time that bible study was ending, Iris was walking William Hughes, Jr. to the door. Again, she turned on the porch light. William reached out and touched her hand as he said his low-voiced goodnight. He jumped into his pickup and drove away.

There was a call for announcements before the bible study session concluded. Jackie Black stood and proceeded to the podium that stood near the altar.

"Good evening, St. Andrew. We were **supposed** to have an announcement from Deacon William Hughes this evening about the church picnic on Saturday, but he isn't here tonight. Sister Murphy isn't here either. That's interesting," she paused and chuckled. "Two of the most beautiful and eligible people in the church seem to be playing hooky from bible study." She chuckled again. "God bless their hearts. Anyway, saints, the picnic is Saturday. The ladies will be preparing their dishes here at the church, while the men will be grilling and smoking all kinds of meat at Deacon Callahan's house on Friday. Please see Sister Karen Edwards or Sister Judith Callahan for information about requesting ingredients. I had hoped Sister Murphy would be here to help with the cataloguing of the menu, but since she seems to be smitten with our most attractive deacon, I'll ask Sister Caldwell to assist me." She turned as if she had concluded the announcements, but then she remembered something else and turned back to the microphone.

"Let us not forget that we will also celebrate Sister Maybelline Crowder's going away to Beijing. This weekend is her last weekend here with us. I'm sure we're all proud of her and glad to see her move on...to **bigger** and better things and new people." She crooked her lips into devious smile and then took her seat.

Maybelline wasted no time standing up and leaving the sanctuary, and she did so without discretion. Jackie Black turned toward the side door, taking note of her Maybelline's exit. She stood again. "I see that Sister Crowder is already feeling the

weight of her departure. I'll go check on her." Jackie Black slunk out of the same door wearing a look of concern on her face. Eddie sat next to his daughter-in-law across the aisle from Locke, noting Locke's expressions and mannerisms. While Jackie Black was making the announcements, Locke looked like a pipe fit to bust. She had pulled her gloves off and on a dozen times, and her lips were drawn tight. She was upset. Eddie looked over at the deacons and the deaconesses, and they were all abuzz about something. He surmised whatever had upset Locke and had folk whispering and nodding had something to do with the announcement or the announcer.

Big Hughes and Clem, retreated to the back like they always did to count the offering taken up during bible study.

"Now, that was uncalled for, Hughes. Completely uncalled for. She had no business sharing her speculations over the microphone like that," Clem said unlocking the door to the deacons' den. "She shoulda just called one of us up there to do it."

"Out of order. Completely." Big Hughes was a man of few words when he was angry. In his younger days, he preferred to talk with his fists.

"Now, I give William a hard time, but he's like my own flesh and blood! We don't even know this woman, and she doesn't know us! Cracking jokes back here is one thing, but putting folk business out over the congregation is a horse of a different color. I got a good mind to…"

"No, Clem. William is a grown man. There's nothing wrong with going to see a pretty girl on a Wednesday evening. I saw his truck parked in front of her house on my way to church. He's 35 years old and past time to settle down. Don't you say a word to that yella woman. She's gonna get hers, and it's gonna be sometime soon. Did you see the way Belle Locke was staring at her? Like she wanted to gouge her eyes out! I almost hollered 'cat fight'!" That got Clem to laughing. "Besides, you just mad that she called my boy the most attractive deacon in the church. Looks like Junior done stole your title."

Although they were laughing and had decided that William could fend for himself, they were just a bit worried about his temper. William Hughes, Jr. was a like a sleeping giant. He could joke, laugh, and talk sports with the best of them, but he had a short fuse when it came to his family, his church, and his money. Both Clem and Big Hughes feared that Iris had gotten under William's skin to the point she'd fall under family. That would mean trouble for Jackie Black.

In the west wing hallway of the church, Jackie Black and Maybelline Crowder were engaged in a discussion of their own. It didn't take much for Jackie to catch up with Maybelline after she'd left the sanctuary. As Maybelline extended her hand to open the side door to the church, she felt a tug at her wrist. Jackie Black's long fingers had wrapped around her flesh and were holding on tight. The five copper bangles she wore clanked as she grabbed at Maybelline's hand. Jackie moved her body to half-face Maybelline. "Sister Crowder. You're upset."

"How dare you, Sister Black. How dare you touch me?"

"No, no, no, Maybelline," Jackie Black pleaded, "you've got it all wrong."

"No, Jacqueline. You've got it all wrong. And you have some nerve to come after me, after you've shown your behind to embarrass me in front of my church family."

"Oh Maybelline." Jackie lowered her voice, as if consoling a child. "I know you're emotional about leaving the states. I'm sure it can skew your judgment about things, about me. I only came after you because this is the second time you've walked out while I was speaking, and the Bible tells us, that even if you THINK your brother or sister has an issue with you, you should go to her, so that your prayers won't be hindered. I want God to be pleased with me. There are some things I'm petitioning the throne for right now. I want Got to hear the desires of my heart, so I'm coming to you. Let's talk this out."

"Jackie, you did not want to talk when you stepped on my dress at the gala. You did not want to talk when you shared my wardrobe malfunction with the entire church. And trust me, you do NOT want to talk to me now. I don't have the restraint to deal with you right now. Bigger and better things. Please..."

"See Maybelline, that's what I mean. Because you're under so much stress, you are misreading my intents. I am happy for you. I'm glad you have this opportunity to go away." Jackie couldn't help but smile at this, but as she enjoyed her own self-gratification, Maybelline had moved her hand from the knob of the exit and faced Jackie full front.

"Don't you dare sit and quote scripture at me Jacqueline O'Shelle Black, as if you are so righteous and true. Lucifer was as close to God as I am to you right now, and he ended up in the pits of hell." Maybelline moved closer to Jackie Black, so close that she could smell the greasy stench of Patsy's Diner on Jackie's breath. Maybelline wore a purple cowl neck tunic of light cotton fabric, and the gathers of material at her décolletage trembled with every breath. She stared into Jackie's bulging eyes and whispered slowly, "I have given you a wide berth for as long as I can possibly stand, and obviously you have no idea that my staying away from you has granted you more favor from me than you deserve. Now, you get out of my face before I go and braid some switches together and wear you out right here in the doorway of our Lord's house! You think you lost some feathers out there on Sister Belle's lawn," Maybelline squinted when she saw Jackie Black's lips tighten. Jackie flinched as if she'd been slapped, "but if you don't move away from me right now, Usher Melvin Collier will find each one of those hideous twists in your head scattered across the church's parking lot. Good evening." Maybelline walked out of the church and resolved that Jacqueline Black was no longer worth her time and energy. The best week she'd had since the dress fiasco had not yet ended, and she would not let Jackie spoil the remainder of days she'd have in Sweet Fields, at St. Andrew. With Prentiss LeBeaux.

Jackie Black stood at the door for a moment watching Maybelline walk away. It surprised her that Maybelline had the guts to stand up to her. Poor Maybelline. She did not realize that she was but a stepping-stone in God's plan for Jackie Black to become Pastor Prentiss' rib. Jackie also wondered how Maybelline knew about what happened at Sister Belle Lynne Locke's house, out on her lawn, where she had embarrassed herself and torn the one good dress she had. She scolded herself silently for underestimating Maybelline as she had and whispered a prayer of confession and forgiveness to God for not having better discernment. But Jackie wouldn't have to worry about Maybelline anymore. She would be in another country by the end of the week, and then Jackie Black's seat on the organ, nearer to her dear Prentiss LeBeaux, would finally be secured. That was enough for her, for now.

Locke, not knowing what had transpired between Maybelline and Jackie Black, was fuming as she walked to her car.

She had decided all the exercise she was getting by walking with Eddie in mornings was enough, so she had driven her car and had parked next to Rev. Edwards' black Volvo.

"Belle, wait." Eddie had opened up his stride to catch Locke before she reached her car. "Something the matter, Belle?"

"Yes. Yes, there is. That woman had no right to broadcast Iris' personal business like that. It was out of order, and I don't like it. I don't like **her**."

"Wait, Belle. I agree that that was the weirdest church announcement I have ever heard, but Iris is almost 30, right? She's not a child. Even if you feel like she is, she won't ever **really** be a part of the community if she isn't allowed to fight her own battles.

Besides, you may not be here always to run interference for her."

"Oh no? Where, pray tell, would I be going? You killing me off now, are you?" Locke huffed. She knew he was right, but she didn't want to hear it. Not right now.

"Well, who knows? I may just take your adorable little self back to North Carolina with me." He paused and tried to pierce her exterior but her armor was up already. He didn't give up, though. He kept staring through hooded eyes and smiling a mischievous smile.

"Oh, hush up, Eddie. I'm not going anywhere!" She swatted at him and in spite of herself, she laughed. He was right. Iris, if she were really going to become a member of the Sweet Fields community, would have to stand up for herself and fight her own battles. Locke just hoped Iris hadn't gone too soft while she was falling for William Hughes.

CHAPTER 12: THURSDAY

Early Thursday morning, Big Hughes called his son. He had questions. "Junior," Big Hughes started right in. He never said "hello" or "how are you" on the phone. He didn't like talking on it. "Are you courting that Murphy girl?"

"Well, I had dinner with her." William was surprised the inquisition had come so soon. "She gave me some chocolate cake. Want me to bring you a slice?" William said shuffling down the stairs of his two-story mission-style home.

"No. You eat it. That tall, skinny woman said you weren't in bible study last night because you were off courting."

"Courting?" William laughed. "Is that what she said, Pop?"

"No. That's what I'm saying. She hinted around that you and that girl weren't at bible study and made it seem like you two were hanky panky-ing around."

"Who did she tell that to?" William's steps were slowing.

"The whole church, boy!" the older Hughes shouted.

"What?!" William's calm and patient demeanor changed in a flash. "I don't care what she says about me, but I don't want her talking about Iris like that. She has no right to say things like that over the congregation. Who is she anyway? Where did she even come from? How did she even get the microphone?"

"Son, those are the same questions Clem asked. He was mad as a wet hen."

"Clem was mad?" he chuckled. Clem was a sight to see when he got going. He'd turn red, and his straight tendrils always seemed to flop right over his forehead.

"Clem was hot as a six-shooter! I think he wanted to snatch a knot in her after bible study."

"Why was **he** so mad?"

"Because she said you were the most handsome deacon in the church," Big Hughes roared in laughter. William laughed too. Both

Hughes men laughed on the phone, but when the laughter subsided, William was the one hot as a six-shooter.

"Boy, you know people in a small town talk. The only thing about this is she ain't from here, so it hits the ear wrong. I don't want you to do anything shameful, but I wanted you to know." Big Hughes was sitting in his recliner rubbing his coal black hair and shaking his head.

"Well, I knew folk would talk, but I didn't expect her. I wonder what got into her to make her do that? She has never said two words to me before, and I have never seen her and Iris talk either. That was a lowdown thing to do, Pop."

"What looks crazy to us makes perfect sense to women, son."

"Well, I been trying to talk to Iris for three months, and she's finally warmed up to me and now this. If this little stunt runs Iris back into her shell, God so help me, that Jackie woman will regret the day she landed here." He ranted. "She's gonna keep Iris' name out of her mouth when I'm done." William stood fuming at his kitchen sink waiting for his coffee to brew while his father leaned back in his chair bearing the smile of proud father.

"You may not have a chance. Belle looked like she could spit nails. I thought her little head was gonna pop right off. So if you're wondering if you should tell her, I betcha Belle already has," Big Hughes said. "And bring me a slice or two of that cake on your way to work. I feel like eating something sweet."

William, dressed in his work clothes, stopped by his father's house to drop off two thin slices of the Mexican chocolate cake Iris had made for him. His father frowned at the two pieces and called William stingy. William laughed and climbed back into his service van and drove on. He slowed down when he got to Iris' block. He couldn't believe his luck when he saw Iris swinging gently in her porch swing. He made a U-turn in the street and parked in front her of house. He smiled when he saw his presence register on her face in the form of a demure smile.

"Good morning, Iris." he called from the sidewalk. "It is a good morning, William. How are you? Want some orange juice or coffee?" Iris asked still swinging to and fro. William cleared the steps to the porch quickly and was sitting beside her before she could make room for him.

"Orange juice sounds good." he said trying to absorb the picture of Iris with her hair down and hanging in thick curls and coils around her face and shoulders and without makeup. She wore light pink tee shirt, matching knit pants, and ballet style slippers. When she returned, he reached for the glass of orange juice. Had I known you sit on your porch in your pajamas, I would have started driving by here three months ago!" He laughed.

"I will have you know these are not pajamas. It's called loungewear."

"Well, whatever it's called, you look good in it." He smiled and took a sip from his glass. Iris said nothing; she just smiled. She started wrestling with her curls to pull them in an elastic band at the nape of her neck. "Ah. Don't do that. I like it loose."

She relaxed her arms and folded her hands in her lap. And focused on his navy-clad legs stretched out rocking the swing back and forth.

"Iris, it seems I was supposed to make an announcement about the picnic last night bible study. Since I wasn't there, Jackie Black made the announcement. She apparently expected you to be there too to assist with compiling the menu items. So when neither of us were present, she took it upon herself to speculate about where we were and what we were doing." William was starting to get vexed all over again.

"Speculate? What did she say?"

"Well, she said that we were playing hooky from bible study together."

"Oh. That's all?" Iris asked as she leaned back in the arm of the swing with a smile.

"That's enough. I don't like her saying things like that about you. When men's names are in stuff like this, it's not a big deal, but women...well, it's a different story. She shouldn't have said it. Not during the announcements. I've decided to have a word with her." Iris laughed.

"Really? You're going to have a word with her to defend my honor?"

"Yes. If you want to say that. She made it seem like we're doing something wrong, and we aren't. Had she said something to us privately, I might have been alright, but to say it to the entire church was classless."

"William, I appreciate you, but people have said worse things than that about me to more people, even. When Lloyd died, people wrote that I was his mistress, love child, servant, child bride, gold digger. You name it, I was called it. And I was none of it. I was a family member. He was like an uncle or grandfather to me." Her voice trailed off.

"Yeah, well, this ain't California. This is Sweet Fields. I've been here my whole life and I know how folks are. They tease and talk, but she ain't from here. Her little antics are adding up, and if she's not careful she's gonna get her feelings hurt."

"But not by you, surely. Not the valiant William Hughes. Surely, he wouldn't hurt a woman's feelings because she's teased him." Iris said with a light laugh.

"Well, she better be able to take what she dishes out." He said stopping the swing's movement. "I just wanted you know in case someone said something to you."

"I appreciate your telling me. That was very thoughtful of you." They were both quiet. William didn't want to leave, and Iris didn't want him to.

"Well, I better go on. I have a busy morning. Can I call you this evening?" he asked standing and turning to look at her curled up on the porch swing.

"Sure. I'd like that." She smiled. She remained curled up in the corner of the porch swing and watched him descend the steps to the sidewalk. He adjusted his ball cap on his head and waved as he drove away.

Prentiss LeBeaux's stomach was already growling, and it was only 10:30 in the morning. He sat in his office busying himself looking over blue prints for the daycare. For the past three days he'd had lunch in his office with Sister Maybelline. She was clearing out her refrigerator before she left for Beijing. On Monday they'd had pulled chicken, coleslaw and baked beans. On Tuesday Maybelline showed up at the church with meatball submarine sandwiches and sweet potato fries. Wednesday was a hodge-podge of delectables, spinach dip and tortilla chips, garlic seasoned chicken wings, drop biscuits, fried green beans and green salad. Maybelline always brought a hefty to-go plate to the church for Francis the Secretary.

Each time she came with lunch, Maybelline would ask Francis the Secretary to join her and Prentiss. Each time, Francis would decline. Instead she took the meals home, divided them out and shared them with Melvin Collier.

Maybelline and Prentiss LeBeaux would sit in the two seats in front of the pastor's desk with the door to his office open. They ate with their plates in their laps, even though sometimes their raucous laughter would almost cause them to topple over. They talked with their mouths full and guffawed between bites with their forks in the air. Every now and then, Maybelline would yell into the reception area, "Did you hear your pastor, Francis?" Francis would nod, and sometimes drop her head quickly to keep from laughing.

Today, Maybelline would bring in the cornbread dressing she had been bragging about since their lunch at Mom and Pop's Fine Southern Dining on Sunday. He wasn't so much concerned about her dressing anymore.

Prentiss LeBeaux didn't want Maybelline to take the job, but he hadn't told her. Not yet. Now he sat rustling the long blue papers around, his stomach an uncomfortable jumble of butterflies and hunger. He had approximately one hour to come up with something to make Maybelline stay, but he couldn't think of anything yet.

Then there was Sister Black. Pastor LeBeaux had become hyper aware of her since his talk with Maybelline, and it seemed as if his eyes were slowly opening to her antics. The convoluted announcement she made could have been summed up in two sentences, but Prentiss noticed how Jackie continued, chattering on, peppering her words with gossip and suggestive language. He noticed how she held the microphone so tightly that her knuckles whitened, the way she panned the room, smilingly relentlessly, almost reeling with the excitement of having an engaged audience. And what did she say when she went after Maybelline? Maybelline hadn't mentioned anything. Maybe the two women had reconciled their differences. Still, it was in that moment, at bible study, that Pastor Prentiss LeBeaux questioned Jackie Black's true intentions, and how those intentions would affect the body of St. Andrew. There was something else. A question that swam around the edges of his thoughts about Jackie Black. Was she really the reason Maybelline was leaving for Beijing? Whatever the answer, Prentiss would make one last stand for Maybelline. He wanted St. Andrew to sound like it used to sound. He wanted his minister of music back. He wanted… He heard the laughing sound of Maybelline's voice. 11:45 had rolled around fast.

"Hi Francis," he heard Maybelline singing out in the reception area. "I think you're going to enjoy this one. I brought you some dressing."

"Thank you, Sister Maybelline," Francis replied. "You know what folks say, you know you're in the south when you're eating cornbread dressing year 'round… that and potato salad."

"You're right about that," said Francis, "I'll call Pastor LeBeaux, and buzz you in."

"Thank you, Francis. And here's your plate. You sure you won't to come on in? You know you're welcome to join us. In fact I wish you would. You're helping me prepare for my trip; I'd love for you to fellowship before I leave."

"No, Sister Maybelline, you go right ahead. I'd rather be at the front, where I can advise people when they come in. I was never good at fellowshipping, anyway. I don't want you to take it personal, but I'm fine right here."

"Sure, Francis. I do understand." Maybelline knocked on Pastor LeBeaux's office door, even though she knew she had already been buzzed in. "Pastor LeBeaux?"

"Sister Maybelline, come on in. I was afraid you would chicken out on me, being that you've bragged on your cornbread dressing. I thought you'd gotten scared."

"Who me? Scared?" Maybelline started taking the warm dishes out of the thermal bag. "I've never been scared to claim my cooking. She took out a small Tupperware dish and handed it to Pastor LeBeaux. "Here. I brought you a sample to nosh on while I get everything else together. Taste that and tell me what you think."

Pastor LeBeaux grabbed the container. "It's still hot." He took the top off the steaming dressing and sniffed. He had to admit, "It smells really good, Maybelline. But the proof is in the tasting. You know how you can tell if the dressing is really good?"

"No, how can you tell?"

"Good cornbread dressing doesn't need cranberry sauce." He scooped a corner of the dressing out and blew to cool it off. He tasted it and then squinted. "You should be ashamed of yourself."

"What?" Maybelline looked startled. She stopped pulling the food from her bag. "What is it? Too much sage?"

"No. No. No. It's perfect. But now I've got to repent.
Early. Gluttony is about to be committed."

"Oh, so now I'm the tempter? Making you eat all over yourself? You work out your own salvation. Don't try to put your sinning on me!" From that sentence the laughing and guffawing began. Maybelline and Prentiss cracked jokes, played the dozens, and threw sarcasms and bad puns around like old friends. "What did you use for your base broth, duck?" Prentiss asked.

"Really, Pastor. I had a lot of bird in my freezer, but duck wasn't one of those birds."

"Turkey necks?"

"No. Just eat and stop talking, you got cranberry sauce flying out of your mouth. Just rude..."

"Tail of rabbit and eye of newt?"

"Look, Pastor. I told you already, I'm not telling you my secret. You'll have every mother in the church cooking dressing for you. This secret is going to Beijing with me and on to my grave."

Francis the Secretary peeped into the doorway of Pastor LeBeaux's office. "Pastor, I'm going to the work room to make the copies for the Sunday bulletin. Then I'm going on down to the sanctuary to load the announcements onto the jumbo-tron. I'll be right back.

"Okay Sister Secretary." Prentiss was glad for Francis' interruption, because the mention of Beijing changed Pastor LeBeaux's demeanor, as it always did. He waited until he heard the quiet click of the door closing and began. "Look Maybelline, I know we're having a good time and all. But I wanted to talk about
Beijing. Well, since you brought it up."

Maybelline dropped her head a little bit. "Pastor LeBeaux, I know you feel like I'm putting you in a bind with you having to find a minister of music, but…"

"Yes, Maybelline you are. But that's not all. You're going to have to let me finish, now, or I'll never get up the nerve to say what I have to say. I enjoy your playing so much. It's true; those fingers of yours are anointed. It's going to be hard to replace you, because you bring so much to the worship service. Not just your playing, but your voice is so sweet and pure, and you work with the choir well. We're not like most churches that I hear about, you know, where most of the foolishness starts in the choir loft. These choir members really love you. The Choral of Children practically run me over trying to get to you at choir rehearsal. And you serve from your heart. You don't bother anyone, and whatever is asked of you, you do without quarrel or rebuttal. You know the Word. You know how to compliment me on that organ, even though I can't tune up worth a dime…"

"You preach the Word, Pastor. That's good enough. I appreciate your compliments, but…"

"Just let me finish. I was praying Monday morning and you fell on my mind. So I prayed for you. In that prayer, I realized that I didn't want you to leave, well, because I'd like to get to know you as a woman, a companion. I've been wrestling with it, because of Ava. It's hard to explain, but I feel guilty sometimes when I see you smiling or hear your voice, and I like it. Anyway, I just wanted to give it try. Now that I've finally gotten brave enough to tell you my feelings, I was just hoping they'd be enough to make you stay, just to give us a try. I don't want a side woman, don't want to go sneaking around. I want to do it right, date you right, so St. Andrew can see me do it right and respect it. I've thought about this thing, Maybelline. I've thought it through, and I know it's at the 11th hour, but if there's anything I can do…"

Maybelline leaned in toward Prentiss LeBeaux. She took his hand in both of hers. "Pastor LeBeaux, I appreciate your honesty. I really do." She let his hands go, but held his gaze, "and I'd be lying if I said I didn't have the tingles, for you too. I can feel that undercurrent between us. I got some discernment too." Maybelline smiled. "But I can't stay." She took a deep breath. "Let me tell you something, I have sat on my back porch imagining something like this playing out between me and you. Then I laughed at myself for being silly. I mean, I KNOW, I'm a catch." They both laughed. "But I didn't know if you were supposed to be the one to catch me. There are some things that we need to work out, separately, and I think leaving is the best thing."

"But I don't see how separating will help that, Maybelline. How can we get to know one another better if we're not in the same space?"

"That's the point, Pastor, at least for me. I have to figure out how I'm going to deal with… if I want to deal with a man who is too nice to be firm, or too compassionate to put people in check, or too concerned about hurting people's feelings, or too blinded by the good to see what needs to be done about the bad." Maybelline paused, leaning into Prentiss LeBeaux again. She took his hand again. "And pastor, a man who is too in love with the past that he can't see his future is not a man I want to be with right now. I know you'll get there, but I don't want to watch you working the middle while you get there. That would be painful for me."

Pastor LeBeaux watched Maybelline lean back in her chair. She crossed her legs at the ankle and tucked them neatly underneath the long pale yellow dress she wore. The yellow complimented her face well, it gleamed, and to Prentiss LeBeaux, her face was sunshine in his office. Her hair was pulled into the thick long ponytail which hung down and swayed whenever she moved her head, and the ends swept at her skin, beneath where the halter of her dress fastened at the back of her neck, and as was her signature look, a side swept chunk of heavy bangs fell to her chin, framing her full brown face. "You're right, Maybelline. But you do know, I am not always aware of those things? That's why I need you here. I believe it's you."

"I know what YOU believe. But I believe that it couldn't be me. Twice, Prentiss. Twice, Sister Black insulted me. Twice, you missed it. You didn't address it. And do understand, I know it's kind of sticky, especially when you feel the way you say you feel. But, if you don't support and address issues in this church affecting me as a **member** of your congregation, I just can't see how you would handle it sufficiently if I were your **lady, your girlfriend, your wife**."

"And you're right, it is sticky. Sister Black has been out of order. She's new. Trying to find her way. Usually the Mothers or Deaconesses will…"

"Prentiss, as a manager, let me put it in perspective. When I see people on my team disrupting the unity and one accord-ness of the team's mission, as soon as I see it, I call that team member in and I address it. It's not the teammates responsibility to address issues. I am responsible for that team, especially if I see it. The team should support each other, but not discipline each other. Time is too valuable. The main goal is too important for us to tiptoe around issues that could ultimately destroy the outcome. That's my job, to be sure people do their part and do it well and work together and make something great, and to properly address those who cause kinks in the plan."

"I see."

"I hope so Pastor LeBeaux, but I'm not changing my mind. I'm going to Beijing, but I'm not going empty. I'm going full of those beautiful words you spoke to me. I have a lot to think about while I'm there. And you'll know what I decide when I decide it. But let's keep in touch in the meantime. We're enjoying ourselves, right now. We're cultivating a good friendship.
Let's keep it right there until God tells us otherwise."

"Let's do, Sister Maybelline. But you can't leave here today without letting me pray for your journey."

"Of course, Pastor. I wouldn't turn down a prayer from you. And you've eaten too much, so you need to confess and get forgiveness too! I'll take responsibility for my part."

"Dear Lord, we come to you heads bowed and bellies full. We thank you for this opportunity to speak to you on Maybelline's behalf. But first of all, I thank you for making me brave enough to tell this beautiful woman what was on my heart. And thank you for making her honest enough to cuss me out without using cuss words. You've shown me so much about myself and her by letting her sit with me and talk with her for a while. Now Lord, if you see fit, touch her heart and her mind and let her stay. That's my will, and I hope it matches up with yours, because I know you like good singing just like everybody else. Now I know this isn't about me, it's about Maybelline, and I want you to speak to her and confirm she's doing the right thing by you. If you see fit to let her leave me, leave St. Andrew, leave Sweet Fields; build a hedge of protection around her. Don't let all those folks over there be mean to her. Don't let one of those Beijing men snatch her up. And Lord, keep the plane in the air, should she take the journey. When she gets there, let your light shine in her there just as bright as it shined in her here. And let this relationship grow while we're together, and strengthen it while we're apart. Open my eyes and give me some of that discernment she has naturally, give it to me by proxy, just cause I'm sitting in her presence. In the name of Jesus we pray these blessings. Amen." "Amen," Maybelline said with a giggle. "Pastor that's the funniest most honest prayer I ever heard.

"That's the way I talk to the Lord. Like he's right here with me. I don't use all of those rhymes and riddles. I have to get right to it. This is serious Maybelline. I feel like I'm losing something that I didn't get a chance to have."

"Keep praying, pastor. I will too. It's going to be hard, because this is something I want too, but I want it good. I want it to be a good thing, so it needs to start off right, right and fresh. Now, I've got to get out of here. I have some more packing to do, and I have to fix refreshments for the ladies tomorrow. I want them to have something to eat while they prepare the food for the church picnic. I don't want to be up all night with that. I enjoyed our lunch, Pastor." Maybelline stood up as Prentiss stood. She kissed him lightly on the cheek. They packed up the remnants of the lunch together. Maybelline left the remainder of the dressing with Pastor LeBeaux, who promised that he'd have the list of ingredients by the time he saw her on Saturday at the picnic. Francis the secretary had made it back with an arm full of bulletins. She looked up at Maybelline and nodded.

"I'll see you tomorrow, Sister Maybelline. Thanks again for the lunch plate."

"Good bye, Francis. Pastor LeBeaux, I'll see you later.

Forty-five minutes after Maybelline left the church, Jackie Black whirled her car into the parking space beside the pastor's spot. She was excited. She had another gift for Prentiss. He had appreciated her gift of breakfast products and clean shirts on Monday. He had appreciated her thoughtfulness of bringing him breakfast to the church on Tuesday. She knew Wednesdays were his long days, so she sent him a *Thinking of You* card that she had sprayed with her White Diamonds perfume. Today was Thursday, and she had the perfect gift for him. She had been up until the wee hours of the morning compiling her favorite songs for Pastor LeBeaux. She included music from Korsakov to Coltrane, from Billie Holiday to Donna Summer, and from Otis Redding to Michael McDonald. There were three CDs in all. If he listened to them, he would know how she felt about him--she just knew it.

She smoothed her canary yellow chiffon dress as she walked into the church annex to the business offices. She had wrapped the CDs in red foil paper and had them tucked into her yellow straw bag. When she climbed the stairs to the second floor, she saw Francis in the kitchenette and saw her chance to be alone with Prentiss. She tiptoed to his door and tapped lightly. There was no answer. She turned the knob, but it did not give way to her.

It was locked. She knocked a little louder.

"May I help you?" Francis asked with an edge in her voice that Jackie had not heard before.

"I was trying to see Pastor LeBeaux. I have a gift for him." Francis stared at her blankly.

"Leave it with me. I'll see to it that he gets it." Francis reached for the gift. Jackie turned away from the locked door sadly and went to the front desk where Francis sat.

"Francis, please make sure he gets these. It's very important." "Of course, Sister Jackie. I'll be sure he gets them as soon as he returns."

"Oh. He's out of the office today? When will he return?" Jackie smiled, and Francis thought quickly.

"I can't say. He said he would be out and about. That's all I know. I will make certain that he gets your gift, though. You may have your basket back, also." Francis retrieved the picnic basket from a nearby closet and presented it to Jackie. Jackie set the CDs on the desk and picked up the basket.

"I must have caught him on a busy week," she said adjusting her grip on the picnic basket. "Thank you, Francis." "Yes, Sister Jackie. This week has been exceptionally busy...with the picnic and all. Good day."

When Jackie left, Francis placed the CDs on her desk and returned to the copier. Prentiss had gotten so overwhelmed from his lunch with Maybelline that he had gone home for an hour or so. He just sat in his favorite chair and stared at the floor. He hadn't felt heartache like this in a long time. Ava had broken up with him once during their courtship, but this seemed worse. After he gathered his thoughts, he strolled back to the church and back to work. When he climbed the stairs to the second floor, Francis looked up at him over her glasses and slid a red foil package towards him with a pencil. She didn't even want to touch it. "Sister Jackie dropped this off for you.

I barely managed to get her out of here. She wanted to wait." Francis turned the corners of her mouth down in derision.

Prentiss sighed aloud and snatched the foil package off the desk, stormed into his office, and slammed the door. Once inside his office, he tore off the wrapping paper. Three CDs were underneath. Each had a cover that looked to be hand-drawn. The contents of each one was carefully penned on the inside of the cover. Prentiss scanned the track lists and could hardly believe his eyes. The CDs were labeled *The Past, The Present, and Our Future.* On the Past CD were songs that Ava liked, that were played at the gala, including Flight of the Bumblebee. He couldn't believe his eyes. On the Present CD were love songs like Billie Holliday's "All of Me," India Arie's "Ready for Love", and Diana Ross' "Ain't No Mountain High Enough." On the Future CD were songs like Luther Vandross' "Always and Forever," and Bill Withers' "Just the Two of Us."

"She's crazy!" he shouted from his office out to Francis. Francis had never heard Pastor LeBeaux raise his voice. She hurried into his office to see what had upset him.

"Pastor, what's wrong?"

"That woman has to be stopped! She made some CDs with love songs on them! She thinks she is in love with me! Father, God, help your people!" Prentiss held out the CDs to Francis to inspect. "Look at the songs on these! She put Ava's favorite songs on the CD labelled "Past." Can you believe this?" Francis took the CDs from his shaking hand.

Prentiss LeBeaux couldn't decide whether it would have been better for him to stay at home the rest of the day, or whether he should just take another hour or so for himself, to go sit in his chair again. He was trying to compartmentalize all that had taken place, and it was only 2:00 p.m. All over again, Prentiss LeBeaux was angry at Jackie Black. It seemed that in every situation that had to do with Maybelline Crowder, Jackie had inserted herself. He couldn't even think about his time with Maybelline without Jackie Black intruding.

He was reminded in repose, that it wasn't just that. To boil everything about Jackie Black down to Maybelline was selfish.

Jacqueline Black could cause a huge fissure in St. Andrew's constitution. His mind wandered back to the announcement. The veiled accusation she'd made against his co-chair of the deacon board, Brother Hughes, Jr. and the newest member of the flock, Iris Murphy, were preposterous. William Hughes, Jr. could handle a few word taps, but Iris Murphy, she was young in the ministry, and Pastor LeBeaux knew that God would hold him accountable should Sister Black's loose lips cause Iris to stumble in the faith.

Finally, Prentiss LeBeaux was beginning to see the bigger picture, and as the under shepherd he owed it to the members and most importantly to God, to be a good steward over the people with whom God had charged him. He'd have to move into unchartered territory and face the principalities that caused a threat to God's church, as much as he hated facing conflict. He'd prayed for the strength to do it, and now it looked as if he'd have to walk on that prayer, and do it soon.

CHAPTER 13: FRIDAY

When Friday morning arrived, the Food Lion and Piggly Wiggly grocery stores were packed with St. Andrew's members buying food and supplies for the annual picnic on Saturday. The men of the church were responsible for grilling the meats and the women were preparing sides. The tradition had been in place for decades. The men would usually gather at Clem Callahan's home, bring their meats, special sauces, and spices, and marinate ribs, chicken, steaks, and burgers. The women would gather in the church's industrial kitchen to prepare a variety of sides and desserts. Everyone looked forward to the fellowship. Even the older members participated, though they usually just came and provided entertainment by taking the younger folk down memory lane.

Locke was up at 6 a.m. having tea on her porch when Eddie walked up.

"Good morning, Belle," Eddie said tipping his hat. "Good morning, Eddie. Come on in. I can't walk with you today."

"Something wrong?"

"Oh no. I just have some teacakes to make for the picnic, and I do my best baking in the mornings. I figure I'll be baking all day if I don't get started now." Eddie climbed the steps to the porch, thrilled to be invited into Belle's home at last. "You're more than welcome to keep me company if you don't mind missing your walk, that is."

"Honestly, Belle. I was only walking so I could talk to you. So there's no harm done," Eddie said with a twinkle in his eye. He held the door open for her as she entered the house *He opened the door to MY house,* she thought. She remembered Clive and his obsession with opening doors for her and smiled.

"I have a light breakfast for you if you haven't eaten yet." She knew he walked before eating his breakfast. She also knew he didn't eat meat in the mornings. She had prepared for him a fruit bowl, a boiled egg, a slice of toast with a small dollop of pear preserves on the side, and a glass of fresh-squeezed orange juice. He saw the dome covered plate, sat at the breakfast bar, and uncovered the food. It was a perfect breakfast. When Eddie looked up and found Locke looking at him, he smiled. "Belle, I don't think I've ever met a woman like you. You're something else. I thank you for making me breakfast."

"You're welcome. Now, you sit there and eat, and I'm gonna start on my teacakes."

Belle had an assortment of flavorings lined neatly on the counter, most of which came from her garden out back. She'd tied bunches of lavender with cooking string. Beside the lavender were sticks of vanilla, then sticks of cinnamon, both bound with string. Further down were two small piles, one of fresh cardamom seeds and another of cloves. Nestled together at the end of the parade of flavors were two nutmeg pods. Eddie looked at the ingredients and thought that if he used a leveler, he'd discover that all the piles were in a perfect line, straight across. The spices gave off a heady cloud of scents that conjured the word "home" in his mind. Eddie closed his eyes to determine whether he could separate the scents out in his head. He opened his eyes to find Locke lining several glass bowls beneath her garden finds. The bowls she lined up in order of size, from large to small. In the largest bowl, she poured flour. She did not measure the flour with a cup, but eyeballed it, placing the bag down on the counter, looking into the bowl, shaking it around a bit then pouring more. Once she leveled it out to her liking, Locke went to the next bowl where she poured raw crystallized sugar. She continued down the line with brown sugar, baking soda, baking powder, butter milk and cut up blocks of butter, a tiny bowl of ginger and an even tinier bowl of lemon and lime zest.

"You'd think you were preparing for surgery, the way you're lining up those ingredients." Eddie smiled wide. He was both amazed and disturbed by the order. "You got those bowls measured up and lined out like a military troop about to go into battle." Eddie scanned the corners of the kitchen. "Where's your apron? I'll get it for you. You don't want to get flour all over your clothes."

Locke looked up at Eddie warmly. His attention to detail reminded her of her Clive. "Eddie, I haven't worn an apron since Huck was a Pup! Watch me work and come out clean." She giggled and commenced to blending her ingredients.

"What's the lavender for? I've never heard of lavender tea cakes."

"I use lavender in everything. I started when my Clive used to leave to go on business trips. He didn't go many places without me, but when he did, I'd get anxious, so I started with this lavender tea. I'd clean up the house and drink tea. Organize and drink tea. Weed my garden and drink tea. It helped me out a lot. So I started boiling it on the stove so I could smell it throughout the house to help me relax. After that, I put it in my lemonade, along with a little something else I can't tell you about yet."

"Aw, you can tell me Belle," Eddie said leaning over the counter, as if he was about to hear a juicy piece of gossip.

"You may as well lean on back, Eddie, because if I tell you, I'd have to kill ya." She laughed again. "Anyway, I make all flavors of teacakes, so I said, why not try lavender and lime tea cakes. And believe it or not, those are the ones the folks in Sweet Fields like the most."

"And, that also explains why it smells so good in here. It smells like home. I'm relaxed and calm and safe. I have a nice view…" Eddie did lean back then.

"Stop all that flirtation. We've gotten too old for that mess." Locke was carefully mixing the dry ingredients. She didn't spill a bit of flour.

"Who says? We're old enough to do whatever we want. Even flirting."

"So is that what you plan on doing, Eddie? Sitting in my house and looking up in my face all day?"

"Yep, that's it. There's nothing else I'd rather do. I think it's the lavender."

"I think it's the view," Locke said. She blushed and noticed that the feeling in her belly was returning. It was good to have a man, this man, in her house. And the feeling was natural; it was right. Yes, the thoughts of Clive were there, but Clive had always wanted the best for her. Locke believed that the best was happening to her right now, for the first time, since her Clive had died, and guilt didn't weigh so heavily on her anymore.

Across town, Maybelline had taken a break from her packing to purchase large quantities of eggs, sugar, and flour for the cake bakers. She had cooked up most of her food for lunches with Pastor LeBeaux and had prepared her home to be closed up while she was away in Beijing. The church florist, Sister Caldwell, was Maybelline's neighbor and very best friend. She had agreed to keep an eye on Maybelline's house and car. Maybelline and Sister Caldwell were headed to the Food Lion with a laundry list of baking items to retrieve for the night's baking.

Karen Edwards and Judith Callahan were at the Discount Mart picking up napkins, plastic ware, and Styrofoam plates. Both Karen and Judith would be baking cakes and pies later that night, but Maybelline insisted on buying and picking up the ingredients. Karen and Judith had become confidants over the few years that the Edwards family had been at St. Andrew's. They were both quiet women who kept to themselves, but their tickle boxes turned over whenever they got together.

The twins, Luceal and Laura, were shelling pecans and watching their *stories*. Even though they could have had Maybelline pick up pecan halves at the grocery store, the pair insisted on shelling their own pecans. They enjoyed it. They sat on their enclosed porch in their rocker recliners and gossiped on the phone with the ladies in their sewing circle. Luceal operated the large-buttoned phone that sat between them, putting all incoming calls on speakerphone so they could both be in the conversation. Everyone who knew the twins knew if you told something to one, the other was sure to know.

Just a few blocks from Luceal and Laura, Clem was blaring Motown hits in his basement kitchen while he made gallons of barbeque sauce. Big Hughes was humming along and mixing seasonings for his famous grill rubs. When they were in their early twenties, Big Hughes, Clem, and two other young men had gone to Atlanta to see a show. Clem had broken off from the group and talked himself into almost being knifed in an alley. Big Hughes showed up and beat the stuffing out of the would-be mugger. The two men had been joined at the hip ever since. Folk had often called them Ebony and Ivory because Big Hughes was the color of chocolate while Clem was nearer the color of chalk. Their wives had been friends, and they had raised their children together.

William Hughes, Jr. and Rev. Edwards had been given the task of picking up the tents and ice chests. The food and the seniors were always housed in tents at the picnic. While William found Rev. Edwards to be a pleasant man and enjoyed talking sports with him, he couldn't help but wonder what Iris would be doing today and wished he could stop by.

Iris had not been given a task for the picnic, but she had discreetly provided a sizeable donation to the picnic committee. Her donation covered almost all of the food and staples purchased. Most people had assumed Iris could not cook, and she let them think that. The truth was, Iris had spent a great deal of time in the kitchen with Ruth, Lloyd's cook and housekeeper. She had learned to make all kinds of dishes, but none of them were southern or soul foods that the people of Sweet Fields would expect. She'd rather be thought of as incompetent than awkward in this case.

She leisurely walked around to Locke's house and was surprised to be greeted by Eddie, Rev. Edwards' father.

"Good morning! Belle said a pretty young lady would be ringing the doorbell any minute. Come on in." Eddie said standing to the side to grant Iris entrance.

"Iris! I'm in the kitchen! Come on back." Locke called out over the mixer. Iris arrived in the kitchen and found Locke standing over a red Kitchen Aid mixer smiling from ear to ear. "I've got some samples. Try one," Locke yelled above the whirring Iris took a tiny cake from the napkin Locke held out and nibbled on it while Eddie pulled out a chair for her.

"So, Iris. How do you like Sweet Fields so far?"

"I'm afraid it has grown on me. And you? Has Sweet Fields grown on you yet?" Eddie looked at Locke pouring cake batter into molded cake pans and smiled. Iris noticed something how his eyes softened when he looked at Locke.

"Yes. I'm afraid the town and some of the people have begun to grown on me." He never took his eyes from Locke, and Locke never looked up. But she smiled. She smiled a smile that Iris had not seen on her before.

The three sat around nibbling on the sample teacakes and talking about the picnic. Iris liked Eddie. She liked the idea of Locke having a companion closer to her own age. She especially like the way Eddie looked at Locke and wondered if William watched her that way when she wasn't looking.

Friday morning found Prentiss LeBeaux sitting in his favorite chair nursing a cup of strong coffee. He had thought long and hard about Jackie Black. The man in him wanted to excommunicate her from St. Andrew, but the servant in him wanted to counsel with her--with Francis and Locke present--to see where her head was or if she had anything in her head at all. He knew there would be some fall out regardless of what action he took. Now that he could see her intentions clearly, he didn't think she would take anything he said peacefully. He was already losing Maybelline because of her. Prentiss had settled on the fact that Jackie Black was unstable, for no one in their fully functioning mind would be so heartless to label a CD of his deceased wife's favorite songs as, "The Past."

After another cup of coffee, he decided he would talk with her after the picnic. He did not want the annual picnic or Maybelline's farewell celebration to be contaminated with Jackie's foolishness. He would not disturb the peace. Not yet.

Jackie Black was the first to arrive at the church Friday night. First besides Francis, of course. She had established stations with signs and utensils and greeted the women as they arrived at the fellowship hall door, handing each a cheap apron she'd procured from the Community Dollar Store across the bridge. "Wouldn't want you to mess yourself," she said as she handed each her apron. She greeted them warmly. Too warmly. As if they were coming to **her** kitchen. Some of the ladies returned her warmth and appreciated her assistance with unloading their cars. Others met her salutations with indifference. The Sweet Fields in all of the ladies wouldn't allow them to not speak at all, so Jackie was content in believing all the women of St. Andrew, at least the cooking ones, were on her side.

Because she had come earlier to visit with Francis, Iris entered the fellowship hall from the sanctuary rather than the back door where Jackie was standing guard. Jackie was befuddled when she saw Iris standing at a workstation. Iris caught Jackie staring at her and smiled and nodded pleasantly. The ladies, amidst the chatter, got right down to the business. Someone had already given Iris a bowl of potatoes to chop for potato salad. Francis sat nearby with her steno pad. No one seemed to notice her presence. Iris had been Ruth's prep cook for years. She knew her knives, kitchen gadgets, and how to cut up anything. The women took note of her skill in this area and were happy to bring their cutting boards of potatoes, carrots, cabbage, onion, and bell pepper to her for prepping. Francis the Secretary sat her steno pad down long enough to lean toward Iris and ask her softly if she needed help. "Oh, Francis. How sweet of you. But I'm content to have you anchoring me back there, and if you want to tell me a story or two about the sweetness of Sweet Fields, I'd be happy to hear them. Besides, you've done enough already. Whether you know it or not, seeing you smile on Wednesday, did more for me than you could ever know."

Francis the secretary sat straight up and looked at Iris. "Why that's nice of you to say, Sister Murphy. But I can't think of anything I could have done that would make you happy. I'm sure you've recognized, I don't get that much attention around here." Iris did not break the rhythm of her chopping, "Oh but you do, Francis." A grin spread across Iris' face, but she didn't look up. "All it takes is the perfect usher…"

Francis shifted in her seat. She picked up her steno pad and sat it down. "I'm so sorry you had to see that."

"See what?" Iris stopped chopping. "What do you mean, sorry? Francis, there is nothing to be sorry about. I was so happy to see the love between you both. It was so pure. So sweet. It affected me. Gave me some hope. Wait." Iris put her knife down and looked around the counter. She held her hands in the air to keep from getting potato debris all over the place.

Francis the Secretary stood up. "What are you looking for, Sister Murphy? Let me help you."

"My purse. Oh there it is." Iris pointed underneath one of the stainless steel counters nearby. "Could you open it up? There's a little something in there for you. Right there. Right on top. The little lavender bag."

Francis the Secretary looked inside the bag and discovered a small pink and white box tucked inside. The word Chantilly was written in gold across the box's front. "Oh, Sister Murphy, you didn't have to. How'd you know?"

"Grandma Maggs loved Chantilly. I recognized the scent when I came up on Wednesday. When I saw it in the little boutique downtown, I thought of you and picked it up. Read the card."

"To Francis. Thanks for showing me what it looks like to be in love. Iris."

Daughter Eliza looked up just in time to see Francis opening her gift. "Hey! It's not Christmas, ladies! Put those gift bags up. We're cooking up in here."

Mother Carrie chimed in, "I know you're right. You give these young folks one job, and they manage to mess it up."

Deaconess Banks picked up the swell of the verbal sparring, "I told you about these city folks. They don't know how to do nothing but spend money and cut ya. They cut ya so they can spend your money."

Luceal and Laura loved this kind of banter and were chomping at the bit to put in their two cents. "Aw, Sister Banks, you should've been on that cutt'n board, because we all know you know about cutting. We ain't forgot about you cutting up Joe Nelson's tires after the 12th grade dance," Luceal said loudly. "You just stick to peas and pecan pies, twin. You'll be in a bad way soon, cause one gives you gas the other pulls your teeth out. You'll both be in a bad way in a couple hours." Deaconess Banks wasn't done with Luceal. "Anyway, we ALL know very well how you and your sister can cut people off, Sister Ceal. My brother is still bleeding from the love scars Laura left on his poor little heart."

"You going too far now, Sister Banks," Laura said slowly. "You don't bring a woman's tenderness into this." Laura was shaking her head slowly, "you just don't do that. We got new blood in here today."

Mother Carrie spoke up then, "That's what y'all do all the time, twins. Gang up on people. Then when you get your mouth tore out, you wanna go all soft. If you can't run with the big dogs stay your sorry behinds on the porch."

Luceal and Laura slunk into themselves to lick their catty wounds, while the rest of the women in the kitchen cackled at Mother Carrie's way of telling the truth and keeping the laughter going, all at the same time.

Jackie's eyes moved from one speaker to the next, as she listened for a break in conversation so she could insert one of the witty lines she'd been practicing in her studio. She heard that timing was everything when playing the dozens with small town people. Just as the laughter died down and Jackie parted her lips to join the chorus of criticisms and cut downs, the familiar lilt of Maybelline's voice singing out, "Time to eat, ladeeeeez," slipped around the corner. All the women stopped.

"Maybelline!"

"Mable!"

"Lena!"

"Girl, git on in here."

"It's about time somebody thought about bringing our poor hungry souls som'n t'eat."

"Ladies, ladies. I know you're hungry from all of this cooking. I brought you some light refreshments." Maybelline floated in toting a large picnic basket in each hand. She wore a black shimmering T-shirt and a denim jacket, complete with a pair of wide leg black linen pants and black espadrilles.

"Light!" Laura exclaimed, "You never cook anything light.
Bring that basket over here!"

"Naw, Naw," said Mother Carrie slowly, "you take care of the old folks first. We need our nourishment to make it through the evening hours."

Jackie took long strides toward Maybelline, "Let me help you, Sister Crowder."

"I got it," Maybelline said quickly, while deftly swinging the basket away from Jackie Black's outstretched hands. She sat the baskets on the table and set up a buffet line of food that rivaled catering at some of the most elegant parties. There were quiche cups and a cheese tray, southwestern eggrolls and sugar cookies. Francis followed close behind with two crock pots, one with meatballs, and the other with hot spinach dip. Maybelline's baskets had no bottoms as she pulled out lemon bars and chicken wings, mozzarella sticks and tortilla chips, fruit dipped in chocolate, Hawaiian rolls and sliced beef brisket.

The chatter continued as the women found stopping points in their cooking and descended onto the food Maybelline brought.

Sister Berry, the Sunday school teacher, craned her neck looking for Belle Lynne Locke, "Sister Belle, you didn't make any teacakes to add to the spread? You know we've been waiting on them."

The sea of women parted just enough to let Locke glide through proudly carrying a large tin of teacakes. "Here you go ladies. Have at it. And eat slowly. There are no more where these came from. Locke's kitchen is closed until Monday morning!" Francis the Secretary had brewed a strong pot of coffee to pair with Locke's gourmet cakes, and the women ate well.

About an hour into the laughter and cooking, the back door of the fellowship hall opened. The ladies quieted to see who was entering unannounced. Iris leaned to look around Jackie, who was standing near her station. She saw a black ball cap with the Atlanta Falcons logo on the front and her pulse quickened. William was coming through the door carrying a large box of two foil- wrapped turkeys.

"Good evening, ladies," William said smiling and carrying the box effortlessly toward the kitchen. The ladies of all ages appreciated him in his fitted black tee and black jeans. They smiled, giggled, and even catcalled a little. One elderly church mother who was wrapping plastic ware said much too loudly "he sho smells good." To which William replied over his shoulder,
"Mother, I think you smell the turkey."

On his second trip in with another box of turkeys, a blue-haired lady whispered "How fearfully and **wonderfully** made is he!" William shook his head and kept walking.

"Who did you say had snagged this tall drink of water, Jackie?" Luceal could not resist the urge to instigate. She grinned showing her dentures all the way to the gums.

"Well, Ms. Ceal," he answered putting the box down on the counter and turning to face Jackie and Luceal, "Iris has snagged **ME** but I don't know if I have snagged **HER** yet. I'm still working on it," he said with a warm smile. Laughter and chatter filled the room.

William had closed the distance between them quickly and was upon her before she could discreetly swipe her lips with gloss. His heady scent invaded her nose and his long muscular arm wrapped around her shoulders. He tilted his cap back off his forehead so he could whisper in her ear. The sheer closeness of him allowed his well-trimmed beard to brush lightly against her cheek. She could hardly make out what he was saying over the thundering noise her heart was making.

"I'll drive you home when you're ready," he said with his lips dangerously close to her ear. He was doing that low gravelly thing with his voice again. The thing that almost turned her into jelly. She smiled and nodded in agreement but remained without words. She caught Jackie's eye and smiled even bigger. William did not retreat. He, too, looked up to see Jackie staring at them and moved in even closer. "What's wrong? Cat got your tongue?" he laughed quietly holding Jackie's gaze.

The women in the kitchen all let out a swelled, "Woooooooo," in unison as they watched William Hughes, Jr. make a show of speaking with Iris.

"I was planning to ride with Locke." Iris had finally found her words.

"Change your plans. Locke was dropped off by Eddie, and he's coming back to pick her up. So, that leaves me driving you home." His arm squeezed around her shoulders, and he turned to leave.

"Goodnight, ladies!" he called out as he exited the room.

"Lord help us if that ain't a fine man. Wonder why he ain't married yet?" Laura said jerking her head in Iris' direction. Laura was usually the quieter of the two. Her responses were often delayed because she followed Luceal's lead—in everything. Delay or no, Iris had had enough.

"Well," Luceal added, "we all know Sweet Fields men won't have just ANY kind of woman. You have to be from Sweet Fields to know how to woo a man from Sweet Fields." "That's right, sister." Laura was beginning to stretch her verbal prowess a little further, "you don't *know* a Sweet Fields man unless you had the opportunity to *grow* with a Sweet Fields man. Wouldn't want to give anyone false hopes and what not."

"What we do know, Laura, is he doesn't have a brother keeping him from dating." Iris shook her head slowly. "That sibling rivalry is something else, isn't it?" Iris said it sweetly. Sickeningly sweet. The whole of the room quieted. Everyone in Sweet Fields knew Laura had been engaged to Mr. Bennett Banks, but her dear sister Luceal, who was said never to have had a suitor, convinced her sister not to marry Bennett. Laura looked a bit sad, but her sister Luceal went to her side to comfort her. The twins were quiet for the remainder of the evening, working on their pies with their friends from the sewing circle. Iris glanced at Locke who gave a proud nod of approval.

Daughter Liza hunched Mother Carrie, "It looks like the new blood ain't so new after all. Heh. Heh. Heh."

Iris went on chopping vegetables. Something about Iris' retort garnered the approval of most of the women of St. Andrew. She was holding her own in the ring of women, and Francis had slipped her a bottle of water, as if to quench her thirst from the verbal sparring. She remained perched on the edge of her chair with her steno pad, in silent support. After several minutes of jovial conversation and peals of laughter, Jackie returned to stand in front of Iris' worktable. The ladies in the immediate area fell silent in anticipation of the next exchange.

"Congratulations on you and William," Jackie proclaimed loudly. "I wouldn't have pegged you as one who would pursue a blue collar worker like him," she snickered. That snicker was the last straw. Iris sighed pleasantly.

"Come now, Jackie. Not every woman is hung up on collars. It isn't the man's collar that's important. Besides, at least the man I'm interested in acknowledges and respects my existence." Iris smiled brilliantly. She held out the knife she had been using like it was a magic wand and lightly tapped at the air around Jackie Black's shoulder.

Francis scribbled in her steno pad.

Locke moaned low in her throat.

Deaconess Banks let out a labored, "Unh."

The sassy blue-haired lady said, "Well, bless His name!" Jackie, though, was speechless.

"Oh, Jackie, could you bring me one of those turkeys?" Jackie waved the knife toward the turkeys. "I'm ready to cut some meat." Iris carefully laid down the wide-bladed chef's knife she had been using to cut up potatoes and was reaching for her carving knife.

"She said she's ready to cut some MEAT!" Mother Carrie said from her corner of the room.

"Mother," Daughter Eliza warned softly.

"Sound like she's already cut somebody's meat. Heh. Heh.

"Mother."

"I bet that new gal won't come racking 'round here with NO more foolishness. Hmph. Ready to CUT some meat."

"Mother! Stop it!"

"What? Don't *mother* me," Mother Carrie said teasingly. "The sister said she wanted to cut some meat." Mother Carrie paused. She blinked. "'Liza have I had my walk today?" Mother Carried peered out the window into the darkness. "I meant to take my walk before it got too dark," she whined.

"Yes, Mother. You had your walk at lunch." Mother Carrie had lapsed back into the haze of dementia that quickly. As always, she asked Liza if she'd had her midday walk, and of course, she had.

Jackie moved near Mother Carrie and one of the turkeys William Hughes, Jr. had brought in. She reached to pat Mother Carrie's hand; Jackie usually found some semblance of solace with Mother Carrie when she was not so lucid. Iris' words had stung, and Jackie needed a soft place to land after the stabbing. Jackie was not prepared for such venom from Iris. As she lugged the turkey over to her, Jackie thought: *How dare that little debutante embarrass me? What does she know about who I am interested in? Does Iris know I love Prentiss LeBeaux?* Francis was writing in her notepad. *What is she writing? Had Francis told Iris about her visits and gifts to Pastor Prentiss? Why are those two so chummy all of a sudden?*

Iris committed to her task of slicing the turkeys. Methodically she sliced and Jackie watched the knife ease through the meat as she imagined all of the women in the kitchen whispering about her unrequited love for Pastor Prentiss LeBeaux. Every time she looked around the room, she swore the ladies were talking about her. For the rest of the night, Jackie's mind continued to play tricks on her. She was unable to enjoy the wit and intelligence of the one-line wisdoms of the women, because she had become so consumed with her own misperceptions.

The women in the kitchen took note of Jackie's introversion, attributing most of her quietness to the verbal lashing Iris served her. Some even thought, Jackie may have had unrequited love for William Hughes, Jr. Who could blame her? But very few knew of her pining for Pastor Prentiss LeBeaux. In this, Jackie Black was mistaken, to think all the women had their minds set on her love for a man who deplored her existence more and more each day.

Finally, macaroni, baked beans, potato salad, yams, and an assortment of cakes, pies, and cookies were all prepared, covered and stored in the fridge. Ladies were washing dishes, wiping down tables, and sweeping the floors. Iris had cleaned her area. Her hand was on the doorknob when the door opened from the outside. Standing on the other side was Clemson Callahan, Melvin Collier, William Hughes, Charles Edwards and his father, Eddie, with Big Hughes bringing up the rear.

"Well, hello, gentlemen!" Iris said as the men stood aside to let her exit building. All of them lined up at the door made her self-conscious, so much so that she had the urge to run. Not one of the men said anything untoward to her, but knowing there had likely been some conversations about her whilst they stood around tending their grills made her uncomfortable. William called for her, as she speed-walked across the parking lot.

"Iris! Wait up." She stopped in her tracks and he caught up to her quickly. "Did you see me standing out there waiting for you? I thought I was driving you home?"

"Yes. Yes I saw you. But I guess I got so worked up from the conversations on the inside and then the sudden parade of men on the outside, I had a hard time grounding myself. Please, don't take offense. Anyway, it's such a nice night, I thought I'd walk."

"But that's not what we agreed on, Iris Murphy." He said in that low voice that she liked.

"I'm not sure what we agreed on in there. You walked into that kitchen and drove every woman in the room insane with lust. Even my thoughts were clouded by all the testosterone you were throwing around." She threw her head back just a little and laughed.

William studied Iris' mannerism. Yes, she'd opened up just a little since she'd been in Sweet Fields, and he wanted to take credit for that, but he didn't want to push her too hard or take her too fast and send her right back into her shell. I'll walk you home, then." He said. They crossed the avenue and cut through the park. They talked about the food and the arguments over recipes. Big Hughes and another deacon had words about when to season the ribs. Clem and Deacon Caldwell had engaged in a passionate discussion about deep frying turkeys.

Iris told him how Mother Carrie ate a slice of Luceal's pecan pie and then swore to high heaven that she didn't. Then to further incense Luceal, a few of the ladies passed the pie around for all to sample—since it had already been cut. Luceal and Laura had been criticizing everyone else's recipe, so the ladies who ate the forbidden pie shared their own criticisms, driving the irritating twins mad with frustration. William laughed at her stories and she laughed at his. As they climbed the porch steps, Iris sensed a change in the air between them.

"Iris, I meant what I said in the church kitchen. I wasn't just saying that for the audience."

"I know. Just keep working on it, Deacon Hughes." She smiled and stepped inside her screen door.

"We're not back at that, are we?" he laughed nervously.

"No, William. We aren't back at that. Thanks for walking me home. I'll see you tomorrow."

"Goodnight, Iris." He sauntered down the steps knowing she was still watching him. And watch him, she did. She liked the look of his bowed legs as he crossed the street and waved at the flickering blinds of Mr. Bennett Banks' window. He shoved his hands in his pockets and Iris watched him as he strolled along until he was out of sight.

CHAPTER 14: SATURDAY

Pendleton Park was just as gloriously colorful in late August as it was in June. The tents were up. Chafing dishes were aflame. Children were already running around with Frisbees and balls. Picnic benches and tables were grouped together for cozy dining. Throngs of people were parking at the church and walking across the street to the park. Iris arrived and spotted Eddie and Locke sitting on a bench under a tree. As she started towards them, she spotted William walking with his father. It was strange seeing the Hughes men side by side, as they looked so much alike. William seemed to be just an inch or two taller than his father, but much thinner. Big Hughes was outfitted in white linen complete with a white fedora, while William wore jeans and a white Lacoste V-neck tee and black Lacoste sneakers.

William saw Iris right away and the sight of her bare legs tempted him to run to her for a closer look, but he restrained himself and continued to walk casually across the park. Iris wore a knee-length green and gold African print sundress and gold sandals. She arrived at Locke and Eddie's bench before William could intercept her path.

"Iris? Is that you?" Locke said peeping over her sunglasses.

"Locke, stop it."

"Stop what? I've never seen so much of your legs before, and you know William is gonna stutter and stammer all over himself. Here he comes now." Locke said grinning from ear to ear.

Iris ignored her and turned her attentions to Eddie.

"Hi, Eddie. How are you?" Iris said exaggerating her shift in attention. Eddie looked like a character she had helped Lloyd create once. He wore khaki golf shorts, light blue University of North Carolina polo shirt with matching hat. The sunglasses he wore were dark and silver-rimmed--the kind secret service agents wore; they gave him a slightly menacing look.

"I'm great, Iris. Don't let Belle tease you too much. You look great," Eddie said looking past Iris and putting his arm around Locke's shoulders.

"Hello, Iris," William said touching her back lightly. "Ms. Belle" William said nodding in her direction. "Eddie, how are you?" he said shaking Eddie's hand.

"Well, I just came over to say hello. You two carry on," Iris said with a wink at the couple before she turned and walked away with William.

"You look beautiful, Iris. Green really is your color." William said stepping back to look at her again.

"Thank you. You look refreshingly casual yourself."

"Thanks, Iris." William turned his gaze toward Locke and Eddie. "It's good to see Ms. Belle with someone. He's crazy about her."

"How do you know?"

"Did you see how he put his arm around her when I walked up? He was marking his territory. I wanted to do the same thing. Especially when I heard him compliment you."

"Hush, William. Just hush." She laughed and tried to speed up.

"Walking fast won't help you," he said laughing while keeping up with her easily. "You'll have to face it one of these days."

"William, the only thing I'm ready to face is a plate of food. I skipped breakfast for this picnic, and I'm starving." To see Iris uncomfortable made him laugh, so he knew he'd have to do it more often. The couple entered the food tent smiling and greeting the members of the church as they went.

Officer Michael Martinez signed up to patrol the annual picnic. His parents, Hector and Olga, attended St. Andrew regularly. Michael was on duty on most weekends, so he rarely attended Sunday services. He parked his patrol car and stepped out into the festive atmosphere. His hot-weather uniform of knee-length pants and short-sleeved shirt showed off this tanned muscles. He walked across the expanse of the park, smiling and speaking to those he recognized. Michael walked toward the tent where Pastor LeBeaux sat chatting. When he arrived,

Prentiss jumped up in great joy and hugged him tightly. The two men were engaged in lively conversation when Jackie interrupted.

"Pastor, can I fix a plate for you?" she asked running her hand over his shoulder. He flinched and then smiled.

"Thank you, Sister Black, but Sister Maybelline is making my plate." He nodded politely and returned to his conversation with Officer Martinez. Officer Martinez saw the hurt in Jackie's face. Prentiss did not.

"They make a beautiful couple, don't they, Eliza?" Mother Stewart said pointing her fork at William and Iris. Eliza nodded and smiled.

"Yes, Mother, they do. They remind me of Big Hughes and me when I was a girl. He looks so much like his father. Those Hughes men are some good-looking menfolk. They'll make some beautiful babies," Eliza said nodding all the while.

Iris heaped her plate with barbecue and savory sides and chatted with Maybelline who was in front of her. William had gotten side-tracked by a conversation with a deacon who was trying to round up some card players. Iris exited the food tent and sat at a table with Francis, who looked cool and relaxed though she still wore her signature color, brown.

Francis, too, was showing more leg than the members of St. Andrew were accustomed to seeing, but the brown of her legs all but blended right into her brown dress with off-white polka dots. The button-down shirt-waist dress was sleeveless and made of stretch cotton that complimented her slim frame. Her waist was cinched with a simple sash that she'd tied into a knot right at her navel. Small brown wooden buttons stopped beneath the sash, and the remainder of the dress flared and stopped at the knee. Francis inherited her pair of toned calves from her mother's side of the family; therefore not much effort was needed in making them appear attractive. On her feet Francis the Secretary had abandoned the 2-inch heeled brown oxfords for a simple pair of closed toe brown espadrilles that tied at her ankle. She also wore Chantilly, the perfume that Melvin Collier loved so much.

Melvin Collier had been directing the traffic of the picnic and returned to find Francis sitting on a bench beside a plate covered in Saran Wrap. Dutifully, she fanned the flies away and exchanged a few words with Iris Murphy. Melvin Collier watched as Francis interrupted her fanning to lift her wrist to Iris' nose. Both the women smiled and continued their conversation. Francis stood as Melvin approached. She beckoned Melvin over to the table. They greeted each other shyly, Melvin cupping both of her dainty elbows with his large hands and leaning in to kiss her on the cheek.

"Sister Murphy," Melvin greeted Iris.

"Hi, Brother Melvin. I'm afraid I've taken your seat.
Come on and sit down. I'm going on over to the dessert table."

"You're fine. I'll just sit on the other side." Melvin sat down and slid the wrapped plate toward him, "For me?" he teased.
"I sure do appreciate you looking out for me."

Francis the Secretary looked up at Melvin, "It was no problem, Brother Collier."

Iris, feeling like an intruder, left the couple and caught up to William.

Jackie, frustrated that Maybelline was in line, fixing a plate for Prentiss, wandered to the tent where Rev. Edwards was deejaying.

"Reverend, is there anything I can do to help you? Have you eaten?"

"Oh no. I got this." he laughed. "I used to deejay in college, and Karen is getting a plate for me. Go enjoy yourself,
Sister Black."

"Do you mind playing a few songs from this?" Jackie held out a copy of one of the CDs she made for Prentiss. Rev. Edwards looked at the CD with its handwritten cover and then looked into Jackie's bulbous eyes.

"I already have a playlist approved by the pastor. You know we have to walk circumspectly in this regard, Sister Black," he said with a gentle smile.

"I see," was all Jackie said before she snatched her CD back. She spun on her low-heeled royal blue mules that matched her polyester jumpsuit and sauntered away. As she walked through the groups of picnicking parishioners, her gait changed to one reminiscent of runway models. Her vintage-styled jumpsuit billowed about her thighs. Trails of blue polyester anchored around her waist floated around her as she walked. Her back was completely exposed, while her less than ample bosom was completely covered by gathered fabric at the front. The only jewelry she wore were enormous brass Fulani hoop earrings which battled for attention with her massive bun of twists set atop her head. She heard their whispers about her backless jumpsuit. *Of course they love the jumpsuit. It was vintage Halston after all,* Jackie thought.

Jackie continued her proud stride until she reached the edge of the picnic area. She sat down on a bench underneath an oak tree. She heaved a sigh of disappointment. Nothing had gone the way she had planned. She hadn't been able to sit with Prentiss. Maybelline had prepared his plate instead of her. Rev. Edwards refused to play her CD. And now, instead of socializing with Prentiss and his inner circle, she was again on the fringes. On the outside looking in. There she sat. Observing. At some point, Jackie realized that she was the only person who was alone. Everyone at the St. Andrew Annual picnic had a close friend or spouse.

Everyone except her.

"Whatcha doin over here by yourself?" Jackie heard a voice say from above her head. It was Mother Carrie Stewart.

"I'm just watching, Mother Stewart. Checking out the festivities."

"Well, that's what you shoulda been doing when you got here a long time ago. Watching. 'Stead of flitting around here getting into all kinds of devilment. Scoot over and let me sit down." Mother Carrie had on khaki walking shorts and a short sleeved denim shirt with sunflowers embroidered on the collar and sleeves. Her hands were a map of veins, and she kept her nails neatly trimmed. Mother Carrie liked pearls, and she bought herself the biggest pearl ring she could find on this side of Sweet Fields. She wore the ring every day. On her feet she wore a pair of cognac colored Munros, her favorite brand of shoes for walking. That, Mother Carrie never forgot. She kept her steel gray hair cropped close, even though she insisted on combing it through with a wide tooth comb. All she needed was a soft brush and a spray of water to keep it neat and tidy. Her skin was the color of fresh baked pecan pie, and she often smelled sweet, like Karo syrup. "I can't stand up as long as I usedta. Now, let's talk about your goings and doings."

Mother Stewart's words offended Jackie, but she was too surprised by their forwardness to react. "Mother Stewart, whatever do you mean?"

"You know what I mean. Don't take that innocent tone with me. You've spent all your time here in Sweet Fields trying to fit in and done ended up way out here on the outside. It doesn't work like that in Sweet Fields. You need to give yourself some time to get to know these people; get to know their ways. Don't dive in too fast around here, 'lessen you'll drown yourself."

"I've done everything I thought I could to fit in, to help build the kingdom, and still people treat me as if I don't exist. I don't know what else to do."

"I just told you! Weren't you listening to anything I said? That's your problem now. You do more busy-work than listening. Get somewhere and sit down, and stop trying to fool yourself like you're so good and perfect. Ain't nobody perfect. No, not one. Just sweet baby Jesus, our elder brother, and the great God our Father. Somebody ought to take a stick to ya." Mother Stewart stood up and turned around slowly to face Jackie. "And keep them eyes off your pastor. The way you're doing, ain't no good gon come of it. Now I'm gone. I advise you to get on up and be around some people, before your mind get to wandering and coming up with some stupid tricks. Being alone too long ain't good for a body, especially one like yours."

But Jackie didn't move. She kept watching. Watching and praying that she could shake the loneliness she felt. Even Laura and Luceal, as annoying as they were, had each other to laugh and talk with. They were sitting under the seniors' tent laughing with the rest of the deaconesses. Maybelline and Sister Katie Caldwell had been best friends since grade school and lived across the street from each other.

They sat at a table with Deacon Ernest Caldwell and two other church members laughing and playing bingo. Karen Edwards and Judith Callahan were an unlikely pair of friends. Judith's children were all grown and away; Karen was young and seemed to enjoy the older woman's guidance and friendship. They sat with their husbands near the music tent laughing at their men trying to do old dances.

Jackie almost laughed in spite of herself when she saw Big Hughes clap Clem on the back so hard that he nearly fell over. She knew how close those two men were; if Clem wasn't with Judith, he was with Big Hughes. When Clem, Judith, Karen and Rev. Edwards started dancing, Big Hughes slipped off to go sit with Mother Carrie Stewart and Eliza. He hugged Mother Stewart and then took Eliza by the hand and walked toward the fountain in the middle of the park.

Jackie continued to scan the attendees and noticed Iris, William, Locke, and Eddie sitting at a picnic table toasting their red SOLO cups and breaking into laughter. William put his long arm around Iris' shoulders and squeezed, while Eddie grabbed Locke's free hand and held on. Locke leaned back slightly into the space of Eddie's arm. She crossed her legs, and her burnt orange linen trapeze shift slipped slightly above her knee. Eddie whispered into Locke's ear. Locke turned to Eddie severely and pulled the hem of her dress up a little further. They both looked at each other and laughed.

Jackie returned her gaze to Prentiss and was shocked to see him making his way over to Maybelline, who looked relaxed and happy as she sat and talked with the Caldwells. She really was pretty. Jackie had to admit that. The short gold and white linen sundress she wore showed off Maybelline's full hourglass figure and revealed a pair of thick muscular calves. And that hair. Jackie had stared and stared at Maybelline's scalp Sunday after Sunday, trying to find the culprit in the form of a lace front, net, weft, or crocheted braid. Nothing. Maybelline's hair was all Maybelline's, and Jackie watched Pastor LeBeaux bend down over her thick mane to say hello. There was something in the way he closed his eyes as his face got closer. *No.* Jackie thought. *Not Massive Maybelline. Anyway, she's out of the country and out of my sights by Monday.* Jackie took her negative thoughts about

Maybelline into captivity. Then she saw Prentiss LeBeaux stand straight up, throw his head back, slap his leg, and laugh loudly at something Maybelline said. Maybelline stood up, too. Her dress circled around the backs of her knees as she slowly rose to walk with Pastor LeBeaux. Their laughter continued as they strolled along.

Jackie wanted to go to him and demand that he stop laughing. As she stood, the ladies of the Health and Fitness Ministry gathered in an open space. The music changed and young people rushed to join the group. Latin music blared and bodies began moving. Brenda Caldwell, the leader of the ministry and sister-in-law to florist Sister Katie Caldwell, ran to Prentiss and grabbed his hands to pull him into the designated dance space. Prentiss laughed and resisted at first but eventually allowed the curvy Zumba instructor in fitted shorts and tank top to pull him away from Maybelline. Though she was glad Prentiss was no longer sharing laughs with Maybelline, she was furious that Prentiss was doing Zumba. *And with the likes of Brenda Caldwell and her group of scantily clad strumpets,* she thought.

Arms were above heads waving while hips were rocking to and fro. Onlookers were doubled over in laughter. The older picnickers were clapping along with the music. Hector and Olga Martinez stole the show when they started dancing the Salsa.

When Olga broke away from Hector and started trying to teach Prentiss basic Salsa steps, Jackie wanted to scream. *Everyone but me. He's paying attention to everyone but me.* She kept repeating the words to herself. She wanted all of these women to stay away from him. When the impromptu Zumba session turned into Salsa lessons and Prentiss and Iris got partnered up while Maybelline and William looked on, Jackie could no longer restrain herself. She stood up and started her walk back into the action of the picnic, but by the time she got close, the crowd had dispersed and returned to the food tent for seconds. She grabbed a cup of lemonade and walked to her car unnoticed.

She sat behind the wheel of her Thunderbird and looked towards the picnic. People were still arriving and games--egg toss, three-legged race, and hula hooping-- had begun. Prentiss had joined the deacons in a game of horseshoes. Jackie watched him. Studied him.

She didn't see why they couldn't be happy together. He loved St. Andrew and so did she. If he wanted children, she could still give him at least one. She could make him happy. She watched as Prentiss and the deacons posed for a group picture. She noticed how Clem hovered around him and Rev. Edwards. Clem was the chairman of the deacon board and one of the most influential members in the church. He was on the advisory board, and so were William Hughes, Belle Locke, Rev. Charles and Karen Edwards. Iris Murphy might have replaced her grandmother on the board for all she knew. "What if the advisory board was advising him on his personal life? What if they had told him to stay away from me?' Jackie wondered out loud. Prentiss needed younger people and new perspectives around him.

"I have to get rid of this advisory board and keep those Zumba strumpets away from him. Prentiss is so nice and kind that he can't see me for them. I haven't asked for much. I haven't been given much either, but I haven't complained. I am so tired of being looked over. All I want is for Prentiss to notice me and realize how much I can help him. God, why would you send me here when he won't even talk to me?" a single tear rolled down her cheek. "I know! You are teaching me perseverance and humility. If I am to be the wife to a leader, I must learn how to be one of the people. I must blend in and become like those he leads. I must earn their trust and respect," she paused a long moment. "I receive it. Amen."

Jackie sat in her car that was parked across the street from the park and continued to watch the festive picnic. She sighed with relief as the plan came together in her head.

CHAPTER 15: SUNDAY

William Hughes, Jr. knew he'd have the run of the conversation in the deacon's den, so he arrived earlier than his normal early. He turned his narrative about his relationship with Iris over and over in his head. He imagined every theory that old Clem would try to poke in and came up with ready answers for the teasing he would probably get. Seated in one of the wingback chairs in the den, William also thought of the truth of the matter, the truth that he and Iris's relationship may be slightly imbalanced. The weight of his heart for her was so heavy that he could feel himself falling hard and fast, while in his mind Iris seemed to float slowly in the air around him, neither fully confirming nor denying the validity of their relationship.

"Aaaaah, I know what you're in here doing, chief." Clemson Callahan's voice boomed as he entered the men's private sanctum. "In here thinking about that pretty woolly-head woman, huh? Yeah, I know how that feels. I remember when I first knew
I had it bad for my Judith…"

"Come on, Clem," William said gingerly, "why does everything have to center around you and your Judith. More people in the world fall in love than you and your precious…" "Fall in love?" Clemson Callahan stopped short and looked around the room, as if to see if anyone else was listening. "Shhhh! Man, what you talking about falling in love? See this is what happens with you Hughes men. You fall in love when a woman looks at you longer than a millisecond. Get a hold of yourself. Sister Murphy just biding time until the man she really wants comes her way."

Slowly, the other deacons filtered into the room, claiming their seats, readying themselves for the word match Clem and William Hughes, Jr. were about to have. William Hughes, Sr. was also present for the show.

"Look, let me tell you something. The woman fed me from her own table. Now if that ain't something, I don't know what is,"

William said stroking a large hand over his trimmed beard. He shifted in the high-backed chair and placed his right ankle atop his left knee.

"William, William," Clemson said shaking his head slowly, "look at you, son. You're thin as a rail. I'd feed you too if I saw you walking down the street. You look like you haven't eaten in months. You and Big Hughes ain't got no woman in the house. Anybody'd feel sorry for that. In love? Man, please…"

From the corner of the room, one of the younger deacons quipped, "You don't hear him stut-stut-stuttering, Clem. Must be something to it." The room exploded in laughter.

"Ahhh. You're right brother, my words come out like liquid gold, and anytime a woman can cure a stutter, there is something to it. Nightly phone calls can fix a lot of things."

"I talk to your daddy every day. It doesn't mean I'm in love with the brother." Clemson turned to Big Hughes. "Aint that right, Big?"

"Yeah, you right, Doc."

"Okay, okay. So y'all were all at the picnic, right? She couldn't keep her hands off me. She was on me like white on rice, right by my side no matter where I went."

"Are you sure you weren't on her like white on rice after she slipped by you on Friday night?" chimed in Deacon Caldwell, "She ran from you like you were the plague the night before the picnic. She saw you standing outside that door and ran from you like you had bird flu! Now, we all saw that."

William had forgotten about that part. He hadn't formulated a comeback, mainly because he didn't fully understand Iris's reaction himself. "I am an awesome wonder to behold." William Hughes, Jr responded. He ran his hands over his soft waves. "And I had already overwhelmed her earlier that night whispering sweet nothings in her ear in front of the women.

Shoot. It's hard for me to stay in my own presence."

"What about Rick Carson?"

William wasn't sure who'd said it, but he noticed the hush that came over the room. "What about him?"

Clemson answered. "Didn't they have dinner Tuesday night, down there at the steak house? I heard he was coming to church today to confess his love for her."

"You don't say?" William replied. "Well, if I'm not mistaken he received a rude Godspeed on both cheeks from someone right here in Sweet Fields. I'm sure he won't be coming back after that."

"Maybe he will. Maybe he won't. But he is one to watch. I never liked him anyway. He's always been a puffed up no-count. I don't know how Belle Lynne Locke can stand him." Clemson shook his head at his own words.

"Speaking of the Duchess of Sweet Fields," Big Hughes said, changing the subject. He could see his son's chest heaving slowly, and knew the signs of when William was feeling a pounding rising up in him. "Belle Lynne was mighty frisky yesterday. She hitched that dress up while she was sitting under Rev's daddy. Know she's too old for that mess. Just fast. No shame at all."

"I don't have much to say about Belle Lynne Locke. She's good people when she wants to be, besides, she has ears everywhere. By the time church starts, she will have gotten wind of this entire conversation. It's almost like she's bugged all of Sweet Fields. I'll ponder my thoughts about her and her little fast self in my head. That's the best place for them. Otherwise, she'll get a hold to every word we've said about her and make us eat 'em."

"It's almost time to go in, fellas," Clemson said looking at his watch. "We don't want to walk in service late, especially after we cut up at the picnic. The mothers'll never let us live it down." William Hughes, Jr. got up slowly. The conversation had taken a turn that had shifted his heart far from worship service. He didn't know what he would do if Rick Carson showed up at church. His temper was never one he could keep in check. The Lord was still dealing with him on that, and it had been a while since William had had an opportunity to test out what the Lord was doing with him in that area.

The men walked into St. Andrew through the side door as was the tradition for the deacons. Clemson, however, was the first to notice an uncomfortable buzz about the church. As he walked in leading the pack, he turned his head toward William Hughes, Jr., who walked behind him. Clem whispered, "What's going on?" William too was curious about the chatter, "I don't know, man. But something has definitely stirred the waters between now and yesterday."

Everyone seated had their mobile phones out. Out and on. Melvin Collier did his best to personally approach each culprit diplomatically and ask her quietly to turn off her phone and put it away, but he was unable to keep up with the chimes and dings that filled the sanctuary. Lights flashed from the little devices signifying received text messages, and poor Melvin Collier's exasperation prompted him to beckon for Francis the Secretary to ascertain whether or not she had a clue as to what was happening.

She did not.

William Hughes, Sr. was not so surprised. He'd watched the workings of the picnic and knew that some of the festivities left a wide berth for misconception, and that sooner or later, those very misconceptions would be brought to the forefront, but by whom was the question.

NOVELLA III: SECRETS AND OLD PEOPLE

CHAPTER 16: THE TEXT MESSAGE

It wasn't until Locke situated herself in the pew after much gathering, sanitizing, and dusting, that she felt the jagged splitting of air in the church. The atmosphere was rigid, and the congregation, though sitting stiff and sanctimonious in their spots, was unstable. Jackie Black was not in her seat, half blocking Locke's view like she normally would. Locke was glad, at first. She felt her spirits lift at the thought of not having to abide Jackie's body oil, a putrid mixture of lemon grass and Johnson's Floor Wax. Locke once told Jackie Black that she should consider something more holistic, and that the oil she used had a sweltering scent. Locke told Jackie that to smell her made her tired. Jackie Black had not listened and continued to walk around during the late fall smelling of rotten summer.

Jackie's attempts to bully her way into the sleepy culture of St. Andrew had not gone unnoticed. Yes, there was disparity in thought among the congregants about Jackie's true intent. Some of the parishioners had even decided that her missteps were fueled by a desire for one of the eligible bachelors at St. Andrew. Which bachelor, was still in question. Jackie had not quite revealed her heart's intent at the church picnic. The St. Andrew church picnic was known for uncovering the secret desires of its parishioners' hearts. Oddly enough, Jackie made herself visible just long enough to showcase her open-backed, low-cut, fitted blue polyester jumpsuit. She walked, in an awkward runway gait, the length of Pendleton Park and was only seen once since, talking with Mother Carrie.

Jackie Black, since that time, had been quiet. Too quiet.
This left Locke unsettled. Locke knew that when a person like Jackie Black became too quiet, too still, for too long, she was probably planning something. Locke just didn't know the plan. At least if Locke could see Jackie Black's face, or even smell the horrible odor of her body oil, she could begin to discern something, anything.

Because Jackie had assigned herself as St. Andrew's new minister of music, she was usually early for church. This Sunday, Rev. Charles Edward, Jr., St. Andrew's new associate minister, was at the piano and doing well in tuning up for a lively morning service. Locke surmised that Jackie would sashay in wearing one of her monochromatic matchy-matchy outfits--combinations of pants, skirts, opaques, shoes, and blouses that made her look like a walking crayon. Locke envisioned the name of the color, **CHARTREUSE** (or whatever the hue of the day), written sideways in bold and capitalized Arial font, up and along the long length of Jackie's body. If the outfit was new, Jackie Black would be fashionably late. But new gigs for Jackie didn't make sense either. *Black's School of Interpretive Dance and Holy Heavenly Bodies* was not doing so well. This was in part due to how Jackie's kingdom work had offended some workers in the kingdom. Word traveled fast in Sweet Fields that the new dance teacher and member of St. Andrew had a take-over spirit. So the number of children in Jackie's dance classes continued to dwindle. Her enrollment had dropped by half. No dancers. No tuition. No money. No walking crayon.

Adding it all up, Locke knew that Black had done something. And it involved the flashing, vibrating, dinging, chiming phones of the women in the church. Anxious whispers and gesticulations replaced the bright Sunday morning chatter of women speaking two octaves too high and the low rumble of the deacons defending a loss from the week's sports events. Eyes were shifty and attentions were distracted to cell phone screens. The phones were visible. Everyone had them out, and the owners in no way tried to make their use of them discreet. Especially the women. Periodically, little round flashes of blue interrupted Locke's sight line. She did not like phones out in the sanctuary; she considered it sacrilegious. A blatant disrespect of the edifice of God. Nobody seemed to care today, and so she knew she must engage.

"I didn't get one," she heard Sister Washington, the church nurse say. Her nurse's hat was askew in Locke's periphery—it annoyed her, and when Locke turned completely around to take in the whole of

Sister Washington's face, she noticed the door to the nurse's station was completely ajar. Locke would have gotten up from her seat to comment on the sloppiness of a door agape, except Sister Washington's mouth was a line, and her heart-shaped caramel face was slack. The contradiction of her expression puzzled Locke. Sister Washington, a short woman who took short steps, palmed her Samsung Note with her tiny hands, and she too glared at the gray glossy screen. She tugged at a tiny pearl earring in her left ear. Locke registered disappointment in her face. Slowly, Nurse Washington slipped her phone into the pocket of her crisp white nurse's uniform, straightened her cap, walked briskly to the church's nurse's station, slamming the door shut.

"That's better," Locke said as she tugged at her lace gloves, removed them, matched up the fingertips, and placed them neatly in her lap. After sanitizing with the small vial of custom made organic spray attached to a silver chain around her neck, Locke reached into her purse and pulled out her phone. She still considered them ridiculous little devices, but understood they were necessary, as they were the bearers of the news she needed to keep her money, her home and the church in check. They kept her privy to matters which, though they seemed trifles, could negatively affect the progress of her dear, Sweet Fields. Now, Locke checked her own text messages. Nothing. She turned her phone this way and that, finally locating the message flash. There she stared, waiting for her notification.

She looked for Iris, and after discovering she'd not yet arrived, texted in short bursts. One after the other.

"Where are you?
Church begins in 5 minutes.
You are not in your seat.
Phones are out.
Jackie Black is not."

At that moment, the choir members took their positions in the loft. Locke could see that almost every other member tried to conceal her phone by tucking it into the bulbous red sleeves of her cream choir robe. Once in position and seated, the ladies began staring at their screens, dipping their heads behind the ornate, shining cherry wood ministers chairs in the pulpit, to whisper and hold their mouths agape at whatever they beheld.

Iris bent down close to Locke's ear and whispered, "Did you get one?"

"One what?" Locke snapped without turning her head to look at Iris.

"A text!" Iris's whisper sounded just as annoyed. She stood over Locke for several seconds, waiting to sit down. "Let me sit."

"I will not! Go sit where you usually sit. I just sanitized. I can't move now." Iris moved up one pew ahead of Locke and rustled around a little before finally smoothing down her pencil skirt and perching with perfect posture onto the pew. She tussled the hair at the back of her neck and looked left and right before retrieving her phone. Iris then looked toward the vestibule door and squinted. "Where's Jackie Black?"

"Not here. But she's done something."

"Yes, Locke. She has." At that, Iris faced the pulpit and held the face of her phone behind her and toward Locke. Locke could not see Iris' face, but the stiffness of her neck told the story. Iris was angry. Her shoulders were rigid and squared, and her fingers gripped the phone in that way that made one's knuckles whiten. Iris assessed the pre-worship goings-on in the pews, as the deacon board filed in from the side door. Iris noticed the chairman of the deacon board, Clem Callahan whispering to his co-chair, William, a man who was after Iris' heart, literally. But there was no time to think about that, as the text message was a matter of urgency. All the while she observed, Iris held up the phone for Locke to read. She continued to read the faces and movements of the congregation. Her head moved slowly as she scanned the church, so slow that if one were to look away from her and then look back, one would think she'd not moved her head at all.

"I can't see," Locke said as she barely leaned forward to read the message. In a huff, Locke put on her right glove and took the phone from Iris.

Dear Ladies,

I bless God for you, because you are the source of my refinement. Your behaviors and attitudes have done so much in preparing me for what is to be an event as glorious as the coming of Christ to meet His unspotted and unwrinkled bride, the church. You will be part of the ceremony, but not in the way you desire. As God made His Son perfect for His time here on this earth, so has the Matchless Lamb fashioned me as the perfect rib for the angel of this house, Pastor LeBeaux. I tell you this only because I don't want you wasting any more of your time pining away for a relationship that will never be. You are not Pastor LeBeaux's Good Thing. That Good Thing would be me, Jackie Black. Direct your flirtations and ridiculous clumsy attempts at a love connection elsewhere.

Your future, your first, Lady Jackie Black

Iris pulled her phone away, right at the moment Locke finished the last three words. As Rev. Edwards struck the chords commencing worship service, Locke sat back into her pew and firmly exclaimed, "The nerve of that atrocious woman!"

The uncertain bursts of wind characteristic of early fall swept through the church as Jackie Black entered. This time,
Locke envisioned the words **PUTRID PUMPKIN** up and along the side of Jackie Black's clothes. She wore a hat with a pointed peak and wide brim. The brim was *broke down*, as Locke's mother would say when a woman maneuvered the brim of her hat to cover one eye. Locke had a hard time deciding whether the hat made Jackie look more like a witch or a crayon.

The blue light on Iris's phone flashed. It was Locke.

She must be stopped, Iris.

Iris flashed back. *Indeed.*

Worship continued; however, Iris and Locke's minds remained divided between the sweet spirit of the service and the evil aura surrounding Jackie Black. One small solace was that the tone of worship changed for the better with Jackie off the keys. Like Maybelline, Rev. Edwards, Jr. was an accomplished organist and pianist, though his training was not formal or classical. His approach to playing was soulful and rich. He played by ear and embellished what he'd heard and mastered with his unique arrangements. The music was refreshing. Karen Edwards was proud. The unified voices of the choir blended perfectly. Had it not been for the awful cryptic text message sent by Jackie Black, the Sunday could not have been more perfect.

Rev. Edwards was happy to be playing for St. Andrew. His zeal for sharing the gospel through teaching and preaching was just as vibrant as his love of music and song. So, while Jackie's decision to yield the keys to Rev. Edwards was a surprise, it was a relief as well. Jackie had surrendered her post as the festivities of the fall church picnic were coming to a close.

"Pastor Edwards," Jackie said as she smoothed the blue polyester of her jumpsuit over her slim hips, "the word tells me that if I ask something in Jesus' name, I SHALL receive. So in the name of Jesus, I'd like to ask something of you."

"Well, Sister Black, if it's in God's will, I'll try to oblige your inquiry. What is it that you need?"

"I need a break from the post of minister of music." Jackie shook her head back, causing the long Senegalese twists to wiggle around her face. "God has been dealing with me regarding my place in His kingdom work. I have to lose some things in my life, so I can hear from God and receive the greater things He has for me."

"Oooookay," Rev. Charles Edward, Jr. said. He shifted his weight onto the long table that held his computer, speakers, and other music equipment. After taking a sip from his bottled water, he asked, "so, what do you need from me?"

"I hear one of your many God-given talents, one that continues to go under-utilized, I should add, is your musical capabilities. I think my stepping down will afford you the opportunity to enlarge your ministry for Christ." Jackie Black stretched her neck and tilted her chin toward heaven as she continued. "Now, before you try to change my mind, let me tell you, I've prayed about this, and you know the prayers of the righteous availeth much. I believe my prayer for direction has revealed you as the best person to minister to St. Andrew in song at this time. I know the congregation will be uncomfortable with the change at first, but once they become accustomed to your playing, all will be well. The people of St. Andrew are a loving people; they will accept your musical offerings with open hearts.

I'm sure of it."

Rev. Charles Edward, Jr. did all he could to keep from chuckling at the dramatics of Jacqueline O'Shelle Black's request. It was during this conversation Rev. Edwards realized that Jackie Black may *not* be wrapped too tight. Karen Edwards, his wife, was already convinced of this fact, and had expressed it quietly to her husband.

"Sister Black. I'm sorry you won't be able to serve in this capacity any longer. And I'd be more than happy to fill in the gap as you seek God for...for guidance. I sure hope you find what you're looking for."

"I know I will, Rev. Edwards. I ask that you petition the throne of grace on my behalf as well." With one swift movement, Jackie Black slid her large cat-eye sunglasses up from the deep V of her jumpsuit and positioned them over her eyes. She slowly surveyed the remnants of the waning picnic conversations, and sauntered toward her car. As she turned to walk away, Rev. Edwards thought he saw Jackie Black's lips moving, though there were no sounds to confirm she was talking. What he did hear was the loud crack of Jackie clapping her hands as she continued on. She lifted her long thin arms up to the sky, and with her bony fingers splayed, waved her hands in the air. "THANK YA" he heard her yell, as she disappeared into the foliage of Pendleton Park.

Jackie's surrender and Rev. Charles Edward, Jr.'s playing is what allowed the church service to slowly return to normal, even after the text message. Rev. Edwards played with such fervor the church almost forgot about Jackie's antics. Even after she walked in looking like a crayon, the parishioners soon dismissed her presence as they would a gnat. Gradually, a sweet smelling savor of worship was ushered into the room.

St. Andrew was overcome. Karen Edwards stood with her arms folded across her chest. Her lips were pressed together, and she shook her head back and forth to the beat of the music. Clem Callahan rocked his head, and the motion loosened a thick black lock of hair, causing it to pendulum about his forehead. If one were to look closely around the edges of his hair line, one would notice small dark beads of sweat, where the jet black hair dye had mixed with the tiny dots of perspiration accumulating on his forehead. Twin Luceal made small jumps up and down at her seat; her ample breasts slightly grazed her chin with each bounce. Charles Edward, Sr. stood ramrod straight, shouting in unpredictable bursts, "Praise Him, son!" Mother Carrie took a brisk walk around the church. Round and round she walked, shouting, "He lives," until Melvin Collier, the head usher, escorted her back to her seat. Daughter Eliza had taken up a posture of prayer at the foot of the pulpit and remained there, entranced, until Pastor LeBeaux took his text.

Pastor LeBeaux stood slowly and spoke. "Praise the Lord, Saints. It's good to be in the house of Lord again. I see you all have decided you won't let the rocks cry out for you!" At that, Rev. Edwards, ran his fingers across the organ, setting off another round of praise.

"Alright. Alright. I know your spirits are high, but let me encourage you with the word of God. We know that praise and worship is good, but it is the *Word* that breaks the yoke. It's sharper than a two edged sword. Cutting left and right. But just because something cuts you, doesn't mean it's from the word of God. You can't take everything you hear 'cross this pulpit at face value. Yes, I'm a conduit for Christ, but you have to read the word for yourself! Don't take my word for it. Read it for yourself." Rev. Edwards followed Pastor LeBeaux's pacing with the organ.

"Turn with me, if you will, to Acts 17:11 where it tells us that some people, particularly the Jews, received the word of God that they heard from Paul, but after they received the word of God, guess what they did?"

"What'd they do, Pastor?" The congregation asked.

"They went back to the scriptures and examined them for themselves. And once they received confirmation from the scripture, they BELIEVED. Now, we know that Sweet Fields is a small town. Am I right, church?"

"Yeah, Pastor. It's small. You're right about that."

"So, we hear all sorts of things. A lot of us take the things we hear at face value. Some of us take what we hear and spread it out into the highways and by-ways--and it's not the gospel either. But how many of us try to find out the truth for ourselves? Why do we rely on the words of others, instead of getting the word for ourselves? Why do we have to trust the middle man? Why do we wait to come to church, to look up in my face, to hang on my every word, before we open the Bible and read it for ourselves? The church is a place of encouragement. It is for the sick at heart. It is for the weary in well doing. It is for the downtrodden. The depressed. The lonely. The heartbroken. The sad."

The point of Jackie's hat shook vigorously in agreement. It looked as if it would shake off of her head entirely. "Amen, Pastor LeBeaux. The lonely! You're right, pastor. Say that!"

"But St. Andrew, we need the word. So why do we wait until we get here to open our Bibles? We are to study for ourselves to show God that we are good workmen. We have to study for ourselves so that we will deal fairly with others. We have to study for ourselves, so that we won't misunderstand, mistake, misuse, misinterpret the word of God, and do the wrong thing.

Hurt people. Trap people. Misjudge people. Misunderstand people. We. Must. Study. For. Ourselves." Pastor LeBeaux paused. He ran his forefinger around his collar, turning his neck uncomfortably. He scratched at the arms of his long burgundy robe. "Cut out the middle man! The middle man may have good intentions, but the word says, at his BEST, he is but a filthy rag. We ALL need to be washed by the word, so that we can be presented faultless to God. I can't present you faultless. Rev. Edwards can't present you faultless. The deaconess board can't present you faultless. You don't need them to be a middle man.

Go straight to the source! Go to the word. Let it wash you!" "Yes!"

roared the congregation.

"Let it cleanse you!"

"Amen!"

"Let it cover you!"

"Preach, preacher!"

"Read it!"

"Yeah!"

"Study it!"

"Amen!"

"Cut OUT the middle man!"

"Allelujah!"

"You got to get to know Him for yourself."

"I know Him, pastor."

"Amen," Pastor LeBeaux shouted, "Amen. Amen." Pastor LeBeaux turned from the pulpit, snatching down the zipper of his robe, and pulling it off violently. He scratched at his forearms fiercely.

The congregation of St. Andrew thought Pastor LeBeaux was overcome by the spirit. They did not know his upper body was wracked with a nasty itch brought on by the heavily starched shirts Jackie Black had procured from Pastor LeBeaux's porch and taken to the wrong cleaners to be pressed with heavy starch. Heavy starch irritated Prentiss LeBeaux's skin to the point he thought it would drive him mad. He sat down in the minister's chair and made a mental note to get the remainder of the shirts relaundered.

As service came to a close, the buzz about the text message began to ramp up again. Locke's mind returned to the matter of handling Jackie Black. She could not be allowed to continue this way, and Pastor LeBeaux's compassion, which caused Locke to have a strong affinity for him, may be the same compassion that would keep Prentiss LeBeaux from doing something about her. *Unless*, Locke thought. *Unless there was a gathering of witnesses to make the case for excommunicating Jackie Black from the church.*

What Locke also needed to know was Jackie Black's intent. It was best if Locke had answers before the congregation could form an inquiry. But this time, neither Iris nor Locke were given the advantage of being informed in time enough to do damage control. For once, their questions mimicked those of most of the congregation. What made Jackie Black send the text? To whom did she send it? And what was to happen next?

The crowd filed out, and as was her habit, Locke waited in her seat until all members had received their ceremonious hugs from

LeBeaux. Iris stood at the end of Locke's pew, fingering the brass plate of the armrest that bore her and Clive's name. The Lockes had bought every brick of the newly renovated church. Locke would probably buy each brick of the new daycare and academic center as well, and unless Francis the Secretary decided to forego her secretive ways, not one member would be the wiser. Locke did not need accolades. Clive had given her enough of all that, God rest his sleeping soul.

Jackie Black stood at Pastor LeBeaux's right elbow, slightly behind him. She stretched her long arms out to hug each member who embraced the accommodating pastor. The width and length of the cape she wore made her look like a pumpkin colored moth hovering over the pastor's dignified figure, as if to devour a tasty morsel. Many who came through the receiving line gently declined her outstretched arms. Those who felt sorry for her gave her a hug, with lots of air in between.

Iris noticed a few members, particularly women, were privileged with a whisper from Jackie Black's lips to their ears. The gesture was wicked; it gloated. Iris wanted to know what was being said. She left Locke's pew, but not before she heard Locke say out loud, "No."

Iris turned and looked at Locke with mischief, "I am going to obey my pastor. I am NOT going to wait and hear what she's saying to those women, second hand. I will cut out the middle man, and hear it straight from the peacock's mouth." So, Locke's admonishment went unheeded, for Iris's curiosity had gotten the best of her, as it always had, and she side-shimmied through the pews and down the center aisle of the church to fall in line as the last member to greet Pastor LeBeaux.

"Iris," Pastor LeBeaux said gingerly. Iris extended her hand.

"Pastor LeBeaux." He smiled warmly, but did not take her hand. He held his arms in an open circle, and Iris noticed the imprint on Pastor LaBeaux's ring finger was not as deep as it was when she first met him.

"You've been a member long enough to give holy hugs like everyone else." LeBeaux paused and looked out into the congregation, only to find Locke staring at him severely. He winked at her and hugged Iris. Locke nodded.

After the brief hug, Iris noticed Jackie Black's arms were no longer outstretched. *The wing'ed creature has perched*, thought Iris. Iris moved toward Jackie Black, and waited for the whisper. For a moment, Iris just standing there gave Jackie pause. She blinked. Still, as Iris suspected, Jackie Black leaned in toward her. "Sister, did you get my text?" Iris did not answer. Instead, Iris turned and smiled the smile with which Jackie was most familiar--the one that did not reach her eyes. On her way to Locke's pew, Iris mouthed,
"Let's go."

Locke had already put on her gloves and sunglasses. She'd freshened her tinted lip balm and stood to walk out with Iris. "I hate when you mouth things."

"Mouth things?"

"Yes. You just mouthed to me, 'let's go.' Mouthing is so disgusting to watch. Next time just say it out loud." Iris did not say it, yet; however, she thought that saying things out loud, or rather, loudly, was just as disgusting to watch.
Locke and Iris walked out of the church together, silently.
They both were thinking about what to do next.

"What do we do now, Belle?" Iris asked as she reached into her yellow Kate Spade clutch for her sunglasses. "We cannot let her get away with this. She has gone way too far."
"I don't know what to do, just yet. But Clem Callahan and
Junior will have set some things in motion before the day is done."
"But, how will they know what happened? I am quite sure
Jackie didn't send William the text."

"You're going to tell your William; that's how they'll find out."

Iris stopped walking and looked at Locke. "Why do I have to be the one to tell it?"

"Little girl, please. You were going to tell him anyway. You tell that man everything. He'll be running out of that church like Jesse Owens looking for you soon. Then you're going to shake all that hair around him, and run your hands up and down that lil old skirt, get him all wool-gathered, and then you're going to tell him everything, like you always do."

"No, I do not..."

"Yes you do. I've been watching you. Junior has pulled you in close to him, and it's taking all of your energy not to let him see that you're smitten. But that's good. You shouldn't show all your hand. Play one card at a time. That's works best with these Sweet Fields men, or else they'll drive themselves cat crap crazy pining for you when they already got you." Locke peeped around Iris and noticed Eddie walking toward her. They were scheduled to have dinner together after church. Locke popped the collar of her crisp white shirt, and flattened the wide linen belt attached to her wide leg black linen pants.

"What are you look-" Iris stopped mid-sentence. "Oooooh, I see the Duke is coming to call. Look who's smitten now."

"Stay out of grown folks business, Iris. We're going to eat. Everybody has to eat something don't they? I'm not going to starve to death."

"Yes, but everyone isn't going to eat with the Mr. Charles Edward, Sr. Look how he has his fedora tilted on his head. He's coming for you, Belle Lynne."

By the time Iris had finished her sentence, Eddie had closed in the space between him and the ladies. "Belle, I thought you'd gone off and left me." Eddie reached around Iris and lowered his hand to the small of Locke's back, and gently placed it there as he moved closer to her. Locke moved in close to Eddie, settling herself into the space right below his shoulder. The gray suit he wore was the perfect backdrop for Belle Lynne's steel gray locs, which she'd pulled up into her signature chignon. She'd adorned the bun with a silver and amber hair pin that glistened in the sunlight. "How are you this afternoon Sister Murphy?"

"Oh, I am fine Mr. Edwards. I so enjoyed service today. Belle and I were just talking about how riveting it was. Were we not, Belle?"

"It was a good service. Pastor LeBeaux preached a fit on us today."

Eddie looked down at Belle, "I wasn't quite sure how service was going to turn out today. Things seemed a bit off when I first walked in. Something had caused a stir; I could feel it in the air. But when my boy started on that organ, I couldn't concentrate on nothing but the music. I hadn't heard him play like that in a long time. I sure enjoyed it."

"Yes," Iris responded. "I did too. I wasn't aware he played, and played so well."

"That's my boy." Eddie smiled proudly. He turned to Locke. "Are you hungry yet, Belle? I'm starved."

"Yes. I've been craving eggplant parmesan since Pastor LeBeaux's last amen. Iris, I'll call you later on. We'll come up with something to work out that issue." Locke said with a quick nod.

"What issue?" Eddie asked.

"Oh, it's nothing with which you should concern yourself, Eddie."

"What do you mean nothing?"

"It's lady-talk. Surely, you don't want to be bothered with something as trite as lady talk." Locke laughed. "You sure get nosey when you're hungry."

"I'm not nosey, Belle," Eddie said as he opened the door of his Denali. "I just want to know what's going on with my lady. That's it." Eddie reached down to Locke's tiny waist to hoist her small frame into the truck.

"Your lady? Who's your lady?" Locke, looked down at Eddie from the seat.

"I told you Belle, we're too old to be taking up time playing. If you don't know who my lady is, I'm not going to waste time telling you." Eddie laughed as he made his way around to the driver's side. He got in and closed the door and turned to meet Locke's smile. "You know you can make some big trouble to be such a little woman," he grinned.

"And don't you forget it," Locke said as she smiled back.

CHAPTER 17: THE ADVISORY BOARD

After the benediction, William broke away from the convoy of deacons who were retreating to the back, ducked out through a side door, and made his way around to the front steps of the church to look for Iris. Surely she knew what had set the congregation abuzz. He waited at the bottom step hoping to see her gold chiffon blouse through the crowd, but he never did. Instead, he saw her white Audi ease by him making a left on Pendleton Street headed in the direction of her home. He sighed and quickly returned to his duties in the deacons' parlor.

"Where you been? Chasing Sister Murphy?" Clem asked sorting the cash from the checks with a pencil tucked behind his ear.

"I was trying to see if she knew what had everyone worked up today," William said with a frown forming on his forehead.

"Whatever it is, it ain't good," Big Hughes shared. "That skinny woman is behind this. She was the only calm woman in the church." Big Hughes pulled the money bags from a nearby wall safe and kept mumbling to himself.

"William, go on and catch up with Iris and find out what's going on. We got things covered here. Call me as soon as you find out something." Clem said after sitting quiet for a moment. Clem didn't like to be out of the loop on things. He had to know what was going on and whether or not the pastor knew.

"Call me too," Big Hughes added with a heavy pat to his son's shoulder.

William said nothing when he exited the deacon's parlor. His mind was on Iris. He navigated his black Infiniti Q70 in the direction of the Murphy Inn. As he approached Iris' house, he saw her sitting in her grandmother's rocking chair and talking on the phone. He stopped in front of her walkway and got out. Her face showed surprise and she beckoned for him to come onto the porch when he paused at the sidewalk.

"Locke, I have company. I'll have to call you back." "Is it William?" Locke asked.

"Yes, it is William."

"Good. Don't forget to show him the text."

"Okay."

"And tell me what he says."

"Okay."

"Our table is ready. I'll just stop by after my dinner."

"Okay, Locke. Try to enjoy your dinner." she said hurrying to end the conversation. William had slowly made his way to the porch, and Iris was able to evaluate the classic-cut, midnight blue, 3-pc suit he wore and the orange floral tie that brought it to life. *If this man can't do anything else, he can dress,* Iris thought to herself.

"I hope I'm not interrupting anything," William said stepping onto the porch tentatively.

"No. You aren't. Not really. We were talking about a piece of communiqué that caused a bit of a stir today."

"A bit? It caused a tornado from where I was sitting. What happened?" William sat down on the swing and rested his elbows on his knees, focusing on Iris. She was still wearing her gold chiffon blouse, matching skirt, and a skinny black belt. She had traded her pointy-toe pumps for purple house slippers. Her hair was still pulled back into a tight bun, and diamond earrings still hung in her ears. He hoped she would take her hair down and move over to sit closer to him. His breath caught in his throat when she stood to move to the swing.

"Here," she said handing him her cell phone. "I can show you better than I can tell you. You read that while I get you something to drink. I have water, tea, coffee, and brandy." When she said brandy, she turned and smiled at him. He was surprised that she would have his favorite liquor. "If it weren't Sunday, I'd take a brandy, but since it is, I'll have coffee."

"Black, no sugar coming right up." she said slipping into the house.

Not a minute later, William was storming into the kitchen where Iris stood waiting for the coffee to brew. Iris heard the screen door slam and whirled around and saw William's lips stretched into straight line, his tie loosened at his neck, and his usually warm eyes were narrowed into cold slits.

"You have got to be kidding me. She sent this to you?" He asked holding out her phone.

"Not just me, William. Several women. Women who she thinks are interested in Pastor LeBeaux."

"But you're not interested in Pastor LeBeaux...are you?" He looked up from her phone to gauge her response.

"Of course not." Iris choked back a laugh.

"Why would she think you're interested in him? Has he said something? Did something happen?"

"I don't know why she thinks that, William. No one has said anything, nor has anything happened." Iris' vexation with William's line of questioning was showing on her face. She snatched a mug from the cabinet, poured in the hot, black liquid, and unceremoniously placed it in front of William on the breakfast bar.

"I'm sorry. I didn't mean to sound like I was accusing you. I'm just trying to figure this woman out. One minute she's accusing us of skipping church to mess around, and now, she's accusing you of wanting the pastor. The way she keeps your name in her mouth, it's almost like she's deliberately trying to make folks think you're..." William thought it was in his best interest to stop talking. But he had to bring some closure to his rant. "I just can't get a clear read on her. What is she after?"

Iris poured herself a glass of sweet tea and took a sip.
"Think I'm what, William?" She asked calmly.

"Aw, Iris. That's not what I'm saying. It's just that, that lanky woman loves putting you in the middle of mess. I don't want her jeopardizing your reputation here in Sweet Fields. I mean, you're just getting yourself to the point where you're a real part of the community. She has no right to do you like she's doing."

"That's the thing William, I don't think it's just me. It's her and her issues. She wants something, and by any means necessary, she's means get it. She doesn't care who she insults or offends. She just wants what she wants."

"But, what does she want? Why does she want it so bad? And why does she think she should have it?"

"William, I don't know, but I don't like it. Look at that text again. Doesn't it make her sound a bit unstable?"

"A bit? You sure like saying 'a bit' when you really mean 'a lot', William said sipping his hot coffee. "I think Pastor should know what she's done. It's all over town by now, and he shouldn't hear it in the streets."

"I guess you're right. It should come from Clem or you, or both of you."

"Clem. I'm going to call him and see what he thinks we should do."

"Have you eaten, William? I can throw together a grilled chicken salad if you like."

"That sounds good. I'm gonna step outside and call Clem. He'll know what to do." William walked back through the house and called Clem from the porch. Iris liked the sound of his footsteps in her house, but it was not a good time for daydreaming about William. She sent Locke a text message: "*William is calling Clem. He thinks we should tell Prentiss.*" She pulled out grilled chicken breasts to chop.

Locke replied, "I will be there soon."

After a few minutes, William returned to the kitchen and found Iris preparing a cheese and veggie tray.

"Clem is on his way. He's called an emergency advisory board meeting. Looks like you're about to have a full house," William said removing his jacket and vest. "What can I do to help?" He began rolling up his sleeves.

"A meeting?" Iris asked trying to focus on William's face. "How many people are we talking about?"

"Seven with us. Eight if Pastor comes."

"Okay. We'll need to use the big dining room. Can you wipe off the table and chairs for me? I haven't been in there in ages." She handed him a cotton cloth and some furniture polish.

In a matter of minutes, the doorbell was chiming and people were filing through to the window-enclosed dining room that once held Murphy Inn guests. Charles and Karen Edwards entered quietly and cautiously. Big Hughes and Clem arrived together in Clem's Lincoln Town Car. The two men sat at the large dining table and grumbled about newcomers and foolishness. Belle Lynne Locke was the last to arrive. She'd received the text from Iris about halfway through her eggplant parmesan. She'd read it slowly and quickly slipped the phone back into the inside pocket of her purse.

"What happened?" Eddie asked with his left eyebrow raised.

"What do you mean? Why do you think something is wrong?"

"You're doing that thing with your fingers, again. When you get annoyed, you pick at your cuticles."

Locke dropped her hands in her lap. "Oh stop being dramatic, Eddie. I do no such thing." Locke began putting on her gloves. "I'll need you to drop me off at Iris' when we're done."

"What's going on over there?"

"Nothing, we just need to talk about some things."

"You and Iris do more talking than any two people I know. I bet this has something to do with church doesn't it?"

"Yes. But that's all I can tell you right now."

"Okay. I can tell when you've said all you're going to say. But you're going to have to let me into this part of your life sooner or later."

Eddie and Locke finished their meals and started toward Iris'. As he neared their destination, Eddie noticed several cars in the driveway. One of the cars belonged to his son, Charles Edward, Jr. "What's Jr. doing here? Maybe I should go in too," Eddie said as he opened his door. He situated his fedora on his head and walked around the truck slowly, peering onto the porch to ascertain who else was in the large house.

"I have it from here." Locke took Eddie's hand, hopped out and looked up at him. "You needn't worry about what's going on in there. It doesn't concern you."

Eddie closed the door and crooked his arm to escort Locke up Iris' porch stairs. "Well, my son is here, Belle. If it concerns my son, it concerns me."

Locke did not rest her small hands in the crook of Eddie's arm as she usually did when they walked together. "Not in this case."

"Not in this case?" The two had stopped walking. "Why not in this case?"

"Eddie," Locke hesitated when she looked at Eddie and saw the telltale raised eyebrow. She took his arm and walked him a few steps away from Iris' front porch. "Eddie, this is church business. You are not a member of St. Andrew, and therefore, cannot be privy to anything we discuss here. The board is meeting. You're not a member of the board. Just go on home, now. We'll chat later." Locke stood on her tip toes to give Eddie a kiss on the cheek. Eddie did not bend to meet her advance, not at first. "If that's the way you want to leave it, Eddie. That's fine with me." She said.

Eddie bent down quickly and kissed Locke's cheek.

"Okay. We'll talk later."

Locke left Eddie standing in the yard as she ascended the porch stairs. He leaned on the hood of his SUV with his arms folded, admiring the well-made red leather Shandals that peeked from underneath the hem of her flowing wide leg pants. For several minutes he watched the house from behind his mirrored sunglasses.

Locke's behavior perplexed him, and her comments, though diplomatically delivered, stung. He felt cut off from her, and he didn't like it. Neither did he like the way she could change moods like an iguana changed colors. One minute she was soft and nurturing, and the next, all business--cold and unfeeling, so much so she'd left him standing outside in someone else's yard. He shook his head as he stood to get into his SUV. He opened the door and got in, placing the fedora on the passenger seat. He backed out of the driveway and slowly drove away.

Locke did not knock. She walked into the house to find William helping Iris bring out a large salad, a cheese and vegetable tray, and a large pitcher of sweet tea.

As they were about to begin, Clem cleared his throat. "I called Pastor. He's on his way. I think he should be here for this.
For all of it."

Finally Locke spoke, "Yes. That was a good idea, Clem."

"Yeah. I thought that would be best, seeing as how he goes soft on stuff like this. I felt like if we talk to him together, he'd get a clear picture. Speaking of picture, Belle, that was some sight to see outside. Charles the Senior looked like Little Boy Blue, sitting out there all alone just now."

"Clem, *Charles the Senior* and his seating position are none of your concern. Don't start that mess with me. I'm not one of your deacon's den cronies. Let's get down to business."

"All I was saying, Belle, was that you could've-..."

Callahan's defense was interrupted by a tap on the screen door. Iris went to answer and found Luceal and Laura standing there with a pecan pie wrapped in wax paper. Iris stepped out onto the porch.

"How may I help you ladies?" Iris said sweetly stepping onto the porch.

"Well, we saw all the cars and thought we'd stop by and bring a pie," said Luceal.

"If y'all doing church business, you need to keep your energy up," Laura chimed in.

"You're not going to invite us in, Iris?" Luceal whined pulling her pie back towards her bosom.

"Luceal and Laura, this is private business we are attending to," Locke said standing in the open screen door.

"Belle, we were talking to Iris. She got us standing out here on this porch like we're strangers," Luceal said getting upset.

"Yeah. And we were her grandmother's closest friends, and we can't even come into her house," Laura added.

"You could at least invite us in and offer us a glass of tea, girl." Luceal said adding a touch of venom on the word *girl*.

"First of all, as far as Iris is concerned, you *are* strangers," Locke snapped at the ladies. "Second, I know who Maggs' closest friends were, and trust, she would *never* yoke up with the likes of you."

"And finally," a husky voice from inside the house boomed. "She doesn't have to invite you in. This is a private gathering, and you ladies are interrupting." William was holding the door wide open and filling up the doorway.

"Junior, what are you doing here?" Luceal snarled curling her lip into a grimace.

"Right now, Miss Ceal, I'm asking you and Miss Laura to leave." William gave her a sweet smile. "And Miss Laura, before you say anything, why don't you turn around and speak to Bennett? The poor man been standing over there waving at you for five whole minutes." William leaned against the doorjamb, crossed his ankles, and chuckled.

Laura turned quickly to look across the street at her lost love, Bennett Banks. He was standing there with one hand in his pocket and the other hand up waving to her. She smiled a smile as big as the moon and waved vigorously. Luceal snatched her sister's arm down.

"Put your arm down and come on, Laura." Luceal sounded as if she would bite off her sister's head.

"But I was just saying hello. There's no harm in that, 'Ceal."

"We've talked about you and Bennett before. What are you waving back at him for?"

"It's rude not to speak back when people say hello, 'Ceal. That's all."

"Well, you don't have to speak to *him*. You'll just be leading him on if you do. That love affair is over. Remember?"

"Yes. I remember, 'Ceal."

"I've never been treated so badly in all my life," Ceal muttered looking back at Iris while exiting the porch. "Don't you wave at him again, Laura. Next thing you know, he'll be stalking you. Remember last time?"

"He wasn't stalking me last time, Ceal. He was trying to avoid *you*!" The two sisters bickered all the way to their old blue Oldsmobile.

Iris and William returned to the dining room, and moments later Pastor LeBeaux rang the doorbell. William met him at the door and walked him back to the dining room.

"Afternoon, everyone!" Prentiss said in a booming, jovial voice. Each member around the long formal table nodded and greeted the pastor. Clem indicated that the pastor sit at the head of the table near him. When Prentiss was seated, Clem cleared his throat and ran his hand through his hair.

"This morning, before service, Iris and several other women in the congregation received a text message from Sister Jackie Black. Iris?" Iris had printed the text message for each member to read. She passed the copies out. Everyone read the printed text in silence. Some eyebrows raised and some wrinkled into frowns. The silence was shattered when Prentiss slammed his open hand down on the dining table.

"What on God's green earth is wrong with this woman?!" Prentiss' face was red and tight. "I have had enough of her foolishness. All last week…"

"All last week?" Clem almost screamed.

"What did she do?" Big Hughes asked quietly leaning forward to rest his elbows on the table. Prentiss took a deep breath and thought about Maybelline. This foolish woman had run off the only woman he was interested in. Just as he was about to answer, the doorbell rang. Iris jumped up to answer it. Francis the Secretary stood outside waiting patiently to gain entrance.

"Francis! How are you?" Iris greeted.

"Fine, Sister Murphy. Pastor asked me to take record of the meeting," she said quietly. Iris stood aside and gestured for her to enter.

"Just follow the voices, Francis. To the back," Iris said closing and locking the front door.

When Francis entered the large dining room, the men stood, and Big Hughes beckoned for her to sit near him. She was given a copy of the text message, and Clem caught her up on the few bits of information that had been shared.

"Francis, will you share with the board Ms. Black's activities of last week?" Prentiss requested rubbing the frowns above his eyes.

"Yes, sir. Just give me a moment." Francis flipped through her steno pad until she found the page from Monday of the previous week. She began to read off the events in a monotone voice:

"On Monday, Sister Black took Pastor's shirts--7 dress shirts--from his porch and had them cleaned and starched by a cleaners of her choice. She returned the shirts to the porch along with a gift bag of coffee, pastries, and breakfast quiches. She enclosed a card."

"Took them from your porch?" Clem asked.

"Yes. I leave them in a canvas bag on the porch. Ray Christmas picks them up early and delivers them later in the day. A handy little system." Prentiss explained. "Please continue, Francis."

"On Tuesday, Sister Black delivered a basket of breakfast to the church for Pastor. The basket consisted of grits, bacon, sausage, waffles, eggs, and hash browns from Patsy's Diner."

"Patsy?! She has sent a plenty of folk to their heavenly reward with her food," Clem exclaimed.

"All that grease will kill ya," Big Hughes said leaning back in his chair, chomping on his carry-along bag of trail mix, Locke always made especially for him.

"You didn't eat it, did you, Pastor LeBeaux?" Karen asked in quiet concern.

"No, he didn't," Francis answered. "I disposed of the food, sanitized the basket, and returned it to its owner. Shall I continue?" Francis asked flipping her pad to the next page.

"Yes, Francis, please go on." Prentiss rubbing the top of his head.

"On Wednesday, Sister Black slipped a note to Pastor LeBeaux in the mail slot. It read: '*I know Wednesdays are your busy days, but I just wanted you to know that I am always thinking of and praying for you. I am here to help should you need me. With Love, Jackie B.*' The card had been sprayed with White Diamonds perfume."

"Oh dear," Karen Edwards murmured grabbing her husband's hand.

"Oh dear is right, Sister Edwards. This woman is crazy, and Pastor, you shoulda known that by Wednesday!" Clem said beating on the table.

"Clem." Big Hughes got his friends attention and leaned back in his chair. Though he said few words, the older Hughes had no problem communicating his feelings through his tone and body language. What he communicated to Clem was clear--*calm down*. Clem sighed aloud and tried to relax in his chair. Prentiss sighed aloud and rubbed his hands over his head repeatedly; his wavy hair was being rubbed enough to fall out. Francis looked around and continued.

"On Thursday, I found Sister Black trying to enter Pastor's office. After a short exchange, she left a gift for me to give him. The gift was 3 CDs wrapped in red foil paper. Each one had a hand drawn cover. The CDs were labeled *The Past, The Present, and Our Future.* On the Past CD were songs that Pastor LeBeaux's wife liked, that were played at the gala, including 'Flight of the Bumblebee.' On the Present CD were love songs like 'All of Me' by Billie Holliday. On the Future CD were more love songs like Luther Vandross' 'Always and Forever,' and Bill Withers' 'Just the

Two of Us'." Francis looked up to see the shocked faces of the advisory board members. Clem Callahan was red as a beet. Big Hughes' mouth was now in the shape of an upside down U. Locke was twisting her cotton gloves in frustration. Iris and William were exchanging awkward looks. The Edwards were holding hands and shaking their heads. Pastor LeBeaux looked irate enough to commit murder.

"She got bolder and stronger as the week went on," Big Hughes said reaching for a carrot on the vegetable tray.

"Yes." Karen said timidly, "like a hurricane."

"What else did she do, Francis?" Clem asked sharply.

"Well, on Friday, she was rather helpful in the kitchen, but she did stir the pot a bit with Sister Murphy and Deacon William, but that's another matter." Francis said flipping the page over.

William looked at Iris.

"What did she say?" William asked leaning in close to Iris.

"Nothing of any consequence," Iris whispered back.

"She said she didn't believe Iris was into a blue-collared worker such as yourself," Locke said impatiently. "Iris is right. It isn't important, but since you want to know, William, that's what she said. And your Iris put her in her place." Locke's use of the term, *your Iris,* was not lost on anyone at the table, as Locke was sure it wouldn't be. "Now, carry on, Francis."

"Yes, she did," Francis added with some excitement. "She said, and I quote, 'not every woman is hung up on collars. It isn't the man's collar that's important. Besides, at least the man I'm interested in acknowledges and respects my existence' end quote."

William's heart almost exploded. So Iris had admitted that she was interested in him after all. He looked over at her, but Iris averted her eyes. She was smoothing down that gold skirt like there were a million wrinkles in it. She looked up and caught the gaze of Big Hughes who smiled and nodded. Charles and Karen Edwards were smiling too. Even Prentiss, in the midst of his anger and anxiety, offered a crooked smile.

"And on Saturday at the picnic, she asked if I would play one of her CDs. I told her Pastor LeBeaux had approved a music playlist for the event," Charles said trying to move the conversation along.

"What?! You didn't tell me she tried to play that mess at the picnic!" LeBeaux shouted.

"You were having a good time, everyone was, and I was not going to let her ruin it," Charles said pleasantly. Prentiss sighed and threw himself back in the chair.

"Sorry, Charles. You're right. You did the right thing."

"And just to put everything on the table," Charles said, "I should tell you that she approached me at the close of the picnic about taking her place as minister of music. She said the Lord led her to me, and she had other kingdom work to take care of, so she was leaving her post."

"Well, that's the best decision she's made so far," Pastor LeBeaux sighed.

"So now, we have this text message that went out to women in the church," Clem said, scooting his chair back.

"Certain women, Clem. Not all women got it." Locke interjected.

"None of the church mothers or older women in the congregation got it," Iris added. "It seems like the women who had direct contact with Pastor LeBeaux during the picnic were the ones she targeted."

"But you were with me most of the time," William said to Iris.

"Yes, but when we were learning the Salsa, pastor and I were paired up for a few minutes. The ladies who were doing Zumba probably got it because they were teaching him how to do the Zumba moves."

"I didn't get it." Karen said looking at her phone.

"You're married. She doesn't feel threatened by you. I would hazard to say that Maybelline would have gotten one if she hadn't planned to leave this morning to go to China," Iris explained calmly. "Pastor, Jackie thinks she is in love with you. I can tell by the way she looks at you during church. She's been trying to get your attention. And this text message was to ward off any possible competition for your affections." Iris sat back in her chair.

"I think she should be put out of the church," Clem said slamming his hand down on the table.

"Deacon Callahan, please don't break up my granny's table," Iris pleaded.

"Sorry." He blushed and stood up to walk around. He was furious. He hated discord and Jackie had sown nothing but discord since her arrival. "I think she gets booted. We didn't have this kind of fool behavior in St. Andrew until she came." He said pausing in front of the china cabinet. "Wait. A. Minute." Clem said slowly. "Wasn't she the one who put that raggedy lace cloth on the communion table?"

Karen looked up sheepishly and answered, "Yes, Deacon Callahan. And she also replaced Katie Caldwell's beautiful floral arrangements with a spray of gladiolas."

"Oh, *she* did that…" Pastor LeBeaux replied, as he began to put the pieces together. "I was wondering why we had a funeral arrangement in front of the pulpit that Sunday. It's all coming together now." Pastor LeBeaux was still scratching his head, but he'd calmed down, just a little. "But Clem, we just can't put her out. We have to do it right."

"Right. Deacon, let us handle this biblically," Charles said scooting to the edge of his chair and resting his hands on the table.

"Stoning IS biblical," Clem spat out.

"Clem! You don't mean that!" Karen gasped.

"Matthew 18:15 says, if you have an aught against your brother, you go to him and him alone. And I think you should do exactly that, Pastor. Talk to her."

"But not by yourself. The woman is crazy," William blurted out. "She could leave and say you did something to her.
Have someone with you, Pastor." "Right,"

Big Hughes said.

"And be *firm,* Prentiss. One MUST be firm with the delusional," Locke advised.

"All of you are right. I found her to be eager to please in the beginning, but then she became overzealous. And offensive," Prentiss said sliding to the front of his chair.

"And out of order," William added.

"And annoying," Locke said.

"And paranoid," Iris chimed in.

"And inappropriate," Karen whispered.

"And desperate to be seen and acknowledged. She feels invisible, but she doesn't know how to cope with that. She wants to be included, but doesn't know how to connect with others," Francis said shyly.

"Well, Francis will be there, right?" Clem asked.

"Yes. Francis is privy to all of my meetings. She is the soul of discretion." Prentiss reached for a bottle of water.

"Be clear when you tell her you don't want her, Doc," Big Hughes instructed pointing and shaking a carrot stick at Prentiss.

"I can't meet with her tomorrow, but I will talk with her on Tuesday."

"Be sure to give us an update, Pastor. Because if this doesn't work, I got something that will" Clem said pointing and shaking his finger towards the ceiling.

"Clem, you keep that inner-hoodlum in check, you hear? You're too old for that now. We all are, or I would have already slapped her back to where she came from," Locke said reaching for her gloves.

"I heard you're good at slapping folk," Big Hughes muttered with a teasing grin. "Y'all hush and end this meeting. It's past time for my afternoon nap."

"First, I appreciate y'all getting together to talk about this. This is a true advisory board. I appreciate all of you." Prentiss stood and adjusted the waist of his pants.

"Well, Pastor, we're just giving you a chance to fix the problem yourself first. We've run folk out of the church and town before. It can be done rather quietly and peacefully if you know what you're doing. We're too small of a community to let the devil take a foothold here," Clem said standing next to Prentiss.

"I sure thank you all for being kind enough to let me handle it God's way. If God is in the midst, everything will work out alright. Now, shall we pray before we go our separate ways?"

"Yeah."

"Of course."

"Go right ahead, Rev."

"Well, let's touch and agree as we go to God in prayer. Let us bow."

"Let me put my gloves back on first," Locke muttered with agitation.

"*Lord, we thank you for yet another opportunity to assemble here together. We thank you for these able minded brothers and sisters who are committed to holding up my arms as I fight your battles. We all know that if two or three of us come together in your name, if we touch and agree in your will, you will be a God in the midst. Well Lord, we are eight strong. And Lord before we go any further, forgive us, for we know we've sinned. Just tonight we've plotted in our hearts against one of your children. Our flesh took over. That's why we need you to be in the midst right now, because one of your sheep has gone astray. She has turned and gone her own way. She is nibbling on the grass of waywardness, evil, and discord. And like you, the good shepherd, I am laboring to bring her back into the fold.*"

At that statement, Clem opened one eye to glare at Pastor LeBeaux. He shook his head, no, and muttered, "We don't want her back, Lord."

Pastor LeBeaux continued, "*...and now Lord, I ask that you be with me and Sister Francis as I follow your word in talking with Sister Black. You promised your people if we follow your word, it wouldn't come back void. And Lord, while I labor in your work, please keep the prayers of the saints in this room ever before me, because I know they are praying with me and for me. They want everything to end well. They want to do things with an excellent spirit. And as I close this evening, I pray a special prayer of protection over Maybelline…*"

Every member of the board squeezed the hand they held. William looked up and winked at Iris. Iris bugged her eyes at Locke. Clem and Big Hughes looked at each other and smiled. Francis' eyes remained on the hardwood of Iris' floor. She smiled too. Karen mouthed, *I told you*, to her husband, Charles Edward, Jr.

"*Maybelline is going to a strange land where people worship a strange God. Hold her in the hollow of your hand, and allow her to return safely to a peaceful church without the spot or wrinkle of Satan's wiles. And now until Him who is able to keep us from falling, and to present us faultless before a perfect and matchless God with great joy and celebration, we submit these prayers with thanksgiving, counting it done in the precious name of sweet Jesus. Amen.*"

Everyone began filing out of the house except William. He stood on the porch with Iris and watched as the members of the advisory board got into their cars and drove away. His father shot him a questioning glance as he sauntered through the living room. William clapped his father on his shoulder and said, "I'm going to help Iris clean up. I'll stop by the house a little later." His father just smiled and hurried off the porch.

When Clem and Big Hughes eased off in Clem's Town Car, William and Iris sat on the porch swing and swung quietly for a while.

"We have a bona fide fool in our church," William said. "I want her to stay away from you and keep your name out of her mouth."

"I know." Iris said quietly. She wasn't accustomed to someone being as protective as William. She stood and went into the house. William followed close behind.

"Iris, you aren't upset with me, are you?" William asked while helping her clear the dishes from the dining room.

"No. Of course not. I'm just thinking. That's all."

"Thinking about what?"

"About Pastor and his prayer for Maybelline. I think he's in love with her."

"Does that bother you?" William asked stopping in his tracks. Iris put the dishes she was carrying on the breakfast bar and turned to face William, but that wasn't enough. She closed the distance between them and then took a step back so she could see his face and look straight into his eyes.

"William Hughes, if you imply one more time that I want Prentiss, you will never step foot in my house, ring my phone, or fall under the gaze of my eyes again. Do you understand me? I. Do. Not. Want. Prentiss. And if you keep up with this insecure, accusatory foolishness, I won't want you either!" She left William standing speechless in her kitchen and returned to the porch. Thirty minutes passed before William joined her on the porch.

"Iris, I'm sorry. I don't mean to sound accusatory. I just don't know where I stand with you. That's all. And then when you add the rumors, hints, and text messages from Jackie, I tend to think the worse."

"Do you know this was the first time, anyone other than you and Locke have been in my house? I don't let people in. I keep them on the porch. Today, I had more people in my house than I have ever had." She was wringing her hands.

"So maybe Jackie is good for something after all, eh?"

"My point is, William, I don't let people in that I don't like or trust. I've let you in. Left you in there for half an hour unsupervised," she said jerking her head towards the kitchen. "I trust you and I like you. There. Is that clear enough for you?"

"Yes." he laughed nervously. "See? See how she got me acting? I don't usually behave like that." He laughed again. "She's a bad seed, but I won't let her come between what we got going."

"No. We got something good going," she said with a laugh. "Because I sat on the porch enjoying the evening while YOU washed the dishes."

"I'll come by and wash your dishes everyday if you want, Iris Murphy," he said waggling his eyebrows.

"Hush, William," she gushed slapping him lightly on his forearm that was exposed from the rolling up of his shirt sleeves.

They went back inside. William grabbed his vest and jacket and prepared to leave.

"So what you got going on this week?" William asked Iris interrupting her thorough enjoyment of watching him redress.

"Well, let's see. I want to visit that new Kitchen and Bath Tile shop, catch a movie, and maybe cook dinner for a certain deacon of the church."

"I can join you for all three of those events if you like," he said with a gleaming smile.

"I'd like that," she said returning his gleam.

Iris walked William out and sat in her grandmother's rocking chair. She watched William's bowed legs carry him to his parked car, and matched the rhythm of her rocking to his smooth, confident stride. She only stopped after he eased away slowly in his car.

It was getting dark, and while very little mayhem took place in Sweet Fields, Clem Callahan and Big Hughes didn't feel comfortable with Belle Lynne Locke walking home alone. The three of them were nearing Clem Callahan's Town Car, when Clem noticed that Belle Lynne was making her way toward the sidewalk.

"Come on and get in this car so we can take you home," Clem Callahan begged.

"It's near twilight. Let us drop you off." Big Hughes confirmed.

"I'm well able to walk home by myself," Locke said with a wave of her gloved hand. "I know where I live."

"Yeah, we know that," Clem retorted, "but what would two men, grown twice over, look like letting a lady walk home, in the dark, by herself?"

"What would one lady, grown twice over, look like getting in the car, with two men, in the dark, by herself?" Locke responded sharply. "Anyway, Clem, you will drive me to drinking with your incessant growling about this meeting. I don't want to hear all of that, now. I'd rather walk and turn over the matter, quietly. You all go on. I'll be fine."

"Have it your way, then." Clem answered.

"She'll be alright." said Big Hughes. "Let's go. I'm hungry. I need a meal. No more rabbit food."

Belle Lynne Locke didn't want to think about the text message anymore. As a matter of fact, her mind was settled that Pastor LeBeaux would handle Jacqueline Black perfectly. His heart was involved, now. His passion for Maybelline would put some fire behind his words. *Maybelline*, Locke thought, *if that isn't something to smile about.* Locke had almost missed the attraction, and if she were honest with herself, she did miss it, but only because Jackie had distracted her with her absence. *Maybelline.*

She'd be good for him. Every man needed a woman who was good for him.

This thought quickly brought Locke's mind back to Eddie. During the low points of the meeting, Locke visualized him leaning against the black Denali, looking down right angry. *He's not going to leave it alone,* Locke thought. *He'll want to fix it, and fix it tonight.*

She wasn't surprised to see the span of her driveway taken up with Eddie's vehicle, though her heartbeat quickened slightly when she saw it there. His hat sat on the seat of the swing, in the space where she would normally sit while they shared their fresh pressed morning juice. Eddie seemed relaxed in the swing, almost as if he'd been sitting there for years. His legs were crossed, and as Locke ascended the porch, he moved his hat for her to sit.

"Eddie." Locke said.

"Belle."

"I knew you would be here."

"How'd you know that?"

Belle took Eddie's hat and sat it in her lap. "I know how you are about leaving things in order. So, I knew you'd be here to line everything up before nightfall."

"So, are you ready to debrief me, now?"

"Well, before we do any of that, Eddie. I need to be sure you understand where I'm coming from. Sweet Fields is my home. St. Andrew is my sanctum. This…" Belle waved her hand around, "is my history. I'm protective of it. And as much as I like you." Belle paused. "As much as I like you, you've not become a part of that history. You're still an outsider. Outsiders are threats until you know their true intent. I've been taught that all of my life. So when it comes to the business of St. Andrew and Sweet Fields, I close my mind off on everything else, eating, sleeping, having fun, finding love… I close my mind off of that stuff, so I can protect what's mine."

"I have a question for you, Belle." Eddie said gently turning Locke's face to his, "Who is protecting you, while you're protecting…" Eddie waved his hand around, "all this?"

To Locke, Eddie's true intent was all wrapped up in that question. Most of her life had been spent taking care of her Clive. The times before and her early years with Clive had been spent being a friend to Maggie, helping her with her girls, her bed and breakfast, her transition to the other side. Now that Clive was gone and Maggie was gone, Locke had taken to hovering over Iris, mothering Prentiss, despising Jackie Black and running from Eddie's true intent.

"Are you offering protection, Eddie?"

"It's one of the best things I have. But of course it comes along with something else. And we don't even have to talk about that now. What we have to talk about is how we handled each other this afternoon."

"Handled. That's a good word for it."

"We have to work out a way that I can become a part of your history. Your history didn't end with Clive. You're still living. You're still getting around well. You're still looking good." He smiled. "I'm here. You can't just reel me in and shut me out with no warning. I can respect the business you have with your church. I can even respect that because I'm not a member, I can't be privy to that business. But I'm a man, Belle. If you're worked up about something, you can't expect me to ignore it. I care about you and what you're feeling. So I get worked up when you get worked up. Then I get even more worked up when you don't tell me what's got you all out of sorts. Don't keep cutting me off like I'm a commoner. Be easy with me, and trust me to understand." "And you be easy with me. It will take some time, for me. I'm set in my ways. There are just things I do, because I've been doing them for so long."

"I'm the same way."

"So you do understand."

"Sure, I do."

"Well I was thinking too, on my walk home. Your son is the Associate Minister at St. Andrew. It just occurred to me how difficult it would be for his father, and my companion, to be out of the loop. I can see how that can be a strange position in which to be. We should do something about that, you know so it won't cause conflict with us. I mean, there is an *us* to consider. And you've been loafing around with your son for the last couple of weeks. You attend church like a regular, so…"

"What are you trying to talk up on, Belle?"

"I don't know yet, but you're here in Sweet Fields a lot. You've almost become a fixture. What are you going to do with yourself?"

"That all depends on you, Belle. You have more control of that than you think."

"I see. Well, I'm not sure how you're going to protect me when you're in the Carolinas, so you need to do some thinking, too. We'll come up with something."

"I'm sure we will. And soon I hope."

Belle and Eddie sat on the porch in silence for a few more minutes before Eddie decided he wanted some of Belle's famous teacakes. He swayed on the swing while she fixed a platter of teacakes and fruit preserves along with lavender infused sweet tea. They munched on the snacks as Eddie regaled Locke with his military stories. Locke was happy, and Eddie was at ease. They both had the same ideas about each other and would begin to see them through.

After pulling into the driveway, both Clem and Big Hughes took possession of the two rocking chairs sitting on the Callahan's front porch. They wanted to ponder the events of the afternoon. The azalea bushes surrounding the fronts and sides were trimmed perfectly and provided just enough privacy for the two men to speak freely. Sitting between the rocking chairs was a large copper planter turned upside down. Atop the oversized planter were two covered plates, flanked by two tall glasses of sweet tea that glistened with beads of water sliding down the sides. Callahan had not called ahead to let his wife, Judith, know he was coming home, let alone bringing company, and yet she had set out the servings just in time for the men's arrival.

"Deacon Hughes," Judith said, tiptoeing to give Big Hughes a light hug and pat on the back. She was standing on the porch waiting for them. "I'm so glad you stopped by for a spell. We live too close to each other for us not to visit with one another more often." Judith turned to Clem. She held out her small arms to him. "Clem. Hoooneeeey. How'd it go?" The two hugged and kissed. "Are you tired? You know how church conflict wears on your constitution. Sit on down and you and Deek. Get you something on your stomach."

Judith was a tiny woman and the color of homemade ice cream, the kind her grandmother would make her churn and churn sitting on the front porch. Her consistent routine of Pond's face cream in the morning and Noxzema at night kept her skin taut and glistening, or so she thought and told every woman in Sweet Fields who asked her how she kept her skin so clear and young looking. It was really in the genes. Still, Pond's and Noxzema could credit
Judith Callahan for keeping their products on the shelf at the local Beauty Bottle, for many women, both young and old, swore by her

beauty regimen to keep their skin looking young and supple and kept their cabinets full of the creams.

Judith and Clem Callahan had been together for so long that they looked more like brother and sister than husband and wife. Like Clem, Judith's hair was soft and wavy. Unlike Clem, she did not bother with dyes and hues to belie her age. She didn't need too; her hair was so white, that to color it would seem a sin, an insult to what God had blessed her with. Tonight Judith's hair hung loose and unadorned, save a small sequined barrette situated at her right temple to keep the front bangs from falling into her face. It was a perfect compliment to the navy and white linen shift she wore. The shift had two large pockets on either side, where in one pocket she kept her glasses. In the other she stashed special things for Clem, to surprise him at odd times, pieces of candied ginger, a new pocket square sprayed with the perfume he liked her to wear, or on frisky days, a small wallet size picture of Judith dressed as a pin up girl.

"Oh, I'm alright, honey." Clem said, smiling at his wife. "Big Hughes was there to keep me calm. I think we worked things out."

"Well good. I fixed you both a plate to refresh you. I know how city folks eat. If Locke was anywhere in the room, there was plenty of rabbit food to be found." Judith nodded at Deacon Hughes. "Ya'll sit on down and eat, before your food gets cold. I'll leave you to your business." Judith disappeared into the house. The screen shushed close behind her as she left. The men could hear the quickstep shishing of her gold Daniel Greens on the hardwood maple floors as she made her way into the kitchen.

Big Hughes lifted the top off of one of the plates and tore off the leg from the roasted chicken quarter it contained. He took a bite and held the chicken leg in his hand and rested that hand on his knee. "Well, I think we handled that."

"We can't count on it, Big. The final say is on the Pastor, and you know he'll go soft at the sign of female distress. That lanky woman will get in there and drop some tears and everything we said around Maggs' table will be null and void."

"God sent him to be our pastor. We gotta trust him on this one." Big Hughes picked up his entire plate and begin to work on the wild rice.

"I trust him, Big. I just don't trust that custard colored woman! I don't like folk stirring up trouble. It's been peaceful for a while. We don't need anyone messing that up. Especially the likes of—."

"Gentlemen?" Judith sang out from the doorway. "I'm bringing some napkins out." Judith sat the napkins onto the planter and shished back into the house.

"We still have to let him handle it first. Do it God's way." Big Hughes answered.

"You know one thing, Big?" Callahan crossed his right leg over his left knee and let his foot dangle. The rising moon glistened on the tip of his Stacy Adams. "I got a mind to sit in on that meeting with Pastor and that woman. Somebody with some backbone needs to be in there to be sure things go along the way they should."

"It's not time for us to intervene, yet."

"What do you mean, it's not time? You know how Pastor LeBeaux is with the flock. He lets them ride the line until things start to get out of control, but this one... she got away with him this time." Clem shook his head. "Sometimes Pastor tries to make everyone too happy. He doesn't want to make anybody mad. He doesn't want to hurt anyone's feelings. You can't send a man like him to handle a woman like that! I think he needs us for support, don't you?"

"Us?" Big Hughes was on the last half of his plate, the collards and kale with cornbread had demanded his attention. He dropped his fork onto the plate and started on them with his fingertips, pressing the combination together and dipping it into the remaining juices.

"Yes. Us. He needs some menfolk to support him so he won't go weak for her tears."

Big Hughes finished his mouthful of food, put his plate back onto the planter, picked up his napkin and wiped his fingers. He looked up at his friend of over fifty years. "You remember the last time you started out by yourself with some foolishness and it ended up becoming us? You were running your mouth, and I handled the business of running my fist across a man's face," Big Hughes dropped his head and muttered, "and a knife across his gut."

"I got you some more tea!" Judith's voice rang out over the porch.

"Judith, honey. Stop running back and forth. If you want to hear, you can just come on out and hear. You don't have to step in and out like that." Clem got up and pulled a rocking chair from the far end of the porch and positioned it near him.

"Oh. That's alright, honey. I'll just…"

"You'll just nothing, honey. Sit on down. You may as well hear. It'll be all over Sweet Fields before dawn anyhow." "Well, I have talked to Sister Karen tonight already." Judith offered.

"Well..." Clem prodded.

"She told me about that awful text Deaconess Black allegedly…"

"Allegedly?" Clem Callahan slid to the end of his chair, "What do you mean *allegedly*? Don't tell me that woman has you on her side?"

"Now, Clem. Honey. How do we know she sent the text for sure? No lady in her right man would do all the things people are saying she's done."

"Judith, Hon. Jackie Black ain't no lady."

"And she sho ain't in her right mind," Big Hughes said after taking a long sip of the tea. "Crazy as a road lizard."

"Let's not scandalize her name, gentlemen," Judith said with conviction. "She is a member of the flock. A woman, just like me. Surely there must be an explanation for all this."

"How would you explain it, Judith?" Clem Callahan was still sitting up in his chair. He was staring at his wife, waiting patiently for her explanation.

Big Hughes stood up and dusted the crumbs of cornbread from his pants. He turned and picked up his plate and glass and headed toward the screen door. "That sure was good, Judith. I thank you. I'll take care of my setting, and walk on home through the back door."

"Big, you don't have to go. Stay on and chat with us."

"Nah, Clem. I'm sleepy now. I'll check you tomorrow."

Judith picked up the conversation with Clem again. "All I'm saying is, we don't have to scandalize her name. We should treat her with the love of Christ."

"You're right, Judith. The word tells us to love our enemies."

"Oh, Clem. You're a mess." Judith got up from her rocking chair to sit in Clem's lap. "What am I going to do with you?"

"Let me think a second and I'll let you know."

The couple giggled like teenagers and eventually made their way into the Callahan house holding hands and turning off lights as they went along. The bedroom light was already off, and within seconds of the Callahans exiting the porch, the light was on along with the music of an old record playing, "Blue Moon." Finally, the shadows of the two dancing appeared behind the sheer curtains, a sight familiar to most residents of Sweet Fields who took evening strolls to walk off their Sunday dinners.

CHAPTER 18: GOLDEN SUNSETS

While Sunday had been a day filled with the drama of Jackie Black's text message, Monday found her in a financial deficit. By ten o'clock that morning, her private-instruction students had all been pulled from her tutelage. That left her with the group of students from the Parrish County Private School--10 girls and two boys. She especially enjoyed teaching them the basics of African dance and was relieved when Monday came and went without a call from the principal of the school cancelling her instruction. That call came on Tuesday.

"Principal Rice," Jackie sung into the phone after recognizing his voice on the other end. "So good to hear from you this morning."

"Good Morning, Ms. Black. I hope I didn't interrupt any instruction you may be giving at this hour, but the news I have for you is a matter of urgency."

"Oh no, Principal Rice. This is perfect timing, as most of my mornings are free," Jackie responded in a trembling voice.
"What's the urgency?"

"Ms. Black, your contractual agreement with this school will end at the close of the quarter. You do remember, the terms of your contract would remain, pending your quarterly review. I wanted to give you fair notice, just in case you needed to make other arrangements, perhaps start calling prospective students from your waiting list."

"Oh, but Principal Rice, the Christmas Cantata is the crowning moment of all performances rendered by the children. Couldn't we keep our arrangement until the end of the year?"
Jackie begged, as she loosened the wrap that helped keep her hair in place while she slept. Her head had begun to pound, and the wrap aggravated the pain all the more.

"I'm sorry Ms. Black, but we must terminate our agreement at the end of Fall Break in October. It has been decided, and there is nothing more I can do about. I do, however, wish you well in your endeavors. Good bye, Ms. Black."

"Good bye, Principal Rice." Jackie placed the phone onto the receiver and muttered, "You didn't sound too sorry, Principal Rice." She took a quick breath, "but all things work together.
God is still in the blessing business. I receive that."

Jackie Black felt her spirits lift, until she checked her bank account. She scratched some figures on paper, and sighed heavily. She would have to get a job.

As she scoured her makeshift closet, comprised of old dance costumes hanging from a wardrobe rack, for something to wear, her cell phone rang. She sighed deeply hoping it wasn't more bad news. She noticed the call was from St. Andrew Church. The possibility of hearing her Prentiss on the other end gave her a small chill. She answered in her most pleasant voice.

"Hello!" She sang out.

"Good morning, Sister Black," Francis' quiet, monotone voice said on the other end. "I am calling on behalf of Pastor LeBeaux. Will you be able to meet with him today?"

"Of course, Sister Francis! Of course! Shall I come right now?"

"Can you come around at 1p.m.?"

"Yes! Of course. Shall I bring him lunch?"

"He has lunch arrangements already, Sister Black. We will see you at one o'clock."

Jackie was ecstatic. *But did Francis say, we? Oh, it doesn't matter*, she thought. She finally was being given an audience with Pastor LeBeaux. *He probably wants to tell me how much he appreciates me and my gifts and thoughtfulness last week*, she thought.

Golden Sunsets retirement home was looking for an activities planner; she would drop off her application and hopefully have an impromptu interview before going to meet with Pastor LeBeaux. She managed to make a conservative ensemble by adding a royal blue blazer to the blue backless jumpsuit she had worn to the church picnic. She fingered through her freshly permed, golden colored pixie cut, got dressed, and set out, determined to get a job and the man of her dreams.

Golden Sunsets was a retirement home situated on 10 picturesque acres of green grass and shade trees on the northwest part of town. The stucco of the sprawling ranch-style building was the color of turmeric. The grounds were immaculate, and the inside was cleaner than most hospitals. The support staff wore yellow smocks and nurses wore brightly-colored scrubs. Their nametags were golden suns with black typeface. Golden Sunsets, with its impeccable interior and capable, professional staff, had the reputation for being run like a machine--a clean, efficient, and pleasant machine. Jackie arrived with her application in a plastic cover. She stopped at the front desk where a fifty-something blonde lady took her application and asked her to wait. The lady went down a nearby hall while Jackie sat erect in an oversized rattan chair and tried to calm her nerves. Just as she finished a relaxation breathing exercise, an extremely tall, dark brown woman floated towards her.

She wore an ivory blouse, black slacks, and shiny black flats.

"Good morning, Ms. Black. I am Nurse Eva, the administrator of Golden Sunsets. I understand you are interested in the activities planner position."

"Hello, Eva," Jackie said with a bright smile.

"**Nurse** Eva," the woman corrected.

"Nurse Eva. I'm sorry. It's a pleasure to meet you. Yes, I'm interested in the position."

"Good. Do you have time for a tour?" Nurse Eva asked placing Jackie's application in a folder.

"Oh! Of course! I'd love a tour."

Without a word, Nurse Eva turned sharply and began walking down a corridor to the left of the lobby. Jackie caught up to her in time to hear that the hallway was for male guests. The name plates on each door were in the shapes of suns. She saw some men fully dressed and some in hospital gowns. Some were walking down the carpeted hallway and some were sitting in their rooms with the doors open. They stopped at the nurses' station toward the end of the hall and greeted three nurses wearing mint green scrubs. They made a right from the nurses' station and ended up at another station. Two nurses in pink were at their post. They nodded at Nurse Eva and kept working. Eva and Jackie turned right down a hallway that housed female guests. There were ladies fully dressed and some dressed in housecoats. A few had small pocketbooks on their arms as if they were going out. They all smiled and nodded at Nurse Eva and Jackie as they passed. The hallway returned them to the lobby.

"As you can see, we don't have many guests. This allows us to maintain an exceptional standard of cleanliness and personal attention. We are like a family here. No one steals, abuses, yells, or bullies. We keep the noise level at a minimum in the residence areas so that we can hear cries of distress and unusual sounds." She pointed to two other hallways on the other side of the lobby. "Down that hallway are the cafe, exercise, and recreation rooms. Down the other are the administrative offices. Would you like to see the recreation room and meet some of our more lively guests?" "I would." Jackie said trying to curb her excitement. The recreation room was large and sunny. It looked like a solarium with its glass wall and ceilings. There were plants, rattan furniture, and game tables throughout. Tucked away in a corner was a nook of books tucked away in a corner. Jackie turned around in the room looking at the details of the ceiling.

"It's perfectly safe. There are storm windows with an internal protection pane connected to the generator in the event of a storm. The windows become white and look like a regular ceiling. It's nice to have on dreary days. Rainy days can be so depressing." Nurse Eva said.

There was a co-ed group of guests sitting around a large table playing bid whist. Only four members of the group were playing. The other two were onlookers.

"Let me introduce you to our guests," Nurse Eva said approaching the table. "Ladies and gentlemen, I'd like you to meet Jackie Black. She is interested in being the new activities director. They paused and looked at Jackie with caution. Nurse Eva continued, "Ms. Black, I'd like you to meet some of our best bid whist players. This is Mr. Robert Endicott and his partner Mr. Silas

Farmer." The two gentlemen nodded. "This is Ms. Hattie Blackmon and her partner Ms. Ivy Nelson." The two ladies offered smiles.

Nurse Eva then turned to the spectators of the game. "This is Ms. Gladys Turner and Ms. Shirley Frye." From Nurse Eva's gestures, Gladys was seated in the wheelchair and Shirley was using Gladys' frail lap to hold her yarn as she knitted. Gladys said nothing, nor did she acknowledge their presence. Though Shirley kept knitting, she did manage a quick up and down assessment of Jackie. She finally smiled and nodded, never missing a stitch.

"Thank you for your time, ladies and gentlemen. Enjoy your game," Nurse Eva said directing Jackie's attention to another area of the room. "Here," she said opening a French door to a smaller room, "is where you, if selected for the position, will hold your activities."

Jackie's heart leapt at the openness of the space. There were mirrors and ballet bars on one side. The hardwood floors gleamed under Jackie's feet as she walked across the space. It was all she could do to keep herself from pirouetting across the floor.

"It's beautiful. It's perfect. We could do ballroom dancing, low-impact aerobics, and tai chi. I love it," Jackie exclaimed. Her enthusiasm had escaped, but the stern Nurse Eva smiled.

"Good. I will show you the chapel and then we can talk in my office."

The chapel was quaint but beautiful. Mahogany pews with memory foam cushions on the backs and seats were in two rows. A matching altar and small podium stood at the front. Large Boston ferns stood guard on pillars on both ends of the altar, while a tall arrangement of flowering plants and greenery knelt in front of the podium.

The two ladies entered a spacious office of sleek white furniture. There were two deep red armchairs positioned in front of the white lacquered desk.

"Please, Ms. Black. Have a seat." Nurse Eva walked around the desk and sat erectly in her chair. "What do you think of Golden Sunsets?"

"I think it is beautiful and peaceful." Jackie could have rambled on, but she didn't want to ruin her chances of getting the job.

"I would like to offer you the position. We need an activities planner badly, but don't let my eagerness to hire you indicate that I run a loose ship. In fact, I run a very tight ship. People who don't do their jobs are fired. This is what happened to the previous planner. She shirked her duties and did not perform to the standard that we have here. If you do the same, the same will happen to you. Pending calls to your references, the job is yours. I will get back with you at the end of the day. In the meantime, read this packet carefully. It explains the responsibilities of every staff member at Golden Sunsets." She stood and handed Jackie a binder with a picture of a sun on the front.

"Thank you, Nurse Eva. I look forward to hearing from you." Jackie said taking the heavy binder.

Nurse Eva, taller than Jackie by about three inches, walked Jackie to the door and bid her good day. Jackie arranged herself in the Thunderbird and drove away. When she got off the Golden Sunsets premises, she squealed with delight. She squealed all the way to the church for her meeting with Pastor LeBeaux.

CHAPTER 19: THE MEETING

Jackie had gone over this moment hundreds of times in her mind. The moment she would be alone with Prentiss. The moment he would share his heart with her. The moment she would pour hers out to him. She had practiced her facial expressions in the long mirrors of her studio, timing her wide smile and surprise-eyes so that the light would hit her skin just so, and then he would love her. But as Jackie parked her car in the lot of St. Andrew, all of the rehearsals she'd performed in her studio melted away. She felt unsure.

"Lord, be my strength where I am weak," she prayed, "You didn't bring me this far to leave me, now. I give myself over to your will and your way." Jackie Black switched off the ignition and opened the door of her Thunderbird, grabbing the royal blue jacket as she exited the car.

As she approached the doorway to the receptionist area, Francis greeted her smartly. "Hello, Sister Black. You're right on time. Please have a seat, and I will let Pastor LeBeaux know you're here. Then we can go right in."

"Thank you, Francis." Jackie sat down on the edge of the tan wing-back chair. "Um. Francis?"

"Yes, Sister Black," Francis replied, looking over the round tortoise shell frames of her glasses.

"Did I hear you say, *we*? I was under the impression I would be meeting with Pastor Prentiss alone."

Francis the Secretary slid the glasses onto her face. "That impression, Sister Black, is incorrect. We will be seeing Pastor LeBeaux together. Those were his specific instructions." Francis turned and dialed the pastor's extension and announced Jackie Black's arrival. Francis stood and made her way around the desk. She extended her hand toward Pastor Prentiss LeBeaux's now open door. "Shall we go in, Sister Black?"

"Why sure, Francis," Jackie said tugging at the lapels of her royal blue jacket.

"Thank you, Francis." Prentiss LeBeaux said with a brief glance up from his desk. Jackie noticed that Pastor LeBeaux had several sheets of typed notes on his desk. "Come on in, Sister Black. No need to be shy. Have a seat."

"Thank you, Pastor Prentiss. It's so good to see you this afternoon. Perhaps after this little pow-wow you and I can go and get a bite to--"

"No. No. Sister Black." Pastor's response was clipped. "No need for that; I've already had lunch." Jackie noticed that his face was pulled tight, and between glances at the type-filled sheets of paper, he rubbed his head slowly with the palm of his hand. Still, Jackie found Prentiss LeBeaux fiercely attractive. It seemed he'd dressed for the occasion of meeting with her. He wore a slate colored suit and crisp white shirt. At his neck was a navy tie, speckled with small orange polka dots. The dimple of the tie was centered perfectly below his strong chin. Jackie almost came undone as she tallied the details of perfection she found in Pastor LeBeaux.

"Yes, Yes. That's right," Jackie stammered. "Francis told me that when she scheduled our appointment."

Francis nodded and began to scribble on her yellow steno pad.

"Sister Black, I want to talk to you about some things, today. But before we get into that, I do want you to know, I've recognized all the contributions you've made to St. Andrew. You really came in and got busy doing God's work. I appreciate your efforts. You should know that." Prentiss straightened his tie and placed both elbows on his desk. He looked at Jackie intently, squinting his sleepy gray eyes. "It's important that you know that your work for the Lord has not gone unnoticed."

"Oh yes, Pastor Prentiss. Anything I can do in service for the Lord, I'll do. And anything I can do for you, to support you in ministry, I'm more than willing to do." Jackie began to fan herself. "I've gotten just a little warm, Pastor. If you don't mind, I'll just," Jackie shifted in her chair, stretching her arms to remove the royal blue jacket. As she turned to hang the jacket on the back of her seat, Francis the Secretary got a full view of Jackie's ensemble. The jumpsuit revealed Jackie's entire bare back and threatened to give Francis an ample view of the custard colored skin right above Jackie's tailbone.

Francis sucked in her breath. "One moment, Sister Black. I'll adjust the thermostat. It's right here on the wall." Francis moved to adjust the temperature; however, on her way back to her seat, she deftly lifted Jackie Black's jacket from the back of her chair and held it out. "Let me help you with this."

Jackie slid her long arms back into the sleeves of the jacket. "Oh Francis, you're so helpful," she muttered and flopped back into the chair.

Prentiss watched the scene play out in disbelief, but regained himself quickly. He must handle business. He recalled Locke's words: *.and be* **firm**, *Prentiss.* He could not let his compassion keep him from being direct, not this time. There was too much to lose.

"This disrobing you've done just now is a perfect example of how something seemingly harmless can be inappropriate."

"Oh no, pastor, I just…"

"Sister Black. Please keep your jacket on, and listen to what I have to say." He paused, waiting for her to comply. He ignored the look of shock on her face.

"Now, over the past month or two, you've been working hard to contribute to the work of the church, but many of those contributions have been done at the expense of others. Some have been without decorum." Prentiss paused. "You took it upon yourself to remove the floral arrangements that Sister Caldwell prepared with some of your own. This was presumptuous and it greatly offended our church florist. You also took it upon yourself to add a tablecloth to the communion table, but as a deaconess, surely you know there is nothing to be placed upon the table. But you disregarded convention and did as you wished, offending the sanctity of communion. You, without permission or authority, took over a Sunday school class because the teacher was a few minutes late. Her students were supervised by another teacher, so there was no need for you to interfere, but you again took it upon yourself to disrupt the children's routine and teach the class. That was inappropriate and inconsiderate on many levels, Sister Black. Most recently, you shared inappropriate information with the congregation while making announcements. The personal lives of members are not to be broadcast over the congregation. You offended the two people you mentioned as well as disrespected the house of God. In these instances, it has been said that you were only trying to help, but in all cases, you took it upon yourself without conferring with anyone else. This will no longer be tolerated. Before I go on, do you have anything you would like to say?" Prentiss leaned back in his chair and released a breath. Just recounting her behavior made him angry all over again. "Father," Jackie said with tears in her eyes looking toward the ceiling, "forgive me, for I did not know." She pulled a tissue from her purse and dabbed at her eyes. "Pastor, I am so sorry. I didn't mean any harm. I was trying to take some initiative. I didn't think I was hurting anything or anyone. I am so sad that you think I did this on purpose."

"I never said you intentionally hurt or upset people, Sister Black. But since you brought up intentions, let's talk about last week. On Monday, you took MY shirts from MY home and had them laundered. What were your intentions behind that?"

"I was just trying to be thoughtful and helpful to you."

"I see. That was a rather intimate chore, as was bringing me food, sending me perfume soaked cards, and making me CDs of love songs. Not only are these actions intimate, but they suggest a level of intimacy that DOES NOT exist between the two of us." Prentiss could feel his anger rising. His neck was hot and fists clenched. He took a deep breath and looked away from Jackie's bulging, watery eyes. Watching tears form in her eyes caused him to think of Maybelline's tears. He became angry. He arranged the typed pieces of paper into a neat stack, slid them into a manila folder, and passed them to Francis.

"Sister Black, I do not appreciate your treatment of the members of St. Andrew--our florist Sister Caldwell, the Sunday school teacher Sister Berry, Brother Christmas whose family cleaners have ALWAYS cleaned the clothes of the St. Andrew clergy, Sister Maybelline, Sister Iris, and Deacon Hughes. I cannot force you to become thoughtful of your brothers and sisters in Christ, only the Holy Spirit can convict you in that regard, but I have a responsibility to protect my flock. If you wish to remain a member of this congregation, you will not continue to behave this way." He paused. Jackie dabbed at a tear in the corner of her left eye. Prentiss forged ahead, thinking of Big Hughes' words *be clear when you tell her you don't want her.*

"It has also come to my attention that you sent a text message to many women of the congregation. The contents of said text message left me appalled. It is normal, Sister Black, for church members to grow fond of their pastor. It is not uncommon for that fondness to take a wrong turn towards romantic notions, but I want to make it clear that I am not romantically interested in you, Sister Jackie. My heart belongs to God and to the St. Andrew Church (*and Maybelline Crowder* he wanted to say). Any feelings I have for you are that of a sister--a sister in Christ. Please redirect YOUR affections and attentions elsewhere." Prentiss released a sigh of relief.

Jackie's face was heavy with hurt. Her penciled eyebrows were wrinkled and raised in sorrowful surprise. Her lower eyelids were swollen with unshed tears. Her cheeks were hollowed and lips pressed tightly together and folded in. She dabbed at her eyes and sniffed, holding back what would certainly prove to be a torrential rain of tears. She took a shaky breath.

"Pastor LeBeaux, I am sorry. Godly sorry for any trouble I have caused. I only wanted to please the Lord by being a helpful servant in His kingdom. I only sent the text message to help you. I noticed how so many women of the church fawn all over you and demand so much of your attention after church; I thought if I *culled the herd* it would help you see the woman God has for you. I have operated in my spiritual gift of helps, and I am so sorry if my helping has not been received as such," she said through quivering lips.

"The old adage says 'hell is full of good meanings, but heaven is full of GOOD works.' Sister Jackie, let us focus on that which is true, honorable, right, and pure. Now, you have relinquished your responsibilities to the music ministry, and I think it best if you relinquish your seat as a deaconess as well. You need time to fellowship and get to know the other congregants as a peer--a layperson."

"I understand, Pastor LeBeaux."

"Good. Walk circumspectly with God and in your service at St. Andrew." Prentiss said standing. "Let us pray," he said, not giving Jackie a chance to say another word. Jackie stood and stuck her hands out so that she could hold Prentiss' hands, but Prentiss placed his hands on his desk. "*Father, we thank you for this meeting. You told us in your word that if we are not disciplined, we are not your true sons and daughters. Today has been a day of discipline. Let the words spoken here fall on good ground. Amen.*"

Jackie didn't have the breath to say "amen," so she just nodded. She fought back tears as she gathered her purse and exited quickly.

"I'll see you out, Sister Black," Francis the Secretary said.

"I can manage," Jackie eeked out. She left the door to Prentiss' office open and started down the stairs. Once she reached her car, she could hold the tears no longer. She sobbed loudly and rocked herself to and fro, causing the seat to creak and moan. Tears poured down her face while she screamed her anguish in her cramped, red Thunderbird. Between racking sobs, she breathed deeply and wiped her eyes. She turned on her car radio and Norah Jones was singing:

I've tried so hard my dear to show
That you're my every dream
Yet you're afraid each thing I do
Is just some evil scheme
A memory from your lonesome past Keeps us so far apart
Why can't I free your doubtful mind And melt your cold cold heart

After hearing the first verse, Jackie turned up the volume and held herself as she listened to the second verse:

Another love before my time
Made your heart sad an' blue

And so my heart is paying now For
things I didn't do
In anger unkind words are said
That make the teardrops start
Why can't I free your doubtful mind
And melt your cold cold heart
There was a time when I believed
That you belonged to me
But now I know your heart is shackled
To a memory
The more I learn to care for you
The more we drift apart
Why can't I free your doubtful mind
And melt your cold cold heart

When the song ended, Jackie sat quietly with her eyes darting hither and yon. Her mind was moving so quickly, she could hardly control her thoughts. There was one thought that stuck in her mind. "Prentiss is a not a cold-hearted person. He looked absolutely distressed. He didn't want to hurt me. Not really," she said aloud. "Someone put him up to this. Someone told him to have this talk...or else he wouldn't have seemed so conflicted."

With resolve, Jackie sucked in her breath, started her car and pulled off the parking lot. As she turned onto the street, she noticed Clem Callahan's car turning into the lot. She drove in tears all the way to her studio and then decided—under what she discerned as the unction of the Holy Spirit—to drive back to the church. When Jackie returned to the church, she noticed Locke's navy Cadillac parked in the space closest to the church entrance. "So, Clem and Locke are meeting with Prentiss," she noted aloud. She imagined how Prentiss was probably recounting every minute of her humiliation to Clem and Locke. "Snobs!" she shouted. "I'll show them. If Prentiss wants a subservient wife, I can be that. I will be just as sweet and quiet as everyone said Ava was."

CHAPTER 20: THE BID WHIST CLUB

Jackie had worked at Golden Sunsets for three weeks before any of the guests would say anything other than a polite greeting to her. As she drove across town to Golden Sunsets, she pondered how different her life had become. She was flying under the radar at church. She came. She sat. She smiled. She left. Everyone seemed to like her all the more for it. People were nicer. They spoke to and chatted with her before and after service. Still she felt invisible. She blended into the large, working and middleclass congregation of St. Andrew. Blending in was *not* what she wanted.

Jackie had read that sometimes people had to do things they did not want so they could later do the things they wanted. She had turned that over in her mind daily, especially after her conversation with Pastor LeBeaux. She had apologized, shed tears, and vowed to behave, as if she were a child. She smiled to herself. She was sure her time would come. Her time to stand out again. Her time to interfere in their lives as they had interfered in hers. Her time to show them they were wrong about her. Until then, she needed to support herself, and she was thankful for Golden Sunsets.

She grabbed her yellow smock, onto which she had bedazzled her name, touched up her gold lipstick, and finger-combed her honey blonde cap of curls. She smoothed down her amber gold velour track pants, and inspected her gold sneakers as she walked away from her car. She was determined to get some participants for her Basic Movements class, and she had planned to go from room to room recruiting people if she had to.

Her first stop was the recreation room. She found the Bid Whist Club at their regular table just as they were when she had first met them.

"Good morning!" she sang cheerfully. "May I watch?"

"Sure you can. Just keep quiet, though," Hattie said adjusting her eye glasses. "We're about to win and don't need any distractions."

"Bout to win? Who? You and Ivy ain't 'bout to win nothing but a hard way to go!" Silas said grinning and showing his teeth.

"What does it take to win?" Jackie questioned quietly but loud enough for them to hear.

"Heaven help us. This child doesn't know how to play bid whist." Ivy said sucking air through her teeth. "Oh. Did I offend you when I called you a child? I mean you are old enough to be my child or grandchild, but I know how grown folk get when someone tells them they ain't grown. I just..."

"Gracious! Who got Ivy started? Once she starts talking, she gets to rambling, and ain't no telling what all she'll say." Shirley snorted between the clicking of her knitting needles.

"I'm sorry. I'll be quiet." Jackie said shrinking into her seat.

"Good, 'cause that's what we told you to do when you sat down," Hattie said rolling her eyes.

"You see, Hun," Ivy began, "the point is to make the highest bid, and to win your bids. So, if my team, that's me and Hattie over there, if we bid seven, we should make seven books, or you can call them tricks, but I hate that word. Tricks. It reminds me of loose women. My mother used to say she could tell a loose woman by the color lipstick she wore; I've worn red lipstick all my life and never have I been a loose woman in any shape, form or fashion…"

"Except for your loose lips." Shirley said sharply. "She'll never learn how to play whist, let you tell it."

"Anyway, Hun," Ivy continued. "The plan is to be sure that the cards you're holding are good enough to win the game. If you've got good cards, you can take every card on the table. Oh, but you must have good cards. They have to work for you, and when you pull out those cards, you know the ones you bid, they better be able to hold their own, because if not, you'll walk away with your tail betwixt your legs. Oh, Mother said that a lot too. Walking away with your tail betwixt your legs. I made sure in all my living, I never had to live with the fact that I'd walked away from something with my tail, tucked betwixt my leg. It's so very unattractive on a woman. I hope you never have to have THAT experience, Dancing Doll."

"Somebody put a cork in Ivy, so they can finish the game," Shirley interrupted. "This woman didn't come here to hear all that."

The game finally ended. The two gentlemen, Robert and Silas, were sore losers and the ladies, Hattie and Ivy, were bad winners.

"Well, Robert Calton Endicott, what do you have to say for yourself?" Ivy taunted.

"You and Hattie won fair and square. There's no need to discuss it further," Robert said straightening his navy blue cardigan.

"Leave him alone, Ivy. You know how the professor gets when he loses," Hattie clipped returning the cards to the box. She looked up to see Jackie's face of surprise. "Robert Endicott is a teacher."

"Was a teacher," he corrected crossing his long, thin legs.

"You still are. You teach us something every chance you get," Hattie said sounding annoyed. "He doesn't belong in here, Jackie. He should be teaching at that school across the bridge instead of here playing bid whist."

"Especially when he still ain't learned how to play good." Ivy slipped.

"Ain't? Play good? Ivy, you speak as if your father didn't educate you. Our bodies are old, but our minds haven't forgotten what we've been taught. You know better." Robert said with a warm smile. He then turned his attention to Jackie. "So, young lady. What has drawn you to our little game this morning? You have crouched around long enough."

"Oh, Mr., Sir, Professor Endicott," she stammered. I'm still rather new here, and I so appreciate the lessons you all have to offer. So, I'm just gleaning from your fields of wisdom. I have no stories to share."

Robert Endicott peered over his small, black, round wire rimmed glasses. He was always suspecting of those who were reluctant to share in conversation, but only because at one point in his life, he'd been one who was reluctant to share. "I'm sure you have stories; everyone does. As a matter of fact we're all making history every day of our lives."

"Why, Professor Endicott, I'd love to hear some of the history you have to share," Jackie said with interest. She was slowly beginning to get the hang of getting to know people before she inserted herself into their lives. She'd also realized that old people, when stroked a little, would tell stories with no end. Robert Endicott, who had not been called Professor Endicott (unless it was a joke from one of the residents) for decades, basked in Jackie Black's interest in his stories. Her big hungry eyes sent him back to his time behind the lectern, as he waxed philosophically to graduate students who thought that history was the only knowledge there was to gain. While Golden Sunsets was a beautiful place: clean, quiet, and full of stories filled with the sparkle and shine of yesteryears, Robert Endicott missed those who would seek out his intellectual prowess, who knew the true value of education and it's magical key to success. Jackie reminded him of those times gone, ones he'd enjoyed so much. He was grateful for her curiosity and would do all he could to feed her ferocious appetite for information.

Robert Endicott

Robert Calton Endicott was a handsome 85 year old. Jackie looked at his caramel colored skin and prayed her skin would be that beautiful when she got to be his age. His steel gray hair was brushed back in thick waves. His eyebrows were white as was his thin mustache. His eyes, though, were bright, happy, and full of something Jackie couldn't place. "Now, young lady, tell me about yourself. Are you from Sweet Fields?"

"No, sir. I'm not from around here. My family is from up north. I just struck out on my own and ended up in beautiful Sweet Fields." Jackie offered a smile with her partial truth.

"I see. Where do you worship? With Rev. LeBeaux at St. Andrew or Rev. Williams across the bridge at Traveler's Rest?"

"St. Andrew with Rev. LeBeaux. I've been there almost a year."

"Do you know the history of Sweet Fields? It's quite remarkable."

"No, but I'd love to if you have time."

"Oh child, he'd like nothing more. You and Robert mind taking this history lesson over there?" Shirley Frye pointed to a nearby table with a knitting needle. "Silas and I are about to put a beating on Ivy and Hattie."

Jackie and Robert did as Shirley said and moved to a nearby table. Robert, the consummate gentleman, pulled out Jackie's chair before taking his own. He cleared his throat and began his lecture.

"After the Civil War, the south was a dirty, defeated mess. Plantations were destroyed, some white people were poor for the first times in their lives, and freed slaves were wandering around like chickens with no heads. They didn't know where to go or what to do. They didn't know anything except how to work. Some traveled in groups and some wandered off alone. The paths of five men from South Carolina, Florida, Alabama, and Georgia crossed somewhere and they had the idea of creating their own *plantation*, if you will. Now, they figured if white men could thrive on their labor, they could thrive on their own labor, so they put their heads, talents, and skills together. Let's see. Jim Blackman was a blacksmith out of South Carolina. Can you think of why he would leave South Carolina and head further south when everyone was scrambling to get north?" He asked the question as if she were a pupil in his class.

"Uhh," Jackie paused. "No idea. Why?" she asked leaning in a bit.

"Jim was looking for his wife Mary who had been sold to a plantation in Georgia. He was determined to find her." "Did he find her?" Jackie asked sitting on the edge of her seat with widened eyes.

"He did. It wasn't too hard. His wife Mary was an unusually tall, thin woman with blue black skin and no eyebrows. He found her cooking and cleaning for two old women who had lost everything. He walked right onto the porch of that house and called her name.

'Mary, Mary, my sweet blueberry,' he called out in his deep, booming voice. *'Come on outta there. You belong wit' yo' husband.'* A few

seconds later, Mary came tearing through that door full speed and knocked him down with a hug most powerful. They sat there and hugged and cried in each other's arms not paying attention to the white women who sat watching. Mary started packing up, and without a word to those women, walked out of the house to be with her husband."

"How beautiful!" Jackie cried holding her clasped hands under her chin. "He called her his sweet blueberry."

"As Mary was arranging her meager belongings, those two old white women gathered up some supplies for Mary. They gave her a little bit of money before she and Jim left. Then Jim and Mary started walking to their future."

"That's a wonderful love story."

"On their way, they ran into two men, one of whom had a small child. Red Turner and John Farmer had worked on a sugar cane plantations in Florida. They had found an abandoned boy on the side of the road.

"How old was the little boy?" Jackie asked.

"Some say he was about three or four years old, but no one knew for sure. Someone had put the boy in a sack and left him; he was kicking and screaming when John heard him. John Farmer had sired a lot of children and never got to see a one, so he decided he was going to keep the boy. Red wasn't too keen on traveling with a young child, but he didn't want to travel alone.

'John, I don't think that's a good idea. A child only gon' slow us down. Dat boy needs a mama.' They had plans to travel as far north as they could, but they didn't know anything about the north. One day, they got to talking about starting their own sugar cane operation right there in the south.

'How come we gotta travel to some place we don' know nuthin 'bout? We knows how to run a sugar cane farm,' Red said to John one evening over a meal of roasted rabbit.

'Yep. We knows, but we ain't got no land, Red. We need some land and some tools. Where we gon' git that?' John asked. Neither man knew how they would acquire land for a sugar cane operation, but they knew they

could run one if they got a chance. So they kept on their travels. Some months later, they met Abraham Callahan. He was a real fair-skinned man from south Louisiana. John's little boy had taken ill and the men didn't know what to do. They cautiously approached the mulatto and asked about a midwife who could help the child. Callahan took them to his little cottage, one he had once shared with his mother.

Abraham was well cared for by his former slave master, who was also his father. Wealthy white slave owners had a different system of slavery in those parts. They took care of the children they had by their mulatto women. Often they'd free their women and set them up in nice brownstones down in the French Quarters. They took special care of their boy children, financing their trust funds, paying their accounts at local clothiers, and even sending them off to get a good education, sometimes in Canada or France. So, even though the war had taken its toll on the south, the Callahans weren't impoverished the way other family plantations had been. Their former masters made sure that their lighter skinned brown descendants would survive the economic crisis that would soon occur. After hosting Red and John for a few months, Abraham decided to leave and set out with his new friends. When Abraham told his father of his plans, his father gave him a large provision of inheritance and bid his only child goodbye.

The trio, along with the little boy, traveled until they came upon an uninhabited plantation that was partially in ruins. Abraham Callahan, in the role of a white man looking to restart his sugar cane business, set out to purchase the land and the surrounding buildings. The owner of the property, in dire straits, accepted Abraham's money and gave him the deed to the property. They repaired what they could, ate what they could hunt, and bartered for the rest. When the little boy took sick again, they sought help from Mary "Blackberry" Blackman at a nearby camp. Mary and Jim became friends with the trio of men and joined them at their run down plantation. Mary cooked and tended to the boy while the men worked on farming and starting their sugar cane crop.

"God blessed them with good friends." Jackie chimed in.

"Then, Paul Endicott, my great, great grandfather, showed up at the meeting they had by the river on Sundays," Robert Endicott continued. "He preached about freedom and hard times, and he read the bible to them. So many of the freedmen hadn't seen a black man who could read. Through the week, he would teach folk how to read for a meal here and there. On Sundays by the river, he'd teach them what the bible REALLY said. After a while, there were more and more people living in camps near that river. They would find work where they could. When they could get a piece of land and sharecrop, there were more women and children that you could count. Paul would sit under a big oak tree with the children teaching them to read while their parents worked the fields."

"But where did he live?"

"He took up with Callahan and his friends. Now, there were camps of people and then sharecroppers nearby, but they were closer to the river. Callahan and his friends lived on the east side of the river kind of separated from the others. There was a shallow, narrow part of the river where people crossed. Eventually, the men built a bridge."

"So your great, great grandfather was the first teacher and preacher here?"

"Yes, he was. He loved reading and teaching. He married a young woman who was the child of what they called a maroon or a Black Seminole. The community was growing. The once run-down plantation had been rebuilt. The crops were growing, and the five families were living as one. When they harvested the first crop of sugar cane, they decided to call the plantation Sweet Fields." "How wonderful!" Jackie gushed.

"Over the years, families began to build houses and the main house became the gathering place for special occasions, community meetings, and church meetings during the winter. Years later, when the population reached about 100 people, it was officially recognized as a town. Because county and state officials thought Abraham was a white man who was trying to have slaves on the sly, they didn't ask any questions. Because of this, the families were very careful about who they let settle in Sweet Fields."

"The people still act like that now. Picky about who they let in their community," Jackie said with bitterness on her lips and a furrow on her brow. "And they're supposed to be Christians."

"What does being a Christian have to do with it? It's God, Sweet Fields, and family-- in that order," Robert choked out emotionally. "You don't understand. We've managed to survive when other black towns were destroyed. We've have lived peacefully without any real scandal here for over 100 years," Robert said leaning back and re-crossing his legs. "We've had people to try to take over the town, but no one has succeeded yet. I always feel a bit sorry for those who try. It's never a pretty sight."

Ivy Nelson

Ivy Nelson mumbled a lot, to keep her thoughts together. Shirley and Hattie often complained about her ramblings, but it was her ramblings that kept her mind firm. She had to say what was on her mind, no matter how out of sync, because once Ivy Nelson said her peace, she could hear herself. She knew she was alive, and that brought her a good level of comfort. All the pieces needn't come together, but in Ivy's mind, everything was connected to something else. She'd make her way around her own conversations, eventually.

She felt that way about people too. Ivy's mother, Lorene, tried to keep Ivy from people and their goings on, but Ivy's mind didn't work like that. Her mind reached out. She was in Sweet Fields, but often times she wasn't of it. She found herself curious about the secrets her mother kept from her. She wanted to know what was behind every closed door and what lay across every bridge. When she found out, she wasn't privileged to tell. So she wrote, but sometimes she couldn't write fast enough, and the words busted from the trap of her mind then came spilling out of her mouth. She felt like that on one brisk October morning, and it just so happened that Jackie Black was walking past Ivy Nelson as she sat at one of the large windows mumbling. She said out loud,

"You can never tell what's going on in that Murphy Inn."

"I'm sorry, Ms. Ivy. What did you say?"

"Just taking a walk down memory lane, Dancing Doll. I wasn't talking about much of nothing."

"Sure you were, Ms. Ivy. Don't say things like that. What you have to say is important, and someone should listen." Jackie Black drew up a chair and sat near Ivy. Ivy turned to look at her and squinted at the little gold bedazzled beads running across Jackie's uniform. She was the only worker whose uniform seemed to send off sparks when she walked through the large room full of windows. Ivy liked that. But she also wondered about Jackie.

Why was she so feverishly curious? Every since she started working at Golden Sunsets, weeks ago, The Dancing Doll would appear everywhere and when Ivy least expected. She soaked up conversations. Her face, while listening to Robert Endicott last week, looked like the face of a child who'd not eaten in a very long time. Ivy squinted at Jackie again and slid her glasses up her nose with her middle finger. *Surely it would do no harm to share a morsel of memory with her*, Ivy thought.

"I was just thinking about the old Murphy Inn. That place was full of surprises, Hun. I hear that Maggs Murphy's gran' is in the place now."

"Yes. Iris." Jackie said frowning and looking down at the spotless tiled floor.

"Iris. Odd name for a young girl, isn't it?" Ivy mused. "Anyway, Maggs' has always been a place for women who couldn't find their way. That's what kept this town hopping. Oh the drama that would darken those doorsteps at Maggs place!" Ivy laughed loudly. Her hands trembled in her lap as she laughed. "I was good and grown when I knew what was going on at Maggs'. Mother was long gone to her mansion in the sky, but I could hear her voice as clear as a bell telling me, *you should never attempt to know more of things you know nothing about. Curiosity, kills the cat and the mouse lives to fight another day.*"

"Wait, Ms. Ivy. I don't know what you mean. Wayward women? Cats? Mice? What are you…?"

"I ain't said nothing about wayward women, now, Dancing Doll. I said Maggs' place was always one for women who couldn't find their way. A place's history never leaves it. That gran' is probably trying to find her way, too. Iris is it? Mother always said, you should be careful what you name your children, especially your girls. It could cause them a lifetime of worry."

"Maggs' place. It sounds vibrant!" Jackie was looking up, toward one of the far windows as if she was trying to imagine it. Her eyelids fluttered with excitement. "What do you know of it?" "One thing I know for sure is that most girls came there pretty, and six or seven months later they left prettier than they came. Another thing I know is that some women came there mighty ugly. Faces swollen. Bones broken. Cuts all over them. But they left there pretty, too. Some women came there tattered and torn. Clothes falling off of them. But they left sharp as a tack. They left pretty. After a while, someone would come and pick them up and take them on away from there. Most of them you never saw again."

"Oh my, what kind of place was that? How did they come one way and leave another? Where were their men?"

"Their men? The men were the reason they were there! Their men and the war and the civil rights movement and whatever other kind of uproar was happening in the world. That's what kept Maggs' place open. The only men you saw around Maggs' place were the ones who guarded the doors, so no more men could get in."

"Was it a bordello?" Jackie's eyes were bigger than ever.

"What you mean?" Ivy turned in her chair to look Jackie in her face. "A *whore house*? Did you hear me say *whore house*? Weren't you listening to anything I said?" Ivy shook her head slowly. "That was one house I knew I'd never want my own daughter to end up in, because I knew even though you came out of there pretty, something real ugly had to happen to you for you to end up there."

"But who brought the women? How did they get to Maggs' place? How did they know to go there?"

Ivy's thoughts had trailed off. She pulled an off-white lace trimmed handkerchief from the bosom of her sky blue dress, the one with layers and layers of ruffles at the décolletage. The one she really liked. After wringing the dainty piece of cloth in her hands and dabbing her forehead, she continued. "Most times, women, teen-agers, even little girls were dropped off at Maggs'. Other times, they walked right up to the door on their own. Matter of fact, I only remember one girl Maggie actually left her house to go and get. Just one." Ivy turned to Jackie again. "And I know this for a fact, because I was there."

Jackie leaned in, clasped her palms, laced her fingers together and rested her narrow chin on her hands. "Oh my, Ms. Ivy! You were there? Please! Tell me about her."

"I was walking toward Maggs' house right before the last light hit her porch. I did that every now and then, just to keep up with things in my neighborhood. We do that here in Sweet Fields, just walk around to keep up with things and report back to whomever looked like they needed to know. I frequented Maggs' street. It's that gnawing in the back of my mind that made me do that. It's Mother's voice that I kept hearing telling me to stay away from that place, that kept me going, even after Mother was long gone. Bless her slumbering soul, dear Jesus."

"Yes. Bless her," Jackie said quickly to move Ivy along.

"Shut up! You don't even know Mother. Anyway, I walked up just in time to see Maggs trying to hold onto a little package of a girl. The girl looked like she was fainting over and over again. She couldn't stand up. I couldn't stop staring. I was across the street, you see. Let Maggs tell it, my bottom lip was on the ground, and I'd dropped my handkerchief down there with it." Ivy laughed. "Heh. Heh. Heeeeeeehhhh. That Maggs know she could tell a story. Anyway, Maggs caught me staring and called me on over to her. '*Watcha looking at, Ives? Come on over and help me with this one! You see me struggling with her.*' Well, I walked on over. Maggs had the girl's head covered with a rose-colored sweater. I'll never forget that. It was a cardigan, and it was so soft. Looked like a teacher should've been wearing it. I grabbed the child at her waist. Nothing but skin and bones, she was. But it became clear to me why Maggs was having such a hard time with such a small girl. Her body was wracked with the shakes. I mean, she was trembling and carrying on so much that I couldn't keep a steady hold on her." Ivy shook her head. "I've never seen the likes of it, Dancing Doll."

"What was wrong with the poor child?" Jackie asked with tears welling up in the corners of her eyes.

"I can only speculate, Dancing Doll. Gladys could probably tell you more about that. That is, if she could talk. The child was one of her kin, you know. And there was another strange thing about her. Her hands were wrapped up in the cleanest bunch of rags I'd ever seen, well except for the fresh spots of blood that kept blooming through." Ivy shook her head again. Her body trembled from a small chill that crept up her spine. "Mmph. Mmph. Mmph. I feel almost ashamed recalling it. I remember thinking that those white rags wrapped 'round that child's hands were the prettiest sight I'd ever seen. Looked like roses blooming from big old white clouds at the ends of her tiny wrists."

Jackie was indulging in a quiet cry, for she felt sorry for the girl that haunted Ivy's memories so vividly. She wanted to know if the girl was alright. If everything was okay. "Oh Ivy. That's so sad."

"We made it onto the porch with her. There was a young fella at the door. Young and handsome. He was tall and rightly built, but young. That surprised me, because Maggs didn't make it a habit of using young men to guard her house. But, here this one was. I'd seen him in Sweet Fields dipping around. Always trying to figure out a way to make some money. '*You need me to weed your flower beds? You need me to tote your groceries? You need me to sweep your porch?*' I always said no, no, and no, because I knew that young joker's service always came with a fee. C.L. what they called him. You know like Rev. C.L. Franklin. The preacher. Aretha's daddy lived round Memphis way. Or was it somewhere in Arkansas?"

"Aretha? Aretha who?"

"Aretha who? Aretha Franklin? Girl, where you been? I remember the first time I heard that Rev. C.L. Franklin. It was on a record. *The Eagle Stirreth Her Nest.* That's what it was. Lawd! I had church by myself that night. I was stirred up in the spirit, justa running and shouting. You can't hardly get preaching like that now, can you Dancing Doll?"

"I think Pastor Prentiss, over at St. Andrew, does a lovely job of rightly dividing the word. I like his preaching. He's…" "Yeah, he's alright, but his preaching got some sadness in it. Still pining over that wife, I hear. How'd we get to talking about that preacher anyhow? See? Now you've gotten me all off track with my story. Do you want me to finish or not?"

"Yes, of course I want you to finish. I'm so sorry Ms. Ivy. What happened to that poor little girl? I want to know."

"Well, we got her on up the steps wrapped up in that cardigan. C.L. opened the door and asked if Maggs needed help trying to get the child inside. You should have seen the look Maggs shot at him. She had daggers in her eyes. Everyone knew that no man EVER entered Maggs' place unless summoned by
Maggs. You don't ask and you definitely don't take liberties to get in on your own, 'lessen you find yourself breathless at the bottom of the stairs with a hole in you somewhere. Whoa Lawd!" "Jeeesus!" Jackie's hand fluttered across her chest as she gasped at the thought.

"We got her on in and to the stairs, then I froze. It looked like a million stairs, Dancing Doll. I'd never gotten this far in Maggs' house. Mother told me if you make it to the stairs, you're really in bad shape. I didn't want to be in bad shape, but that frail little girl had to get up the stairs. She'd stopped shaking a little, and Maggs pulled the pretty teacher sweater from her head. The child was about eleven or twelve years old, I surmised. But she was so small, like she was eight or nine. Pretty little something with dark brown skin that was cool to the touch. She had nice hair, too. Real thick and bone straight. Somebody really knew how to work a hot comb on that head. And right over her left ear was a patch of gray hair. It hung way down past her shoulders, and the gray was shiny, it caught the light just so. Pretty little girl, she was."

"Did you get her up the stairs, Ms. Ivy? Did you all get the blood off her hands?"

"We got her up there, but I froze again when my foot hit the landing, and I saw all those rooms. I knew Maggs had a big house, but I just didn't know how big. There were four bedrooms upstairs, all occupied but one. Two on the left, two on the right. The first one to the left housed a lady whose face I never got to see. Her back was turned to me, and she sat at a desk. Us, walking that hallway didn't phase her. She never looked up. Rude indeed. Her hair was pulled back in a bun and she was writing. She wore glasses. I could see the tiny gold chain hanging from the sides of her face. I still have good eyes, you know." Ivy took her middle finger and pushed her glasses up her nose. "That second room on the left was where I saw the dancing lady, the one that kind of reminds me of you. Tall. Skinny. With a shape of no kind at all. Her legs were long, and she waltzed around the room with real grace. Like when the white folks on TV dance with their waists bent and their arms circled." Ivy held out her arms gracefully. "Her head was tilted to the side and she didn't have a lick of hair on her head. But this was the kind of woman who was so pretty, she didn't need hair. If she had it, she'd cause a world of trouble. Funny thing. There was no music. That woman was flitting around the room to no music."

Jackie sat back in her seat and sighed. She secretly wished to be that woman, even if she didn't have hair. "That's so beautiful, Ms. Ivy."

"Beautiful? See, that's your problem, Dancing Doll. You are so busy trying to look at the pretty stuff outside, you miss the real stuff that's going on underneath the surface. But there was one more woman there. Her room was the first door to the right. She sat in the door of her room as if she had been waiting for the three of us all day. She was the color of black coffee. Her hair was black, too. Long and bone straight it was, straighter than that shaking child we carried. It looked like the woman was actually sitting on her own hair. I remember it was parted down the middle. She didn't have a lick of shine on her lips, just a blank face. Mother would have turned over in her grave if she'd have seen me sitting around the house with no color at all on my face like that woman. The woman wore overalls with a white shirt underneath. She had on brogans too, you know those work boots menfolk wore in the field. That's what she had on. She was whittling, working on a piece of wood with a small knife."

"What was she whittling?"

"Heck if I know. I was too distracted by the little white wooden cradle sitting behind her in the corner of her room. There was a baby in that cradle, and the baby was cooing and gurgling as we walked up. All three of us stopped when we heard that baby make that sweet noise. The woman sitting in the door stopped her woodworking and looked at me dead in the face. She said to me, 'Don't worry about that little one. He's going to be alright, now.' That woman left Maggs' pretty too. Pretty and alone. But that cooing, grinning baby, he stayed. Stayed and grinned until he was grown. Grinned himself on 'way from Sweet Fields." "We got the girl to the last empty room, and when I reached to close the door as we all entered, I realized the room had no door. I'd heard about that mess at Maggs' place, all these rooms with no doors. I never understood it. I also heard that out of all those bathrooms in that house, Maggs had only one she designated for what she called the *cry room*. I hear it was in the basement, that cry room. They say she told those women when they first came in, 'You can bathe yourself two ways in this room, with soap and water or with your own tears, but this is it. No crying anywhere but here. And one at a time, because we can't have all you ladies crying at the same time. It's not prudent.'"

"What happened to the little girl, Ms. Ivy?" "I really don't know about her time at Maggs'. But of course you know everything turned out fine for her. She found her way. Maggs dismissed me from the room when she started unwrapping the girl's hands. They were both very quiet. I would have left anyway. I felt like I was interrupting a church service. Maggs wasn't rude. She just said to me '*Thank you, Ives. C.L. will let you out.*'

She was the only one in Sweet Fields that called me Ives, you know. Then I asked when she started letting young boys keep the door at her place. She told me that younger boys move faster, think quicker, and long to be heroes. She said young boys thought they'd live forever, so they'd risk more of their lives outside to save the ones inside. It made sense to me. I'll never forget, though, that girl's face when she looked up as I walked out. She whispered *thank you* with the voice of a child, but beneath that young face was some old worry, like she'd just found out something she could have lived her entire life without knowing. And I reckon she did. But of course, Gladys could tell you more about that, if only she could talk."

Shirley Frye

Mr. Endicott had explained that Shirley Frye was a descendant of Abraham Callahan and a relative of Clemson Callahan's, so naturally Jackie wanted to know more. One morning, she arrived at Golden Sunsets before her shift and spotted Ms. Frye sitting alone in the television room knitting.

"Good morning, Ms. Frye. How are you?"

"I'm fair. How are you?" Shirley managed a small smile for Jackie before she returned her attentions to her knitting. "Come have a seat and grab that ball of yarn for me," she said directing Jackie's attention to the yarn that was about to fall to the floor.

Jackie did as she was instructed.

"Now. Tell me everything," Shirley said with a straight face, her fleshy jowls jiggling slightly.

"Pardon?"

"Tell me what Endicott told you about my family. I heard him telling you about the founding families. What did he say about the Callahan clan?" Jackie repeated a short summary of Abraham Callahan's role in the inception of Sweet Fields.

"He didn't tell you about the raiders did he? The Klan?" she asked pausing to look at Jackie. "No. Of course not. No one likes to talk of the night raids."

"Night raids?" Jackie asked loosening more yarn.

"Yes. Sweet Fields came close to being burned down many times. Real close."

"What happened?" Jackie asked. Shirley tugged on the yarn to signal she needed more unraveled from the skein.

"I can't believe Endicott skipped over parts! As much as he likes to tell the story of Sweet Fields! He ought to be ashamed of himself. Well, the slaves were free and white people didn't know what to do. They started raiding houses and camps to keep the black folk scared of them--you know, keep them in their places. The raids would take place at night. A group of them would come in the middle of the night, burn barns, sheds, houses, steal horses, and anything else they could get to. They would pull women from their homes, rape them in front of their husbands and children, and throw them back like used rags. Well, one night, they came to Sweet Fields hollering and hooting with torches and such. They fired a shot in the air and waited. Abraham Callahan came out on the porch of the big house with a shotgun and asked what they wanted."

"Abraham lived in the big house? I thought…"

"No. He lived behind the big house, but the drill was to come out the front door like it was his house. He came out angry. 'What y'all gentlemen want this time of night?' he asked them. 'This here is my property and these folk work my land. Ain't no cause for trouble, is there?' Then, he prepared to shoot. The men on the horses backed down. One got off his horse and walked almost to the porch. 'We don't mean to trouble to you. We just making sure these darkies don't think they can take over just 'cause they free.' Abraham swallowed and said, 'Well, I got mine under control. They know who's in charge. Now, I appreciate y'all checking on me, but I got to get back to bed.' When it was all over, Abraham lost his stomach right there on the porch."

"Lost his stomach?"

"Vomited. He was so scared, he threw up all over the place. After that, those men would come around every now and then to 'keep the peace'. That went on for a long time.

It looked strange to outsiders. Abraham Callahan, a darn near white man working beside everybody else during the day, but if the Klan came around, he'd have to pretend to be a white man who owned the plantation. Of course there were questions. 'Why was a white man choosing to work in the cane fields with a bunch a darkies?' Little did they know, Abraham Callahan never considered himself white. He just played the role to keep the folks off of him, his people and this beloved Sweet Fields."

"But didn't he buy the plantation with the money his daddy gave him?"

"Yes, but everyone worked and shared all of the yield and money from the crops. Callahan didn't build Sweet Fields alone. Everyone made Sweet Fields what it is today. No one owned anybody. Everyone was free and to come and go as they wished. No one lived in the big house. It was for show. Abraham, when the time came, would go in through the back door and step out on the front porch like he owned the place. They used to joke that he'd go in the back door a black man and come out the front door a white one. Loosen that yarn, will you?"

"Did Abraham ever marry, Ms. Frye?"

"Sure! He married someone just like him. He found him a mulatto that looked whiter than he did, and he looked as white as they came. Her hair was red and wiry, and it was that hair that gave her away. You know, it wasn't bone-straight like it should have been if she were actually white. They married and started having children--all boys. Story has it my grandfather was the worse Callahan of them all."

"What?! Your grandfather?"

"Yes. My grandfather. You know who's another worrisome Callahan?"

"Let me guess," Jackie said with a wide grin, "Clemson Callahan."

"You better know it! You know him?"

"I know of him. I go to church at St. Andrew with him."

"Ahh yes. St. Andrew. He's still there bossing people around, is he?"

"Well, he's never bossed me around. He's a nice man."

"That's what you think. Bossing people around is in the Callahan blood. We don't know how to do anything else. Unroll some more of that yarn, dear." Shirley said, nodding her head toward the tangle of yarn.

"How are you related?"

"We're first cousins. Two brother's children. He comes to see me from time to time. Now his wife, Judith, is an angel. I don't know why she married a big-mouth like Clem."

"He can't be that bad, Ms. Frye. He's the head of the Deacon Board."

"My point exactly. He always has to be the head of something. He can't ever follow. Even as children, playing outside in the backyard, he had to run things. He ended up outside by himself many a-day. No one can deal with a bossy know-it-all for too long.

Jackie peered out of the window in deep thought. "But taking charge of things can come in handy sometimes. You said it yourself Mrs. Frye." Jackie was thinking about how she was taking charge of her destiny, her life and her love for Pastor LeBeaux.

"I guess being in charge can come in handy, as it pertains to protecting Sweet Fields, anyway. Callahans have always taken pride in protecting the town with their abilities to pass for white, so much so that none of them ever married a brown skinned woman. Callahan girls didn't marry brown people either. I had my mind set on a beautiful brown skinned man when I went off to college, but when I brought him home, the whole family liketa had strokes. Light skin had become a family tradition--a way to protect the town, I guess, but when you're young and in love, you don't care about tradition or skin color."

"Yes, you're right, Ms. Shirley. Love has no color. It doesn't matter what the Callahans say." Jackie dropped her voice just a little. "Even Clem Callahan can't boss you about who you love."

Shirley paused a while. "I guess Clem's okay. He just talks too much for my liking."

"Did you marry your brown-skinned beau?" Jackie inquired.

"Yes. Yes, I did. My daddy was mad as a wet hen, but I did it. Callahans are stubborn too. It's the Irish blood, I think. I married Alvin Frye and had three pretty brown babies. They came out looking white, but they browned up as they got older. They all live in Washington, D.C. now. That's where we lived and raised our family. I came back here to spend my last days in the peace and quietness of Sweet Fields.

"But Ms. Shirley, if there were so many rules and restrictions here, why would you want to come back and spend your last days here. Where's the peace in that?"

Shirley Frye turned to look at Jackie. She put down her knitting needles and thought for a moment. "Where's your home, girl?"

"Oh, it's far from here, Ms. Shirley. I don't have fond memories of that place."

"See, you wouldn't understand. Home means a lot to me. Love is everything, but love of home means a lot. So, when love leaves, you ought to be able to go home, especially when that home was built from the ground up all for you. The Callahans, Farmers, Blackman's, all the founding families worked hard to make a place we'd all be proud to live in. Just because I left doesn't mean I'm not proud of my home. Just because me and my family had different ideas about love and protection doesn't mean there's no peace here. Just because I moved away to make my own way doesn't mean I'm never coming back. Sweet Fields is my home. And if you can't have peace in your own home, dear. You can't have peace anywhere."

Jackie dropped her head. "I guess you're right, Mrs. Shirley."

"I know I'm right about it. And since I know you don't have a place to call home, I already know you don't have a tablespoon of peace. I sure do hope you find it, because it ain't no way for a woman to live."

Hattie Blackman

Hattie had been watching the new Body Movement teacher move about Golden Sunsets. She really did look like a ray of sunshine. The streak of gold the woman wore each day hurt Hattie Blackman's eyes and made her squint. But, Hattie had to admit, she was a little miffed that Jacqueline Black had talked to everyone in Golden Sunsets but her. Well, almost everyone. There was Silas. But Silas, as much as he grinned, had funny ways. He'd soon chat her up when he felt moved to. Then there was Gladys. Gladys was nothing to worry about, though. The dancing teacher would probably never get her to talk. Nobody could.

Hattie Blackman had chosen Golden Sunsets to get away from most of the folks she spent time with everyday. She was the first one of the crew to choose to convalesce at the place. That was on purpose. She *needed* to get away from smart mouth Robert Endicott, rambling Ivy, grinning Silas, and silent Gladys. She'd been with them all her life, and frankly she was tired of them.

Hattie enjoyed her solitude from them for two weeks before one by one, they all began to trickle in. Her happy days had ended, and she felt like she'd never left high school when they came to Golden Sunsets, reminding her of days past, conjuring up old loves and happiness that hurt her, because she'd never experience them again.

Everyone had stories for the new worker. She sought them out, fed on their stories and had been doing so for over a month, and yet she'd not visited Hattie Blackman. Hattie had stories. She'd married into the Hughes family. There were giant stories to tell. But the new girl hadn't sought her out, and Hattie was miffed when she finally did.

"Ms. Hattie! Finally, we get to chat."

"Yeah. What took you so long?"

"Well, I was making my rounds here and there. And you know, Mr. Endicott can stretch a story for miles and miles. Ms. Ivy is also a big talker. I love her to pieces, but she can get so hard to follow." Jackie was gushing by now, high with the knowledge she'd obtained from her new friends at Golden Sunsets.

Hattie Blackman sat looking at Jackie with the corners of her mouth turned down. Now that Jackie was in close proximity, Hattie surmised that she really didn't want to talk to her at all. "So what do you want to talk about? I know you want to talk about something. Hmph. Been 'round here sucking up stories like an anteater."

"Well, Ms. Hattie. Whatever you want to talk about." Jackie put a stray piece of Hattie's wiry gray hair back in place as she answered.

Hattie returned the hair to its original unorganized position. "I like it like that," she said flatly. "Those Hughes men still dying their hair?"

"Excuse me?" Jackie said sitting beside Hattie.

"Are. The. Hughes. Men. Still. Dying. Their. Hair." Hattie spoke slowly. She looked at Jackie intently, her eyes getting bigger and bigger with each word.

"I've never seen a Hughes man with gray hair."

Hattie Blackman crossed her legs at the ankle and bent over slightly to pull up her knee highs. "You know that's what they call a myth. They do get gray hair. My man got gray hair. There were just a few strands, right above the ears. But it was gray. Didn't make me no never mind, though. My Hughes was the best looking Hughes in the clan."

"Well, Ms. Hattie, the Hughes men aren't short on looks, at all. The two I've met are easy on the eyes, so if you had the best looking one… hmph, I don't know how you kept yourself together."

"I can't lie. I kept him wrapped in my arms as much as I could. But…"

"But what, Ms. Hattie? How could you have a *but* with the most handsome man in the Hughes clan?" Jackie leaned in. "You know Walter William Hughes, Sr.? They call him Big Hughes nowadays. He's always copping for a meal. I always said, one day he's gonna eat himself on 'way from here. His boy's named William too. William, Jr." Ms. Hattie chuckled. "But Junior wouldn't let *nobody* call him Little Hughes. They're some proud men, you know? Anyway, Big went over 'cross the bridge and brought home a long tall gal. A lot of folks thought she was pretty. Caramel colored. Had all her teeth, big pretty teeth. Her eyebrows were thick and black and she kept them shaped up. Arched. Yes, arched is what they call it nowadays. Didn't wear much makeup, but she wasn't plain either. Shined her lips up with Vaseline. I had to teach her how to dress you know." Hattie straightened her own collar and spread the hem of her dress over her knees. She began running her thumb and forefinger down the pleats of her dress, arranging them in neat little rows. "Edith was her name. Clumsy, country Edith. But folks over here took to her like flies to sh-–"

"Oh my! What was it about her?"

"I guess it was her voice. That voice pulled folks in. Sometimes she'd lumber into the room and some idiot would say, 'Say something Edith; we want to hear you talk.' And she'd hem and haw around reciting poems and speeches she'd learned at some fancy college up north. Every church meeting had to have her on program saying something. I hated to see her coming, because I knew she'd fall and trip over something on her way to the front of the church, her and her big feet and sloppy clothing."

"She sounds a mess!"

"If it wasn't for those big pretty teeth and that long pretty black hair," Hattie paused, "and that skin that didn't need a lick of powder, and the voice, that round silky voice that demanded your attention. Oh yeah, and those big old long legs. She could cook too. And she loved on the men in her house. Bout smothered those boys to death with her love. I believe that's what run the oldest one off from here. Well, that in those fast tail bridge women. Anyway, if it wasn't for that little stuff, and my helping her out with her wardrobe and what all, Edith would have been a mess. She really wasn't what folks made her out to be. Not too many bridge people end up amounting to nothing. Edith just happened to be a bridge girl with an education."

"Were you not friends with her, Ms. Hattie? Did you get along okay?"

"Oh yeah, we got along fine for sister-in-laws. It's just I got tired of going places with her. She was awfully clumsy. I got tired of store owners moving stuff around when they saw us coming. And then the thing with her voice. People made such a hullabaloo over that. We couldn't go anywhere downtown without people on the street stopping her and telling her to recite some scripture in Psalms or some kind of poem or another. Sometimes, people wouldn't speak to me trying to get to Edith. Whether she was talking or walking, she got all the attention. It just got to be such a bother."

"You said she had two boys. Where's William, Jr.'s brother?"

"Wesley? I don't know where he is, now. But just go on 'cross the bridge; you'll see his fruit. He spread his seeds all across that bridge. But William Jr., I've always liked Junior. He's a good boy. Good looking, too. Not as handsome as my Hughes man was. Not even as handsome as his brother, Wesley. But he's good looking. Tell me something. Does he still stutter?"

"I haven't heard him stutter since I've known him."

Hattie shrugged her shoulders. "Hmph. He must done gone and got him a woman. The tall tales are really about to start now. You know Junior always could stretch a story from here to Tallahassee, 'specially when he had a woman."

"He may have someone special, now."

"Is she a bridge girl? Those Hughes act like they could never get a nice, quiet Sweet Fields woman. They had to go off and pick up those common girls. Mmph. Mmph. Mmph." "Well, she's related to Maggie Murphy somehow. She's living in her house, now."

"Oh. She's Maggie's kin?"

"Yes. Her granddaughter, I believe."

"Well, well, well. I wonder if Silas knows?" Hattie turned to the window and smiled. She looked as if she was smiling at something, not someone. "Well, if she's any kin to Maggs Murphy, I'm sure she got a figure that'll make cars turn off they own engines. Yep. I used to have a shape like that. That's how I got my Hughes man." Hattie grinned. "If she's Maggs' kin, she's good people. Good and smart, if she's Maggs' kin. But if she's really like Maggs," Hattie turned back to Jackie and pointed at her, "you better not cross her."

Jackie stirred in her seat. She stretched her long legs and pointed her toes. "Well, Ms. Hattie, I don't know much about crossing her. But I do know, I'd like to hear more of your story. Especially about Edith. What happened to her?"

"You wouldn't believe it."

"Oh. Try me."

"Remember, I told you she was clumsy, right?"

"Right."

"Well, she had a nail for everything in her house. Trying to be so organized and everything. Like she was so much neater than everyone else. She was coming up her own stairs, at her own house, with an arm full of cosmetics from down there at the Beauty Bottle. Somehow, someway, she tripped right at the threshold of her front door. Fell sideways, and hit her head on a nail."

Jackie winced and fell back into her chair. "Nooooooo."

"Yes. They say that long nail slipped right into the soft spot in the side of her head. Right at the temple. Say she died quick. Didn't feel a thing. When Big got home, he thought she was leaning her head on the side of the door to rest. But…"

"Oh my God!"

"Yep. And to this day, Big doesn't walk through the front door of his own house. He goes in through the back door, like a dutiful slave. He can't bear to cross that threshold. Said it's full of bad juju. I say, that's what you get for messing with gals from across that bridge."

Silas Farmer

One Tuesday evening in late October, Jackie was preparing to leave work. Just as she turned the light out in her small office and slipped on her yellow, bedazzled windbreaker, she heard a loud crack of thunder. Terrified of driving in rain, she flicked her office light back on and removed her jacket. She wandered into the recreation room where some residents were finishing up their evening meals. Jackie looked for Robert, Ivy, or Shirley, but she didn't see any of them. Nor did she see Hattie or Gladys. She sat down in a club chair and watched the ceiling close over the glass. She picked up a nearby magazine and was completely engrossed when a voice interrupted her read of "*Get the Man You Want.*"

"You waiting for the storm to pass before you go home?" A man in a wheelchair asked.

"Yes. I'm terrified of storms. I'll stay here all night if I have to," Jackie said shivering even though it wasn't cold.

"Ain't nobody at home to worry about you?"

"No, sir."

"That's a shame," he said clucking his teeth. "I'm Silas. And you're the new activity lady."

"Jackie Black."

"Ah. Ivy calls you Dancing Doll. Sweet little Ivy." He shook his head with a grin.

"Yes. She has called me that before. I remind her of someone she saw at Maggie Murphy's house." Jackie lifted herself to tuck her long legs under her. Silas wrinkled his brow a bit and paused. Eventually, he smiled a wide toothy smile.

"Yes. I know exactly who she's talking about. You do look like her 'cept you have hair."

"You knew the Dancing Doll too?" Jackie asked closing the magazine and putting it back on the table beside her.

"Yes. I knew almost everyone who ever visited Maggie Murphy's house. I worked there."

"A guard? Did you have a gun? What were you guarding?"

"A gun? Oh no. I was handy with a gun, but I was better with knife," Silas' grin reached all the way to his eyes. He was a jovial fellow with an easy smile and clear, expressive eyes. He rubbed the front of his white shirt and hooked his thumbs in his suspenders. "I could cut a man up before he even knew I had a blade."

"So how did you end up working for Maggie?"

"Well, I'm sure Ivy's told you about the women who came there. They needed protecting. They were all running from a man or being protected from the wrong man."

"I don't understand."

"Well, Doll. There were some men who treated their women like they were chattel rather than God's fine handiwork." He raised his brows a bit. "Some women came there looking like they had been in a juke joint brawl. And there were others, during the war, who didn't have the protection of family. 'Magine living by yourself with some young ones. No husband to provide or to fend off the jackals in the neighborhood. Black and white jackals for that matter. Those women ended up at Maggie's, and I was there at night to be sure no jackals got into the hen house, so to speak."

"I see," Jackie said with her mouth wide open in awe.

"Do you?" Silas asked wheeling a little closer. "I don't think you do, Doll." Jackie smiled at being called Doll. She decided that she liked Silas.

"Did you ever have to fight?"

"Sho! There was always someone coming through that gate talking 'bout he wanted his wife back. I would step out of the shadows and tell him to git moving or else he would never move again." Jackie gasped. "That was my line, you know. Most of the time it worked. Sometimes, it didn't."

"What happened when it didn't?" Jackie asked rocking in her seat.

"Well, let's just say I know what a man's intestines look like. I have seen a plenty of them."

"Oh dear!" Jackie gasped aloud.

"Awww. I shouldn't be telling you this. This ain't no conversation for a lady." Silas unhooked his thumbs from his suspenders and rubbed the tops of his thighs.

"No. Go on, Mr. Farmer. How did you start working for Maggie?"

"Now, that's a long story. Well, Maggie came to Sweet Fields when she was awfully young. Oooo wee! She was a pretty thang! Tall with curves from here to yonder. She was bout 16 or 17, I guess. Maggie set every man's mouth to water when she got outta that truck. But she was promised to Darvil Murphy. Folk used to call him Devil Murphy when he wasn't around. He was a hard man. Never smiled.

Mean as a rattlesnake. They got married after Sunday service one day. He didn't even allow a real ceremony."

"Oh no! She didn't have a wedding with flowers and cake?"

"No. None of that. Preacher married them right after church. He dragged her right on home and put her to work. "

"No reception? No cake?" Jackie's eyes welled up with tears. "Every woman wants to be fussed over on her wedding day. That's awful."

"It was a sad day. We all felt sorry for Maggie. My mother took her a cake, but Darvil made her leave it on the porch and yelled at her to stay away from his house. Maggie was like a prisoner in there. We saw her on Sundays only. She wouldn't talk. Couldn't talk to anyone. Darvil controlled her. Sometimes during church, a single tear would roll down her cheek. I felt so bad for her. She wouldn't let anyone touch her or hug her, but one Sunday my grandmother, Rachel Farmer, reached out and hugged her."

"What happened?"

"Maggie hollered like a scalded dog."

"Why? What was wrong?"

"Turns out everyone was right about old Darvil Murphy. He had been beating that poor girl. When my grandmother hugged her, she was agitating those bruises and cuts. Darvil heard Maggie scream. He ran over and snatched her away from Grandma and dragged her on home."

"My granny started screaming 'someone has got to do something 'bout that man!'"

'She ain't from here though, Rachel,' my grandfather said.

'What did you say, Famer? She ain't got to be from Sweet Fields to need help! Now, if y'all deacons don't go help that girl, I swear fo' heaven and earth I will!' My grandmother was a tough woman. She taught me how to fight and wield a knife. I looked at her narrowed eyes and figured she had planned to kill Devil Murphy if someone didn't beat her to it." Silas shifted in his wheelchair.

"So, what happened? Did your grandmother kill Mr. Murphy?" Jackie asked impatiently.

"Nope. He died before she could get to him." "What?! How?" Jackie was disappointed.

"Well, it was about three in the afternoon when Darvil dragged Maggie home. By eight that night, he was dead. Maggie said he ate his dinner and took a nap. When he slept longer than he usually did, she went and checked on him and he wasn't breathing. She ran next door and asked for help."

"How did he die? Did he have a heart attack?"

"Heart attack? Not at all. My grandmother told me on her deathbed that when she hugged Maggie, she slipped her a piece of paper with some powder in it. When Maggie called for help that night, she knew Maggie had used that powder. Folk suspected Maggie killed him, but there wasn't any proof. Besides, Maggie had fresh bruises, a busted lip, and a black eye. They figured Old Devil Murphy got what he deserved. They had his funeral, buried him, and never said another word about it."

"What strong, wonderful women they were! I wish I could be like that."

"Don't say that. They were strong 'cause they had to be. They didn't have the luxury of being anything else."

"So how did you come to guard Maggie's house for women?"

"Oh yes. After Darvil died, she went away for a week or so, and came back with a woman who looked like a scarecrow. She was the first one. Maggie fed her, read to her, fixed her up. She stayed a few months, and when she left, she was a mighty fine woman to see! Then, there was always someone climbing those stairs needing shelter from something or someone. When husbands started coming to look for their wives, that's when Maggie hired someone to stand guard. A fella kicked in her front door one evening as I was walking by. I ran up those stairs and threw his behind off the porch. I jumped on him and beat the stuffing outta him. I had my knife to his throat when Maggie called my name. I woulda killed him if she hadn't."

"Oh my goodness, Mr. Farmer! Did you cut him?"

"No. I told him he didn't have no wife and if he came back to Sweet Fields, he wouldn't have a life either. We never saw him again."

"So Maggie hired you after that?"

"Yep. She knew I had been keeping an eye on the place anyway. She said, 'since you so nosey and good with a knife, why don't you help me protect these broken birds of mine?' I've always been a night owl, so keeping watch at night suited me just fine."

"Did you ever marry, Mr. Farmer?"

"No. Never married. I had my heart broken one time and didn't care for it happening again."

"No!" Jackie said in surprise. "Who broke your heart? It seems like it would have been the other way around," she said with a smile.

"I was in love with someone who didn't want to be married. We had an affair. Real hot and heavy stuff, but she didn't want to marry. So I moved on. Worked for the railroad, had a few jobs here and there, and just recently came back to Sweet Fields a few years ago."

"I bet you were something else, Mr. Farmer, especially in your younger days."

"That bet would fatten your pockets, Doll. I was a dangerous tomcat if there ever was one." He laughed and stood from his wheelchair. Bent down to touch his toes and stretched his long arms high in the air.

"Mr. Farmer! You can stand and walk?!" Jackie was shocked.

"Sho! I was pullman porter after I left Sweet Fields, and every job after that, I've had to rest on my feet. I think I deserve to roll around in this comfy chair for a while, don't you?" Silas Farmer threw his head back when he laughed his hearty laugh. He walked around behind the wheelchair and pushed it on out of the recreation room. "It has stopped raining, Doll. You better get on home before it starts back again," he called over his shoulder.

Jackie did as Mr. Silas Farmer told her. And sure enough, just as she was pulling into her parking space at her studio, the rain and thunder started again. She thought about Mr. Farmer and decided he was her favorite. She would talk to him again. She was dying to know about Gladys, and thought he might be the one to tell her.

Gladys Turner

Almost two week passed before Jackie saw Silas Farmer again. She saw him roll into the recreation room from the library. He wore a straw hat with a blue and white band, a white shirt, green suspenders, and navy blue pants. His socked feet were in leather huarache sandals.

"Good evening, Doll. What are you doing here so late?"

"Hi, Mr. Farmer. I just wasn't in a rush to get home. I thought I'd sit around for while."

"You're not a good liar, Doll. Not at all," he laughed hard. He stood from his wheelchair and gracefully walked over to where Jackie sat. Jackie was in awe. There was nothing wrong with Silas Farmer. Not a thing. "So, what do you want to talk about? I used to be a bartender. Folk who want to talk have a certain look about them. And you, Doll, have that look."

"Well, I did have a question."

"Hmm mmm," he said stroking his chin. "Ask away."

"What happened to Ms. Gladys? Why doesn't she speak?" Jackie asked turning to look Silas directly. Silas closed his eyes, and his head shook from side to side ever so slightly.

"Was it that bad?" Jackie asked.

"Bad doesn't even begin to describe it. No one ever talks about it, but the old timers still think about it from time to time." Silas took a deep breath and then continued. "Well, it had to be the late 40s or early 50s. Gladys was almost a woman. She was an energetic little thing. Always smiling. Always talking. Friendly. A little too friendly. Anyway, you know about the bridge people?"

"Yes. The people on the other side of the river?"

"Yes. Well, it wasn't like we didn't like them or anything. It was just that they were a little rough around the edges. They didn't carry themselves the way folk in Sweet Fields did. Three young men, teenagers really, from the west side of the river started coming over to Sweet Fields. They'd come and visit the candy store, loiter around, and folk were nice to them---to a point. Then one Sunday, they came to church. They tried to clean up as best they could, and we welcomed them in---as much as we could. But we were suspicious. Bridge folk had a church and a store. We didn't know what they wanted when they came and walked around our little town. Everyone was warned to be polite, but careful. One of them, the tallest one, took a liking to Gladys. And Gladys, the sweet, naive thing she was, chatted with him a bit."

"She wasn't afraid of them?"

"No, and that's the problem with naive people. They are so innocent, they don't know to be afraid. Those boys had a look in their eyes that grown men recognize, and Gladys' father, Frank Turner, told her to stay away from those boys. Well, we had the annual sugar cane festival, and we celebrated well into the evening with a bonfire. Those three boys came, and the next thing we knew, everyone was at home safe and sound except Gladys. Some of the men went out looking for her.

"Oh my goodness! Where was she? Was she alright?" Jackie's eyes filled with fear.

"They found her in the woods," Silas' voice dropped with his eyes. "Covered in blood and seed." Silas hung his head. "Those jackals had violated her in every way they could think of. Poor Gladys. She was too trusting. When they went to cover her with a blanket, she had a wild look in her eyes. Kinda like an animal."

"Oh no!" Jackie cried out in anguish with tears running down her face. She held herself in her bony arms and began to rock back and forth in the chair.

"The men took her to Maggie's first to get her cleaned up some. They didn't want Frank and Rose, her daddy and mama, to see her like that. When they finally caught up with Frank and told him what had happened, he went mad. Frank Turner had a wicked temper about his wife and kids. Word got around to Frank, Jr. who was at home with his wife and daughter. Frank, Jr. wasn't stable either. When he got mad, seemed like his eyes changed colors. Folk didn't too much mess with Frank, Jr. on account of he never knew when enough was enough." Silas rubbed his eyes and looked at Jackie.

"Go on, Mr. Farmer. Tell me what happened," Jackie begged.

"Well, Frank, Jr. went and saw his sister at Maggie's while they were still cleaning her up, and he turned to the devil right then and there. He asked *'Them bridge boys did this to you? Answer me, Glad.'* Frank walked up to Gladys, rubbed the spot where they had pulled out her pretty hair and put his ear to her mouth. 'Tell me, Glad. Was it them bridge boys?' When Gladys whispered yes, Frank, Jr. calmly left. The women folk stayed with Gladys cleaning her up. The men were too busy keeping an eye on Frank, Sr., so they didn't pay attention to Frank, Jr. Lawd, have mercy on me for telling this." Silas covered his face with both hand and shook his head from side to side.

"Oh, Mr. Farmer. Are you okay? What happened?"

"Frank, Jr. stayed gone all night. Around sunrise, he walked back into town covered in blood. Blood was dripping from his hands. He walked just as calmly as you please back to his house, leaving a trail of blood on the sidewalks. His wife, a quiet little woman, didn't say a word to him. She took him out back and filled a tub with hot water and soap and washed him off. She didn't ask him anything and he didn't volunteer."

"What had he done? He killed the boys?" Jackie asked wiping fresh tears from her face.

"That family found those boys swinging from trees with their manhood cut off and stuffed in their mouths." "No!" Jackie shrieked and covered her eyes.

"There were bottles in them too… you know in the place where they would normally do their business." Silas paused and grabbed Jackie's long bony fingers. "I'm so sorry. You're a lady. You shouldn't have to hear the nastiness of it all. But if I couldn't say it, I wouldn't believe it myself. He violated them the way they had violated Gladys. It was a terrible sight."

"You were there?"

"No, but we heard about."

"Did the boys' families try to get revenge?" Jackie asked. Silas laughed and shook his head.

"Oh no. They weren't sure who did it. Frank, Jr. was smart that way. He killed them the way the Klan woulda done. The boys' family thought it was a Klan attack."

"Did anyone know it was Frank, Jr. who killed them?"

"Yep. The town council knew. Frank's wife, daddy, mama, and Gladys knew. But no one ever spoke of it. The head of the council back then, Calvin Callahan, had a talk with Frank, Jr. He said 'Frank, I know how you feel about your family, but you shoulda let us handle it. We got a way of dealing with folk that helps us keep the peace.'

Frank kept staring at his hands, but he finally said, 'Peace ain't fit to mention, Calvin. My baby sister ain't gonna ever have no children. She jump every time someone touch her. She ain't right no more. They broke her. They ruined her. I handled it. That's all that matters. If you wanna call the law, you go right ahead.' I heard him say it. Truth be told, Frank, Jr. wasn't right no mo' after that either."

"He avenged his sister! He did the right thing! Didn't he? What happened to him? Why wasn't he right after that?"

"Frank, Jr. went stone crazy after that. I 'magine he kept seeing all that blood he brought back on him. He couldn't stop washing his hands. He'd wash his hands and arms til the skin on them busted. He made his little wife scrub and clean day in and day out. His little girl too. I guess he thought the people of Sweet Fields knew what he had done, so he stopped going to work and never left his house. As he got older, he stopped leaving his room. He stayed that way til they put him in a mental hospital over in the next county."

"What about his wife and daughter?"

"Well, they managed the best way they could. His wife, Sarah, kept on with that habit of cleaning and started taking in laundry. His daughter, Belle, did the same. Neither one of them could get over that cleaning spirit Frank, Jr. brought into that house."

"Belle? Did you say his daughter's name was Belle?"

"Yep. Quiet little girl. Small like her mother. She left Sweet Fields as soon as she could. She didn't come back this way for a while, but I hear she's back now. They say she's still small but she sho carries a big stick." Jackie sighed and wondered if he was talking about Belle Lynne Locke.

CHAPTER 21: BUDDING LOVES

While Jackie was learning about Maggie and the Murphy Inn, William was easing up to the Murphy home to pick up Iris for dinner at the Argentine Steakhouse. He ran up to the porch with giant umbrella deployed and rang the bell. When Iris opened the door, he held his breath and smiled.

"Hi, William, come in. I'll just be a minute," Iris said turning away from the front door to rush up the stairs. He admired the firmness of her thighs in her black skinny jeans as she climbed the stairs and noticed she wore no socks or shoes.

"Iris," he shouted from the bottom of the stairs "we don't have to get out in the rain. I can go get the food and we can eat here."

"Oh no! I'm fine. I just need to put on my boots," Iris shouted. "I'll be down in just a second." William stepped to the right of the stairs into the parlor where he could tell Iris spent most of her time. He saw her home improvement catalogs, lists, and budget sheets. Just as he was about to look through her folder marked "kitchen," he heard her coming down the stairs. Her firm legs looked even longer stuck in her high-heeled ankle boots. She wore a V-neck cream sweater that seemed to hug every curve she had and gave William a stunning view of her neck and collarbone. Her hair swung about her neck in thick curly tresses. She smiled at William as she reached the bottom step.

"My coat and umbrella are in the parlor, and then sir, I'm all yours," she said playfully.

William helped her slip her arms into her cream pea coat and grabbed her umbrella.

"Are you sure you still want to go out in this weather?" he asked while they stood on the porch.

"Yes. I've been in the house all day thinking about my new kitchen. I need to get out," Iris explained taking her umbrella and opening it. William looked at her.

"I understand," he said taking the umbrella back. "Off we go." The two ran out into the rain. William escorted her to the passenger side of his car and opened the door for her. Once she was seated inside the warm, dry car, Iris unlocked his door. William stowed the wet umbrellas on the back seat floor before sliding behind the steering wheel.

Just as they pulled away from Murphy Inn, Iris' phone rang. It was Locke.

"Are you still going on your date with William?" she clipped out.

"Yes. We just left."

"In this weather?" Locke fussed. "Let me speak to William."

"Locke, he's driving."

"Well, put me on speakerphone." Iris sighed and did as she was told.

"William?" Locke tried to soften her tone a bit, but failed.

"Yes, Ms. Belle. How are you?"

"I'm wondering why you didn't order that food and bring it to the house. Y'all shouldn't be out in this storm."

"I know, Ms. Belle. I suggested it, but Iris wanted to get out." He paused. "And I aim to please her. Would you like me to bring you a nice juicy steak?"

"Ooo! No, indeed, William Hughes!" she shouted in disgust. "You know I detest the consumption of meat. You said that to vex me. Y'all be careful. Goodnight." Locke ended her instructions with a click. Locke immediately called Eddie's cell phone. He was in town.

"Eddie, they went to dinner anyway. Out driving to the edge of town in this weather. It makes no sense. It would have been safer for them to stay in."

"Is that what you're doing, Belle? Staying in?" Eddie asked smiling into the phone.

"Of course. I'm not getting out in this terrible weather. I'm a firm believer that all the earth should keep still when God is doing his handiwork."

"Good. I'm coming over. Be decent...if you want." Eddie laughed and hung up the phone before Locke could protest.

By the time Iris and William arrived at the Argentine Steakhouse, the rain had subsided. William deposited Iris at the front entrance and had walked around to open her door and escort her in before parking the car. Jorge's face lit up to see Iris back at his restaurant again.

"Ahh, Senorita! How good to see you again," he gushed. "I have a special table for you and Senor Hughes. Let me take your coat." Iris was shocked that he remembered her. While Jorge checked her coat into the coatroom, William joined her, and Jorge showed them both to a table set for two in a cozy nook near a fireplace with a blazing fire. William dismissed Jorge and pulled out a chair for Iris before taking his own. Iris looked around at the fireplace, the candlelit table setting and smiled.

"William, this is a beautiful restaurant. How romantic." she leaned in and whispered. She noted the open collar of William's sateen gray shirt and wondered how warm the curve of his neck was.

"I'm glad you like it. I hope you don't mind that I ordered for us already," William said tentatively. "But you're welcome to choose your own meal, if you like."

"Oh no. I trust your judgment." Iris smiled at him and sipped from her water glass. She noticed how William released a sigh of relief. She also noticed how he nodded at Jorge in the distance. Moments later, Jorge brought a tray of appetizers and placed it on the table. He then presented a pitcher of Sangria and poured two glasses of the dark red liquid.

"Thank you, Jorge." William said. Jorge nodded and disappeared.

"William, this looks delicious. Tell me what all of this is," Iris said placing her napkin in her lap.

"This is provoleta; it's a grilled cheese with olive oil and spices. Use the bread to eat it. This is chorizo; a grilled sausage. And these are the beef empanadas you like. The drink is sangria made of red wine, oranges, sugar, and my favorite...brandy."

"Delish!" Iris smiled and rubbed her hands together. "I am starving. I've had my head in catalogs all day and didn't eat very much."

"I figured as much," William said placing a serving of each appetizer on her plate. "Tell me what you've decided for the kitchen."

"Oh no. We don't have to talk about that now. Not over dinner. It's exciting for me, but it's work for you. You tell me about your day." She said dipping a piece of bread into the provoleta.

"My day was boring. There's a house near the church that is going up for sale, and the owner wants some updating done on it before she puts it on the market. I'll let some of my guys do that house. I'm keeping myself free to start on yours," he said taking a bite of chorizo.

"Really? Well, I know what I want for the kitchen. White cabinets with dark hardware, slate countertops, and a big garden window over a dark apron sink," she said proud that she had finally made up her mind.

"What about the wall and the flooring?" William asked as if he were challenging her.

"Sherwin Williams Antique White on the walls and cabinets and African Blue Artesia slate tiles on the floor," she replied.

"That will look very nice. Start date?"

"Whenever you can get started."

"Next week," he said making a note of it on his phone.

"See how easy that was?"

The conversation moved seamlessly from topic to topic. They talked about home improvement, Sweet Fields, San Francisco, and their love of clothes. At some point before they had finished the appetizers, Jorge brought their entrees of mini parrillada--grilled flap steak, chicken breast, Argentine-styled sausage, and a side of seasoned vegetables.

"William, I can't possibly eat all of this!" Iris said while picking up her fork.

"I don't expect you to. When you have it for lunch tomorrow, you'll think of me," he said with a wink. Iris could only wink back because her mouth was full of succulent grilled chicken. When Jorge stopped by to refill their water glasses and offer another pitcher of sangria, William informed Jorge that their plates would be packed to go.

"Senor, would you and the lovely lady like dessert?" Jorge asked smiling at Iris.

"Iris, how do you feel about bread pudding?"

"I've never had it, but I'll try it."

"Jorge, we will have the bread pudding with two spoons, please." William said with narrowed eyes. "Iris, you have an admirer. Jorge likes you."

"No. Jorge finds me attractive. He doesn't know me enough to like me. But whatever he's got going on is of no consequence to me. I'm here with the man I find attractive AND like." William was speechless. He smiled.

"You know me enough to like me?"

"I do. You wash dishes, dress impeccably, defend my honor, and you are a perfect gentleman. And I'm sure that's just the tip of the iceberg."

"Yes, Iris. This is just the beginning" he said peering at her over his glass of sangria.

The two enjoyed laughs at the antics of the residents of Sweet Fields while they nibbled on bread pudding. When Jorge arrived with their packaged meals, William paid the check and slid Iris' chair out when they were ready to leave. As Iris walked through the dining room to the exit, she thought of her last visit to the Argentine Steakhouse with Rick Carson and almost laughed out loud. She remembered what Lloyd had taught her "*the first one is always the imposter.*" He had said that with the creation of every villain or suspect. Rick had definitely been an imposter; he was charming and handsome, but he was a self-centered idiot of massive proportions. William, on the other hand, had been a perfect gentleman in every way. She laughed to herself when William almost snatched her coat from Jorge and helped her into it before Jorge could. Iris, watching William put on his black driving coat, wondered how he kept his abs so taut and chest so firm when he had such a hearty appetite. She stood in the door and watched him trot out to the car in the cold drizzle of rain that had started again. When he pulled the car to the door, he hopped out and escorted her the few steps to the open passenger door. The chivalry was almost too much for her. She hadn't been treated like this before… but she liked it.

The ride home was accompanied by music by the O'jays. They sang along to "Love Train." The night ended with William unlocking the front door to the Murphy Inn. She stepped inside, and he placed her keys in her hand.

"Thank you, Iris, for making my Tuesday night dinner a night to remember."

"It was my pleasure, William," Iris smiled as she stepped forward. She tiptoed up and he bent down. She placed a gentle kiss on his lips and stepped back quickly and let the screen door close.

"Goodnight, Iris. Sleep well." He felt his tongue tying up and afraid he'd stutter and stammer, he decided that's all he would say. She stood behind the screen door and watched him until he drove away.

The next morning, Locke called to invite William and Iris to dinner with her and Eddie later in the week.

"You two come over here and eat dinner with me and Eddie on Friday night," she instructed. "Because you need to clean that meat out of your system. Tell William I have some brandy he might like, too."

Bennett Banks was still up when William and Iris got in from their Tuesday night date. He sat, alone on the glassed-in front porch, holding several lavender sheets of stationery. The delicate papers quivered in his hand and were lit only by a soft glow coming from a white three wick candle sitting on the side table near his rocking chair.

The letter was from Laura. It was the last one he'd received from her since he saw her a few weeks ago, waving from Maggs' porch. He'd not seen her since that time. Bennett assumed that Laura's sister Luceal had made a big stink over Laura waving at him that Sunday. They'd have to be more careful.

That's what the letter said, and that they couldn't become,

...overwhelmed with our feelings for one another. It would surely raise suspicion. It's not that I am ashamed of you, or of us; timing is of the essence. To uncover this relationship we have too soon will surely kill Luceal. I don't want to hurt her. You remember what happened the last time we tried to be together, to stand our ground with her. It didn't end well. She put up a fight.

But it wasn't just a fight. Luceal lied. She schemed. She manipulated and brainwashed Laura into leaving Bennett Banks. Laura didn't see it at first, but once she'd given up on herself and on Bennett and the possibility of the two of them being an us, once she caught a 15-year glimpse into her future through Luceal's anger and bitterness, Laura began to come around. It was almost too late by then.

I know it seems like forever, sweet Bennett, but this is why we worked out this system. The letters. The extended visits to Golden Sunsets to take puzzles and socks. Luceal has no idea that I don't sit and talk with the residents; that I drop the items off at the front desk and make my way to you, to drop off your dinner for the week. That I spend my extra money on Tupperware dishes I keep shoved in the top drawer of my chifferobe. And by the way, don't forget to leave the last set on the bottom step in the laundry bag. But that will only be for a little while longer, Bennett. I feel a change in the air. The Christmas winds always bring new beginnings for long time lovers. Luceal will be consumed with helping with the Christmas cantata. While she is out, we can make a plan, a plan to live and love together, out in the open, not in secret.

Bennett dropped his head and turned the letter over on his knee. These promises landed in his mailbox around this time every year. With his other hand, Bennett took off his reading glasses and laid them aside. That was when Bennett saw William Jr. and Maggs' grand running up the steps from their date. Bennett thought they were a good looking pair, and his mind went back to the day Laura had said, yes. That was 30 years ago. It was the cool of the evening, late fall, at the cusp of Christmas time. The rain had just begun, right after she'd said yes. She ran for several blocks screaming "Yes!" They were young. Sweet Fields didn't mind the noise much. Luceal, on the other hand, hated it, hated the noise, hated Bennett. She'd chided Laura for screaming in the streets like a banshee, for flailing her arms wildly and running like a feral child. That was the happiest she'd ever seen Laura. Bennett had done that, he had made her happy.

It was hard for him to imagine how and when that happiness changed. How quickly he became the enemy of his best friend, a recluse after reuniting with his community. The warmth of the Sweet Fields "Homecoming for our Veterans" parade slipped from his memory. The hugs and congratulatory greetings meant nothing. With the withdrawal of Laura's love came the withdrawal of Bennett Banks. Luceal had done that to them, but Bennett wasn't a vengeful man. He was patient. He sulked and brooded and fell into a depression brought on by one visit from Luceal, an encounter he would never forget.

"You stay away from my sister. You'll never be good enough for her." Luceal was standing on Bennett's step, dressed in a pair of burnt orange, wide legged pants. The seams of the pants were not ironed in, but sewn in, as was the fashion for 1975. The hem covered a pair of off-white Mary Janes. Her shirt was a button down of white polyester and covered in large yellow sunflowers with ugly green leaves shooting from the stems. Bennett remembered the flowers looked as if they would ease off of the fabric and choke the life out of him.

That's what Bennett Banks' imagination had begun to do since he came back from the war in 1966. He was only 18 years old when he left in 1962, but he felt like an old man when he returned four years later. It was Laura who made it all better. She wrote down all of his imaginings, his 3-D musings. She made them into poems, songs, stories, stories that made him laugh. Bennett knew then, that Laura was a good woman.

"Don't you mean I'd never be good enough for *you*?" Bennett had remained at the top of the stairs, so he could look down at Luceal. He was more than put off by her insolence. "This is none of your concern. Laura is a grown woman. She makes her own decisions."

"She is just a CHILD!" Luceal spat out. "Barely 25 years old. I will NOT let her waste her life away with you, a man almost 10 years her senior."

"I'm only 31, Luceal. You act like I'm an old man. I can love her right. I can provide for her. We've already made our plans to be together. You can't get in that. It's not your call."

"We'll see about that, Bennett. I will not let Laura leave me for the likes of you. I know about the war. I know what it does to people. You're no different. You're just as crazy as the rest of them that come back. I know, because I read her little diaries. The crazy poems you make her write. Those creepy stories. You're certified crazy. I won't let you make her crazy, too. I can't let you do that. I can take care of her better than you can."

"Luceal," Bennett put his hands in the pockets of his olive colored pants. He wore an olive colored button down shirt with an ecru sweater vest decorated with small green and brown squares, "go home."

"I am not leaving this door step until you promise that you will NOT go through with this marriage. Promise me you won't do me...I mean, Laura like that. Don't burden her any longer. Don't strap her down with your post war crazy. That would kill me if you did."

Bennett remembered looking across the street and seeing Maggie's second floor curtains flutter just a bit when Luceal screamed the words *post war crazy*. His heart fluttered too. Yes, it had been almost ten years, but there were still some nights when he didn't sleep at all. There were times when Laura wasn't there to help him deal with his wild imaginings. But that would end soon. Laura would help with all that; she always did.

"Luceal, I can't let you stand on my doorstep and challenge my manhood too many more times. Now, I'm going to ask you one time to get off my porch. If you don't move, I'm going to have to make you move."

Luceal looked up at Bennett Banks. She squinted and whispered, "And if you don't leave my sister alone, I'm going to have to do everything in my power to move her heart far away from yours." Laura reached up and put her finger on the tip of Bennett's nose. "You can bet on that Bennett Banks. Ask anybody in Sweet Fields. I'm a woman who makes good on her bets." At that, Luceal took her forefinger and stabbed Bennett's chest, twice. "Watch me."

In one quick move, Bennett made the biggest mistake of his life. He took his right hand out of his pocket, grabbed Luceal in the crook of her arm, and walked her down his steps.

"Bennett Banks, you take your hands off me," Luceal screamed as she tried to wriggle from Bennett's grip. Bennett kept his grip tight as he walked her down the stone path of his yard. "Get your hands off me Bennett! Maggs! Maggs!" Luceal called as she tripped over her own feet at Bennett's coercion.

Maggs had come to her front door by then.

"Everythang alright over there, BB? Do I need to make a trip across that street?"

Bennett didn't answer Maggs. Instead, he shoved Luceal outside of the picket fence of his home and slammed the fence closed. He placed his hand back into his pocket and went into his house.

The trip Luceal took from Bennett's front door to the sidewalk in front of his house was the undoing of Laura and Bennett. By the tame Laura got wind of the scene, the verbal sparring had turned into an all-out fist fight.

Persuading Laura was easy, as everyone on the street had heard Luceal screaming for Bennett to take his hands off her. Maggie, though she knew how messy and vindictive Luceal could be, witnessed Bennett Banks' grip on Luceal's arm, as she stumbled out of the yard yelling. She used this fact for leverage.

"Maggie saw the whole thing. You can go ask her. He put his hands on me, Laura." Luceal was shivering and crying when she got home to her twin sister. "I don't know what got into him, but before I knew it," Luceal broke down, but it was more from the guilt of her breaking Laura's heart than from Bennett Bank's grip, one that she still felt in crook of her left arm. But she'd started the break in Laura's heart, and she wouldn't stop it now. Luceal didn't want Laura to leave her all alone. They'd always been together, and if Luceal had anything to do with it, they always would be. "Maggie saw it, Laura. She was standing there, right on her front porch watching the entire thing."

This should have been a clue for Laura. Everyone in Sweet Fields knew that Maggie never turned a blind eye to a woman in distress. When people witnessed her taking one of her girls in (she called them her little broken birds) they whispered in jest, *Maggie to the rescue.* The fact that Maggie never left her porch should have softened the blow for Laura. It should have given Bennett a reprieve with her; it had with the remainder of the community. But Laura missed the clue and did not engage its importance until some years later.

"What triggered it, Luceal? I mean, I know you two never really got along, but that doesn't sound like *my* Bennett." Laura was pleading for more, something to justify Bennett's behavior. She was hugging Luceal, hugging her and rocking her, back and forth. "I just don't think he would have done it without…"

Luceal snatched away from Laura's embrace, "What are you implying? That I did something to him? No man has cause to put his hands on a woman! Not for love nor money should he hurt her like that. No matter what is said."

"No. No. Luceal. I'm not saying… I can't make sense of it all. I just saw Bennett. We talked about the wedding, about our lives together. He was so happy; I wonder what changed?"

Luceal fell back into her sister's arms. "I don't know, Laura. But I do know this, if he put his hands on me, it won't be too long before he puts his hands on you. He wasn't far from it today. If he could do it to me so easily, and I'm your twin sister, more of your blood than anyone on this earth. If he could do it to me, Laura, he's bound to do it to you."

On that night, Laura's *yes* turned into a *no.* That is all the letter said, the one Laura had written and left underneath the fence in front of his house. "No. Love, Laura."

Bennett shook the memory of those days from his mind. He picked up his reading glasses and turned the delicate pages over, reading the last four words over and over again. *I promise.*
Love Laura.

CHAPTER 22: MEMORY LANE

After his date with Iris, William started stopping by to drink coffee with Iris in the mornings and have dinner with her in the evenings. On Friday morning over coffee, Iris announced that she would start removing the tile in the upstairs hallway bathroom.

"Iris, why don't you let me do that? I don't want you to hurt yourself." William looked concerned.

"I won't hurt myself. I'll wear goggles and gloves. I've been watching HGTV. I'll be fine," Iris assured William with a pat on his shoulder as she took his coffee cup into the kitchen. Iris remained true to her word. After William left, she donned a pair of jeans, a long sleeve tee, and some old sneakers and gathered her tools-- a hammer, garbage bags and a crowbar. With India Arie playing in the background, she started on the hallway bathroom. She actually enjoyed breaking the aqua blue tiles. After she cleared one wall, the one beside the sink, she noticed imprints of rectangles in the wall plaster. The lines were too big to be imprints of the tiles. She tapped the area with her hammer and heard an odd, hollow thud. She found a large box cutter and followed the imprint with the sharp blade, praying she didn't cut herself.

After hours of scoring and cutting and scratching at the rectangle imprints, Iris unearthed a set of built-in drawers that had been sealed shut. She used the crowbar to pry the top drawer open and found a small metal box. A part of Iris wanted to squeal with delight while the other part shrank in fear. She took the metal box into the hallway and she sat down on the hardwood floor. Glad for her work gloves, she pulled the rusty lid open and found a stack of pictures. There were about 15 in all. Several of women, a few of children, and some of a woman who Iris was sure was her grandmother. In one picture, Maggie stood in front of the Murphy Inn with a tall young man on one arm and small handbag on the other. Her granny wore a floral front-pleated dress with a scoop neck. On her head sat a velvet ringlet with a small veil. Always a fan of sensible shoes, she was wearing lowheeled pumps. Maggie was tall and voluptuous. Her smile was tight like she wasn't sure about having her picture taken. The young man, though, had a smile as a big as all outdoors. His shoulders and chest were broad and upright in his suit. His hand covered Maggie's hand, and he looked proud to have her on his arm. Iris flipped the photo over hoping to find some information. All she saw was initials M.M. and F. and the year 1964.

Iris was speechless. She flipped through the pictures and pulled out the ones of babies. Most of the pictures were so old and deteriorated and the babies were so young, she couldn't tell if they were boys or girls. She just hoped that one was her father. Iris, determined to demolish the remainder of the tile and clean up before William came to pick her up for dinner that evening, set aside her metal box of pictures and returned to her work with renewed vigor.

"Iris, I don't know why I doubted you," William said when he stepped into the tileless bathroom. "You did a good job. Maybe you could work part-time for me," he joked with a short laugh. "The guys make such a mess when they bust up old tile." William slid his arm around Iris' waist and kissed her cheek.

"Let's go. I found some pictures in a drawer in the wall that I want to ask Locke about," Iris said descending the steps behind William. William reached the bottom of the stairs first and turned to see her down the remaining few steps--a gesture she had only read about.

Dinner with Locke and Eddie was a show, and William and Iris were spectators. Iris had suspected this from the two. They were comical and quirky enough alone. Doubling the trouble would yield much fodder for her coffee talk with William the next day.

"Y'all come on in," Eddie said, standing at the door to greet the two. Eddie gave Iris a big bear hug, and Iris could have sworn she heard a low growl coming from William's throat. As Iris went into the house, Eddie extended his hand to William. William obliged and was surprised as Eddie pulled him in and gave him a hug as well, clapping him on the back with his free hand. "Hey man, how ya doing? We're so glad you could join us. Y'all go on back. Locke is in the kitchen finishing up things."

Both Iris and William had underestimated the power of the aroma produced by vegetarian cooking. Locke had promised to keep it simple, spaghetti. That was the agreement. But the smells that rose from the kitchen testified that this spaghetti was no ordinary spaghetti. Iris giggled to herself as she made it to the counter, *if only I could eat an aroma.*

"You got it smelling good in here, Locke! I can't wait to taste." Iris hung her bag underneath the kitchen bar, where Locke had William install little decorative hooks, just for that purpose.

Iris walked around and began to peep in pots.

"No ma'am!" Locke said tapping Iris' hand. "You don't come in here messing with stuff. That's rude! I don't like folks in my kitchen."

"Oh yeah? So why is Eddie in your kitchen, Locke? I see he's dragged a stool over to sit in the kitchen with you. I guess he doesn't count." Iris said sarcastically. She smoothed down the dark wash skinny jeans she had on. Even though she didn't let on, she saw William's reaction when she came downstairs with a similar pair on for their date. She liked that reaction. Her yellow tunic was accented with red, orange, and turquoise designs down the front, and stopped just below her hips. The cognac colored bootie she wore extended her calves and accentuated her strut down the stairs. Iris was happy that even this simple outfit had the same effect on William. She flitted around him like a schoolgirl.

Locke pulled the wooden spoon out of the spaghetti sauce and sat it on the stove. She wiped her hand on a white dishcloth she'd tucked into the string of her sage apron. Pointing toward the kitchen's bar, she said to Iris, "Get over there and get your man something to drink, and y'all go sit down. There's a fruit and cheese tray on the table. Teacakes are in the…you know where they are. That'll hold you until everything's done." She turned back to her work at the stove, but only after she said, "and stay out of grown folks business."

Eddie walked into the kitchen laughing. He placed his hand at the small of Locke's back and bent to kiss her lightly on the cheek. From that point until Locke had begun to set the table, William and Iris felt as if they were invisible.

William watched the interactions intently. He too had chosen a dark wash jean, and marveled that they both were likeminded in their wardrobe choices. He wore a deep red shirt, because he knew spaghetti would be served. Should he waste a little sauce, it wouldn't be so noticeable. Iris had complimented him on the way he dressed at dinner, he didn't want to mess that perception up. William continued to watch for nuances from Iris to confirm that she was all his. He wanted to be sure.

In watching everyone, William realized Eddie was a good guy. He had to be to break through Belle Lynne Locke's tough exterior. Locke was malleable in Eddie's company. Eddie chatted quietly with her in the kitchen, and William noticed how at ease Locke looked with him. When Eddie extended affection toward Locke, she floated into it gracefully, as if she knew it was there all along.

William became embarrassed. His assumptions that Eddie was a little too free with Iris made him feel ashamed. They were unwarranted and were more about William's insecurities than anything else. Now he saw Locke liked Eddie. It was evident in the way she looked directly at him when she talked to him. In how she moved closer to him, in how she let him answer her door. William decided that he would apologize again to Iris, for being silly, possessive, paranoid and…

"Let's eat!" Eddie said, breaking Williams' train of thought.

"What do we have here?" William asked, pulling Iris' chair out from the table.

Locke decided they should eat by the bay window in the small intimate space that overlooked her garden. She'd brought up a bottle of wine she'd been aging in her basement for the past three years. The bottle in which it was housed was clear, and the wine inside looked as if it had been made in the finest winery, beautifully burgundy, not a cloud in sight. The oval label on the front was the color of parchment paper and accented all around with creeping ivy. In the center of the label were the words, Bee Elle Elle: 2011, written in beautiful script.

"Wait a minute," William said picking up the bottle and leaning back. "Ms. Belle, surely you're not making wine in your basement."

"Yes, I am." Belle said, as if the answer should have been obvious.

"You know that's against the law, right?" William said with his eyebrow raised. Iris put her hand on Williams' thigh, as if to stop him from talking.

"Who's law?" Locke asked. "Not Sweet Fields' law. We make our own laws here, and if it's okay with the council..." "Council?" Eddie asked.

"Yes," William answered with a grin, "Sweet Fields is almost a self-governed place, except for the great and powerful *council*." William used air quotes. "A council that hasn't met in a hundred years."

Eddie shook his head in disbelief. He grabbed Locke's hand, "Let's us pray, before our food gets cold. We can talk about this council while we're chewing. Our heavenly father, thank you for this food we are about to receive. Thank you for the small garden of Eden that you've placed right in my Belle's back yard. Thank you for our guests and the budding relationship you are gifting to them. Bless the hands that prepared the food and the bellies that will enjoy it. In Jesus name…"

After the amens and sanitizing ended, the eating commenced. Belle had made homemade pasta using a spinach base. The pasta was a beautiful green color, which was complimented all the more by the deep red sauce made from tomatoes and herbs from Belle's own back yard. Christmas on a plate is what Iris kept saying between bites.

A wooden salad tong peeped out of the Caesar salad which was plated in a large wooden bowl in the middle of the table. Arranged neatly atop a bed of spinach, kale and romaine were green peppers and large black olives. A tall green glass bottle housed homemade Caesar salad dressing. Locke had bought a large loaf of garlic bread from the bakery downtown; however, she knew about Iris' penchant for sweet cornbread. She'd placed a basket of her own special recipe near Iris' seat and sat a few pats of honey infused butter nearby. Eddie had grilled the corn and asparagus, and Locke's steamed lemon pepper broccoli rounded out their choice of vegetables. There was tea for everyone and wine for anyone who dared try.

"So what's everyone been up to?" Eddie asked, stuffing a forkful of salad into his mouth.

"I've been working." Iris chirped between swallows.

"Working on what?" Belle asked, surprised. "You don't have a job, little girl."

"She's been working with me, Ms. Belle." William chimed in.

"Mmmhm, working with you doing what?" Locke pried.

"Like you say," Eddie interjected, "stay out of grown folks business."

"It is nothing like that. I've started the renovation on my house."

"Yeah, she has. Against my better judgment. A woman watches a couple of shows on HGTV and all of a sudden she's a demolition man. I tried to warn her, but she wouldn't listen. That's how she got that little scratch on her hand, right there." William reached for Iris' hand, "Show 'em how you hurt yourself."

Iris pulled her hand back playfully and gently tapped William on the shoulder. "I decided to go ahead and demo the wall in the hallway bathroom upstairs. It was a good workout. And yes, I learned how to do it on HGTV. But I found these," Iris pulled out a small blue box. She opened it and revealed the stack of pictures she found in the wall of the bathroom. "I realized that I had a whole lot more to learn, about my Grandma Maggs. Locke, who *are* these people?"

Locke wiped her hands with her white cloth napkin and reached for the box. She took out the pictures and fanned them out on the table. Eddie leaned over to look at the old photos. He noticed a stark white streak of hair interwoven between one of the long plaits on either side of the child's hair on the picture. "Why, Belle, that one looks like you, a very young you."

Belle shook her head, no, and quickly restacked the photos and put them in the box. After replacing the top, she dropped the box in her lap. "Let me keep these and take a closer look at them. These photos are so old that I may need some time. I want to tell you the truth as well as I know it. So, I'll need some time."

"But, those are *my* photos, Locke. I'll need them back. I can make you a copy." Iris reached across the table to retrieve the box. Eddie and William sat quietly, each holding his breath, a little bit unsure of why the air in the room had changed; their eyes shifted from each woman as if watching a tennis match.

"I'm not going to keep them. And, no, I don't need a copy. I need some time. That's all. And don't reach across my table again. You're going to get sauce on the sleeve of that pretty blouse." And that was the end of the conversation. Everyone released a quiet sigh and returned to their meals. Locke brought out more teacakes, and to Iris' surprise, a homemade pound cake. They took their desserts to the enclosed deck out back and finished their meals by the light of several oversized candles. "Anybody heard from that hideous Jackie Black?" Locke asked.

"Nah, she's been mighty quiet. I guess Pastor handled his business. Anyway, I don't want to see her, or hear from her. She talks too much for my liking. She'll break up a happy home talking all over herself." William offered. "I've had enough of that Black woman."

"What's her deal anyway?" Eddie inquired. "I've observed her. I think she's one to watch. Just because she's quiet doesn't mean she's not up to something. It's the quiet ones you have to question. I learned that in the service."

"She's a wounded bird, that's all." Iris was surprised at her own sympathy. "I'm more curious about where all her crazy comes from. And I'm determine to find out."

"So you're an investigator and a demolition man, now?" William chuckled.

"I've always been an investigator. That's what I used to do in my other life, dig up information on characters like that Jackie Black. You'd be surprised how investigation and demolition go hand in hand. Most times, investigation is its own demolition project."

"We should stop talking about her. We may talk her up. She's been quiet all this time. Let's keep it that way." William's suggestion was well taken, and Iris decided to return to the subject of the picture box.

"So, Locke. You mean to tell me you don't recognize *anyone* on those photos?" Iris kicked off her shoes and tucked her legs underneath her. Her socked feet grazed William's thigh, as she leaned back onto William's chest, who was sharing the chaise lounge with her.

"Yes. I recognize myself and I recognize Maggie. If I were to guess, that's Silas Farmer standing behind her on one of those photos. He used to work for Maggs. Nobody grins like Silas. And nobody laughs like him either. He'd throw his whole head back when he laughed. It looked as if he would break his neck. When I was a little girl he used to scare me to bits. I just knew one day he'd laugh too hard, and his head would roll off his neck right on down Maggie's front porch steps."

Iris threw her head back and laughed. "You're too much! Really? Break his neck from laughing?"

Locke crossed her leg. "Yeah, break his neck laughing." Locke had a curious look on her face, as if she was trying to remember something. He eyelids were almost completely shut, but she was staring at Iris and fidgeting with her cuticles. "Just like you're laughing right now." Locke was examining Iris closely, taking in her long legs, and the warm brown of her face, the yellow undertones that made her look as if she housed a personal sunshine right beneath her skin. She assessed the big white pretty teeth. Perfect teeth that were probably all hers. No caps or cavities. She measured the circumference of her face and the thick, shiny dark brown, almost black coils framing her cheekbones. All she needed was a pair of suspenders and a deeper voice. But… No… It couldn't be.

Eddie was too busy visualizing a man laughing until his neck broke to notice how Locke had begun to pick furiously at a hangnail on the inside of her right thumb. He too was laughing at the image Locke portrayed of the man on the picture. William was too busy watching Iris' hair bounce and shimmy to the music of her own laughter to notice Locke's demeanor suddenly change. She'd become uncharacteristically quiet and unbothered by their simultaneous outbursts. All four friends were too preoccupied with themselves to see Laura Baxter pass the backstreet that could be seen from Locke's backyard. She'd circled the block twice.

Bennett Banks peeped out of the blinds of his parlor window, counting the seconds it would take for Laura to pass his house, circle the block, and pass again in the blue Oldsmobile. She'd seen William and Iris coming out of Iris' house and walk in the direction of Belle Lynne Locke's home. Laura wasn't sure if the friends would all meet up and take an evening stroll, if they were eating dinner together, or if they would return to Iris' to sit out on the porch to talk. Laura did not want to risk being seen by anyone who would carry her secret back to Luceal. Iris had already proven herself a sleuth by bringing up her history with Bennett Banks while they were preparing for the St. Andrew fall picnic. Of all people, she did not want Iris to see her car pulling into Bennett's garage.

When Laura felt safe enough to park, she exited the car, smoothing out her wool, navy pants. She'd worn a crisp white button down shirt and a short string of pearls, an outfit similar to the one she wore on her first date with Bennett Banks. Back then she'd chosen a slim navy skirt that stopped right at her knee and pointed toe kitten heel pumps. Her strand of pearls then were long and fell right at her navel, which was covered by a fitted white turtleneck that accentuated her full bosom. She wondered if he would notice.

"C-Come on in, Laura." Bennett said from the screened in porch. Laura opened the door and walked slowly onto the neat space of Bennett's glassed in front porch. It was completely furnished, like an outside living room. In the back corner was a rocking chair, where Bennett often watched the street and the people occupying. Near the rocking chair was a small side table upon which sat a stack of stationary, lavender in color and turned with the writing facing down. This was also where he watched her when she dropped off his meals, picked up his Tupperware dishes, left him all those letters. Stacks and stacks of letters.

"Thank you, Bennett. You know it's been a long time." Laura reached for Bennett, but stopped herself short, her pinky just grazing the back of his hand.

Bennett's, who'd not had human contact in years, entire body was paralyzed by Laura's small touch, and he walked quickly into the house, beckoning her to follow him. He shut the door. The two stood, right past the threshold, facing each other, staring. Bennett, suddenly, grabbed Laura and hugged her. He wouldn't let her go, and Laura couldn't let Bennett go either. They stayed in that position for several seconds before Bennett tilted his head slightly to whisper in Laura's ear. "Laura, we've got to talk. We've got to talk before anything else."

"Yes, Bennett I know."

"It's been too long, Laura."

"Yes, I know."

"I don't even know if I can, be… be a man for you anymore."

"You can. You've been a man for me forever."

"What are we going to do?"

"I don't know, Bennett. I just don't know." The tears began then. There were many tears. Tears from the pain of old hurt and the prospect of new beginnings flooded Laura's face. Bennett did not move to wipe Laura's tears. He watched her cry and pushed her to let it all out, to flood his entire house with tears. He promised her love. He told her that she needed to be at his house with him.

Laura looked up at Bennett. "Let's sit down." They moved to a tan loveseat near another window Bennett often looked out of to watch Laura. "I know you love me. And I know I need to be here. But you can't keep me locked up behind glass like your service medals. I have a life outside the walls of my home. You need a life like that too, with me."

"But, you know my condition. You know I can't…" "Why can't you, Bennett? How long is your condition going to keep you from us?" Bennett shrugged. Laura took Bennett's hands. They were trembling. "Before, we let Luceal come through that gate and keep you from getting to me. We're not going to do that this time. Together, we need to go through that gate and keep Luceal from getting to *us*. We can do this. If we don't, we are still living like we did decades ago, by her rules. A lonely, mean-spirited, gossiping woman's rules. We were too old for that when we started out together. I was too stupid to figure out that you never meant me any harm. We've made mistakes..." "Yes, and those mistakes look like they're going to cost me again. I've been in this house so long, I don't think I could ever leave... not even for you, Laura." Bennett took off his glasses and sat them on top of his bald head.

"But I can help you with that. It doesn't have to be this way. I'm ready to be my own woman, a woman who can help her man, if you let me. I helped you before. Remember the journals? The stories? The poems? I still have them, locked away. I always dreamed of us taking them out and reading before we went to bed. We'd read them and laugh and laugh about how silly we were then."

"I don't know, Laura. It's just been so long."

"It has, but a new year is coming. There's change in the air. I feel brave and strong, like I have a fever that can't be broken. I want to run outside in the cool air like I did on that rainy day when you proposed to me. I need you to make that happen, Bennett."

Laura stood up and clapped her hands together. Her pearl charm bracelet rattled with the motion. " I know!" Laura's voice went up two octaves. "You can come to church with me. The cantata is always nice. The children outdo themselves with their performances. And Luceal says that the production will be extra special this year." Laura turned around in a circle, "And then there's the tree trimming, when everyone brings his special ornament to decorate the tree. Oh, Bennett, I'll bring a pen ornament for us, for all those years we were lovely pen pals! And church! Bless his name, church will be a wonderful experience to behold." Laura took a deep breath. She was winded from all of her musings, her dreams, wishes, and hopes had raised her heart rate, and she was crying all over again. Through the tears, she saw Bennett shaking his head, no. Laura's voice dropped. "You're not ready."

"No, I'm not ready. I mean I'm ready for you. I'm ready to have you gliding around my house. I'm ready to have you… to have you in my bed. I'm ready for your good cooking. I'm ready for your stories. But here. I'm ready for you right here." Bennett pointed toward the floor. "In this house. Not out there. I'm a sick man. My head ain't well. I hasn't been well since I lost you. I ain't well enough to weather the outside, the people, the whispers, the stares. Surely, you can understand that?"

"I can't Bennett."

Laura exited, all alone, out of the same gate Bennett used to dump Luceal out onto the sidewalk over thirty-five years ago. She didn't care who saw as she made her way around to the garage attachment. She waited patiently for the door to lift; Bennett opened it from the inside. Slowly, she got into the Blue Oldsmobile and backed out of the driveway. She did not turn on the radio, but drove in silence to pick up her sister, Luceal, from St. Andrew where she was rehearsing for the Christmas Cantata. She did not bother to wipe away the continuous stream of tears spilling from her eyes.

"What's wrong with you Laur-Mae?" Luceal asked as she slammed her girth onto the passenger seat of the car. She was winded from the walk from the church to the car. Luceal didn't wait for Laura to answer before she started in on the Christmas Cantata.

"Ooooh girl! The Cantata is going to be goooood this year!"

"That's nice."

"That Sister Black has so many hidden talents. St. Andrew won't be ready for what we have to show them this year."

"Really?"

"Aw yeah, child. Sweet Fields will be talking about this Christmas Program for years to come."

"I'll bet they will."

"I'm so glad Sister Black went on and asked me to help her. She would've never got that done all by herself"

"Probably not."

"Yeah, Sister Black and I, we work well together. I think we're going to be great friends after this. Great friends. Finally, somebody in that church that got some sense. Got sense enough to see that more people got talent and say-so than that old Belle Lynne Locke. That's why she sitting over there lonely, now. She's mean as a snake. Think she knows everything. Well, this one is going to knock those little linen pants off of her, Laur-Mae. You know those little overpriced pants she's wearing all the time? Gonna knock them off of her. Sure will. Now, wipe that water out your eyes. It's going to be a good Christmas. No more crying for you. Sister Black has a wonderful gift for us all this Christmas."

Laura drove home in silence, without wiping her eyes, as Luceal cackled on and on about Sister Black and her remix of St. Andrew's Christmas Cantata.

CHAPTER 23: CHRISTMAS CANTATA

The Christmas season arrived in Sweet Fields with great haste and much fanfare. Almost overnight, lights were hung on houses, evergreens were adorned with twinkle lights, and colorful wreaths on front doors welcomed visitors. Picture windows in both houses and shops were decorated with trees and fake snow. At St. Andrew, the children were rehearsing every chance they got for the Christmas Cantata. The sunshine band, youth choir, and praise dancers were all teeming with excitement. The adult choir was also buzzing with energy, as there was an attractive addition to the music ministry. Charles Edwards had invited his college buddy, Sampson, to sit in with the musicians on the biggest occasion of the year.

Jackie, who had been as quiet as a mouse, was working with praise dancers on a very special interpretation of the arrival of the wise men to Jesus' manger. Mother Emmadine Walker, the town seamstress, had designed and sewn the holiday choir smocks for the little ones in the Sunshine Band. When Jackie approached her about sewing the costumes for the wise men, she readily agreed and asked Jackie if she would be performing as well.

"Oh, no, Mother Walker. This is about the children. I have everything I need. Just robes and headdresses for the twelve wise men," Jackie declined graciously.

"Twelve? There were only three wise men, Sister Black," Emmadine said with straight pins between her lips.

"Oh no. The Magi, that's what they were called, were often groups of 12. But since they brought three gifts, people just assumed there were three men," she explained. "We will have 12 for the cantata." Mother Emmadine Walker smiled and nodded.
She was so glad Jackie had behaved herself in the past few months that she said nothing more.

But the foolishness began with the arrival of a package from 1-800-COSTUMES. When the UPS delivery man tapped on the studio window, Jackie was ecstatic. She threw open the door, signed for the medium-sized box, and leapt into the air with joy. When she cautiously opened the box, she smiled until water filled her eyes. This was the finishing piece to her costume for "Gift of the Magi Interpretive Dance." She was convinced that *everyone* would notice and appreciate her beauty and talent when she performed in her piece de resistance.

On the night of the Cantata, the sanctuary was alive with parental pride, stage fright, excitement, and Christmas spirit. Pastor LeBeaux was seated in the audience on the second row. Rev. Charles Edwards was on the light and soundboard. Sampson, still a strange figure to the parishioners, mainly because he had no last name, was on the organ, and John Martinez was on the drums. It was customary for all the men of St. Andrew to wear black suits and red neckwear for the annual Christmas program, but Sampson wore his white shirt open to the chest and his red tie hanging loosely around his neck. Everyone noticed, but no one said anything; he was a visitor. They assumed he didn't know any better.

When the cue was given by Luceal, who had always wanted a part in the Christmas program, the lights went low and the baritone voice of the narrator began. Through the first set of songs, Locke sat beside Eddie fidgeting with her gloves.

"I have a bad feeling about this program, Eddie," Locke whispered during a brief applause. Eddie said nothing. He grabbed her hand and held it tightly with his fingers interlocked with hers.

Luceal gave another cue and the lights dimmed again. Very low. Too low for Locke's liking. Locke stood and looked around in the darkness, but sat down again after Eddie gently tapped her wrist.

Silhouettes moved across the front of the church and got into place. Low music began, and the lights brightened just a bit.

The music was foreign to the audience, so they remained silent. They couldn't really find the rhythm. The melody seemed to be a combination of high-pitched strings, flutes, and tambourines. Twelve wise men appeared vigorously dancing in a circle while the narrator explained the magi who came from the east were Persian, Indian, and Arab. The narrator described the Magi's journey to Bethlehem being guided by a star.

When he mentioned the word "star" the dancers changed. They began bowing and making large movements with extended arms in dramatic intervals. Just as they crouched down again, the music slowed, and a drum got louder. Then there was an arm stretching up out of the center of the circle of wise men. Then another. The hands and wrists of the arms were making fluid circles. The wise men began their dance again in a circle around the rotating wrists. The narrator continued.

A thin long leg joined the arms. The toes on the foot were severely pointed. Eventually the leg and foot disappeared, leaving the slim arms, wrists and hands to continue their circular motions. A head wearing a pointed tiara appeared, and the emerging silhouette that followed was reminiscent of the statue of liberty with no gown or tablet.

The music sped up. The wise men danced faster, bowing and reaching to the emerging figure. Gradually, the lights came up, and the audience gasped when they saw Jackie in a flesh colored leotard stretching and writhing in a seductive, cat-like manner. The music had grown louder and faster, and at the clash of the symbols noting the end of the song, the golden star atop Jackie's head lit up. With the push of a button on her sleeve, Jackie's entire body lit up in twinkle lights. The wise men fell to their feet, and Jackie stood above them prepared to speak.

While her mouth was still agape, and before she could say a word, Rev. Edwards motioned to Sampson, who then started playing "Away in a Manger" on the organ. Rev. Edwards motioned to Luceal for the wise men and Jackie to exit. Luceal shrugged her shoulders and the "star" and her wise men exited the sanctuary through the side door.

The abrupt change threw everyone off. The spirit of Christmas seemed to have up and left the remaining participants in a frenzy of confusion. The senior choir was assembled but not yet in the choir loft, so Sampson continued to play, dutifully, as he awaited a cue from somebody as to what to do next.

A still anticipatory fog descended on the room, and a familiar voice began singing from the back of the church. Heads turned and mouths hung open as Maybelline moved out of a rear pew. She beckoned for the senior choir to enter the sanctuary from the vestibule, and headed down the main aisle.

"Oh Happy Day," she sang in a low rounded voice. She took her time walking down the aisle, and the choir slowly organized themselves in two lines behind her. Sampson played the organ until Rev. Edwards slid onto the bench; then Sampson picked up his guitar and joined in.

Maybelline had never looked better. She was wrapped in a charcoal cashmere sweater dress. The form fitting dress revealed that Maybelline had lost about two dress sizes and had retained her curves. The bodice was a series of soft drapes of the sumptuous fabric across the front of her and about her arms, and drawn in at her naturally cinched waist. The skirt of her dress lay neatly atop her curves, maintaining a delicate balance of modesty and sexiness. Her legs were encased in a thin layer of charcoal silk, and gray suede pointed-toe pumps finished her ensemble.

The choir members had made it into place just in time to sing the bridge of the song:

He taught me how to
watch, fight and pray
(fight and pray) and live
rejoicing every day
(everyday)

When the song reached the call and response, Maybelline sang with an energy St. Andrew had never seen before. She rocked from her waist causing her thick, straightened hair to swing from side to side.

Prentiss LeBeaux couldn't contain his excitement. It was all he could do to not run up and hug her in the middle of the selection. They had spoken just two days earlier. Maybelline had said nothing about returning to Sweet Fields for Christmas. Pastor LeBeaux grinned so hard, he didn't notice that he had developed a headache. He just kept smiling, clapping, and hoping the program would end soon.

Locke was so happy to see Maybelline that she stood up and clapped--only she didn't clap along with the song. She was applauding

Maybelline. She had taken care of herself. She looked beautiful, and she saved the program from becoming a total shamble.

Iris was sitting in her customary place on her favorite pew, and Francis the Secretary was sitting with her. Francis grabbed Iris' hand and squeezed it tight when she recognized the familiar voice singing from the back of the church. Iris returned the squeeze and decided not to be unnerved by Francis holding her hand through the song and wiping at tears that slipped past her tortoise shell frames.

The song ended, and Pastor LeBeaux took the microphone. He thanked the youth director for all of her hard work, the children for their discipline, the support crew and many ministries that assisted with the production. He applauded the music ministry and made special mention of the visiting musician Sampson. He recognized Mother Emmadine Walker for her annual contributions and hard work making new and adjusting old costumes, to which she mumbled too loudly, "I had nothing to do with that leotard."

"We know, Mother Emmadine." Someone from the congregation muttered in response.

Prentiss couldn't hide the joy in his heart when he said, "Let's welcome back Sister Maybelline Crowder. She came back from China to spend the holidays with us!" He tried his best not to say "spend the holidays with me" and breathed a sigh of relief when it came out right.

He passed the microphone over to Rev. Edwards who announced there were light refreshments in the fellowship hall, and reminded everyone to attend the Tree Trimming Fellowship the next evening before concluding the program with the benediction.

A small crowd formed around Maybelline. Friends, coworkers, and choir members. She hugged them all and blushed when people mentioned how beautiful she looked. The crowds thinned as everyone moved into the fellowship hall for homemade Christmas cookies and punch, but Prentiss remained behind. He walked up and hugged Maybelline and squeezed her tightly.

"I had no idea you were coming home. You never said anything."

"I know. I wanted it to be a surprise," she said smiling. "You look good Prentiss." Maybelline, from her seat in the back had noticed Prentiss had trimmed down. His waist was more streamlined, his back more defined, and his face thinner under his thin graying beard.

"And I feel good, now that you're back, Maybelline. Back where you belong." Prentiss took her arm, looped it under his, and quickly kissed her on the lips before starting toward the fellowship hall. They did not see Jackie standing in the musician's corner. She had covered her atrocious twinkle-light nude body suit with an even more atrocious yellow caftan and replaced her starry crown with a matching turban.

Jackie was disappointed. She had prepared to receive the congregation's acceptance and adoration and wanted to look beautiful as she returned the smiles and hugs she'd predicted. The performance was to be her triumphant return to the spotlight and a heartfelt appeal for Prentiss' heart, but Charles Edwards had rudely interrupted her, and Maybelline had stolen the show.

If all had gone as planned in Jackie's mind, things could have ended differently, for everyone. She would have obeyed the sentiments tugging at her heartstrings, sentiments that had been planted by the residents of Golden Sunsets. But Jackie found herself on the outside and upstaged, yet again. She was hurt and angry, and because of this she would have to resort to her back up plan. She fluffed her caftan, retrieved her handbag from its hiding place and retreated to her car. She had no interest in sharing cookies and punch with the people she was about to bring to an open shame at the largest holiday event of the year.

CHAPTER 24: TREE TRIMMING

The St. Andrew tree trimming was a legendary and ceremonious event in Sweet Fields. The ornaments represented families or individuals and something special that happened to them during the year. Their names and the year were penned somewhere on the ornament and placed on the tree. The placement of the ornaments was done with much flare and pomp and circumstance. When the tree was taken down on January 2nd, the ornaments were returned to the owners.

The tree trimming fellowship usually took place in the afternoon in the fellowship hall. There were platters upon platters of finger foods. The deacons had brought up the giant Balsam Fir Christmas tree from the basement and set it up in the fellowship hall. Emmadine decided it was time to replace the tree skirt that had been used for the past seven years. She had sewn a beautiful pale gold skirt complete with gold lace and scalloped embroidery. The tree was in place and the food was being arranged on the long buffet rows. Rumor had it that there would be several out of town guests attending as well as some church members from long ago returning to visit.

When the clock struck 4 pm, Rev. Edwards said a brief prayer of thanks and the buffet lines were formed. Prentiss and Maybelline arrived together, but only a few people noticed. William had gotten to the church early to help set up the tree and the tables for the buffet, but when Iris arrived, he greeted her warmly and remained by her side. Locke and Eddie arrived together, and the congregants had come to expect nothing different.

As was customary, Laura and Luceal arrived together. Little did Laura know, Bennett Banks (who hadn't stepped foot in St. Andrews since he had come to ask for prayer before shipping out to war) had made his way quietly into the fellowship hall, and deposited himself on the back seat. Mother Carrie and Daughter Eliza had chosen seating closest to the tree, for Mother Carrie loved Christmas trees more than any other holiday decoration. The Edwards were tucked away in a corner whispering and smiling to each other, as were Clem and Judith Callahan. The deaconesses were watching the buffet line like guards. They kept the platters stocked with chicken wings, cheeses and crackers, vegetables, chips and dips, pinwheels, fruit skewers, burger sliders, bacon wrapped chicken bites, and a host of other savory delights.

After a short while of dining, Big Hughes, who rarely made announcements, stood and said, "Let's begin presenting the ornaments." Big presented a gold dollar sign from the deacon board and joked that the church had experienced its best financial year ever, even with the groundbreaking of the new daycare facility.

The Edwards presented a pacifier. Rev. Edwards said, "God has seen fit to bless us with a child. The baby is due in June!" Everyone applauded.

Mother Carrie stood. "Babies are blessings from God, and that one is gonna be pretty as all get out!"

Maybelline presented a globe ornament. "God took me around the world, and brought me back safely, and for that, I am grateful."

Sampson, who was starting to cause quite a buzz among the single's ministry, stood and presented a wooden ornament of five choral singers. "To the best choir in all of Georgia!" he shouted, and the choir members hooted and hollered. He then put a finger to his lips and said, "save your voices for tomorrow."

Clem and Judith stood together and presented an ornament of a giant golden needle with a thin thread wrapped around it on behalf of Emmadine Walker. "She's not going to pat herself on the back, so we decided to do it for her," Clem said. "If Emmadine can't sew it, it can't be made. So we present this on behalf of Emmadine who made the tree skirt and all of the smocks and costumes," said Judith dabbing at her eyes as she went to hug Emmadine who was also crying.

Iris stood and presented a crystal ornament in the shape of a church. She paused before she spoke. "St. Andrew is a wonderful example of a how a church should be--full of love, acceptance, and the spirit of God."

Luceal stood and Laura took her time standing up with her. Laura lagged behind as Luceal walked to the tree to present her traditional golden pecan. The parishioners of St. Andrew joked every year, that Luceal and Laura hung enough gold pecans on the Christmas tree to make a pecan pie Christmas ornament. Just as Laura reached to hang her golden pecan, she felt someone grab her hand.

"I got this one," Bennett Banks whispered into Laura's ear. He reached up and hung a golden pen onto the Christmas tree. Bennett had to catch Laura, because she'd almost fainted. She righted herself quickly and turned around and gave Bennett a big hug. Everyone clapped and hooted and almost forgot that there was more trimming to do, when Luceal spoke.

"Who let this one in? What are you doing here and what are you doing to my…"

Laura turned to her sister and looked her in her eye. "Not today, Luceal. You won't do this to me or Bennett today."

Bennett took Laura's hand and escorted her to a seat near the Christmas tree. They held hands and cried together softly.

Many others presented ornaments. Families presented the ornaments their children had made during children's church. The deaconess board presented an angel in memory of Maggie Murphy. Just as ornament presentations seemed to wind down, Jackie stepped forward with a wicker basket.

"Members of St. Andrew, I have gotten to know so many of you, and I have come to love you all dearly. I have a few ornaments I would like to present. Now, it is because of the love I have for St. Andrew that I want to present these ornaments. They represent the history of Sweet Fields that I have come to learn while working at Golden Sunsets. Some of my friends from Golden Sunsets are here. Say hello!" The crowd turned and applauded the faces they hadn't seen in ages. The entire Bid Whist Club sat together nibbling on their food and whispering to each other.

"Well, everyone knows that successful pastors have a strong advising team, and Pastor LeBeaux's advisory board does exactly that. They advise him in everything. So I thought you all should know some bits and pieces of information that I have learned about this advisory board, you know, so that it will help you appreciate them more."

Jackie reached into her wicker basket and pulled out a salt dough ornament with the imprint of a hand on it. "This is for the lady who keeps her hands covered. Had her father worn gloves, maybe her life would have turned out differently, as most killers wear gloves before they commit cold blooded murder." Jackie turned and smiled at Locke. Locke nodded and offered her a smile in kind. She sat with a remarkable amount of poise, though her blood boiled on the inside.

"My next ornament is for the man who likes control. His family owned most of your ancestors, and it seems his tyranny continues. She pulled out a bracelet of large chain links painted black. They looked like shackles. Someone shouted from the back, "sit down and be quiet!" But Locke held up her gloved hand and said "let her finish. Go on, Jackie, say your peace." The crowd started whispering amongst themselves. The Bid Whist Club remained quiet with straight faces.

"To the new owner of the Murphy Inn, Iris." Jackie pulled out a small red light bulb, complete with a short silver pull chain.
"For perfect little Iris, I present this bulb. The Mae West of Sweet Fields, the late Maggie Murphy, ran a brothel of sorts. It has become evident that Iris may be a lot like her grandmother. Watch out, St. Andrew, Sweet Fields is about to have a red light district, if Iris follows in her granny's footsteps."

Mother Emmadine Walker stood up with her mouth stretched into a straight line. "You take that back, you lying hussy! Maggie didn't run a brothel!"

Iris said loud enough for everyone to hear "It's okay. She's entitled to her version of the story. Go on, tell it your way, Jackie." Iris offered her a smile while William's blood was boiling.

"To the rest of the advisory board--Charles Edwards, William Hughes, both father and son, I have an ornament for you too." Jackie pulled out three sachets bags filled with dried oats. "If you didn't know, Charles and Karen Edwards have been pregnant before---before they were married, so the right reverend hasn't always been right. William Hughes, Sr. has grandchildren all over the county from both sons. I had a 10 year old boy as a dance pupil who stuttered like you Will Junior and was as clumsy as Edith Hughes. Iris, did you know William had fathered a child by a woman from the wrong side of the bridge?" Iris held William's hand and whispered something in his ear that made him smile.

Prentiss released Maybelline's hand and stood up.

"And I mustn't forget, Pastor." Jackie pulled out a bright red heart covered in glitter. "And for you, Maybelline," she said smiling pulling out a miniature cardboard label of a Spanx package trimmed in gold glitter. Prentiss turned red from his ears to the "v" of his burgundy sweater. "I'm sure she knows what to do with that, Pastor." Jackie turned to Maybelline and bent down close, but not to close. "Use it wisely, Maybelline. It holds in a multitude of, ahem, faults." Maybelline smiled, a real smile. She shook her head from side to side, her hair following the motion in long heavy waves brushing the sides of her cheeks. She squeezed
Prentiss' hand tight and muttered, "Bless your poor black heart."

"Have a seat right there, Sister Jackie. We, the members of St. Andrew, have a special presentation for you too," Prentiss said through grimacing lips. "Sister Murphy, we're in your hands." Iris stood and greeted everyone.

"On this joyful occasion, Sister Black's intent today was to sow seeds of discord among the St. Andrew family with special attention to the advisory board. She targeted the advisory board because she believes we have influenced Pastor LeBeaux to reject her affections," Iris said calmly walking to the front of the room where Jackie was seated. The audience gasped. "But Sister Jackie," Iris said addressing her directly, "we have had nothing to do with Pastor LeBeaux not being romantically interested in you. You have attacked us and attempted to slander us for no reason. Since you have put forth so much effort in trying to destroy the unity and camaraderie of this church, we--the advisory board--decided to come together and share a little bit about you as well." Jackie's already large eyes bulged in surprise.

"You know nothing about me," Jackie said trying to stand. But Maybelline put her hand on her shoulder to keep her seated.

"No. No, Sister Jackie," Iris said waving her index finger at Jackie. "We let you spew all of your venom, now you will be quiet and let us present the anti-venom, so to speak." Iris moved to the place where Jackie had placed her offensive ornaments and began to pick them up one at a time. She picked up the black-colored chain that resembled shackles and looked a Deacon Callahan.

Clem Callahan stood, pulled at the lapels of his jacket and spoke. "It's no secret that my great, great grandfather was one of the five founders of Sweet Fields. You all know or at least heard about how the Klan tried to come and terrorize our town. They tried time and time again to shut us down. But we devised a plan, together. And that plan worked. No one here believes that my family owned anyone. The Callahans worked the sugar cane fields just like everyone else. You cannot let this stranger who knows nothing of our history have you believe what you know to be true. We take great pride in our beloved Sweet Fields and the peace that comes along with being a member of the Sweet Fields community. That's why, in spite of all, when folks leave Sweet Fields, they always come back home." Clem looked over to his cousin Shirley Frye. She smiled and offered a nod of approval. Clem returned the smile and nod and took his seat.

Iris then picked up the red light bulb and crooked her lips into a smile. She said, "I have heard many stories about my grandmother, Maggie, but I've been told that Ms. Ivy Nelson knows more about my grandmother than anyone in the room."

Ivy Nelson stood confidently. Sampson offered her a cordless microphone. She grabbed it, almost snatched it away from him. "There is no way on God's green earth that Maggie would use a woman like this gal here claims. Maggie didn't stand for abuse on account of she had been abused herself. She took in women who had been body beat, spirit beat, heart sore, and wandering--that came from a poem, you know. I believe the writer's name was Owen Dodson, but it makes sense all the same. Anyway, she would have beat a man with her own hands if anyone had tried some funny stuff with one of her broken birds--that's what she called them." She paused and moved a bit closer to where Jackie sat. "When I told this gal about the Murphy Inn, I told her how Maggie helped women. I didn't say *nothing* about prostitution. That tells you where her mind is—in the gutter, and people who says such things ought to be put out! Put out, I say! I loved Maggie and I think she'd be proud of you Iris. I don't know who named you Iris, but you'll grow into that name just fine. Here, honey." She held out the microphone to Sampson and returned to her seat.

Iris held up the glitter-trimmed Spanx ornament. "Maybelline, do you want to address this foolishness?" Maybelline stood and smoothed down her high waist, red pencil skirt. The bright white of her button down shirt complimented her perfect teeth, and the multi-strand of pearls at her neck lay gleaming on her chest, barely peeking from the collar of her shirt. Her newfound confidence allowed a smile to spread beautifully across her face before she spoke.

"At the benefit gala, after my performance, Jackie deliberately stepped on my dress while I walked by her, causing the skirt to tear completely away from the bodice. As you can imagine, I was mortified, so much so that I refused to play the organ or even come to church. Because of her and the embarrassment she caused, I took a project in China. What I have learned is Jacqueline Black is black indeed. Her thoughts, her deeds, and very existence is dark and depressing. So I want you to know, Jackie," Maybelline said turning to look directly at her tormentor. "I am no longer embarrassed or ashamed. I was a happy person who gave and received love. And the fact that you were the only one in all of St. Andrew who talked about my wardrobe malfunction should have been an indicator to you (and to me) that my church community isn't petty like that. We love, respect, and support each other. It is my prayer that your poor dark heart will someday be able to be a part of something as rich and sweet as the Sweet Fields community." The entire audience clapped. The choir stood and hooted, while Sampson shook his head for them to be quiet and save their voices.

Iris held up the bags of oats meant to symbolize the fornication of Rev. Edwards and the Hughes brothers. "Rev.

Edwards, why don't you go first?"

"My sisters and brothers, when my wife was in college, she was assaulted by someone she knew. I had been in love with Karen since the 9th grade, so when I heard about her attack and the pregnancy that resulted from it, I offered to marry her. I loved her and wanted to protect her from the hateful gossip that was sure to surface once her pregnancy became obvious, so we married. Soon after, she miscarried and we went on with life. I don't know how Jackie dug up this information or why she would use such a hurtful experience, but it doesn't hurt and we aren't bitter. This is a testimony. What the devil meant for evil...God meant it for good. Maybe this will bless someone today. Hurt doesn't last always, as long as you're willing to let God heal you." "Amen!" a deaconess responded.

"And the hurt and healing is not just for our good!" Rev. Edwards continued.

"Oh Lord!" Daughter Eliza hollered.

"But it's for the good of the kingdom," shouted Rev. Edwards. Rev. Edwards stood up and began to walk around the fellowship hall.

"The kingdom!" the crowd roared.

"In the kingdom, my maladies help me to minister!"

"Minister to us, Reverend!"

"In the kingdom, my grief can be a gift!"

"Praise Him!"

"And it's all...all...... all!"

"All!"

"All for my good! And for God's glory! Allelujah!" Rev. Edwards began jumping in place. "Ain't he good?!" He sat down, and Karen put her arm around him, rocking as she cried along with her husband.

Charles and Karen both turned to Jackie. Charles said "We pray that you let God heal you of your hurt, Jackie, so you can be at peace and stop hurting others." Eddie had never been more proud of his son than he was at that moment.

Big Hughes put his plate down and took long slow strides to the front where Iris stood. "Everyone in here knows Edith and I had two sons. As two good-looking parents, we had no choice but to make some good-looking children. Y'all know children can come from the same parents but be as different as night and day. My son, Wesley, is nothing like his younger brother William. Wesley was a ladies' man. He has made me grandfather to 2 boys and 3 girls. And I love them all; how they got here is not their fault. The young man you mentioned, Ms. Black, is Wesley, Jr. He is not William's son. My boy William would never be as indiscreet as you have accused. He's an honorable man. I'm proud to call him my son, and any woman," he smiled at Iris "would be glad to have a morally sound, God-fearing, hard-working man like William as her husband."

Iris held up the salt dough imprint of a hand that was meant to offend Belle Lynne Locke. Locke stood up and walked to the front with a full skirt of green linen flowing about her legs. She held two small boxes in her gloved hands.

"St. Andrew," Jackie called my father a murderer. "And maybe she's right. But the book of Ecclesiastes reminds us there is a time and season for all things." Locke recited the third chapter of Ecclesiastes verses 1-8.

1*For everything there is a season,*
a time for every activity under heaven.
2*A time to be born and a time to die.*
A time to plant and a time to harvest.
3*A time to kill and a time to heal.*
A time to tear down and a time to build up.
4*A time to cry and a time to laugh.*
A time to grieve and a time to dance.
5*A time to scatter stones and a time to gather stones.*
A time to embrace and a time to turn away.
6*A time to search and a time to quit searching.*
A time to keep and a time to throw away.
7*A time to tear and a time to mend.*
A time to be quiet and a time to speak.
8*A time to love and a time to hate.*
A time for war and a time for peace.

Jacqueline, your timing has been off since the day you drove that Thunderbird into Sweet Fields. It is not the time for you to love anyone," she said picking up the red heart ornament for Prentiss "because you don't love yourself. It is not the time to tear down a community by bringing up its history because it didn't accept you and your take-over ways."

Locke turned to the congregation and said, "It is not the time to be quiet, but the time to speak. I spoke with my Aunt Glad. Gladys Turner, Jacqueline, is my aunt, and she told me of your plan here today. She also told me about my father and what he did. I am not ashamed of my father. Not one bit!" Locke jabbed the table with two fingers. "His baby sister had been treated worse than an animal by people Sweet Fields let into their community, and he avenged her. Much like I'm doing today." Locke felt the tears welling up in her eyes. She opened the two small boxes she carried in her hand. One was a peacock feather on a gold string.

"Here, Jackie. This is for you. It represents a time to tear-remember how you tore your dress to pieces in my front yard, because Prentiss was not giving you the attention you thought you deserved? Well, we at St. Andrew, are tired of you tearing things up and tearing people down." Locke recomposed herself, for her pulse was racing. Eddie walked up and placed his hand on her back, as if to calm her, but Locke was not done. She continued. "When I think about it, Jackie. You're just like a peacock: proud, manifold in color, and weighted down by your own feathers. Peacocks, because of their heavy over decorated plumage, can't fly, and they never will. You, Jacqueline O'Shelle Black, seem to be experiencing the same lot in life. But you will not continue to drag your destructive feathers around here, kicking up dust where it has already settled." She opened the second box and revealed a suitcase ornament on a gold string.

"This ornament represents a time for turning away. We are inviting you to leave Sweet Fields. You cannot appreciate the uniqueness of our community regardless of the many chances we've given you and the countless warnings we've issued." Locke dusted her hands off as if she were shaking dirt from them. She nodded at Iris and reclaimed her seat beside Eddie.

"May I say something?" a voice called from the very back of the room. A tall man in a casual suit stood and walked to an opening in the middle of the room. "My name is George Pryor, and I pastor Bread of Life Christian Center in Jericho, Georgia." Jackie's eyes closed in disbelief. "Jacqueline Black was a member of my congregation about seven years ago. She sowed seeds of discord in every ministry she touched. She fixated on the chairman of the deacon board and stalked the poor man until he moved to Florida to be with his children." Rev. Pryor shook his head in great sadness. "You people have been nice to 'invite her' to leave. We weren't so nice. You've done the right thing and in the right spirit." The man returned to his seat at the back of the room.

"How did you find him? Why did you bring him here?" Jackie burst out.

"You aren't the only one who can investigate people, Jackie." Iris said shoving Jackie's ornaments into a plastic garbage bag. "And we aren't done just yet. Sister Francis, the letter, please." Francis stood and read.

Ms. Jacqueline O'Shelle Black,

This document serves to inform you of Pastor Prentiss LeBeaux and the Church Board's decision to dismiss you from the St. Andrew Church of Sweet Fields, GA. This decision was made in accordance with the Holy Scriptures and by-laws of this, our beloved, church. As of today, you will no longer be permitted to attend any St. Andrew church services or functions.

As outlined by the Matthew 18 model, you have been made aware of your offenses both in private and public as situations have escalated. As outlined by the aforementioned scripture, the final step of this process is excommunication from the church, to give you the opportunity to confess and repent and finally learn from the errors you've made.

To recap, you were welcomed into this body in keeping with the compassion Christ showed to others, in spite of the fact the letter preceding your acceptance here was not favorable. You continued in the same practices not in alignment with the principles of scripture. You have shown that you are not a new creature in Christ. You have not exhibited that the old habits you practiced at former churches have become new. You have done many of the things that God hates, as listed in Proverbs, the most profound being, you have sown discord among the brethren. You therefore have been marked, and as scripture recounts separated from this body.

The St. Andrew community is a traditional tight knit group, who welcomes true brothers and sisters in Christ into the fold with open arms; however, you have not shown this love in kind. And because you remain unrepentant of your infractions and have made a mockery of the true cause of Christ, this decision will remain final unless otherwise revealed by the Holy Spirit.

Cordially,

Pastor Prentiss LeBeaux,

The Board Members of St. Andrew Church,

On behalf of the St. Andrew Church Community

Pastor LeBeaux stood to speak, "St. Andrew, you have all heard the contents of the excommunication letter as read by the church secretary, Sister Francis, here. Are we all in agreement?

"Yes." The church responded in unison. Jackie Black flinched.

"Jackie," Iris turned to speak to someone near the back of the room, "we have called in someone to assist you with your departure. Mrs. Helen Black, did you have something to say?"

Jackie stood up and shouted "You called my *mother*?!" A tall, slender woman in her late fifties with Jackie's coloring stood up and told Jackie to sit down. "Ladies and gentlemen, I sincerely apologize for the distress my daughter has caused. Ever since her father died, she has been fixating on men at different churches. She has a twin sister, you see, and Jackie has always believed that her sister, Janice, was my favorite, and she was her father's. His death did something to her. This is the third church she's been expelled from, but I am grateful for the gentility you have shown her. We will leave now."

"Wait!" Sister Berry called out. "Mrs. Black, your daughter needs help with her grief. Here's the card of a Christian therapist I know in Atlanta," she said hugging them both at the exit door. Deacon William Hughes took great satisfaction in escorting Jackie Black and her mother out of the church. Officer Michael Martinez sat waiting in his police cruiser to escort them to the edge of Sweet Fields.

Finally, Prentiss stood and presented an ornament in the shape of a diamond ring. "I want to say how much I love each of you. You all have become my family, but there is one person I would like to become an official member of my family. Sister Maybelline, would you come up here for a moment?" Maybelline's bosom was heaving and tears were welling up her eyes. "Maybelline, would you marry me?" Prentiss asked while on bended knee. Maybelline, unable to maintain her composure, burst into tears. Maybelline sang out in a strong alto voice, "Yeeeeeess! Yeeeee--eeess! Yeees Prentiss! My soul, My soul says, yeeessssss!" The church body of St. Andrew roared with excitement. From all corners of the room, parishioners rushed the newly engaged couple with congratulatory hugs. There was a loud shout from the wings, and Maybelline stood on her tiptoes to witness her dear friend, Katie Caldwell, letting out a loud, "Lawwwwwwwd, I thank you!" Katie Caldwell had always been blamed for starting impromptu praise breaks; however, several of the members joined her in her celebration.

Voices of praise filled the room, and Sampson slid onto the fellowship hall's keyboard just in time to join in the chorus. Prentiss LeBeaux clapped his hands loudly and walked around and around in circles. Maybelline held her lips and eyes tight, but that didn't stop the tears from rolling down her face. She rocked from side to side with her hands clasped in front of her chest.

The celebration finally dissipated to a dull murmur, and Pastor LeBeaux was able to compose himself to close out the service. "We've had a high time in the Lord, this afternoon, haven't we church?" He reached for Maybelline to join him at the front of the fellowship hall. "I'm going to take a cue from our newest guest, Sampson. Y'all save some of that praise for tomorrow!" Everyone laughed and gathered together for the closing prayer. "Let us pray saints."

"Lord, I don't know where to start, for there are so many things to be thankful for. You are a great God, as evidenced by this tree trimming fellowship. When it looked as if things would take a turn for the worse, you made yourself manifest to your people, and showed us that all things work for your glory and our good. Thank you for that manifestation. You worked a mighty work in the building today. The enemy of the saints came to steal, kill and destroy our fellowship. He tried to spread his seeds of discord among the brothers and sisters of Christ. He tried to present us full of faults in front of a Holy God. But you, God, took what looked like a dirty nasty past, and brought your people even closer together. You used the past to remind of us of just how far we've come. And we thank you Lord. Lord thank you for giving us a mind to please you, even though we had to turn one of your children away. But we know that the word was preached here. And if Sister Jackie Black heard it, it will NOT come back void. We believe that. And even though she had to leave, we can take comfort in knowing that we dismissed her using your way and your word. And we can rest well and prepare ourselves for a wonderful praise celebration in the morning, since we've been cleansed of the fiery darts of the enemy. I know you're going to be in the building to pour your glory out onto your people. Bless St. Andrew and give them hearts of peace as they walk with you. Draw them closer to you. Let them feel your love. I thank you for this congregation. They've been good to me, even when I didn't always make good decisions in a timely manner. And bless the board of advisors. They've been patient, kind and obedient. And Lord, bless this help mate you've sent me. Thank you for opening my eyes to my good thing. I feel your spirit between us, and right now, I place you in the center of our courtship. Help us to be a good example of Christ's love for his church. Help me love her well, because I'm thankful for you

bringing her to me. Until Sunday morning, we will await your presence in our hearts and in this house. In Jesus name,
Amen."

It took close to an hour for everyone to vacate the fellowship hall. The Bid Whist Club of Golden Sunsets was showered with hugs and kisses from St. Andrew parishioners. Many of the older members hung around to reminisce about old times, while some of the younger members became reacquainted with their elders. As the Golden Sunsets van pulled up to collect its group, Locke caught up with Silas Farmer.

"Silas. How long will you be up tonight? I know you don't do much philandering nowadays, but I have a matter of very urgent business to discuss with you. It must be discussed tonight." Silas looked up from his wheelchair and grinned at Locke. "Of course I'll wait up for you Little Belle. If it's that important, it's worth staying up an extra few minutes."

"I'll be there shortly after you arrive. Please be decent, Silas. I won't be alone."

Silas threw back his head and laughed. Locke turned her head away from the sight. "I'll be decent, Little Belle. I promise."

"Thank you, Silas."

Quickly, Locke scurried over to Iris, who was accompanied by William. Francis and Melvin Collier were with them as well.

"Locke, Francis was just telling us about when she and Melvin…"

"That's very nice, Iris. But we must go. I may have something to share with you." Locke turned to the other couple. "Francis. Melvin. You are certainly an attractive couple. I want you to stay that way. Come along Iris. William, I'll have her back before curfew," Locke said with a wink.

Iris was not yet ready to lose the camaraderie she was enjoying. "But must we go now Locke? I was really enjoying…"

Locke moved closer to Iris and whispered, "It's about the pictures."

Iris' interest had been officially peaked. She said quick goodbyes to Melvin and Francis, waved to the remaining congregants, and planted a quick kiss on William's cheek.

"No wonder the residents from Golden Sunsets look so happy." Iris said as she looked around marveling at the beauty of the place.

"You know, I don't half do anything. I put my people on this building project, and they made sure it was a place folks could come in and be at peace in their latter years. I have an entire wing reserved behind the seventh sunray, right over there in that corner."

Iris stared at Locke with her mouth open. Finally she was able to speak. "Don't tell me this is your place, too."

"Why sure. My Clive left it for me. Now go sit over there while I make sure Silas is decent."

The lights in Golden Sunsets were low, but the bright yellow of the walls and furniture cast a soft glow over the lobby and down the facility's hallway. Locke tapped lightly on Silas' door with her fingertips. There was no answer from inside, so she tapped again, this time with her fist.

"Come on in," Silas said gingerly.

"Silas, I hope it's not too late, but this matter is of great urgency." Locke walked over to Silas' window where he sat looking over the lawn.

He turned his wheelchair around. "I was just about to doze off on you, Little Belle." He wheeled over to her. "What has you so wool-gathered this evening?"

Locke pulled out the blue box she'd gotten from Iris. One by one she spread the pictures out on the colorful red and green quilt covering Silas' bed. "These were found in the wall of Maggie's house. I wanted you to take a look at them." Locke pointed at three images that were of the small child. "Especially the ones with the babies. Do you remember any of this, Silas? It's important that I tell the truth to someone, as full as I know it."

Silas picked up each picture; one by one he examined them. At the photo of himself and Maggie Murphy he produced a wide grin, shaking his head back and forth. "That Maggs… I tell you. She was my one and only. But these children, I can't place them. 'Course there were several children running around when Maggie and I… when we. When I left Maggs' place, there were no babies there. Not that I can remember. But, I left bad. Not bad. But sad."

"What happen with you and Maggs, Silas? It's not a secret that you were sweet on each other. She kept you around the place the longest. I never told Maggs, but I'd seen you coming inside from the side door a few times. You all weren't fooling anybody."
Locke laughed. "If you were trying, you failed miserably."

"Maggs has always been her own woman, even when she was a child, I hear. She didn't like people making a fuss over her. I'm a fuss-maker by nature. I think when Maggs saw too much of that, she went off me a little bit."

"What was the last thing you made a fuss about? What really did it for you both?" Locke asked.

Silas looked at Locke intently. "I thought she was sick. I'd show up every morning for my shift, and usually she'd be waiting at the porch step for me, with my coffee, you know, because usually we would have a pretty long night, you know. For a couple of weeks though, she said she was sick. She looked sick. She stopped making coffee because she said it made her stomach sick, couldn't stand the smell of it, she said. That's when I started getting worried. I tried to carry her to the doctor uptown. You remember we used to have our very own Sweet Fields doctor? I wonder why we got away from that, having our own doctor in Sweet Fields? Now, we have to go way to the county doctor to get some decent medical care."

"Focus Silas."

"Okay. Well, after the sickness didn't let up, I put my foot down. I knocked on her door when I came to work one morning and told her we needed to sit down and talk about her illness. I had gotten myself all worked up about it, thinking she may have the stomach cancer everyone had been catching 'round that time. I told her if she didn't go to the doctor, I wouldn't come back and guard for her in the mornings. Told her I couldn't watch her waste away to bits, looking pale every morning. She lost her stomach one time right off the side of the porch. Landed right in those pretty pink azaleas of hers. I told her, I couldn't abide it, so she'd either go to the doctor, or I'd go away from Maggs place. And you know what she told me?"

"She told you to go."

"Yep. So I left. It ain't right for a woman to see a man cry over her, but when I went down those porch steps, I was crying on the inside. I knew I had to follow through, though. For two days I went to my home and slept something powerful. I slept and waited for God to give me a sign as to where I should go. And he did. That's why I left Sweet Fields. I came back to visit a couple times, but Maggs had taken a liking to raising a boy. I figured it was the child of one of her broke birds. I didn't question it. I could see she didn't have room left for me. So the last time I left,
I stayed a while. When I came back, she was gone."

"Silas, I have a very important question for you. Did you know you had a son?"

"Little Belle, stop all that foolish talk. I was frisky when I left Sweet Fields, but I was careful."

"No. No. You had a son in Sweet Fields. Maggie's son."
Belle left the room quickly. She never knew what to do with people when they became overly emotional, so she found the quickest exit. Before she exited, though, Locke explained to Silas, that she had someone she wanted him to meet.

"Here take this." Locke placed the box in Iris' lap. "Now, come with me."

Iris was a little foggy. The comfort of the couches in the lobby of Golden Sunsets had put her right to sleep. She grabbed the box and followed Locke, dutifully. Locke tapped on the door of Silas' room.

"Come on in."

"Silas," Locke said quietly, "this is Iris, Maggs' granddaughter."

"Well, hello, Iris. I'm glad I got a chance to see you up close. You're a pretty little thing. Just as cute as you can be, and you favor your grandmother, Maggie."

"Hi, Mr. Silas. It's good to meet you. I'm not sure why I'm meeting you, but I hope it's for good reason."

"Iris go on over there and stand beside Mr. Silas. Silas, get on up out that chair." Locke was waving her hand to and fro, directing the pair to the middle of the room. "That's right. Now just a little bit closer, and let me look at you."

All the movement and Locke's serious tone gave both Iris and Silas the giggles. At first, they both tried to contain themselves. But Locke and her gloved gesticulations set them both into a frenzy of laughter. They threw their heads back and laughed and laughed at the awkwardness of it all. Locke placed a gloved hand over her mouth.

"I knew it!" She gasped.

"What, what is it Locke?" Iris said between giggles.

"Iris, this is your grandfather."

"Silas, this, is your granddaughter."

The pair turned and stared at each other for several seconds before Silas broke the silence. "I knew you looked like Maggs' Murphy, but I never thought for a second you'd be my kin. You belong to me…" Silas moved closer to Iris and held his arms out to embrace her. "May I?"

Iris hesitated. The news had come too fast too soon, but she was happy to feel as if she really belonged somewhere and to somebody, especially in Sweet Fields. She leaned into her grandfather's hug, though she couldn't bring herself to put her arms around him, not yet.

"Y'all talk." Locke said briskly. "Y'all talk and look at those pictures there. It'll come together. And Iris, you know how to investigate it, if you need proof. But I'm never wrong about these things. Go on now. Talk. Iris, call me when you're ready. I'll be around the corner, checking in on my suite." Locke left the room quickly, but all Iris could say to Silas was, "You can walk?"

CHAPTER 25: CELEBRATION SUNDAY

The whole town was abuzz with the excitement that took place at Saturday's tree trimming. Members of the congregation could hardly wait to join together again for Sunday's Christmas
Celebration Service. They thought of it as an extension of the Christmas program. Celebration Sunday was always a special time.
Sister Washington was on call as the church nurse since the Bid
Whist Club from Golden Sunsets would be attending. The Deaconesses were in their white shirtdresses and wore bright red poinsettias on their lapels. The deacons had gathered in the back as usual, and parishioners sitting on the far right side of the sanctuary could hear their raucous laughter. Iris had ridden to church with William and was planted in her favorite seat. She turned to find Locke nestled in her favorite place on her favorite pew next to Eddie. The Bid Whist Club wanted to sit together, but Silas insisted on sitting next to Iris.

In the choir loft, Maybelline sat at the organ. John Martinez was playing guitar that morning instead of the drums.
Folks laughed about the Martinez brothers. Officer Michael Martinez got the muscles while his little brother got the musical talent. Sampson, who felt less of a newcomer, was on the drums.
A tucked and dusted Pastor LeBeaux entered the pulpit with Rev.
Edwards. Once they were in place, Maybelline gave a nod to Melvin who stood at the rear doors and the choir began their processional to the old song "We've Come This Far By Faith." The audience stood and sang along.

We've come this far by faith
leaning on the Lord
trusting in His holy word
He never failed me yet
Oh, oh, oh, oh, oh oh oh!
Can't turn around

We've come this far by faith.

After the choir had gotten situated in the loft, Rev. Edwards stepped forward to begin the service with prayer. The congregation stood.

Our father, who is in heaven. We come to worship you today with a spirit of thankfulness. God, we are thankful to have our lives, our health, and strength to make it to your house of worship. Lord, we thank you for protecting us as we slumbered and slept. We thank you for blessing us to see the close of another year. The enemy set snares for us, God, but you were with us, protecting us, guiding our every footstep. Now, today as we worship you, take joy in what we offer to you, dear Father, for we love you and seek only to please you. In Jesus' name we pray. Amen.

As the congregation sat and the ushers allowed late arrivals into the sanctuary, the choir prepared to minister in song. The audience mumbled when Laura Baxter stood and went to the microphone that was set up for the lead singer. Laura hadn't led a song since she was a child. Luceal had always discouraged her from singing, because her voice was a little raspy. Laura grabbed the microphone and yanked it from the stand. She started the song a-capella. She sang it slowly and full of emotion. The audience was shocked into silence, for they had never heard Laura sing before, and her voice was beautiful. She had the voice of sultry jazz singer.

Real, real. Jesus is real to me.
Oh yes! He gives me the victory!
So many people doubt Him, but I
can't live without Him. That is
why I love him so He's so real to
me.

When she repeated the verse, she added more riffs and runs in the song, and the audience clapped and cheered her on. Everyone, except her sister Luceal. Even Gladys Turner, dressed in navy wool plaid suit, raised her hand and waved it back and forth as she enjoyed the song. Bennett was sitting on the end of a middle pew dressed in black suit, white shirt, and no tie. When Laura repeated the second verse with fervor and with one hand raised in praise, Bennett Banks stood up and shouted, "Sang my song, Laura!"

What people didn't know was Laura often sang that song to Bennett on their secret visits when he was feeling off kilter. He had confided to her that during his most trying times, right after Vietnam, he would sing that song to himself to steady his mind. He pulled out a wrinkled handkerchief and dabbed at his eyes. The choir joined in, and the song sped up to an up-tempo beat. It morphed into a congregational song with everyone standing, clapping, and singing along.

After the song ended, there was a shift in the musician's corner. Maybelline slid off the organ, and Rev. Edwards took her place. Sampson traded places with John Martinez; Sampson began picking at the bass guitar while John started with a quick beat on the drums. When Charles came in strong on the organ, Katie Caldwell picked up her tambourine and gave it all she had. When Maybelline took the microphone, the congregation went crazy with applause. The music to Dorinda Clark-Cole's song was fast and hearkened back to the rhythms of church music of old. Maybelline started with the verse:

Been through the storm
Been through the rain
I've experienced so much hurt
I've experienced so much pain
He's always there
No matter what the snare
If He brought me this far
He'll take me all the way

Karen Edwards, thinking about all her years of trying to conceive, took the words to heart and stood and waved her handkerchief in the choir's direction. When the choir sang the chorus "*He brought me this far, He'll take me all the way*", the audience sang clapped and shouted praises to God. The energy in the sanctuary encouraged the singers and musicians through to the next verse.

Economy is still down
Enemies trying to run me down
I got my faith in You
I know your word is true
Said you'll never leave me You'll
always there
If You brought me this far
You'll take me all the way He
brought me this far
He'll take me all the way.

The deacon board, in reflection of how God had provided the funds for the daycare couldn't help but stand and rejoice. Clem stood and clapped as hard and smiled as wide as he could. Charles did something fancy with the organ keys to take the choir to the bridge of song, and the harmony was impeccable.

All the way
I had to cry sometimes, You wiped the tears from my eyes
All the way
I put my trust in You,
You know what to do
All the way
When I wanted to scream about everything
Oh you brought me
All the way
I want to praise You lord until I get my reward
If he brought me this far
He'll take me all the way

When Locke thought of all the tears she had cried for her beloved Clive and how God had never left her and even brought her Eddie to wipe away her tears, she was overwhelmed. Standing in her place, Locke waved both her gloved hands high in the air as tears streamed down her face. Whilst the congregation reflected on their times of trials, sorrow, and deliverance, Maybelline kept on singing. Rev. Edwards was bouncing on the organ bench hardly able to contain himself, Sampson's face was screwed up in concentration as he plucked the guitar, and John had beat the drums so passionately that his black hair had fallen loose from its side-parted position. In preparation for the third verse, the music cut off abruptly except for the beat of the bass drum. Maybelline sang the last verse thinking about her own life.

I've been through the fire
I've been through the flood
Thank God, I'm covered (I'm covered, I'm covered)
Hey I'm covered by His blood
If it were not for Him, for the Lord
I'd' never, I would've never make it this far
If he brought me this far
He'll take me all the way

Something in the third verse touched both Bennett and Gladys. The both had carried their trauma as a result of acts of violence for so long, spending a large part of their lives shut off from the world and dwelling on their pasts. Bennett threw his arms up and walked to the front of the church. He knelt at the altar and cried tears--tears of sorrow, relief, and joy. For the first time since he returned from Vietnam, he felt forgiven for the lives he had taken during the war. He felt thankful that God had spared his life and given him a second chance to have a happy existence with Laura and be accepted at St. Andrew.

Gladys had been sitting on the inside aisle in her wheelchair tapping her hands on the armrests. But when Maybelline dug deep in her voice to sign "*at times I wanted to scream about everything...I want to praise you Lord, until I get my reward,*" she could no longer remain quiet or seated. She stood slowly from her wheelchair and gingerly made her way to the altar with Bennett. She walked with her arms extended waving them to and fro as if she were clearing her own path while shouting as best she could "God did it!" Melvin, the usher, and Sister Washington moved closer without interrupting Gladys' praise, but they wanted to be sure she didn't fall. Gladys made it to the altar where Bennett was still kneeling. She placed her frail, wrinkled hands on his back, and he stood to face her. She grabbed his hands and pumped them up and down. She was smiling and crying at the same time. She kept saying "God kept us! God kept us!" The church went into an even higher praise to see the two most emotionally scarred people in their community rejoice together. As Bennett walked Gladys back to her chair, Maybelline and the St. Andrew choir continued to sing, ad-libbing the call and response. Each musician had a brief solo before the song ended.

Through all of this Pastor LeBeaux was so full of emotion that his face was a red as the poinsettia arrangements at the edge of the pulpit. Tears streamed down his face as he sorted through his emotions. He was happy for Charles and Karen because he had fasted and prayed with them for a baby. He was proud of Maybelline singing like she had never done before and was ecstatic that she was going to be by his side in ministry. He looked at Bennett Banks and Gladys Turner, two people who thought God had turned His back on them, who were now realizing they, too, had something to be thankful for. He looked at Belle Lynne Locke who was no longer a grieving widow, but a woman who had been given a second chance at love. Though Iris had not been overly emotional as others had, Prentiss noticed how she stood in a half hug with Mr. Farmer from Golden Sunsets. Even Iris had realized she was not alone in the world, and that she had family all around her. He smiled as he turned to look at the choir and musicians who had never sounded better. This is how God worked. He had tested them, and when they maintained the integrity and spirit of Christ, he delivered them.

"It's been a long time, saints, since we've praised him like this. I can already tell that the saints of St. Andrew won't let the rocks cry out for them. We can all think back to where God has brought us from," Prentiss nodded at Maybelline, "and cry out a hallelujah, anyhow! We can all look back to yesterday, just last night, and see how God has brought us. How he has kept us through dangers we couldn't even see, and protected us from those we could. He's a great God. A mender of broken hearts…" "That's right, Pastor." The crowd shouted in agreement.

"A lifter of bowed down heads."

"Won't he lift you?" Gladys yelled. She was fanning herself with a small blue handkerchief and gently rubbing her throat with her free hand.

"A repayer of joy for tears."

"Praise Him." The congregation roared.

"Turn with me, if you will, to 2 Corinthians 5:17. Y'all know the scripture. It's about becoming new in Christ. That scripture tells us that those of us who accept Christ are new creatures. We put away the old things, and we become new, *all* things become new! We know that Christ came down to earth as a precious little babe, so that we could have the opportunity to become new. That's why we're celebrating today. But that celebration shouldn't end. We shouldn't forget the importance of that babe who was wrapped in swaddling clothes and laid in a manger. No. No. No. Every day, we should thank Him for newness."

Prentiss LeBeaux looked around at the St. Andrew congregation. "Have you ever just sat down and thought about newness. New opportunities. New friends. New relationships. New mind. New homes. New love. The ability to see things with new eyes. All of these things come with newness in Christ. God made this happen for us, by sending us His Son. Let me put this in perspective for you. Just last night, we were given a grand opportunity. Now, nonbelievers wouldn't see this as an opportunity, but when you're in Christ, you have a unique perspective. God allows you to look back at the old, so you can better appreciate, better enjoy, better navigate the new. So when the devil reminds us of the old, God can always show us the new. Look around you today, St. Andrew. Don't you see new faces? Yes, I know, some of the faces are up in age, but they are new to you. God did that. The morning God gave us, that's new! The next breath you breathe is a new breath. *Behold*, the word says, ALL things are become new. Can you say all, St. Andrew?"

"All!"

"That's right, all. And guess what else you get?"

"What do we get, Pastor?" Clem said, loudly.

"You get brand new mercies. Everyday you open your eyes, you are staring at a brand new mercy! That's the kind of God we serve. A God who sends down his only Son, as a precious little baby, so that we can have all things new. A brand new life. Brand new experiences. Brand new testimony. Brand new memories. Brand new stories of the grace of God. Sit back and close your eyes, and think of your new. What comes to mind? Just shout it out!"

"A new voice!" shouted Gladys as new tears began to roll down her face.

"New family!" Silas followed up with the same vigor. He grabbed Iris around her shoulder, shook her, and grinned. "New friends!" Locke shouted as she shook one glove at Eddie and the other at Iris.

"New chances!" Laura shouted as she blushed and looked at Bennett Banks.

"New babies!" Karen Edwards cried out.

"And I got a new love, St. Andrew. A good thing." Prentiss LeBeaux said with a smirk on his face. "Christ offers us newness. You know how the old saints say it. Help me out, Golden Sunsets. When you come to Christ, you get a new walk!"

"Yeah!" The Bid Whist Club yelled.

"A new talk!" shouted Prentiss LeBeaux

"Amen!" The crowd chimed in.

"A new shout!" Prentiss yelled.

"Hammercy, Jesus!" St. Andrew began to rev up for another round of rousing corporate praise.

"A brand new life!" Prentiss moved from behind the pulpit and began to walk toward the aisles of the sanctuary.

"Praise the Lord!" The deaconesses joined the chorus of responders.

"And if we continue on in Him, we will have a new home!"

"That's right!"

"Over in glory!"

"Glorrrrraaaaay!"

Rev. Edwards, couldn't resist. He jumped on the organ, sliding his hands up and down the keys, following Pastor LeBeaux's cadence.

"And it's yours!"

"Yesssir!"

"And mine!"

"Amen"

"And we are gonna sing and shout all over the place when we get there, because Jesus has made it possible for all things to become new. He loves us, church. He loves us more than we can ever know." Pastor LeBeaux clasped his arms around himself and twisted his body around vigorously from left to right.

Mother Carrie took off in her traditional walk around the sanctuary, except this time she added a clap or two as she reached the corner pews. Bennett Banks slid his way into the aisle and began marching in place. The heave and swell of the spirit descended on St. Andrew once again, producing a new answer to the question, "Didn't we have a good time in the Lord today?"

Eddie stepped out into the aisle with his arms crossed while Pastor LeBeaux was preaching, and for a change, Belle Lynne Locke rubbed his back. Iris stood as well, straight, erect, and thankful for God, community, family, and home.

St. Andrew received many gifts that Sunday Celebration morning. They received the gift of Bennett's rededication to Christ. They received a commitment from Golden Sunsets administration that the Bid Whist Club would be prepped and primed for church at St. Andrew each Sunday. And with the Bid Whist Club's attendance came one of the greatest gifts, the gift of wisdom from the elders. Prentiss LeBeaux was thankful for that and expressed his appreciation by giving one of the Bid Whist members an opportunity to close out the Sunday Celebration in prayer.

"I'd be honored to close us out," Robert Endicott said, making his way up to the front of the church. Melvin Collier walked slowly behind him, just in case; however, Robert Endicott had proven to be one of the spryest members of the group, and made his way just fine. He was especially neat. His brushed-back silver wavy hair gleamed under the lights. His gray tweed jacket, complete with navy corduroy elbow patches gave off an air of poise and intelligence. His chocolate ankle high Stacey Adams shined with each step he took.

"Brothers and sisters, Professor Endicott," Prentiss announced as Robert Endicott approached the podium.

"Praise the Lord, Saints." He said in an excited, but still dignified manner. He was excited to be amongst community and the saints of St. Andrew. But the microphone excited him even more.

"Praise the Lord." The crowd responded.

"It's been a long time since I've had the opportunity to have a word of prayer in public. But I promised the Lord, should that opportunity present itself, I'd like to recite portions from a most appropriate prayer penned by James Weldon Johnson called 'Listen Lord: A Prayer,' from his book *God's Trombone.* If I remember correctly, Bigs' wife, Edith, God rest her slumbering soul, used to recite this same prayer beautifully at the close of every Christmas service.

O Lord, we come this morning
Knee-bowed and body-bent Before Thy
throne of grace.
O Lord--this morning--
Bow our hearts beneath our knees,
And our knees in some lonesome valley. We come this morning--
Like empty pitchers to a full fountain, With no merits of our own.
O Lord--open up a window of heaven,
And lean out far over the battlements of glory, And listen this morning.
Lord, have mercy on proud and dying sinners-- Sinners hanging over the mouth
of hell Who seem to love their distance well.
Lord--ride by this morning-- Mount Your milk-white horse,
And ride-a this morning-- And in Your ride, ride by old hell,
Ride by the dingy gates of hell,

And stop poor sinners in their headlong plunge.
And now, O Lord, this man of God,
Who [broke] the bread of life this morning-- Shadow him in the hollow of Thy hand, And keep him out of the gunshot of the devil.
Take him, Lord--this morning-- Wash him with hyssop inside and out,
Hang him up and drain him dry of sin.
Pin his ear to the wisdom-post,
And make his words sledge hammers of truth—
Beating on the iron heart of sin.
Lord God, this morning--
Put his eye to the telescope of eternity,
And let him look upon the paper walls of time.
Lord, turpentine his imagination,
Put perpetual motion in his arms,
Fill him full of the dynamite of Thy power,
Anoint him all over with the oil of Thy salvation,
And set his tongue on fire.
And now, O Lord--
When I've done drunk my last cup of sorrow--
When I've been called everything but a child of God--
When I'm done traveling up the rough side of the mountain-O--
Mary's Baby--
When I start down the steep and slippery steps of death--
When this old world begins to rock beneath my feet--
Lower me to my dusty grave in peace
To wait for that great gittin'-up morning--Amen.

Robert Endicott's prayer left the congregation of St. Andrew in tears. The congregation filed out, hugging Robert and complimenting him on his diction, elocution and ability to remember a poem from so long ago.

Bennett Banks returned from the New Members' room to find Eddie and Belle Lynne Locke standing on the church parking lot chatting with Gladys Turner and Hattie Blackman. He looked for

Laura, but found her engaged in deep conversation with Karen Edwards, so he joined Eddie, Belle and Hattie.

"Hattie, you would think this church service would smooth out those rough edges on you. What are you fussing about now?" Locke was asking as Bennett approached the group.

"Robert Endicott didn't have to be the one who ended the church service. He ain't no preacher." Hattie replied.

"But he did a good job with the prayer," Gladys whispered. She had overworked her vocal chords during the service. She considered that she probably should have eased into talking as Locke had advised a few nights before.

"Yeah, he did fine," Hattie retorted. "I'm just saying. He just got his ego stroked today; now he's going to think he's supposed to pray all the time."

"So what if he does?" Locke asked. She looked up to find the Golden Sunsets van pulling around to pick up the residents. "Aunt Gladys, you want me to wheel you over to the van?"

"I'd sure appreciate it. Come on Hattie and stop being so hateful." Gladys whispered.

Eddie extended his arm to shake Bennett Banks' hand. "Welcome back to the fold, soldier."

"Glad to be back, Brother. Glad to be back."

"So what's next for you on the home front? You think you've found your footing?" Eddie asked him, seriously. "It can be tough out here, trying to navigate the real world again. That PTSD is a real thing, and once you think you got it conquered, it'll creep up on you again. You've been out of circulation for a while, I hear. It's going to be challenging. But, I want you to know, you can call me to talk, anytime you get ready. I'm here for you. We're brothers twice over, in the service of the Lord and in the service for our country."

Bennett hadn't met anyone who could commiserate with his experience, and he was glad that Eddie had offered him an outlet. He'd be sure to use it. "How can I get in touch with you?" "Here's my cell number, and you know I'm over at my son's house, when I come in town to visit with my Belle. I stay over longer and longer each time I come. They'll tire of me after while, especially with the baby coming. They'll need their space. Belle and I have been talking about it a lot."

"Well, can I offer you an alternative 'til you get settled in?" Bennett asked.

"Sure, what you got?"

"Come on over and bunk with me until you find you a more permanent place. My house is waaaay too big for one person, as most of these houses in Sweet Fields are. Some of those rooms up stairs, I haven't been in for years. You can have the whole upstairs to yourself."

"That's a big step, Bennett. You sure that's something you want to do? I mean, I see you and Laura are… I don't want to be in the way."

"Oh, naw." Bennett shook his head. "You won't be in the way at all. It'll be good to have someone around who's conquered this thing. It will be good for us both. You can stop mooching off your son and daughter-in-law, and I'll have someone to hold me accountable. Someone to help me out with this dating stuff, too. You know it's been a while. And don't worry, I keep a clean house. You know how it is when you've been in the service. Everything is in order."

"Bennett man," Eddie shook his hand. "I'm going to take you up on that offer. Now what are the monetary terms here?
What you want me to pay you for this?"

"We can work that out later. Let's not talk about money now. I see our ladies are making their way back to us."

Laura was walking, almost running, a few steps ahead of
Belle Locke to get to Bennett Banks. "Bennett! Bennett!"
Panting, Laura caught up with the two men. "Let's go get us some Sunday dinner from Mom and Pop's Diner." Turning back to address Locke, Laura asked, "You and Eddie wanna join us?" Taking her time, so as not to get a speck of dust on her cream wool pantsuit,

Locke replied. "I like the owners, Laura. But it's too much meat in that establishment. The smell alone messes with my constitution. Y'all go on. You have enough catching up to do without me butting in."

Laura and Bennett walked on toward the Blue Oldsmobile where Luceal sat in the back, waiting for the couple. They dropped her off at home and continued on.

Iris waited for William to finish settling up the money. She sat on the back pew of St. Andrew Church picking at small imaginary pieces of lint that had fallen on her cream cashmere pencil dress. "You didn't have to rush," Iris said to him as she noticed him speed walking down the aisle.

"I didn't want to have you waiting too long. I knew you'd be hungry soon. A service like this will leave you famished." "Oh, no, I was fine. I wanted to chat a little with my grandfather before the van came. The time waiting was well spent. Anyway, I would've waited for you all day, William Hughes, Jr." Iris said with a sly wink and wide smile. They walked hand in hand out of the door of St. Andrews, recounting the worship of the day and making plans for a juicy steak at Argentine's.

Mother Carrie and Daughter Eliza bundled up and walked home from St. Andrew. Mother Carrie insisted that the cool air was good for her lungs and helped her fight walking pneumonia. They were in deep conversation about Golden Sunsets. "But I want to go, Daughter," Carrie argued. "All my friends are there. I'd be comfortable and out your hair. And maybe you could get you an old man like Laura and Belle did."

"Mother Carrie. I'm your friend. I'm your daughter, Eliza. You know me. Don't I take good care of you?"

"Yes, you do. But I've been worrying you long enough. That van was a sign from God. He wanted me to get in it and leave you to finish out your life in peace."

"God didn't say that, Mother."

"Oh, yes He did. He told me to get in that van and go with my friends."

"I'll take you to visit your friends."

Mother Carrie got quiet. "I reckon that's good enough. Good enough for now." Mother Carrie placed the palm of her hand over her forehead. "Did we go to church today, Liza?"

"Yes we sure did, Mother."

"Did I go for my walk?"

"Yes, you walked round and round St. Andrew, praising God."

"Won't you tell me about church, Liza? I think I've forgotten." And the two women talked all the way home.

Big Hughes, Clem Callahan, and Judith rode through Pendleton Park in Clem's Lincoln. They too were still on a church high.

"Oh, wasn't it lovely!" Judith exclaimed clapping her hands.

"It was beautiful," said Big Hughes.

"You can't beat a service like that." Clem said, dabbing at his hairline with a handkerchief Judith had sewn for him. His initials, CC, were embroidered in burgundy in one of the corners. "That kind of service'll make you hungry!" Big mumbled from the back seat.

"Glad you're hungry," Judith chirped, "because I made a big meal for us. So, you come on over and sup with us. And don't try to tip out of my house early. I won't have it today. Sit around and let your food digest. You both have had enough excitement for the day." Judith put on her glasses, which were hung on a dainty silver chain around her neck. She was digging in her purse for something. Finally, she found the small parcel covered in wax paper, which rattled noisily in her hand. "That's why I brought some candied ginger for Clem." She handed Clem a small piece. "Here you go, honey." She continued talking, turning half way round toward the back seat to finish her conversation with Big. Her seat belt restrained her from turning around all the way. She looked over her glasses. "You know how excitement messes with his stomach. You want one, Big?" "Naw, I'll be alright. I'll stay for dinner. Can't stay too long, though. William,

Jr. and Iris invited me over for dessert this evening. I reckon I'll go over there and get acquainted."

The Edwards retired to their home to enjoy a quiet dinner alone. They sat at the breakfast nook, peering over a small black and white picture. It was their first ultrasound.

"Isn't she cute?" Karen said, sliding her fingertips across the glossy image.

"She? What do you mean she? That's a boy if I've ever seen one." Charles Edwards grin was wide.

"Either one of us could be wrong. The baby's not old enough for us to tell yet." Karen giggled.

"Yeah, but it's a mighty fine baby. Thank the Lord; it's a mighty fine baby."

Old time gospel music was blaring from Pastor Prentiss LeBeaux's office, and Maybelline Crowder was singing her heart out, loud and crystal clear. Francis the Secretary was collecting a few things from her desk while Melvin Collier waited. They'd made plans to join William and Iris at Argentine's. Francis was a little worried about it, but Melvin was excited. He'd wanted to take Francis for the longest, but he knew how she was a stickler for routine. Somehow Iris convinced her to come along, and Melvin couldn't be happier to take his favorite lady to a fancy restaurant.

They walked out to Melvin's Toyota Forerunner and hopped in. Francis situated herself and looked up to see Sampson, the guest musician, running along the trail at Pendleton Park. He was dressed in a navy tracksuit, though the jacket was unzipped almost halfway to reveal a white ribbed tank and the slightest outline of muscle along his chest and torso. "It's too cold a day for even the best athlete to be running outside!" she exclaimed. "You know how city folk are, Ms. Francis. They have some strange ways. I guess he's no different."

Maybelline and Prentiss couldn't think about food. They'd not seen each other in almost four months, and for a few minutes they just stared at each other, exchanging very few words.

"You look good, May."

"You do too, Pastor."

"You know I've missed you, don't you?"

"I've missed you too, Prentiss. I've missed you terribly."

"I thought you weren't going to come back to me."

"Here I am. And I'm not going anywhere."

"So what are we gonna do now?"

"We're going to plan a wedding," Maybelline answered. Then, she closed the pastor's study door.

ABOUT THE AUTHORS

Hazel Lindey and Rosee Garfield are pseudonyms for Cicely Wilson and DiAnne Malone, respectively. These two college professors started creating humorous church and community scenarios as a way to decompress from everyday stressors. But then, the scenarios turned into stories of desperation and drama, community and pride, love and lasciviousness. The final scenario was "what if we wrote a book, just to see if we can do it?" Over a few months, those possible plots turned into an entire trilogy chronicling the lives of some very quirky inhabitants in the fictional town of Sweet Fields, Georgia.

Both natives of small southern towns, Hazel and Rosee enjoy escaping the hustle and bustle of their busy lives to sit and enjoy the southern comfort of Sweet Fields. Hazel resides in a Chicago suburb with her husband, while Rosee resides in Memphis with her husband and three adorable children.

Visit our webpage at www.irisandlocke.com

Follow Iris and Locke on Facebook:
https://www.facebook.com/pages/Iris-andLocke/762259863829111

Follow Iris and Locke on Twitter: https://twitter.com/IrisandLocke

Made in the USA
Coppell, TX
27 June 2021

58165141R00215